Select praise for the no

T0005569

"A beautifully written story about s
women's fiction won't be able to pu

—*Publishers Weekly* on *The Secret of Snow*

"Viola Shipman knows relationships. *The Clover Girls* will sometimes make you smile and other times cry, but like a true friendship, it is a novel you will forever savor and treasure."

—Mary Alice Monroe, *New York Times* bestselling author

"The perfect winter warmer!"

—*USA TODAY* bestselling author Sarah Morgan on *The Secret of Snow*

"Viola Shipman has written a love song to long-lost friends, an ode to the summers that define us and the people who make us who we are. The minute I finished *The Clover Girls*, I ordered copies for all my friends. It's that good."

—Kristy Woodson Harvey, *New York Times* bestselling author

"Reading Viola Shipman's novels is like talking with your best friend and wanting never to hang up the phone. *The Clover Girls* is her most beautiful novel yet, and her most important."

—Nancy Thayer, *New York Times* bestselling author

"Oh, the joy! *The Clover Girls* may be [Shipman's] best yet.... A redemptive tale, celebrating the power of friendship while focusing on what matters most. Perfect for the beach!"

—*New York Journal of Books*

"Every now and then a new voice in fiction arrives to completely charm, entertain and remind us what matters. Viola Shipman is that voice and *The Summer Cottage* is that absolutely irresistible and necessary novel."

—Dorothea Benton Frank, *New York Times* bestselling author

"A blissful summer read sure to please the author's many fans, and fans of writers like Elin Hilderbrand or Kristin Hannah."

—*Library Journal* on *The Heirloom Garden*

Also by Viola Shipman

FAMOUS IN A SMALL TOWN
A WISH FOR WINTER
THE EDGE OF SUMMER
THE SECRET OF SNOW
THE CLOVER GIRLS
THE HEIRLOOM GARDEN
THE SUMMER COTTAGE

For a complete list of titles by Viola Shipman,
please visit www.violashipman.com.

Viola Shipman

The *Wishing* Bridge

If you purchased this book without a cover you should be aware that this book is stolen property. It was reported as "unsold and destroyed" to the publisher, and neither the author nor the publisher has received any payment for this "stripped book."

Recycling programs for this product may not exist in your area.

ISBN-13: 978-1-525-80486-1

The Wishing Bridge
Copyright © 2023 by Viola Shipman

Christmas Angels
First published in 2016 by St. Martin's Press. This edition published in 2023.
Copyright © 2016 by Viola Shipman

All rights reserved. No part of this book may be used or reproduced in any manner whatsoever without written permission except in the case of brief quotations embodied in critical articles and reviews.

This is a work of fiction. Names, characters, places and incidents are either the product of the author's imagination or are used fictitiously. Any resemblance to actual persons, living or dead, businesses, companies, events or locales is entirely coincidental.

Graydon House
22 Adelaide St. West, 40th Floor
Toronto, Ontario M5H 4E3, Canada
www.GraydonHouseBooks.com
www.BookClubbish.com

Printed in U.S.A.

To Kathy Talsma

One of my most beloved readers, a friend and bright light in this world taken too soon, whose love of family and Michigan's beauty was as big as the lake and will inspire me forever.

prologue

If there were one sound that defined my childhood, it would be the chiming of the glockenspiel.

Every hour of my youth was punctuated by the sound of the five-bell Westminster chime. Clarion bells echoed through my little Bavarian hometown of Frankenmuth, Michigan, across the Holz Brücke and the Cass River, through the woods and directly into my heart.

Memories serve as the voice to our souls, the soundtrack to our lives.

I bet you can remember—clear as those bells—the following sounds: the call of a whip-poor-will off the cabin's screened porch, your grandmother's singing as she baked after Sunday church, the crack of a baseball off a bat as your father watched a game, the crunch of fall leaves under your boots, your brother's giggle, the sound of tires on a gravel road and the scratching of a mouse that's found its way inside your home on the first frigid day of winter.

You can, can't you?

No matter how much time has passed, you can recall that memory—just as clearly as you can smell your mother's perfume right now—as if it were yesterday.

The glockenspiel became as ever present as the sound of my own heartbeat drumming in my ears.

I ran as far away as I could from the sound of those bells.

But, like any memory, there was much more to the glockenspiel than its sound.

There was a history.

There was a myth.

There was a story.

There was a fable that unfolded before your eyes, wood figurines that told the tale of the Pied Piper of Hamelin.

The glockenspiel was a constant reminder of home and Christmas that scratched in my ears, just like that winter mouse and the ones that danced on its bell tower.

And from that…

Well, from that memory, I could never run.

Part One

1

December 7

I hit the brakes, my car fishtailing on the slippery road. I come to a stop just inches from the car before me.

Ah, the hazards of winter in Michigan and Detroit drivers who think snow is a reason to hit the gas.

I cock my head and see an accident just a few cars in front of me. A man is out of his car, screaming into the window of the car he hit.

Merry Christmas!

I take a breath, sip my coffee—which miraculously didn't spill—hit my blinker and wait to merge into the next lane.

That's when I notice it: the abandoned house I drive by every day to work.

There are many abandoned homes in many forgotten neighborhoods in this proud city whose shoulders were slumped by the mortgage crisis, layoffs in the auto industry and never-ending winters that used to be as brutal and mind-numbing as a Detroit Lions football season. Neighborhoods stand like ghost towns, and, in winter, they look even sadder, the grass dead, the green gone, broken glass shimmering in the sun before the snow arrives to cover their remains.

This particular home is a three-story redbrick beauty that looks like a castle. The windows are broken, the walls are collapsing and yet the wooden staircase—visible to the world—remains intact. I slow down just enough every day to admire the finials, worn and shining from the hands that have polished them over the years.

There is a line of shattered windows just above the ground, and as you pass by, you catch a glimmer of red in the basement. Coming the opposite way, you swear you can see a man smiling.

I stopped years ago to investigate. I parked, careful to avoid nails, and wound my way in high heels through the weeds to the broken window. I knelt and peeked into the basement.

Santa!

A plastic molded Santa smiled at me. It was a vintage mold—like the one my grandparents centered in the middle of a wreath on their front door every year—of a cheery Santa with red cheeks, blue eyes, green gloves, holding a candy cane tied in a golden bow.

I scanned the basement. Boxes were still stacked everywhere. Tubs were marked Christmas!

In the corner of the basement sat a sign overrun with cobwebs that read Santa's Toy Shop!

December 1975

"They're here! They're here!"

My voice echoed through my grandparents' house. I ran to the front door, grabbed the first catalog, which seemed to weigh nearly as much as I did, and tottered down the steep basement stairs. Back up I went to retrieve the next one from Mr. Haley, the postman, who looked exactly like Captain Kangaroo.

"Don't move!" I said, disappearing and returning moments later.

Then back down the stairs I scrambled once again.

Mr. Haley laughed when I returned the final time, out of breath.

"Last one," he said. "Oh, and a bunch of Christmas cards for your grandmother."

I bent over, panting, as if I'd just done wind sprints on the track.

"Tired?" he asked.

I shook my head. "No! Think of what Santa carries! Not to mention what you carry every day!"

"You got me there," he said. "Here's the cards. I'll see you tomorrow. Merry Christmas!"

I watched him trudge through the freshly fallen snow, just enough to dust the world in white. If there's one thing we never had to worry about in our town of Frankenmuth, it was a white Christmas. My dad said it was one of the gifts of living in a Christmas wonderland.

"Merry Christmas, Mr. Haley!" I yelled, my breath coming out in puffs.

I shut the door, tossed the cards on the telephone desk sitting in the foyer and hightailed it back down to the basement.

I looked at the catalogs where I'd set them on the shag carpet and ran around them in a happy circle doing a little jig.

I turned on the electric fireplace. It was so cool, fake brick, and it just faded into the Z-BRICK walls. The flames seemed to dance, even though they weren't real.

I went over to the card table where my grandparents played games—bridge, canasta, hearts—and I grabbed my marker from a cup.

The red one.

The one I used every year.

The one Santa would recognize.

I took a seat on the orange shag and arranged the catalogs in a semicircle around me: the Christmas catalogs from JCPenney and Monkey Wards, and my favorite, the *Sears Wish Book*.

The catalogs were heavy and thick, big as the Buick my grandpa drove. They were brand-new and all mine. I began to flip through the crisp pages, turning quickly to the ones that showed all the toys, clothes and games I wanted for Christmas.

I was lost for hours in the pages, dreaming, hoping, wishing.

"Yes, yes, yes!" I said, my marker in constant motion.

"Are you using a red marker so Santa will see?"

I looked up, and my dad was standing over me. He was tall, hair as fair as mine. He had just gotten off work. He was an accountant at a car dealership, and he never seemed happy when he got home from work.

Until he came down to my grandparents' basement.

"Of course!" I said. "Finn gets green. I use red!"

"So what do you want Santa to bring you this year?"

I patted the carpet, and my dad took a seat next to me. I began showing him all the things I'd marked in the wish catalogs.

"I want this eight-room dollhouse, and, oh! this Shaun Cassidy phono with sing-along microphone and this battery-operated sewing machine! It's the first ever like this!" I stopped, took a deep breath and continued, "And this dress, and this Raggedy Ann doll, but—" I stopped again, flipping through pages as quickly as I could "—more than anything I want this game called Simon. It's computer controlled, Daddy! It's like Simon Says, and you have to be really fast, and..."

"Slow down," he said, rubbing my back. "And what about your brother?"

"What about him?"

"What does he want?"

"He'll want all the stupid stuff boys like," I said. "Stars Wars figurines, an erector set, a Nerf rocket and probably a drum set."

My father winced at the last suggestion.

"Maybe a scooter instead," my dad suggested. "What do you think?"

"Good idea, Daddy." I placed my hands over my ears.

He laughed and stood up.

"Hey?" I asked. "What do *you* want for Christmas?"

My dad headed over to the workshop he had on the other side of the basement. We lived in a small ranch house on the other side of town that didn't have a basement, much less any extra room. My grandparents let my father convert this space a few years ago so he could pursue a second career and his true passion: Christmas.

"You know what I want," he said with a smile.

My dad picked up a sign and turned it my way. It was a hand-carved wooden sign that read *Frohe Weihnachten!*

Frankenmuth is a Bavarian town filled with all things German: a wooden bridge flowing over a charming river, a glockenspiel that—on the hour—played the Westminster chimes followed by an entire show complete with dancing figurines, a cheese *haus* and competing chicken-and-noodle restaurants. I was named Henrietta, my father Jakob, my brother, Finn. Only my mother, Debbie, escaped the German name game with the very American moniker.

"What's this mean, Henri?" my dad asked.

"Merry Christmas," I said.

"And what do I want?"

"Christmas all year long."

"Exactly," he said. "Just like you. Except as a grown-up." He looked at his sign. "That's my Christmas wish."

For a long time, everyone thought this was just a hobby of my father's, sort of like other dads tinkered on car engines, went fishing or coached baseball. For an even longer time, people thought my dad was nuts.

Why would a man spend all of his time creating Christmas signs in July, or designing ornaments in March?

They didn't know my dad.

They didn't how serious he was, that he often worked until three in the morning from October through December and countless weekends the rest of the year.

"You have a good job, Jakob," friends would tell him. "Don't ruin your life over some silly notion."

But my mom and grandparents believed in him just as much as I believed in Santa.

I watched my father work. As he did, he began to whistle Christmas tunes.

The world was finally catching up with my father's dream. He was now creating window displays for two of the biggest stores in town: Shepherd Woolen Mill and Koch's Country Store.

My dad picked up a big piece of lumber.

"Do you know what this is going to be, Henri?" he asked.

I shook my head.

"This is the same as having a dream," Dad continued. "No one knows what it's going to look like. But I do."

I smiled.

"Let me ask you another question," my father said. "What do you think of the holiday decorations downtown?"

I crinkled my nose. In my mind, I could see the tired old wreaths, no longer green, wires protruding through the lights, only half of which worked.

"They're icky," I said.

"That's why I'm designing all new Christmas decorations for the downtown lampposts," he said. "This wood I'm holding will become miniature Christmas cuckoo clocks that celebrate Frankenmuth's history."

My dad set down the wood and looked at me.

"Did you know *Franken* is in honor of the province of Franconia in the kingdom of Bavaria and *Mut* is the German word for 'courage'? Our town's architecture is inspired by Germany—our shops and homes are recreations of the timber-framed buildings found in the Franconia region of Germany. My decorations will honor our heritage. Christmas should continue our beloved traditions and memories."

My dad came back to where I was sitting.

"One day, I will be the Christmas König," he said. "The Christmas King." My dad took a seat on the shag next to me. "And you will be the Christmas Prinzessin." My dad smiled. "The Christmas Princess. You love Christmas even more than I do. And what I start, you will make it your own. Not out of obligation to me, but because you have the spirit of Christmas inside of you. I can feel it in my heart."

My dad tapped the wish catalog with his finger.

"One day, I will have one of these for the entire world," he said. "All my own Christmas decorations—signs, ornaments, villages. Can you imagine, Henri?"

I looked at my dad and then down at the wish catalog.

Did he realize the world was changing? Games were going from batteries to computer controlled. What would be next? Would people always love Christmas the way we did now? Or would that change, too?

"And you will be on the cover of that catalog, because nothing embodies Christmas more than the innocence and joy of a child." My father took my hand in his. "I want you to know something, Henri."

I looked into my father's eyes.

"When we go to see Santa downtown this year, and you tell him all the things you want for Christmas, I want you to ask yourself after you see him what you wish for, more than anything in the world."

I cocked my head. "I don't understand."

"It's not *things* that make our lives meaningful and our

Christmases happy—it's what we already have. Each other." My dad's voice deepened into a hum as low and vibrating as the fireplace. "Just remember to always keep a catalog of wishes and dreams right here."

My dad touched my heart.

"You'll forget about all these toys one day, but you should never forget your wishes and dreams." My dad was silent for the longest time. Then, as if reading my mind, he said, "Some things should never change, but they will. And when they do, we'll wish we had them all back again."

He stood, headed back toward his workshop and began to carve.

"Henri! Phone!"

My grandma's voice echoed into the basement.

I went running upstairs and picked up the receiver.

"Hello?"

"Hi, Henri? This is Sofie from Sears."

I giggled like mad.

"As a customer service representative," Sofie continued, "I have a direct connection to Santa."

Sofie and I did this routine every year. As soon as we received our wish catalogs, we called each other and acted like customer service representatives, our dream jobs because we'd have a link to Santa Claus.

"When did you get yours?" I asked.

"Just today! You?"

"Same!" I cleared my throat. "This is Henri from Sears. May I have your order?"

As Sofie rattled off her Christmas wish list, I wrote it down on a pad of paper my grandma kept next to the big, black rotary phone. I recited it back to her, and then she did the same.

"One day," Sofie said, "we'll take over our families' businesses. We'll never leave Frankenmuth, and every day will feel like Christmas."

When we hung up, I returned to the basement.

I glanced at the wish book and then began to collect the scrap pieces of wood from Dad's workshop and stack them this way and that—like my brother did his LEGOs—until a city of skyscrapers rose before the fireplace.

"What are you building?" my father asked.

I shrugged. I couldn't put it into words at the time, but in my heart I already knew there was more to the world than Frankenmuth.

I was building my future. I was creating my own destiny.

My dad smiled.

"My Christmas Prinzessin."

As he said this, I could still hear the words he said to me earlier.

Some things should never change, but they will. And when they do, we'll wish we had them all back again.

A car honks, knocking me from these childhood memories. A driver is motioning for me to merge. I ease into the lane and give the driver an apologetic wave.

"I'll Be Home for Christmas" begins to play on the radio.

When was the last time I was home for Christmas?

I grip the steering wheel hard and shake my head to steady myself as I continue past the abandoned house.

And then I change the station on the radio.

2

TOLLIVER & CO. MONDAY MEETING AGENDA
HAPPY HOLIDAYS!
December 7

*Report on TaterTot Toys closure & turning a year-end profit
—Maya Jenkins

*Report on Vance Enterprises Takeover & Scandal
—Benjamin Tolliver

The light from my colleagues' laptops brightens the conference room. Outside, the sky is as gray as Detroit steel.

My mind flashes to the city of wood I built as a child, the light from the fireplace streaming through the blocks.

I take a seat at the end of the massive conference table and stare at the agenda before me. My name is not on the agenda. Your name should *always* be on the agenda.

I see a flash of pink.

"Morning, Henri."

I look up. Maya Jenkins has taken a seat across from me.

Maya is a grown-up Barbie doll with the soul of Linda Hamilton in *Terminator.*

She's a former Miss Michigan, who told the Miss America judges she was going to be an attorney for the underrepresented but ended up earning her MBA at the University of Chicago and now represents the very privileged. Maya was my intern, my assistant, my protégée and now my competition and pink pestilence.

"Maya."

No one really greets each other at Tolliver & Co. There are no warm hugs, no happy talk at the water cooler about family, even at the holidays. Working here is like waking up every morning and participating in *Squid Game*. It's an endless battle to survive, and money is the carrot that keeps us going.

"You look nice," Maya says in that soft, husky voice of hers. "Very—" she stops and gives me a slow-mo once-over with her dark eyes "—festive."

She doesn't mean it. Maya's compliments are delivered in a way that results in you feeling like crap.

Maya is wearing a perfectly tailored pink power suit. The jacket is low cut, and she is not wearing a camisole underneath it. Her jet-black hair is long and beautiful, coiffed like Kate Middleton's and swept across one shoulder.

"Thank you," I say.

I actually do look nice. You have to bring your A-game to the Monday Meat Market when you're face-to-face with the bigwigs. I am wearing a beautiful red blazer and camel trousers with a winter white turtleneck. I am not sultry like Maya. I am from a long Bavarian lineage so I look more like a *Game of Thrones* queen—or a German nanny perhaps—blonde, pale, sapphire eyes, as if my blood may have a layer of ice floating atop it. And that faux facade has served me well in my career.

"I don't see your name on the agenda."

Just not recently.

"Not formally," I say. "You know how these meetings go. Anything can happen, especially as the year draws to a close."

"Tell me about it," she says with a big smile. Maya waits until I look her in the eye. "But that's why I'm glad my name is on it."

She taps her laptop with her perfect nail and then shoots me a pitying look.

When she was new to the company, I took Maya under my wing. She had worked hard to succeed, growing up in rural Michigan and entering the pageant world to earn scholarships, juggling jobs in college and grad school, believing in the American dream. I not only taught her the ropes, but I also instilled her with a cutthroat mentality to survive as a tigress in a lion's den. She became like a sister to me. She became the family I sacrificed for this career. We vented and gossiped over pizza and wine at midnight in my office. We often spent holiday weekends working together when everyone was off with their families.

And then…

Benjie Tolliver bounds into the conference room in a pinstriped suit that fits like a wetsuit.

…she slept with the boss.

And the world was hers.

He wasn't the boss at the time, mind you; his father—the inimitable Quentin Tolliver—was. Quentin hired me, and he was everything his son is not. But Maya knew where her future, pardon the pun, lay, and when Quentin died of a massive heart attack, Maya had a golden ticket to a corner office.

She also used all of my late-night confessions against me, essentially letting Benjie know that I perhaps was getting a bit old and a bit soft for such a cutthroat career.

I look at Maya. She glances up, and I smile.

She beat me at my own game.

Benjie is wearing a crisp white shirt, no tie and a Patek Philippe watch that costs more than most people's homes. He purchased his watch—he proudly told us last year at this time—with a bonus he received for closing a company and laying off twelve hundred people.

My mind whirs back to last year's performance evaluation.

"It's been a tough year for you," Benjie had said. "A tough few years actually. You still think you're up for this? My father is gone, and I don't need Herz Henri anymore. I need Hart Henri."

My heart—quite literally—had broken that day.

Benjie changed—with intention, motivation and cruelty—the beloved moniker his father had given me: Herz Henri meant I had heart and soul. Hart Henri meant "Tough Henri" in German.

Mr. Tolliver had given me that nickname in such a loving way, like when my father would whisper, "You are my Christmas Prinzessin."

Twenty-five years ago, Tolliver & Co. acquired small companies for larger companies. But Mr. Tolliver didn't just gobble them up like Pac-Man, rampaging along without a second thought. He ensured that employees were retained, often with better wages, more hours and benefits, and stock options.

Today, companies are streamlined to make more profit. People are a byproduct of the greed, human widgets, a line item that can be quickly eliminated.

I earned my MBA from Michigan, and my specialization was transitioning smaller companies into larger ones. I retrained management, altered best business practices, revamped manufacturing and sales strategies. People were valued. Profits rose along with skill levels. It was rewarding and fulfilling.

My job has changed dramatically.

Now, I am the equivalent of the Grinch, who sleds into town like a deranged outcast to wreak havoc on the sweet townsfolk's lives just before Christmas. I lay off almost everyone, retaining a skeleton crew to squeeze the remains out of a toy store in Raleigh, North Carolina, or a home goods store in Boulder, Colorado, pilfering every last dime from every last product—75% Off! Everything Must Go!—and then sneaking out of town in the middle of the night with their Roast Beast. When they wake up, their homes, hearts and lifestyle malls are as empty as the Grinch's heart.

Have you ever gone into a store having a clearance sale, and you're so excited because you are able to buy that pricey, beautiful comforter you always dreamed of having for twenty bucks? Well, your well-decorated bedroom comes at a high cost.

Quentin Tolliver rehabilitated companies. Benjie Tolliver tears them down and sells them to the highest bidder, salvaging their scraps for pennies at the end.

How have I gone from a Christmas princess to the Fräulein of Firing?

Stop being a softie, Henri, I think, looking up and down the table filled with young, hungry twenty- and thirty-somethings who don't sleep at night like Dracula, only consume protein and desperately want my corner office and salary.

Eye of the tigress, Henri.

"When I was younger, I always wanted to live in a house like this!" Benjie shouts, shaking me from my thoughts. "Who knows what movie this line is from? Dinner on me!"

Benjie plays this game of movie trivia at the start of every meeting. I know the answer, but I can't bring myself to shout it out over the testosterone-amped males surrounding me.

"8 Mile!" Maya shouts.

And that includes Maya.

"And whose house is this?" Benjie yells.

"Tolliver's House!" the executives yell.

Benjie has all the energy of a game show host who's had a quad-shot latte, six Red Bulls and a cup of sugar merged with the adrenaline of a thrill seeker who just bungee jumped off a cliff into the ocean and who then went cage diving with sharks.

Although it's 8:00 a.m. on a December Monday, I feel like I'm a contestant on *The Price Is Right.*

A fifty-two-year-old woman going through menopause, still on her first cup of coffee and sweating through her winter white sweater does not particularly respond well to this type of behavior.

"Welcome to the Monday meeting," Benjie says, falling into a sleek, ergo-friendly Herman Miller chair, which he rolls to the massive, gleaming wood conference table. "I'm going to let Maya kick off what is going to be a massive Monday and drop-dead December with her report on the TaterTot Toys takeover." He stops. "See what I did there again?"

People actually clap.

"He's so clever," Maya says.

Oh, he's a whiz with alliteration all right, I think. *Hart Henri. TaterTot Toys. Massive Monday. Drop-dead December. And you don't even know I heard him call you Moaning Maya to his buddies late one night. Such a clever guy.*

"Maya!" he yells. "It's all yours, my lady!"

And there's a lawsuit.

Maya taps her keyboard, and a report pops up on our laptop screens.

It's not a presentation per se—*Oh, no, now I'm doing the alliteration game!*—but bullet points, bold letters and lots of capital letters.

Benjie doesn't like to read. He likes bullet points. Scribbles on napkins. Arrows that go straight up.

- 1220 LAID OFF!

- ONE-TIME LAYOFF BONUS REDUCED SEVERANCE PACKAGES BY HALF!

- EARNED $12 MILLION IN 2 MONTH CLEARANCE & CLOSE!

- FOLEY PRODUCTS LOOKS TO CLEAR $120 MILLION BY 4th QTR 2024!

- PLUS! DES MOINES BUILDING & PLANT SOLD TO ANOTHER COMPANY FOR $5 MILLION IN NET, YEAR-END PROFIT!

"Look at that two-month clearance and close!" Benjie yells. "And the sale of the building and plant is sheer brilliance, Maya. That's the way we do it around here! No meat left on the carcass. Only bones. Everyone up!"

Benjie leads a standing ovation.

Maya stands and takes a bow, leaning way too far forward for comfort in that suit jacket.

"Wonderful presentation," everyone murmurs.

But business is not a simple bake sale graph.

No one asks what Foley Products plans to do with the beloved toy company that grew from the ground up. No one asks whether over a thousand employees were being assisted by Foley to procure new jobs. No one asks anything because it would hurt too much to care.

I had to stop asking to survive.

But that caring part… Well, that's another thing.

"I'm up next," Benjie continues. "If you'll look at your laptops."

Benjie taps his keyboard, and his report illuminates our laptops.

"It's a video," Benjie says, his voice as excited as a child's. "Push Play."

We all do as one.

It opens with Benjie and Maya standing in the snow in front

of a Bavarian inn that looks so similar to the buildings in my hometown that I can feel the floor, the building, the entire earth disappear below my feet until I'm floating in the snow that has once again started falling outside the window. Benjie and Maya are wearing stylish ski outfits, Maya in vivid pink, Benjie in blinding yellow. They look so beautiful, so perfect, as if they are not real, but anime characters. They point at a sign; they are in the Swiss Alps.

A camera is trained on the duo as they leap into a ski lift and drift into the air, hovering over the Alps, before being deposited into a thicket of snow. They ski up to another sign. It's a black diamond, the most dangerous of ski runs. Benjie gives a thumbs-up and then swats Maya on the rear. Suddenly Maya takes off, a whoosh of white enveloping the camera. Benjie laughs, and then he is gone with one big push of his poles.

The video changes to a firsthand view of Benjie skiing. He is obviously wearing a GoPro camera. It looks as if he is traveling at the speed of light. I grew up ice-skating and cross-country skiing, but I didn't downhill. Benjie swerves left and right, just missing pines. It doesn't look as if he's even on a groomed trail but skiing directly down the side of a mountain. It is breathtaking to witness; I cannot lie. You can hear Benjie's breath; you feel as if you are standing in his skis.

You feel as if you are capable of doing the impossible.

I look up at the team. They are mesmerized. Benjie is a master at seizing people's attention, motivating underlings to admire and emulate him, capturing the current zeitgeist.

I feel eyes on me. I skew my eyes toward the head of the table, and Benjie winks at me.

He knows that my BS detector goes off every time he pulls a stunt like this, and it galls him that he cannot win me over like his father did. I do not fall for the superficial. I've been taught since a child what is a real decoration and what is simply ornamental.

His father was, like mine, a good man at heart.

His father knew I wanted to make my own mark on the world.

Benjie is bitter he's still living in the long shadow of his father's legacy, and he's tried using that to motivate me as if we are the same.

And it infuriates me that it has worked to some degree.

Am I jealous of what my father created out of my grandparents' basement?

Or did I simply want to walk in my own light?

I catch Maya looking at Benjie.

Is that love in her eyes? Or greed?

I turn back to the video.

Benjie jumps an old bridge crossing a frozen stream.

My heart hiccups.

Or did I run because of what happened on that wooden bridge so long ago?

Benjie is flying down the hill, taking air with every mogul he hits, zipping to and fro, a blur of white. Finally, from his perspective, he comes into a clearing, and you can see not only the end of the run at the bottom of a hill but also a blip of pink.

"Yes!" Benjie says on the video, gasping for air.

He zooms past an unaware Maya and reaches the bottom of the hill first, stopping on a dime and sending snow flying. When Maya finally catches up to him, he lifts his hand. When she raises hers to high-five him, he drops it and says with a laugh, "Nice try, babe, but you will never beat me."

Everyone laughs. I look at Maya. Her cheeks are as pink as her suit, and yet she manages to laugh, too.

"So what's the lesson here?" Benjie asks. "Why did I show you this?"

"That no one will ever beat you?" asks Theo, a pale, very serious, twenty-something Ivy grad built like Superman who consumes only protein bars and, I'm pretty sure, others' blood.

"Truth!" Benjie yells. "But that's not what I'm looking for."

I glance around the table.

Seriously? I ask myself. *I have to do this?*

"That even though you give someone a head start, and even if it's someone you—" I stop, searching for just the right word "—trust, you never give up. There's always someone faster, better, smarter coming for you. The goal is to be the first one at the finish line. Everything else is second place. Everyone else is just a loser."

People's jaws drop. Maya is staring at me.

Benjie's eyes grow as big as the windows behind him. He gets to his feet and begins to slow clap.

"Get on your feet, everyone," he says.

The room stands.

"Henri, stand up and take a bow," Benjie commands.

I stand, but I don't bow. I am not, and will never be, a trained seal.

"Hart Henri is a legend around here," Benjie says. He looks at me and then adds with a twinkle in his eye, "*Was* a legend around here. But she's showing us she's still got game." Benjie stares at me. "Are you still in the game, Henri? Show me what you've got."

I suddenly feel as if this is a threat, as if I am the one on skis and a mountain lion is barreling down the mountainside directly for me.

I stare out the window at the city before me.

I came to Detroit in order to make my mark, but that's beginning to fade, my career becoming the equivalent of a long-ago tattoo on an aging bicep.

Everyone is staring at me.

I am sweating like a madwoman.

For the last few years, I feel as if I've been living in a sweat lodge, perimenopause consuming my body at the same time the young sharks began to swarm the corporate waters. I swam for survival, trying not to drown. And now menopause, coupled with the growing realization that perhaps, just perhaps, my dream career has turned into a never-ending nightmare, has made me feel like Albert Brooks in *Broadcast News*. I get the flop sweats every time the cameras and lights pop on.

My mind whirs. My entire career was built thinking on my feet.

I'm the one who secured that first store location for my father while taking a run through Frankenmuth on break from college, finding that swath of land on the outskirts of town for sale cheap.

I'm the one who, in my thirties, helped Quentin Tolliver expand his company by wooing corporate investors to back us during an elevator ride in which I shared how my father started his company in a basement.

I was the first woman to sit on the executive team here, and…

I see my reflection in the glass.

…I'm still standing.

I stare into my own eyes and ask, *But do you want to be Herz Henri or Hart Henri?*

I begin to speak in a calm, modulated tone. I've learned—in an environment of toxic masculinity—that if you speak without shouting, people are forced to still and listen.

"As we all know, Victoria Vance recently took over the company from her father, Malcolm Vance."

The room nods.

"She's working hard to send the right message that the future direction of the company will be different under her leadership, but it's still deeply tainted by her father's insider trading scandal, and as a result—" I stop and type on my laptop "—its stock price is a quarter of what it used to be." I look around the table. "It's not been helped at all by the fact that Vance Enterprises has tried to take over an aging media conglomerate as well as a hot social media company, both hostile takeovers the SEC is fighting. None of this has helped their image."

I look around the table. "Does anyone here remember how Malcolm Vance started his company?" I ask. "No, not fair. No googling." I turn to Benjie. "Oh, c'mon, you should know your history."

His face turns red. I smile.

Two can play this game, sweetheart.

"He started with a single home furnishing store in Wisconsin, and Malcolm actually sold mattresses and beds on the sales floor," I say. "He then expanded into home goods, selling not only furniture but linens, kitchenware, art and other home accessories. They were HomeGoods before HomeGoods. They were TJ Maxx before TJ Maxx. They need to return to their roots, especially in this time of inflation. These types of home goods companies are going to do exceedingly well over the next few years, which will help their bottom line. They need to focus on solid cash and their roots rather than navigating the ups and downs of social media and the tech train wreck in stocks."

I close my eyes.

"We could position this in the media as Vance Comes Home Again," I continue.

People gasp.

"And with investors, we could position it as 'Take a Chance on Vance.'"

I open my eyes. Benjie is nodding, mesmerized.

"I like it," he says. "But I feel like we need something more, something concrete to take to Victoria as a first step." Benjie drums the table with his fingers. "A real company that makes her see the value in returning to their roots."

Benjie looks at me and then at his hundred-thousand-dollar watch. I know my time is limited.

In so many ways.

I look up and see myself again in the window: my reflection against the city.

Don't do it, Henri. Don't you dare do it.

"What if I were to convince my parents to sell Wegner's Winter Wonderland?"

The entire room gasps.

"Your father's Christmas store?" Benjie asks, eyes wide again. "The largest independently owned Christmas store in the world?"

I nod.

"Can you do that?" Benjie asks.

"Watch me," I say.

Benjie slow claps again.

The entire room stands and begins to chant my name.

"Hart Henri! Hart Henri! Hart Henri!"

As we file out of the meeting room, Benjie sidles up next to me and whispers, "Where has this Henri been?" He puts his hand on my arm to slow me and waits for the room to clear. "It's almost like you have ESP."

I cock my head at him.

"What do you mean?"

"I mean, I was seriously considering letting you go before the end of the year," he says.

My head nearly explodes.

"Oh, really," I say. I try to remain calm. "I had no idea."

"Your revenue production has declined more than the stock market the last couple of years," Benjie says. "Your output just didn't justify your salary any longer. We have people that make less who are way hungrier than you are." He shakes his head. "But today it's like you knew or something. You were like Ebenezer Scrooge being visited by the three spirits of Christmas, and you chose to ignore Christmas Past. I'm proud of you." He looks me right in the eyes. "I just hope you don't change and become a kinder, gentler person like Scrooge did at the end," Benjie says. "We need Hart Henri."

He doesn't add, *Or else*. But it's implied.

"I won't disappoint you," I say. "Christmas? Bah humbug."

Benjie laughs.

"She's back, and I love it!"

I rush to my office—people congratulating me as I pass—shut the door, close the blinds, remove my suit jacket and shove Kleenex under my sweater to stop the deluge.

But I can't slow my heart or the voice in my head screaming, *What have you done, Henri?*

3

There is a soft knock on my office door.

"Come in."

"I thought you could use this."

I look up from my laptop as my assistant, Bea, delivers a mammoth coffee.

"It's a triple-shot pumpkin-spice latte, oat milk, with only half the pumpkin spice but an extra shot of white chocolate and a drizzle of gingerbread," she says, setting the cup on my desk. "It's the equivalent of a caffeinated Christmas."

I smile.

"Thank you," I say. "Is this what Santa drinks before he drives his sleigh across the world?"

"Santa has one of these in each time zone," Bea says with a wink. "And I have one every morning in December."

"Thank you, Aunt Bea."

"You're welcome," she says with a laugh and shake of her head at my nickname for her. "And you wanted me to update your Microsoft Teams, right?"

I nod and scoot my office chair back so she can get to my laptop.

Beatrice Schneider is diminutive and pretty with raven hair that falls in perfect ringlets down her back. She looks like the actress Lacey Chabert, and—yes, if you return to my house for the holidays, you must watch Hallmark at Christmas with my mother.

I think of this morning's meeting, my stomach drops and I take a sip of the latte to rekindle the holiday spirit.

Beatrice is a Columbia grad who's getting her feet wet working alongside me, and I've been trying to teach her to walk the high wire that is working at Tolliver & Co. without falling to her death. She is smart as a whip, unaffected and deeply kind, attributes that can lead to your downfall here.

She reminds me of me when I was young and fresh out of school.

During a follow-up interview lunch, Beatrice told me how hard it was being named after your grandmother in a world of Ashleys, Madisons, Hannahs, Tiffanys and Britneys.

I had laughed and nearly broken my neck nodding my head in agreement.

"Tell me about it," I said. "Try growing up being called what everyone believed was a boy's name."

"It actually gave me strength," Bea had said. "And now I understand why my parents did it. My grandma was a wonderful woman, and her name instills a sense of pride in me."

Her sentiment had nearly and unexpectedly brought me to tears, and I hired her on the spot. However, during the luncheon, I had remarked that she looked like Lacey Chabert.

"Who?" she had asked.

"*Party of Five*? The TV show?" I asked. "In the '90s."

"I wasn't born yet," she had said.

Gut punch.

"She was in *Mean Girls*?" I had pressed. "The movie?"

Bea had shaken her head. "I think I was two when that came out."

That spurred a nonstop attempt on my part to pepper Bea—as well as our young waiter—about celebrities from my youth.

"Jane Fonda?"
"Walter Cronkite?"
"Burt Reynolds?"
"Farrah Fawcett?"
"Shaun Cassidy? Goldie Hawn? David Bowie? Tina Turner?"
Bug eyes, head shakes.
"Are you kidding me?" I'd yelled. "Not even a rerun of *Andy Griffith*?"
Nothing.
"All right, Aunt Bea," I'd called her jokingly. "If you're going to work for me, I've got to get you up to speed a little bit on how I grew up."
And the nickname had stuck and become a term of affection.
"Done!" Bea says, knocking me from my thoughts. "Oh, and speaking of Christmas, I'll be right back with your mail."
"Mail?" I call after her as she zips out of my office. "What's that?"
I remember when Mr. Haley would bring the mail. My grandmother would line her kitchen cabinets with Christmas cards from friends and family.
When I started working here, we'd use interoffice mail, printing out letters and documents and sticking them in large, lined envelopes on which we'd write the name of the intended recipient.
Now, our lives are email, Zoom, Facebook, TikTok, Instagram and online shopping.
As if on cue, my laptop dings, and I open an email.
I hear a grunt. I glance up to see Bea carrying a massive package enclosed in a bright red, glittering padded envelope.
"Did someone send me a microwave?" I ask.
Bea laughs and drops the package on the edge of my desk with a thud.
"What is it?" I ask.

She shrugs her shoulders. "Don't know, but it sure is pretty," Bea offers, nodding at the shimmering red packaging.

"Pretty big," we say in unison with a laugh.

I open my desk drawer, remove a pair of scissors and open the end of the envelope. I slide the surprise free.

Wegner's Winter Wonderland Wish Book, 2023.

Christmas past.

The cover of the catalog features a photo of me as a little girl sitting on the shag carpet in my grandparents' basement—my wish catalogs spread before me, my father's early Christmas signs in the background—staring into the glowing faux brick fireplace.

I look as if I am making a Christmas wish.

The type below the photo reads:

What Do You Wish for This Christmas?
We Already Know!
To Be a Kid Again!

"Is that…?" Bea starts.

I nod. "It's me."

When my dad was building his new world, and I was dreaming of building mine.

"Talk about timing," she adds.

"You know, the real Aunt Bea was never ironic or sarcastic," I say.

She smiles. "Sorry. Just trying to deflect after this morning's bombshell." Bea catches my eye. "Are you okay?"

I shrug.

Didn't I do the exact same thing when my dad asked what I was building?

"Let me know if you need anything else," Bea says.

"Thanks."

She closes the door behind her.

I stand, pick up the wish catalog and sit on the floor in the middle of my office, just like the girl in the picture.

I stare at the cover.

How old was I? How young were my parents?

I open the catalog and have a flashback of me as a girl wondering if my dad realized that the world was changing. I remember long ago admonishing him and my mom for continuing to produce this costly catalog in an online world.

"You could save so much money," I argued, presenting them with a printout of what I'd estimated. "Just put everything on your website, send e-catalogs..."

"No!" my dad had suddenly said. "Some things should never change."

He had pushed away his plate filled with late-night, pre-Christmas pizza and challenged me with his eyes.

"Somewhere, right now, there is a little girl just like you looking through this catalog and dreaming about what she wants for Christmas. Kids at school have probably told her it's silly to still believe in Santa Claus any longer, that board games are dumb or it's stupid to make a Christmas wish. This catalog, like our store, is something tangible and real, something people can touch and feel, something that is magical and not marketing. I will never stop doing this no matter how old-fashioned you think it might be. This connects people. It still matters to people. And that's all that matters to me."

How many years ago was that? I wonder. Was that the last time I was home for Christmas?

I turn a page, and it is filled with one-of-a-kind snow globes. Some are cardinals on a branch, some happy snowmen. And then I see it, the snow-globe scene my father created so long ago of a miniature Bavarian village—just like Frankenmuth—in a Christmas blizzard. My eyes drift like the snow in the glass toward the main attraction: the Glockenspiel Tower just like the one downtown.

I shut my eyes and can still hear the music.

The German word *Glockenspiel* quite literally translates into "bells play."

I open my eyes and study my father's craftsmanship.

A perfect miniature replication of the Bavarian Inn's magnificent thirty-five-bell carillon complete with dancing figurines and an illuminated clock.

I shut my eyes again and can hear the clock chime, just as it did on each quarter hour. Starting at noon, the glockenspiel would play the Westminster chimes followed by several musical selections followed by a figurine theater come to life depicting the legend of the Pied Piper of Hamelin.

My heart sinks again thinking of the legend.

I am a rat.

I open my eyes, shake my head and that's when I notice in the globe—just beyond the glockenspiel—the Holz Brücke. *Holz Brücke* is German for "wooden bridge" and is Michigan's largest covered wooden bridge. It crosses the Cass River, which magically runs through downtown Frankenmuth.

I lean my face toward the wish book and run my fingers over the bridge.

I can still feel the splinters in my heart.

Winter 1988

Snow fell lightly on the Cass River. The flakes swirled around my head, whispering, *Welcome home, Henri.*

White lights outlined the entrance to the Holz Brücke, whose latticework architecture tossed a beautiful illuminated pattern across the darkening, still river.

Frankenmuth was bustling, as usual, at Christmas, but the closer I got to the wooden bridge, the quieter the world became.

"It's good to have you home! I missed you so much!"

I nearly jumped out of my winter coat. Sofie, my best friend in the world, was standing in front of the tiny, two-lane bridge, waving. She always knew how to shatter the silence.

"I missed you, too!" I yelled.

We ran into each other's arms and hugged until a car honked for us to step out of the way.

"Look at you," Sofie said. "You look like such a college girl now. No! You look like one of those Robert Palmer video girls!"

I was wearing all black with bright red lipstick, dark eye makeup, my hair pulled back off my face.

"A blonde Palmer girl," I said with a laugh. "Look at you!"

Sofie twirled. "Some things never change."

She was wearing a dirndl—a Bavarian costume consisting of a tight bodice with a low neckline, a blouse underneath, a wide, high-waisted skirt and an apron. A small floral wreath known as a *jungfernkranz* was in her blond hair, topped by a bonnet called a *goldhaube*.

Sofie's parents owned Z's Chicken Haus of Frankenmuth, which had been in business since the horse-and-buggy days in the mid-1850s. It was a local, national and international dining hotspot now, known for its amazing all-you-can-eat dinners consisting of heaping platters of home-cooked German food, namely their signature cabbage, mashed potatoes, dressing, buttered egg noodles and the best golden fried chicken in the world. Just ask the one million guests who visited every year.

Sofie was majoring in business at Michigan State, but she returned home nearly every weekend to help her parents with the restaurant, which she'd been doing since she was a girl and why she was dressed in a dirndl.

I smiled. Sofie hadn't changed much since we became friends during May Day long ago.

"Aren't you cold?" I asked.

"Yes," she said with a laugh. "But I'll be sweating like crazy the rest of the night."

I turned to look at the downtown sparkling in the snow and holiday lights in the near distance.

"Beautiful, isn't it?" Sofie asked. "Miss it?"

I ignored her question.

"Miss me?"

"Of course," I said, grabbing her hand and giving it a good shake. "Every minute of every day. So? What do you think is going on?"

Sofie's blue eyes grew wide. "I think Shep's going to ask you to marry him."

The snow and lights blurred around me.

"No way," I said. "We've never even talked about it. The timing is all wrong."

"He's going to take over his family business, I'm going to take over my family business and so are you," Sofie countered. "We'll all be here together forever. Like a storybook. Nothing will ever change."

"Hey, Sofie. Hi, Henri."

Sofie yelped.

"Heya, Shep!" she said, opening her arms. "It's been a minute."

He laughed and gave Sofie a brotherly hug around her shoulders. "It's not like we see each other pretty much every weekend, although neither of us has time for any fun."

"Speaking of which…I'm going to be so late," Sofie said, taking off. "And frostbitten."

We watched her bolt toward downtown, her body becoming smaller and smaller until it, too, was just another snowflake in the sky.

"It's good to see you," I said.

Shep opened his arms. I merged into the warmth of his body and then he kissed me.

"I've missed you so much. This has always been our magical place, hasn't it?" he asked, dusting the snow off the shoulders of my coat and leading me inside the Holz Brücke. "That perfect spot we've always come to talk, laugh…and, well, other stuff."

I slugged him playfully on the shoulder to hide my anxiety.

He continued, "Being here with you, Henri, always makes me feel as if I'm floating in midair, as if anything is possible, as if our past is meeting our future, and we can go anywhere we want together."

My heart raced.

"I just want to hold you right here on the bridge, in the quiet of winter, forever."

I put my head on his shoulder and closed my eyes.

It had always been me and Shep.

Together. For as long as I could remember.

Brandon Shepherd had gone by the nickname Shep—just like his father, grandfather and great-grandfather—since birth. It was perfectly fitting, too: the Shepherds had founded and owned the Shepherd Woolen Mill in town since the late 1800s. They used to process wool from local farm flocks into warm wool bedding to help families survive the harsh Michigan and Midwestern winters. Then, the company began to make major league baseball uniforms, hats and even the balls themselves. Four layers of wool yarn—as Shep has told me so many times—or 316 yards' worth, were compressed around the cork-and-rubber core before being sealed with tanned cowhide and stitched with bright red string.

Over the years, the famed mill had transformed into making the highest-quality wool comforters and bedding in the world. Shep said one day the world would move to buying things on computers, and though many laughed at him, I believed in his vision.

Things change.

"How's senior year going?" I asked, trying to change the subject.

"Flying by," he said. "I can't wait until it's over. How about you?"

"Busy," I said. "Sometimes I still feel like Melanie Griffith in *Working Girl*, a scholarship kid completely out of place and totally out of my league."

Shep shook his head. "Not you. My Henri's always been the smartest in the class. And your dad's business is really taking off. We may never have it as easy as your fellow Michigan grads with fancy jobs in big cities, but we'll always do okay. Our kids will never want for a thing. Small-town life."

Our kids.

Small town.

Shep stared into my eyes.

Shep was the most handsome boy I'd ever seen in my life. He looked a lot like Rob Lowe: longish, dark hair, eyes the blue of the bay in the middle of summer, full lips that curled when he was about to tell you something funny and cheeks that flushed pink in the cold like they were doing right now.

I met him the same day I met Sofie. I was in class 1A in first grade, and Sofie and Shep were in 1B. The entire school gathered in the gym to make the long ribbons to decorate the Maypole, an annual and beloved tradition in Frankenmuth. Sofie and Shep got bored and began to wrap themselves in ribbon, and I laughed so hard I just had to join in the fun. We had been bound together—literally tied by similar histories—ever since.

Shep reached out his hand, and I followed him to the pedestrian walkway on the edge of the bridge.

Although the bridge looked ancient, it was actually just a few years old, built recently, the dream of the town's leaders to mark a bridge to the future and the past as well as to connect the downtown to undeveloped property across the river that had no access. It was still the talk of the town.

I knew all about the building of the bridge. I had to, working in retail at Wegner's alongside my family. Every tourist wanted to walk across it. Every visitor wanted to know its history.

I scanned the lattice-truss bridge as we walked. The Holz Brücke weighed 230 tons and stretched some 240 feet across the Cass River. It was built mostly of Douglas fir and clad with some 25,000 cedar shingles. Everyone in town came out to the river every day in January when I was a girl to watch a team of oxen pull the completed bridge into place over twelve days at a pace of three inches per minute.

Shep stopped. He ran his finger over a board that faced the water and looked out at the river. He looked at me and then I followed his gaze back down.

He was tracing his finger over a heart we had carved into the board a few years ago, our initials in the middle of it.

And that's when I saw it.

A velvet box tied to the rail with a ribbon next to our initials.

My real heart thumped in my chest.

Shep untied the ribbon.

In slow motion, I saw him drop to his knees.

"I think I've loved you since the moment we got tied together in first grade," Shep said. "I know I will love you forever."

"Shep," I started.

"This bridge was built to connect our past to our future, and that's what I want to do with you, Henri Wegner."

He opened the box.

A diamond ring glimmered in the bridge's lights.

Shep pulled out the ring and held it up to me.

Inside the band were our initials. Not just any initials engraved by a jeweler, but replicas of the initials—along with the heart—that we had carved right here on the bridge.

"You are a part of my heart," Shep said. "We are one. We will always be one. Henri Wegner, would you do the honor of marrying me and making me the happiest man in the world?"

The ring glimmered before me, a stationary snowflake.

In the distance, Frankenmuth twinkled.

I shut my eyes. I could see my entire future before me. I could see dirndls, wool sweaters, working at Wegner's.

My life would be the life I already knew.

"I love you more than anything, Shep," I started.

He looked at me, eyes narrowing as if preparing for pain.

"It sounds like there's a 'but' in there, Henri. You're scaring me."

"But I have my senior year still to finish," I said. "It's very stressful. And I've been interviewing with an incredible company in Detroit called Tolliver & Company. They only hire one new graduate every year. I'm one of the final five, the only woman."

Shep stood.

"When were you going to tell me all this, Henri?"

"I *have* been telling you all this, Shep. You just haven't been listening."

Shep stared at me and then into the river.

"Aren't I enough? Isn't this life good enough?"

The tone of his voice shattered my soul.

"I think I just want the chance to build something of my own first," I said. "I've lived my father's dream for so long. It's nice to be seen as Henri Wegner, not as Jakob Wegner's daughter, the Christmas kid. And I just don't think I'm ready to know what the next fifty years are already going to look like at this stage of my life."

"What if they can always look like this?" he asked, gesturing at the winter scene around us. "What if they will always be filled with love?"

"Can you give me a little time to figure it all out?" I asked.

Shep sighed, releasing all the air from his body. His head sagged, like a balloon losing its helium.

"I will, but we already know the answer, don't we?"

"Shep, please understand. The timing just doesn't feel right."

"This bridge only leads me back to Frankenmuth, but it's leading you far away from here," Shep said. "We see the same thing, just in totally different ways."

He put the ring back into the box and snapped the lid shut.

It was as if—at that exact moment—I could feel his heart do the same.

"Will I see you at Christmas?" he asked.

"Nothing's changed," I insist.

The saddest, most knowing smile crossed his face.

"Right, Henri. Nothing's changed."

He turned and trudged off into the snow.

"Merry Christmas, Henri," he said, sliding the box into his coat pocket. "I do love you. More than anything."

My entire being wanted to call after him, *Stop, Shep! I made a mistake! I love you more than anything, too.*

But then the glockenspiel chimed again in the distance, as if adding a resounding period to this chapter of my life.

Shep turned, lifting his hand and striking the air in sync with each and every chime. A knowing smile came over his face.

"It's all about timing, isn't it, Henri?"

I watched Shep walk off the bridge and disappear into the snow.

I collapsed into tears, heaving, holding on to the wooden bridge for support, our heart blurring before my eyes, and then I turned and walked the other way.

I jerk upright when a stray tear hits the cover of the wish book, a wet bull's-eye on the face of a little girl who once believed in Santa and love, a woman who gave up the known for a world of adventure, who gave up safety to do it all on her own.

I wipe the tear off the cover and then trace my finger over my face.

"I can still see me in you," I say to the image. "Trapped in there somewhere."

I dab my eyes and then shut them.

I can still see Shep's face—and anguish—on that bridge.

Did I create my destiny that day?

Or did I throw my future away on that bridge?

I'm still haunted by the ghosts of that long-ago decision, the memories making me feel as if I have some sort of sensory survivor's guilt.

What if the timing had been different?

I have dated many men in my life, some good, some not. But none have compared to Shep, either in looks or heart. He was a kind person, a good man, and I've learned those are as rare as finding the perfect Christmas tree.

When I fall asleep alone, a fifty-plus-year-old woman, I wonder to this day what my life would look like if I had turned and run to him across that bridge.

Maybe I'm just scared.

Maybe I've been scared my whole life and worn my faux bravado like a winter coat.

Perhaps that has been my Christmas curse: I'm too scared of reliving that heartbreak so I choose not to live—and love—at all.

Over the years, my heart has become a lot like the baseballs Shep's family used to make: wrapped in layers so it won't feel too much when it gets hit by emotion.

I get up to grab my laptop off my desk and return to the floor, just like the girl on the cover.

Of course, I've stalked Shep on Facebook over the years. I mean, what totally normal, self-respecting ex-girlfriend doesn't do that?

For many years, I would look him up on social media—after a glass of wine in a hotel room in some city—to follow the Frankenmuth family that might have been mine.

After I accepted the job with Tolliver and moved to Detroit, Shep and I gave the long-distance game a go for a few months.

But our relationship was already on life support after that day on the bridge. I was working eighty-plus hours a week, every weekend, and Shep was overwhelmed trying to modernize his family business. One Friday, Shep called to say he couldn't make it to Detroit for the weekend, and we just sort of stopped talking after that. There was no major blowup, just a sad dissolution. Since I turned down his proposal, our relationship felt like a sandcastle on the edge of the ocean: you knew it was going to collapse; you just didn't know when.

And then one Christmas when I was working on a deal and couldn't make it home for the holidays—the start of a very long pattern—Sofie called.

"Shep's dating Hannah."

My sandcastle caught a massive wave.

Hannah Clausen.

The Pukey Palindrome, as Sofie referred to her since we were kids.

Hannah's family owned Clausen's Chicken Haus, the rival to Sofie's family's business. The two restaurants sat right across the street from one another.

Hannah and Sofie always disliked one another. And I disliked Hannah for that alone, not to mention she was rich and rude, acting like her family put Frankenmuth on the map.

Do you know how you feel as if you're finally feeling emotionally healthy after a breakup, and then you hear your ex is dating?

But Hannah Clausen?

How could Shep have ended up with *her*?

When MySpace started, and then Facebook took over the world, I began to open photo albums of Shep and Hannah. It was like a View-Master of their entire life: Hannah the bride, Hannah pregnant, moving into a new home, first-day-of-school pictures.

I wished for Hannah to gain weight after the birth of her two children, a beautiful boy and girl.

I wished for Shep's cheeks to pale, his lips to narrow, his hair to thin and his waist to expand.

None of those wishes came true.

They seemed as perfect as the pictures they posted.

And then Sofie called me late one night.

"They're getting divorced," she announced.

That was five years ago.

My laptop trills with a FaceTime from Sofie.

"It's like you can read my mind," I say after I accept the call.

I hear dishes clattering. I am staring at a serving tray filled with dishes stacked a mile high with chicken, noodles and mashed potatoes. I see parsley fall like snow from above.

"Winner, winner, chicken dinner!" I hear Sofie say, clapping her hands. "This is the way one of Z's Chicken Haus of Frankenmuth's famous all-you-can-eat dinners should look! Presentation, people! Smile! Now, go feed the troops!"

The platter disappears.

"Hello?" I call. "Sofie?"

I see a hand grab a cell. A red-faced Sofie appears.

"Oh, my gosh, I'm so sorry," she says. "I think I dirndl dialed you."

I laugh. It feels good to laugh.

Sofie lowers the phone to show me where she had it placed: in the band of her apron over her little Bavarian dress, which every waitress at Z's wears. It's tradition, and the customers love it. *Bavarian branding*, Sofie calls it.

"They'll bury me in a dirndl," Sofie says. "What's up, my Bavarian boo?" She peers at the camera. "Are you sitting on the floor? When did you become a kindergarten teacher?"

"Yes, and I wish," I say. "Well, it was meant to be that you called. I was just thinking of you."

"You know how December is around here," Sofie says. "The

entire world comes to Frankenmuth to shop at your parents' Christmas store and then bus over here to fill their bellies with chicken."

I think of Hannah and Shep.

Their world has always been constant.

"Speaking of which," Sofie starts. "I saw the Pukey Palindrome. I mean, I see her almost every day, but this time she actually spoke to me."

She *can* read my mind.

"One of the tourist buses parked in front of Hannah's restaurant yesterday letting people off," she continues. "We had a big snow, the streets hadn't been plowed and the lots were full, so drivers didn't have anywhere to park, and, well, you know old people and snow."

I laugh again.

Sofie continues, "Hannah came out, and I thought she was going to try and steer everyone into *her* restaurant like she's done before. Instead, she said, 'Merry Christmas, Sofie.' I couldn't believe it. I mean, there was no one behind her with a gun to her head or anything. So I said, 'Merry Christmas,' and asked how she was doing. She just sort of shrugged. She looked kind of sad. I actually felt sorry for her, Henri."

"Wow," I say.

"So I walked over and gave her a hug," Sofie says. "She just stood there, stiff as a board, but finally she put her head on my shoulder and just let me hold her. It was surreal."

My heart pings. For the first time of my life, I actually can see Hannah as a real, flesh-and-blood human being, not as my longtime frenemy or the woman who swept in on Shep after I left.

"The holidays must be hard for her," I volunteer. "After the divorce."

"I think so. The holidays are hard for a lot of us," Sofie says. "Too many people acting like the world is perfect when others are battling lots of bad memories, or loss. You've been through the wringer a time or two at the holidays."

She's not wrong.

"Speaking of which, what century might I expect to see you again for Christmas?"

"Ha-ha," I say. "Actually..."

Before I can finish my sentence, she screams, "You're coming home for Christmas?"

"I am."

"That's amazing! But why?"

I take a breath and try to decide how much to tell my best friend.

"It's time to come home."

A lie that is actually not a lie.

"We're going to have so much fun!" she sings. "I can't wait to drink wine and break stuff with you."

I laugh and then—as if on cue with her joke—I hear a cacophony of glass breaking in the background. Sofie shakes her head.

"Speaking of," she says. "I have to go before someone gets a piece of glass in their cabbage. It's hard being an adult, isn't it?"

"Amen, sister," I say.

"I love you! Can't wait to see you soon IRL!"

"Me, too."

Sofie's phone suddenly goes waist level again, and she is on the move, navigating into the restaurant. She stops before a mountain of chicken and noodles on the carpet and ends the call.

I glance down at the wish book again.

"You're going home again for Christmas," I say to the little girl.

4

December 11

I'm standing at the floor-to-ceiling windows in my penthouse condominium overlooking the Detroit River. Snow is falling lightly, the city set against the water, beautiful Belle Isle in the near distance.

Belle Isle is a 982-acre park developed in the late nineteenth century, an island in the Detroit River featuring historic, environmental and cultural attractions that have been beloved for generations, as well as several surrounding islets. The US-Canada border is in the channel south of Belle Isle.

I wonder how my father would draw this?

Perspective in art quite literally means drawing solid objects on a two-dimensional surface in order to give the impression of their size in relation to one another when viewed from a particular point.

I have zero artistic talent. Zero. And yet I am a student—and admirer—of those things I cannot do, art and unabashed creativity topping that list.

My father might replicate this scene in a snow globe or intricately on the front of a Christmas ornament.

In life, perspective is a way of considering an issue from another perspective.

Essentially, as in art, we draw our own way of seeing the world.

My perspective has changed over the years.

So have my borders.

Winter 1988

Have you ever lain on your back underneath the Christmas tree and stared into its branches?

A Christmas tree looks entirely different from this perspective, as if you're lost in a great forest, searching for the North Star over the top of the tallest tree to guide you home again.

And yet this viewpoint makes you look at the familiar in a different way: the known—the decorated tree—looks unrecognizable from here. It is an assortment of branches, wires, hangers, backward ornaments. But, when you look long enough, you begin to appreciate the symmetry of the branches, the way the unseen structure supports the beauty on the outside.

This was my vantage point—my head resting on my grandma's felt appliqué tree skirt, staring into the branches, something I hadn't done since I was a girl—two days before Christmas, two days after I'd rejected Shep's proposal, two hours after I received the call at home from Mr. Tolliver offering me a job after I graduated from Michigan.

My entire world was upside down.

I heard the front door slam, footsteps leading up the stairway, the refrigerator opening and closing numerous times, more footsteps. My father's face appeared among the branches, his mouth munching a sandwich.

"I thought you were coming down to the store to help?" he asked.

The lights on the tree made his face look like a kaleidoscope.

"Okay, what gives?" he continued. "You've been acting oddly for days. Is something going on at school?"

"Shep asked me to marry him," I said.

"What?" my father yelped.

"I said no."

"Well, you're both still young. You have all the time in the world."

"And I just got a job offer from Tolliver & Company, the firm I've been interviewing with for the last couple of months. Starts in May when I graduate." I hesitated. "In Detroit."

"Congratulations," my father boomed. "I'm proud of you. But that's a lot to digest in a few days." He took a bite of his sandwich. "Way more than this bologna. So? What do you think you're going to do?"

He asked this without judgment.

I scooched my body from underneath the tree, sat up and looked at my dad.

"I'm going to take the job."

"I'm very proud of you, Henri," he said again. "Making your dreams come true. You've worked very hard for this." His left eyelid twitched. He lowered the sandwich. "But I also extended you an offer. I'd love to work alongside you, Henri. Expand this business. It's finally beginning to take off after all these years. I just want you to know I would love to have you on board just as much as Tolliver." He looked thoughtful. "May I ask what they are offering that we can't?"

"Oh, Dad," I said. "It's more than money or benefits. It's a new start in a new city. I can prove myself with Tolliver, make my own mark. Please don't be mad."

"I'm not mad, Henri," he said. "I'm just a bit sad. I feel like we started Wegner's together, when it was just you and me in that basement. Is it really so bad here?"

"Dad…" My voice broke.

"I don't mean to be selfish, Henri, I really don't, but I can't imagine Wegner's—and Christmas—without you. You found the property for our building. You've had so many ideas about branding. You see the future."

"You created your own destiny, Dad. I want to do the same."

"You can do that here, Henri. You will be able to travel the world searching for the best Christmas decorations. You will be able to build something that is ours, something that you can believe in, something that makes your hometown and its people stronger." My dad's voice was so soft, it was as if he was the wind whispering its secrets to me. "And we can do that together. Leave a legacy that will last forever."

"I've always wanted to build something of my own, Dad. I think I need a shot to do that. I hope you understand." I stopped. "Please understand."

He nodded, but I could see his fingers tighten around his sandwich, crumpling it between his fingers.

"You will always be my Christmas Prinzessin."

I watched him head to the door, and then it was quiet.

I lay back down and stared at my familiar world, completely upside down.

I stare out the window.

Ever since then, I have been Belle Isle, so close to home, but an island, adrift and isolated, especially at Christmas.

The lights come on in a condo across the street. Moments later, a Christmas tree blinks in the window. It's a big tree, limbs heavy with decorations, and a woman moves next to the tree and touches an ornament. My first thought—as it has been my whole life whenever I look at a tree—is: *I bet those ornaments came from Wegner's.*

The woman catches me watching, and she waves.

I return a wave, my legs growing shaky. I feel as if I might just faint, and I move to the sofa and take a seat.

The *Wegner's Wish Book* stares at me from the coffee table.

"What have you done?" I ask myself aloud.

I've created my own version of *Squid Game*. I have to sacrifice my family to save myself.

My stomach somersaults, and I feel as if I might get sick.

My father started Wegner's in my grandparents' basement, working himself to the bone to make his dream come true. Everyone doubted him, except his family. And he created a successful business all on his own.

I feel as if I have the proverbial angel on one shoulder and devil on the other.

The angel is whispering, *But your parents are getting older. You can ensure they will be taken care of forever, along with Finn and his family. Wegner's will continue and have massive backing to expand it, perhaps take it globally. Good job, Henri.*

But the devil whispers, *You know the business will never be the same once it's sold. It will be dissected, gutted, turned into quick pop-up shops in abandoned malls all over the US, just like all those Halloween stores, to make as much profit as possible off the cheapest products. In a few years, the Wegner's legacy will be gone.*

What possessed me to promise Benjie I could get them to sell?

He was planning on firing me, with zero warning. My father would never do that.

I have become so consumed by career and money—making it in a male-dominated industry—that I've lost all perspective entirely. Am I just a grown-up version of the girl who walked away from her father and Frankenmuth so long ago?

Have I made my own mark?

Or have I simply left a stain on society and my family's good name?

And what will I say to my parents?

Hi, Mom and Dad! I'm home! Merry Christmas after, what, a decade? Just here for some eggnog and Santa cookies! Oh, and to steal your business out from under you in the middle of the night just like the Grinch. You'll never know because you love and trust me.

I stand and race to the bathroom. I put my head in the sink and splash water on my face.

When I look up, I'm—literally and figuratively—green.

My doorbell buzzes.

"I brought the pizza," Bea says as I pull open the door.

"I have the wine," I say.

Then she looks at me. "You don't look well. Are you okay?"

"Wrestling with the outcome of my decision," I say. "Think I'm on Santa's naughty list."

Bea doesn't laugh.

"I'm sorry we have to work on a Friday night," I continue, trying to be nice and change the subject.

"You've worked every Friday night for as long as I've known you," Bea says.

She's not having it tonight.

I lead Bea to the kitchen. She places the pizza on the counter, and I grab a bottle of wonderful Cab, two glasses and plates.

"Nothing like Detroit pizza, is there?" I ask, still trying.

Finally, she nods. "My favorite."

While Chicago is famed for its deep-dish pizza, and St. Louis is known for its thin crust, Detroit loves its rectangular pizza with a thick crust that is both crispy and chewy. Our pizza is traditionally topped with Wisconsin brick cheese that goes all the way to the edges and caramelizes against the high-sided heavyweight rectangular pan.

"I forgot how beautiful your home is," Bea says, looking around.

"Thank you," I say, leading her to the dining room table. "I love living in the clouds."

I think back to my childhood home, the one my parents bought after our starter ranch, the one that makes me feel as if I am living in a tree house when I go home for the holidays.

My condo is a large open concept design. The big, contemporary kitchen with two islands opens to the living room and dining room, a modern fireplace against the far wall.

"Why don't you have any holiday decorations up?" Bea says, taking a sip of her red wine. She looks at me. "Considering... You know."

I smile, take a bite of pizza and glance around the room. "Ah, me and Christmas. A complicated couple."

"Do you need a holiday therapist?" she asks. "I'm game."

"I just might actually," I say. "Truth? I have boxes upon boxes of ornaments, lights, snow globes, signs, plaques, wreaths...you name it, I've got it. It's just sort of hard to look at all of that this time of year."

Bea cocks an eyebrow.

I swirl my wine in my glass and continue. "My childhood boyfriend asked me to marry him over Christmas break my senior year in college. I said no. Then I was offered the job with Tolliver just a couple of days after that. I broke my boyfriend's heart and then I broke my dad's heart when I told him I was going to accept. Christmas has never really been the same since then." I take a sip of my wine. "I think I've let this job consume me. I offered, year after year, to work on the holidays, travel, stay on the road just so I wouldn't have to see my ex or face my family again this time of year." I hesitate. "Actually, so I wouldn't have to see the hurt on their faces or face my own decisions."

Bea tilts her eyes toward her plate and finishes a piece of pizza.

"You know, I lost my mom when I was young, and it's still hard, especially at the holidays. The last thing I wanted to do when I went away to college and then got this job was to go home again because the hurt was too great. But I did." Bea looks at me. "Not for me, Henri, but for my family. They needed me there. Avoiding them just made that void even bigger."

Bea sips her wine. "You can't take anything for granted,

Henri. Not one moment, not one Christmas, because one day, your family will be gone, and you will never get that back. If you don't celebrate what you have, you will look back and not be able to forgive yourself. It will be much worse than the guilt you feel right now. You don't want to live with that regret. You have to try and enjoy these moments while they last. Because, trust me, they won't last forever, Henri."

"How old are you again?" I ask. "You certainly have the wisdom of Aunt Bea. Seriously, thank you."

"So then, why don't we give it a try?" Bea says, clapping her hands and standing suddenly. "Let's decorate for the holidays tonight. Try to reset how you look at Christmas. Maybe starting in your own home will make you see things differently."

Perspective.

"But I'm leaving town soon. We're exactly two weeks away from Christmas. My entire life is on the line. Tonight is supposed to be a working dinner. If you're going to step in for me, I need to show you the ropes."

"I know the ropes already," she says. "It's not like you haven't prepared me. Tonight should be more of a holiday party, don't you think? For the both of us. You're going home to the world's largest Christmas store. I'm going home to a three-hundred-square-foot apartment. We both need a little Christmas."

"We have so much work to do," I protest.

"We can discuss work while we decorate."

She begins to walk away as if I have already agreed.

"Where are your decorations?"

I lead her to my guest room.

"You have a walk-in closet in your guest room?" she asks. "I think I hate you."

I open the closet door.

"Hello, Christmas!" Bea gasps.

The entire closet—save for a corner big enough for a guest to stack a suitcase and hang their clothes—is stuffed with red and green bins, wreaths and signs hanging on hooks, shelves lined with snow globes.

Bea unsnaps the top of a tub marked Frankenmuth & Santa Ornaments.

She turns, eyes wide.

"How many ornaments do you have?"

"How much time do you have?"

"They're all so well organized," she marvels as she peeks beneath the lid.

"You grow up and work in the world's largest Christmas store, you learn how to organize and merchandise," I say. "That's the way my parents have always laid out the store. Each area is dedicated to a specific ornament design my father created—Christmas trees, snowmen and Santas, religious, Old World, family and friends, kids, hobbies and occupations, spun glass, snowflakes and icicles, not to mention areas for nativity scenes, lights, stockings, Christmas trees and every kind of miniature village you can imagine, from Peanuts to Precious Moments. There are millions of ornaments for every type of Christmas collector."

"I would be in heaven!" she says, yanking out a tub and then another into the bedroom. "Where's your tree?"

I point at a stack of long boxes in another corner. "Which one?" I laugh. "I have two traditional green artificial trees—one ten-foot, one slim-line—a silver and a pink, both with rotating color wheels. At home, we used to go to a tree farm and select a live tree together. We love balsams, Douglas and Fraser firs, Scotch pines and blue spruces. After Christmas, we used to plant a tree on the acreage surrounding our Silent Night Memorial Chapel in honor of the one we cut down and decorate it with a plaque stating the type of tree and year."

"Your silent what?" Bea asks.

"It's a replica of the original chapel in Austria where 'Silent Night' was first sung on Christmas Eve in 1818. It's open year-round, and lots of customers visit our store not only to shop but to pray and meditate."

I think of the many hours I used to spend in there.

"I think I have to visit one day."

I nod. "You would love it. It's less than a hundred miles from here, but it's a world away."

A different world.

Bea drags a giant box containing the ten-foot tree into the bedroom.

"I want traditional," Bea says. "And go big or go home, right?"

The irony of her words strikes me.

I sigh. "If we're going to do this right—and I mean, *everything* right—we have a lot of work to do."

I play some Rat Pack Christmas music, a favorite of my grandparents' and now mine as I've grown older, and we begin to put up the tree in the large windows overlooking the river. While we extend and fluff branches, I run through all the projects Bea will need to manage while I'm gone as well as all the details with the Vance Enterprises deal I need her to oversee.

"I know Benjie," I say, "and at some point, he'll lose patience with how slowly things are progressing and will want to take over, but we cannot let him. Got it?"

Bea nods.

I continue, "I have two weeks to convince my parents." I inhale sharply. "And that will not be easy. I'm going to need a few days just to work up the courage."

Bea gives me a look but doesn't say a word. I pretend not to notice.

As we begin to open the boxes upon boxes of ornaments that I've received since I was a girl, I—without realizing it—switch from talking about the takeover to sharing stories about each ornament. I tell Bea all about the ornaments featuring my father's art—like the girl catching a snowflake on her tongue, to

Mabel, my family's beloved, now ancient mutt, snuggled on the tree skirt amid the gifts under the twinkling lights.

When we finally finish hanging ornaments, I grab two more glasses of wine, and Bea and I sit on the couch and stare at the tree, mesmerized, just as I did as a girl.

"Don't do it," Bea says, breaking the silence.

She pivots on the couch to look at me.

"You're making a huge mistake. Your job is not worth this, Henri. Your family is more important."

"I'll lose my job," I say, my voice barely audible over the holiday music. "Benjie will fire me. He told me that. My career will be over."

"So what? Is that more important than your family?"

Silence.

"Just go home for the holidays," she pleads. "See your family. Think about what they built. Think about what they have. Think about what *you* have." Bea turns to face the lights again. "This could fracture your relationship with your family forever. It could end the legacy your father built. It could end everything."

"Bea, you're still so young and, I'm sorry to say, a bit naive," I start, "but this is the real world. I need this job. I need my health care, retirement and IRA."

"No, you need your parents!" Bea shouts.

Her outburst surprises her, and she takes a moment to gather herself.

"I'm sorry for yelling, but one day, your parents will be gone, you will be all alone and this job won't mean a damn thing. Tell me exactly why you want to convince your parents to do something they haven't said they want to do yet? Tell me why you want to impress a man who you don't even respect? Tell me what the legacy of your family's company would look like in the hands of Benjie and Vance? More importantly, tell me what your legacy would look like without your family?"

The wineglass trembles ever so slightly in my hand.

"Don't do something you'll regret," she urges. "You are not a Scrooge, Henri. I know you."

"Bea," I start.

"Everyone has a story with a few heartbreaking chapters, Henri. Take it from me." Bea sips her wine. "Just go home like you're a normal person that's taken a couple of weeks off for the holidays. Take a break. Celebrate the holidays with your family and friends. Remind yourself why your father built that company and why he still believes in—" Bea leans over and grabs the catalog off the coffee table "—Christmas, in this little girl and in making wishes come true."

"It's n-not that easy," I stammer. Her words unnerve me.

"Your father did it all on his own," Bea says. "Why can't you? It's not too late. It's never too late."

Timing.

Bea points.

"Look into the tree, Henri," she continues. "Really look."

I stare into the lights. I look at each and every ornament. I remember lying underneath it.

"I'm so confused, Bea."

"What do you wish for this Christmas, Henri Wegner, more than anything else in the world?"

I shut my eyes.

When I open them, the tree lights shimmer as if I'm underwater.

"There's still time to get on Santa's nice list," Bea says.

5

The two large glasses of wine have not done their trick: my mind is filled with static, as if my brain had been tossed into the dryer without a sheet. For some reason, I could not turn off the lights on my tree tonight, and they shimmer just beyond my bedroom door, just like my cell, which I have hovering above my face. I pull the electric blanket up to my chin with one hand.

Seeing the tree lights makes me feel like a girl again, which is supremely comforting and utterly unnerving at this crucial juncture in my life.

Facts are facts: my parents are getting older, and one day they will not be able to run Wegner's Winter Wonderland. Who will take it over?

Finn? Could he even handle it all by himself? My parents were always a team.

Plus he doesn't have a background in business.

My parents could be taken advantage of in the sale of their beloved business if I weren't to intervene. I could make their golden years truly golden.

And isn't Christmas just a business like any other? My parents make a wonderful living off of fantasy and glitter. I know they are people of great faith, just like my grandparents were, but aren't they responsible for putting the "mass" in Christmas merchandising?

Bea's comment at the end of the night floats through my head like the tree lights in the condo: *Your father did it all on his own. Why can't you?*

Is that what it all comes down to? Did I run from Shep and Frankenmuth because I wanted to forge my own path? Because I didn't want my entire future to be written at the age of twenty-two? Or was I afraid—somewhere deep down inside—that I'd fail, both in business and love?

Do I have the talent, perseverance, moxie and unparalleled fight and faith of my father? Or am I, like Benjie, just a silhouette of my father?

In so many ways, my life is like a Hallmark movie meets *Twilight Zone* mash-up: I ran from small-town life, young love and my father's business to be a big-city loner who dismantles the dreams of dreamers.

I had a psych professor in college who once said, "Pride and stubbornness share a fence," the exact words my father told me he once used on a former coworker at the car lot where he worked. That coworker told Dad he would fail in his new job venture. Those words have stayed with me forever.

Ah, borders.

How do we overcome our pride—the fragile image of ourselves and our desire not to fail—with incredible determination to succeed?

I illuminate my phone again and begin to scroll through TikTok. It's my dirty secret. Fifteen-second videos of people tripping and falling, makeup and hairstyle tutorials, dancing to the trendiest tunes, eating pasta and drinking ouzo on vacations in Italy and Greece, or teaching you how to decorate your mantel with pine cones for Christmas.

I scroll through the videos. So many are about quitting: Food. Toxic relationships. Alcohol. Your job.

I listen to a young woman talk about "quiet quitting."

"Quiet quitting is not outright quitting your job, but you're quitting the idea of going above and beyond," she says. "You're still performing your duties, but you're no longer subscribing to the hustle-culture mentality that work has to be your life."

I can't help but roll my eyes. I came of age watching my grandparents work hard so their families would have an easier life. I grew up watching my father work countless hours to ensure his dream would come true. My career was forged in the fire of an era dedicated to going above and beyond. To me, "quiet quitting" is the equivalent of not only cheating those for whom you work but also cheating yourself out of career opportunities that call to and challenge you.

I can't do that.

Can I?

And yet I know there is irony in my anger because I can hear Bea's question ring in my head yet again.

My eye twitches, and I finally put my phone down on my nightstand, plugging it into the charger.

Perhaps I haven't been able to sleep well as an adult for a very long time because I know that, in my heart, I yearn to be that little girl who wakes on Christmas to a home filled with excitement, joy, family, friends…

And hope.

Or perhaps, I'm simply unable to sleep because I know what I'm going home to do is wrong, and that I will regret it for the rest of my life.

Part two

6

December 15

There is nothing more magical than Frankenmuth in a December snowfall.

From the north end to the south end of Main Street—and in every direction in between—the town twinkles from the nearly two hundred trees wrapped in red, green and white lights.

I've forgotten how beautiful it is.

I ease my car into a parking spot by the visitors' center. I grab my coat from the passenger seat and slide it on. I wrap my scarf around my neck and then slip on my gloves. From the floorboard, I pluck the stocking cap I keep in my car during winter in case my car breaks down. It is a red one with a white ball on top that reads Wegner's Winter Wonderland in bright green stitching. I snuggle it atop my head to ward off the chill.

And to clamp down the guilt.

I step outside and am immediately immersed in a Bavarian Christmas village.

I turn in a circle, à la Mary Tyler Moore, opting to keep my cap firmly on my head. Although it is just as cold in Detroit, it feels colder here in the hinterland. The city's concrete and skyscrapers seem to trap the heat. Out here, winter greets you like a drunken uncle.

I can't help but smile at the holiday beauty of my small hometown. I feel as if I have flown across the world and am standing in a beautiful German Christmas market.

As if on cue, the bells on the glockenspiel chime a few blocks away and echo through the downtown. I shut my eyes to steady myself, the chiming echoing through my body, reverberating in my soul. When they stop, I open my eyes.

Standing smack-dab in the middle of town is a forty-foot Christmas tree drenched in lights.

How many lights?

I already know the answer: *twenty-three thousand.*

Suddenly, the tree goes dark, as if a fuse has shorted.

A crowd gathers.

I check my watch: 6:00 p.m.

Things never change in Frankenmuth, even down to the minute.

"Welcome to the most wonderful time of the year in Frankenmuth!"

The tree talks, a cheery female voice greeting visitors.

"We wish you a joyous and healthy holiday season, and invite you to celebrate every magical moment of the Frankenmuth Christmas Spectacular!"

The towering tree begins to blink. Sections spring to life, as if Tinkerbell is flying branch to branch lighting them with her magic wand.

A jazzy, instrumental version of "We Wish You A Merry Christmas" begins to play. As it does, the tree comes to life. It explodes in green, then red, then blue, a meteor shower of white pouring over it. Short segments of holiday songs play, and the tree seems to dance along with every beat, flashing lights making it appear as if it is moving, a sort of Christmas tree version of the dancing waters at the Bellagio in Las Vegas.

The crowd sways and sings, recording the tree with their

cell phones. Kids are lifted on their fathers' shoulders, and they watch, eyes wide, mouths open.

The show goes on for nearly ten minutes, and when it ends, bystanders explode into applause. It takes me a second to realize I am applauding, too.

"This never gets cheesy, does it?"

I jump at a man's gravelly voice.

A big whiskey barrel of a man with red cheeks, kind eyes and a dark beard flecked with gray—wearing a big block of cheese atop his head like a Green Bay Packers fan—opens his arms.

"Mouse!"

He picks me up and twirls me in a circle as if I weigh little more than his nickname.

"Henri Wegner! How long has it been? What brings you to town this early in December?" he asks. "It's a Christmas miracle!"

His questions swirl around my head like the cold wind. I do not answer. I cannot answer.

"It's so good to see you!" I say. "How are you? How's the family?"

He points.

His two children, a boy and a girl—both teenagers now—along with his wife, Tammy, are handing out samples to the crowd in front of the Cheese Haus.

I last saw Mouse's children when they were just kids.

The Cheese Haus has been in Mouse's family for three generations now, and they sell local cheese as well as cheese from around the world, not to mention cheese curds, cheese spreads, chocolate cheese as well as mustards, marinades and meats. Sofie and I used to stuff ourselves with his family's cheese when we played hooky from school, were depressed or were allowed to go off campus for lunch as seniors.

The reason for Mouse's nickname is apparent: the Cheese

Haus logo features a happy rodent in a bowtie emerging through a hole in a piece of cheese.

We are a community of nicknames, quirks and characters. All linked by a connection from so long ago that continues to flicker just like the lights on this tree.

Is the magic real, though, or is it just a fantasy that blinds you from reality? Was I the smart one who moved away so that I wouldn't be forced to forever wear a Wegner's elf costume just as Sofie continues to sport a dirndl and Mouse a block of cheese on his head?

Or have I missed…everything? Every holiday, every triumph, every one of life's important moments?

I reach up and guiltily pull the Wegner's stocking cap off my head.

"The Mouseketeers are all fine," he says with a laugh, knocking me from my thoughts. "We've had great crowds already this year, and chamber is projecting a record number of holiday visitors. Of course, your parents are to thank for much of that."

Mouse spreads his arms and lifts his face to the night sky. Soft flakes gather on his beard, and he seems to transform into Santa before my very eyes. "Snow makes the town so magical, doesn't it?"

I look around and nod.

"Dad, we've got a line!"

Mouse's son is yelling at him.

"I gotta go. How long you here?"

"TBD," I say.

Mouse cocks his head, and his cheese hat goes askew. "Stop by and see me, okay?"

"Promise," I say.

"Merry Christmas, Henri!" Mouse says, giving me another big squeeze. "It's been too long. Tell your parents hi."

"I will."

He turns at the last minute. "And tell them they need to leave Santa's shop on occasion. I never see them."

"It's Christmastime," I point out.

"It's *always* Christmastime for them, no matter what the calendar says. See ya, Henri!"

I wave goodbye and turn to watch the tree dance to "Here Comes Santa Claus." Although I want to move, I cannot force my feet forward.

I came downtown on purpose: to steel myself with the Christmas spirit and to delay the inevitable.

I stand and watch the tree for just another few seconds like all the other tourists.

The irony of this particular holiday song is not lost on me.

I know where I must point my sleigh next.

7

I click on 101.1, "the Muth," Frankenmuth's local radio station.

Starting at midnight on November 1, the second Halloween ends, before the pumpkins are tossed and toilet paper is cleared from neighborhood trees, the Muth begins to play holiday music.

And it doesn't end the second the clock strikes the New Year. No, in this town, it goes until the first day of spring.

Guess who started that?

"As always, this year's holiday music is brought to you courtesy of Wegner's Winter Wonderland," the baritone-voiced DJ says. "If you can't make it to the North Pole, don't worry! Wegner's has brought Christmas to Frankenmuth. Make your holiday wish come true at Wegner's. Open daily, except for Christmas Day and Easter, all year long."

"Why should Christmas ever end?" my dad used to say.

The announcer launches into the seven-o'clock news update.

"Deer crashes abound all over the area tonight. They are active little boogers when it starts to snow. Use extra caution as you drive."

I immediately turn on my high beams. I slow my car, lean

over the steering wheel and scan the sides of the road, glancing into the woods just beyond the snowy ditch.

If there is any phrase used as much as "Merry Christmas" in my hometown, it would definitely be "deer crash." As fall turns to winter, the cold air seeps in and hunting season starts with a bang, deer begin to move.

They run through downtown as if they're late to work or across the high school football field as if they're a wide receiver. They mow down gardens all year long if you're not diligent. Mostly, they try to cross the road in the dark this time of year.

Growing up, the local paper used to print a graphic showing the time of day and year that deer crashes were most prevalent. September through January were the high points, with November and December serving as the crescendo.

I remember that the local paper's graphic used Rudolph—a wide-eyed deer with big lashes and a red nose leaping over a car in the middle of a road—to make it all seem so sweet.

"All the deer are on the move because they're headed to the North Pole to audition for Santa," my dad used to tell me.

But ever since Sofie nearly hit a deer on our way to a football game—she swerved and went off the road, our cheerleading pom-poms flying into the front seat, barely missing the leaping animal but nicking the side of a pine—I had been on high alert when driving this time of year.

I love deer. They are wondrous, magical creatures. Muscular bodies, their winter coats beautiful, and their eyes—they're called "doe eyes" for a reason—melt your heart. When I ran cross-country in high school, the deer and their fawn would playfully run alongside me in the morning when I trained, bouncing as I moved down the wooded country roads, curious as to why I was in their neck of the woods.

"Hi, babies," I used to call. "Run with me."

Coincidentally, I saw a deer that looked like Rudolph—save for the red nose—standing on a vacant lot that was for sale during a long run when I was home from college. It was, literally, a sign to me. I sprinted home and told my father about the property that would eventually become Wegner's.

I glance up at a Wegner's billboard. Ironically, it features a giant Rudolph standing alongside the road, his nose flashing, his hand motioning: This Way to Wegner's!

A car flashes its lights, and I look back just in time to see a deer leaping across the road. I hit the brakes, my heart racing. The deer bounds directly underneath the billboard and into the woods.

Something seems to happen to deer when they get in the middle of the road. They simply stop, as if paralyzed, looking directly at you, helpless, unsure as to which way to go.

I can relate completely to your conundrum right now, deer.

I slow my pace as I head farther out of town.

The countryside is dark, a contrast to Detroit, which—even in the dark of winter—seems constantly aglow from a variety of headlights, streetlights and the soft glow of fluorescent lights from office towers and high rises.

There is a glow in the distance. As I drive closer, it grows brighter until it nearly blinds me, as if I'm driving directly into the sun during rush hour.

Home.

I turn at an old-fashioned street sign in red with fancy gold lettering that reads 25 Christmas Lane.

As soon as I turn, I am no longer in the real world. I am in a winter wonderland, a Christmas cartoon, a child's dream.

The drive through 25 Christmas Lane is like driving through that favorite neighborhood when you were a kid, where every homeowner decorated his house and his yard à la Clark Griswold.

Wegner's 25 Christmas Lane is that times a million.

My grandparents' neighborhood was the quintessential Christmas street growing up and a main reason my father brought it to life again here. So we could all remember the joy of being a kid again at Christmas.

My heart pings. Lighted arches—like illuminated wickets—frame the narrow lane that leads to the parking lot. A line of cars drives at a snail's pace to take in the spectacle, windows down, arms dangling out the door holding cell phones, even in the cold and snow.

Christmas Lane is lined on both sides with hundreds of illuminated decorations, from inflatable snowmen and Santas, to twinkling trees and candy canes. The old-fashioned light posts are wrapped in greenery and bows, each holding a vintage candle flickering in the night.

The darkness shimmers with icy blues, bright whites, holiday reds and greens, and the snowy quiet is filled with holiday music blasting from well-hidden speakers.

I realize as I near the end of the lane that my mouth is hanging open yet again.

I scan the mammoth parking lot searching for a spot and chuckle as Perry Como begins to sing "(There's No Place Like) Home for the Holidays."

There is nothing particularly "homey" about the parking lot to Wegner's. It's like pulling into the lot for a Detroit Lions football game: massive.

As if on instinct, I find a spot a fair distance from the store and park. I think of my father, who always parks a million miles away from the front door, leaving the best spots for customers. I step out of the car, and the wind whips across the lot, the cold knifing through my body.

I race toward the building, stopping before one of the giant outdoor Santa figurines standing guard over my family's business.

"Hi, Santa!" I call, as I've done for as long as I can remember, looking up at the twenty-foot Kringle towering above me.

The Santa—like his wife flanking the other end of the

store—has not aged a day since I last saw him, unlike Mouse's kids. He is shiny, smiling, chuckling, his suit still red, gloves green, beard and fur trim snow-white, boots black, eyes twinkling. He is holding an open scroll dangling from a golden rod that states:

Welcome to Wegner's
The World's Largest Christmas Store!
Open 363 Days a Year

Santa stands between two giant pine trees flocked in snow. My father landscaped the exterior of the building and planted the parking lot with pines to make it feel more like a home than a business.

I touch a branch of the tree. They were just saplings when I helped my dad plant them here. In fact, they were so small and fragile that I called them "Charlie Brown Christmas trees," just like the one Bea said she put in her apartment. My dad staked them so they would not be crushed by the winter's snow.

I look from the trees to the store and back again.

Everything has become bigger than any of us ever imagined, grown to unimaginable heights.

Wegner's is not billed "the world's largest year-round Christmas store" for nothing.

My parents own the thirty acres that make up Wegner's beautifully landscaped grounds. The store itself covers three of those acres—roughly two football fields.

I smile at my mental analogies. In Michigan, everything comes back to football.

My feet kick up the snow on my way to the entrance. A line of buses—even at this late hour—is dropping off holiday shoppers under the porte cochere. I stop at the entrance to the store and take in its stunning majesty.

In a way, Wegner's resembles one of those new megachurches.

It is comprised of many minibuildings, additions upon additions, some that soar over the original roofline, some that span out like a bird's wings.

Its roof is sharply angled, metal and holiday red. This roof was chosen for both aesthetic and functional reasons: its Christmas color, of course, as well as to allow Michigan's heavy snow to slide off the top. My father learned early on that you cannot have four feet of snow atop an aging flat roof for too long. Either it will collapse under the weight or, when warmer weather comes, it will drip, drip, drip, damaging the ceilings and walls before turning to mold. A good portion of my young life was spent using a roof rake to pull the heavy snow off the flat roof of the original building.

Many of my father's original wood signs and cutouts—Christmas trees, wreaths, North Stars, bells—line the building's exterior.

But the one thing that makes Wegner's so spectacular is…

I look around, lifting a mittened hand to shield my eyes from the brightness.

…the lights.

Everything—and I mean everything—is drenched in lights.

White lights, multicolored lights, twinkling lights, blinking lights, small bulbs, big bulbs, old-fashioned strands, newfangled ones.

If memory serves correct, over one hundred thousand lights illuminate 25 Christmas Lane each night, from dusk 'til first light.

In the falling snow, the red roof juxtaposed against the deep green of the pines, the lights twinkling in the darkness, Wegner's looks as if it might actually be Santa's Workshop filled with hundreds of elves scurrying around to make holiday wishes come true.

Excited groups of shoppers rush past me and throw open the front doors.

I see a sea of employees decked out in the traditional Wegner's garb—red vests dotted with white snowflakes, an oval nameplate attached to it that says Hi! I'm One of Santa's Elves & I'm Here to Help!

They are elves, I think. *And I used to be one of them.*

I follow the warm air spilling outside and head through the doors.

"*Frohe Weihnachte!* Welcome to Wegner's!"

Frohe Weihnachte is German for "Merry Christmas." It quite literally means "consecrated night."

I smile.

"That used to be my line," I say. "And my wardrobe."

A pretty girl with red hair—I'd guess her to be no more than eighteen—smiles. She is outfitted in a completely over-the-top elf costume that my mother—along with my grandma—created decades ago. In fact, they worked together to sew the original just for me.

Her green stocking cap rises from her head and ends in a curl thanks to the wiring inside. A gold bell on the end jingles with every breath or movement. Her leggings are green-and-red-striped like a peppermint candy, and the ends of her red elf shoes—like her cap—also curl upward and are topped with gold bells. She is wearing a short green velvet skirt and a red jacket with felt trim decorated in the shape of holly leaves around her neck. A black belt with a massive gold buckle—matching the gold buttons on the jacket—cinches it all together.

"When they made that outfit, they didn't really ever consider someone might need to use the bathroom, did they?"

The girl's eyes grow as wide as the ones on the shoppers entering the store.

"I was the original Wegner's '*Weihnachten* woman,'" I explain. "My mom and grandma made the first costume for me. I earned the right to criticize."

The girl's face lifts and then she erupts into a fit of giggles, putting a gloved hand over her mouth as if trying to stuff them back inside.

"I've learned not to drink any liquids before or during my shift," she says, tilting her hand to turn her words into a whisper.

"Before my very first day on the job here, I stopped at the new 7-Eleven and got a Big Gulp," I say.

"Oh, no!"

"Oh, yes," I say. "Let's just say I tore that elf outfit off just in the St. Nick of time."

The girl whoops in laughter. "So you know the question I'm going to ask next?" she says.

"Would you like your picture taken on Santa's throne?" we say together.

"Of course," I say. "You can't visit Wegner's without a photo."

I get in line and wait my turn, watching the Christmas chaos around me.

If you think the elf costume is over-the-top, the Santa throne is "over the top of the North Pole."

It resembles a theater set in scope and drama. This was one of the very first things my father built when he started his "sign business" on the side and then expanded it to focus on the holidays. Tingleman's—the old department store in town—used to hire a Santa to come on holiday weekends to listen to children's Christmas wishes and take photos with all the kids. My father built two wooden signs for them—one for children and one for adults, each on opposite sides of the store. One read What Do You Want for Christmas? Whisper it to Santa! And the other one read What Do Your Kids Want for Christmas? Buy It at Tingleman's!

Tingleman's then asked my father to build a Santa set to place in the front window to draw in more customers, and my father's elaborate creation proved so popular that families from all over the eastern part of the state would drive to town just to have their photos taken with it.

When Tingleman's closed, they gave the Godzilla-sized set back to my father, who installed it here.

For a moment, I stare at the throne, remembering Tingleman's and why it closed: no one in the family wanted to take it over.

"You're up next!"

I shake my head, take a seat and instantly feel like a kid again.

The throne is truly a throne, a king-size chair of red velvet with an ornate gold scroll outlining it. A forest of Christmas trees surrounds it, drenched in white lights and snow-blue ornaments. Two big candy canes flank the throne, giant old-fashioned multicolored bulbs in red, green and yellow hang over the chair, and behind the scene a circle of lights that resembles falling snow twinkles. A Wegner's Winter Wonderland sign—white with green lettering, encircled in red with a flocked pine Christmas tree branch behind it—is centered so it appears in every photo.

It is magical, and there is always a line of shoppers—from eight to eighty—waiting to get their photos taken.

When my father opened the original store, he and my mother did it all themselves. They were so busy helping shoppers and fulfilling orders, or sitting in the back room balancing the books, they felt they didn't have time to greet customers.

When this set was returned to my dad, he said he felt as if the magic of Christmas returned as well and that he remembered why he had started the store in the first place. I was installed as the first elf—the face of the store—and handed a Polaroid camera to take photos of everyone who walked into Wegner's. That tradition has never changed, although technology has. Today, the girl uses a Polaroid Now, which produces an instant photo much faster and much clearer than the Polaroids of my past.

But the feeling is just the same.

"Every single person who walks into our store should feel like family," I can hear my father saying.

Guilt bubbles inside of me, and my stomach churns. I burp acid.

"Smile!"

The elf clicks the camera and then waits for the photo to emerge.

"Maybe we should do another," she says, looking at it. "You look—" she stops and cocks her head, the bell on her cap jangling "—distracted."

My face cannot lie. Neither can I.

Yet.

She holds up the camera again and repeats, "Smile!"

This time I produce a megawatt grin that belies my emotional state and point my fingers at the Wegner's sign over my head. And this time, the girl is pleased when the photo pops out.

"That's a lot of pressure," she says, shaking the Polaroid in the air, just like I used to do. "The picture has to be perfect. I mean, you're the daughter of the man himself."

"Santa?" I ask with a laugh.

"No, the man who fills Santa's sleigh!" she says. "Would there be Christmas without Mr. Wegner? Would there even be a Frankenmuth?"

More guilt.

She hands me the picture.

I stare at my face. *Who is this woman?*

I look at the girl.

Bea's words drift in my head, like the snow falling outside. *What would your legacy be without your family?*

"Are you okay?" the girl asks.

"I don't know."

She gestures to the store behind. "I guarantee you all that will make you feel better," she says. "Even when I'm having a terrible day—like when my parents are mad at me, or I'm in a fight with my best friend—I feel all my troubles fade away when I step foot in here."

I smile. "My parents certainly hired the right person for this job," I say.

"Thank you. I'm sure you set the bar pretty high."

I might as well rip my heart out, set it on the floor in front of this sweet soul and have her stomp on it with her elf shoe.

"Have fun!" she says, as I head inside. Then she turns to a group waiting anxiously and says, "*Frohe Weihnachte!* Welcome to Wegner's!"

I take a deep breath to steady myself and head inside.

Wegner's is, to put it mildly, overwhelming.

You feel as if you have emerged inside a never-ending airport—sprawling in all directions—with every single square inch of space decorated for Christmas.

But the reason most shoppers travel to Wegner's is the ornaments.

They go on forever.

They dangle from trees and shelves, hangers and ceilings.

Room after room is filled with ornaments by category: animals, babies, food, flowers, Santa, snowflakes, snowmen, hobbies, professions, Old World and brand-new.

Wegner's has ornaments made in the US as well as ornaments from over seventy nations.

I glance around.

Shoppers' mouths are wide-open, and they are moving at a snail's pace, their carts traveling only a couple of feet before someone yells, "Look!" or "Mom, stop!" or "Grandma would love this one!"

I zip through the different departments and head to a quiet place to gather my thoughts before I spring my unannounced Christmas arrival—but not my intention for being here—upon my parents.

I head through trees to outdoor decor, back through lights and villages, until I come to the original part of the store.

It is a small space, half-filled with reproductions of my father's vintage wooden holiday signs. A small café—Frosty the Doughman—occupies the other half. It looks as if it has stopped in time, furnished with Formica tables and retro chairs.

A sign my father made shows Frosty holding a doughnut instead of a pipe, which is what the café originally served: doughnuts—glazed, cinnamon sugar, apple cider—homemade by my grandmother.

The only thing that has changed is the menu. Now people want coffee and lattes, and I can see my father has bent somewhat to the changing times. A line waits for coffee. I sniff the air and then follow my nose to the counter.

Under the glass is an eye-dazzling display of German desserts: apple cake, apple strudel, bee sting cake, linzer cookies, dipped gingersnaps, stollen, almond spritz cookies.

"Is this from Z's Chicken Haus?" I ask a man behind the counter.

He nods.

Sofie!

I smile.

This was actually my idea. I told my dad years ago it would be more cost-effective to eliminate the kitchen—do away with the hot dogs, French fries and fast food smell—and purchase true German desserts from the only place that could hold a candle to my grandma's legacy. I told him Sofie would be delighted, and it would still honor the original café.

A few years back, my parents converted the kitchen space to expand their tiny offices. They needed the room for online sales, marketing, events and a business manager, although my father still does all his own accounting.

Which will make the numbers easy for me to access.

My gut rumbles again as I glance at the desserts.

"Must be hungry?" the kid says.

Not exactly.

"When did they start selling desserts from Sofie?" I ask. "I mean, Z's?"

"Just a few weeks ago," the kid says. "Been a nice change."

I shut my eyes and listen.

I am again in my grandparents' basement, the *Sears Wish Book* spread before me.

I open my eyes and cock my head.

There is a signature sound to Wegner's, and it's not the holiday music.

Over the tune of "Jingle Bells" and over the never-ending hum of classical Christmas crooners—Sinatra, Martin, Clooney, Dolly—there is an ever-present jingling.

And I mean that quite literally.

All day long, the thousands upon thousands of holiday ornaments hanging throughout the store jingle and jangle as they're picked up and placed in carts, admired and hung back on branches and shelves, or sway in the current from the circulating air or passing of shoppers. The jangling sounds much like you might be having a fancy dinner during a minor earthquake, and all the stemware and dishes rattle in the background while you pretend nothing is happening.

You get used to it after a while, much like you get used to the crash of waves living next to Lake Michigan or sirens living in the city.

I cock my head again, shut my eyes and listen.

The jangling sounds as if it is getting closer, like a mosquito that has moved close to your face.

I open my eyes.

"Mabel!" I cry.

My parents' old mutt, the one I got them after the death of my grandma, the one named Mabel in memory of her, the one who grew up in this store and seems to know the moment I return home, runs toward me.

Well, *run* would be a generous description. Mabel sort of limp-trots to me, her arthritic right front leg giving out a bit with every step she takes.

I jump from my chair, take a seat on the floor and hug her with all my might.

"My baby," I say.

She looks directly into my eyes, smiles and releases a howl of delight that echoes throughout the café.

I gently take her face in my hands. The shaggy puppy who was once all black is now all gray. Her beautiful brown eyes are cloudy. But her happy spirit—defined by the insane wagging of her tail—hasn't diminished.

I've been holding my breath since I walked into Wegner's, hoping I would see her once again.

"How's my girl?" I ask. "How's my beautiful baby? I'm sorry it's been so long. I'm so, so sorry, Mabel."

She jumps onto my chest, licking my face, and then releases another howl.

Forgiveness.

I put my hand on the floor and play with her feet. She dances in delight for a few seconds, before suddenly crawling into my lap and promptly falling asleep.

"Henri?"

I look up.

My parents are looking down at me.

"Surprise!" I gingerly ease Mabel off my lap and stand to greet my mom and dad.

"What are you doing here?" my mother asks.

"Well, Merry Christmas to you, too," I say. "Aren't you glad to see me?"

"Of course," my father says. "But we're a little bit in shock."

"Hey, it's not like I don't visit," I protest. "I was back for your birthday, I visited in the summer, I was here for Finn's fiftieth."

"But how long has it been since you've been home for Christmas?" my mom asks.

"How long *has* it been?" my dad asks.

They look at each other.

"I wasn't collecting Social Security yet," my dad says.

"I wasn't getting Medicare," my mom says.

"Okay, okay, point made," I say. "I get it. But I'm home now."

My dad gives me a long look.

"Can't a daughter come home for Christmas to see her family?"

"Some daughters, yes," my dad says. "But you? No."

I clench my teeth to keep a smile on my face.

"I'm sorry it's been so long. I just wanted to surprise you."

Elation replaces the confusion on their faces.

"Well, it's so good to see you, honey," my mom says. "I feel like I've already gotten the only Christmas present I ever want. I missed you so much. Give me a hug."

"I love you," they whisper into my neck.

"How long can you stay?" my dad asks.

"How long will you have me?"

My dad laughs. "Well, this is a Christmas miracle. And, this time of year, we can use all the help we can get."

"That's not how you greet your daughter, Jakob," my mom scolds.

"It is if she's a Wegner." He looks at me. "I'm sorry. It's good to have you home, Henri." He grins. "At Christmas."

"Why don't you go home to unpack and get settled," my mom says, playfully punching my father in the shoulder. "We'll stop at Giuseppe's and pick up a pizza. We'll try to be home by nine."

"Nine?" my dad asks. "We don't close until ten. Then we have..."

My mom shoots him one of her patented *Don't mess with me, the decision has been made* looks.

"Nine it is," my dad says with a laugh. "Santa could use some pizza."

My phone trills with a text.

Day one. How are things progressing? Tick-tock.

Benjie.

I've only been home a couple of hours, and I already have to move into *Mission: Impossible* mode.

My mom and dad are watching me, smiling.

My heart sinks.

I didn't really come home to see you, I think. *I came home with a mission.*

My cell vibrates again.

Don't ignore me, Henri

I think of the sign hanging by the throne at the entrance to the store.

What Do You Want for Christmas? Whisper It to Santa!

I want a way out of this mess, Kris.

8

My childhood home sits on the other side of town, across the wooden bridge.

When most people think of a wooden bridge, they tend to dreamily picture the quintessential covered section of the bridge, à la *The Bridges of Madison County*.

Many do not realize that the actual bridge floor that spans the water is made of wood as well.

As I drive into the Holz Brücke, my tires sing to me, the bridge as much a musical accompaniment as the ornaments at Wegner's, Mabel's collar or the glockenspiel.

Clickety-clack, clack, clack!

I am the only car on the bridge.

My lights illuminate the burnished wood that surrounds me. I feel as if I've gone back in time, entered an old barn on horse and buggy.

My mind tumbles to a time long ago when the town gathered to watch the bridge being built. It was a fascinating mix of science and art, logistics and architecture. Each piece of lumber was individually hewn, each section of bridge meticulously drawn and raised.

I remember that after the team of oxen would pull another

three inches of the bridge into place, everyone would stand back and collectively breathe a sigh of relief. It was more than relief, I now understand as an adult; it was visual evidence that what they had dreamed of building was actually coming to fruition before their very eyes.

I can see my parents' faces in my mind, the lights and sounds of Wegner's surrounding them.

What they dreamed of building actually came true.

And this ox is here to knock it all down.

As if on cue, my cell blinks.

I glance down.

It's a text from Bea.

Did you make it okay?

I made it.

But I'm not okay.

Benjie is asking about progress...what should I say?

Yes, building a wooden bridge is just like building a business. It takes a team...of oxen, of dreamers, of tireless workers and optimists, just like my parents.

Clickety-clack, clack, clack! go, my wheels on the bridge.

But perhaps building a bridge is like building a lasting relationship.

I've done it on my own, in life and business, and I'm starting to believe that isolation has rendered me as cold and icy as the Cass River.

I think of the two local residents who were the first to drive across the Holz Brücke. They were a couple who had been married sixty-five years and owned a local business.

Were they scared the bridge might collapse? Or did they

travel across it clutching hands, squealing in delight, taking risks, doing it…

Together.

My mind whirs to Shep. Our initials are forever a part of the history of this bridge.

What would my life look like right now if I'd said yes?

Would it be less messy, less lonely than what I've created?

I've been so consumed with building my own bridge that I never considered it might crumble below me when I least expected it, leaving me to free-fall into the river below without any safety net.

And that's where I am right now.

Clickety-clack, clack, clack!

I make it across the Holz Brücke.

When I emerge, the snow begins again in earnest.

9

Just like their store, my parents' home glows from a distance.

You can see it shimmer a mile away through the bare branches of the trees, a canopy of lush green in the summer, a silhouette of skeletons in the winter.

The lights make the dead branches look as if they are dancing in the snow.

This is why we decorate in the winter, to distract us from the reality of what surrounds us.

I pull up to the gate at the front of my parents' property.

My father did not want this gate. He said it would send the wrong message to the community that he was being elitist, but the township—and my mother—forced him to install it.

Years ago, this quiet road led to horse farms. My parents discovered their quirky house long before minimansions were erected upon large swaths of acreage, long before Wegner's became a destination, long before this country lane morphed into Woodward Avenue in Detroit following a traffic accident.

Cars are lined up to get a peek at the real-life Santa.

You can almost hear people ask, *Is Jakob Wegner's home as magical as his store?*

My dad promised the city these folks were harmless, and as soon as the holidays ended, things would return to normal.

But my dad has always been an optimist.

Social media influencers, Instagrammers, TikTokers and nosy old women began to pull into the driveway and take photos as well as record videos dancing to Mariah's "All I Want for Christmas Is You." When my mother walked out one morning to find a couple on her front porch drinking coffee, you could hear her scream of *"Jakob!"* all the way to Chicago.

The gate went up the next day.

When I finally reach the entrance—waiting for people to take their pictures and drive on—I punch in the code and chuckle.

It's not difficult: 1225.

Twelve twenty-five.

Christmas Day.

Anybody could figure it out.

And yet there is something about a gate—like a stern look—that keeps people at bay.

I roll my window back up as the gate opens, and I see my reflection.

Hart Henri.

I head down the long driveway, which already is in need of a plow.

Hart Henri is home.

"For the holidays, to wreak havoc or both?" I say out loud.

I shake my head and pull into the circle drive in front of my parents' home.

The yard is filled with vintage plastic figures—from happy reindeer to holiday candles—all of which glow from within, as if you can see their bright souls. These, too, were my grandparents', and my parents love them dearly.

"You can try and re-create them," my dad says, "but you can't re-create the nostalgia and memories."

The pines surrounding the house are draped in white lights, which makes the snow on the branches shimmer, while multicolored lights line every rafter and pitch of the roof and twinkle lights are wrapped around the front porch and door.

And, as always, reindeer pulling Santa's sleigh sit on top of the roof while the jolly man's plump rear end pops directly out of the chimney.

I grab my cell and quickly respond to Bea's text.

I made it home. Tell Benjie it's all good, and he'll have his present gift-wrapped by Christmas.

Three dots undulate.

Okay, I will. But, Henri, just rest & relax right now. This has to be overwhelming. Don't do anything rash. Just enjoy being home and with your family. The answer will come to you. I'll cover for you until it does.

More guilt.

More dots.

Have a glass of wine, or two...have a cookie, or two...and sleep on it for a day, or two...once you broach the topic of selling with your parents, you will never be able to walk it back.

The phone glows in the dark along with the house.

I stare at it, then at a plastic mold of a gingerbread man with the happiest, most content face you've ever seen.

Just keep Benjie off my reindeer tail for a while, and I promise I'll start with the wine and cookies.

I drop the cell into my purse, step out into the snow and grab my bags from the back of the car. I trudge up the snowy steps, stomp my feet on the rug by the front door and set my bags down. I stick my hand into the pocket of my purse, searching for the side pocket where I keep the key to my parents' house. I pull it free.

The key is on an ancient plastic key chain featuring a boy in Bavarian garb dancing with a girl in a similar outfit on May Day. Shep gave it to me long ago. It was not only his first gift to me but also a tribute to how we first met.

Every day should be as magical as May Day.

I run my mittened finger over the key chain, as I have done in secret for the last four decades.

A gust of wind whips through the woods, and in the distance, I can hear a tree branch crack, then break and fall.

"You're an ironic mother, aren't you, Mother Nature?" I mutter.

I slip the key into the lock, stomp my feet once more, grab my bags and head inside. I flick on the light in the foyer.

"Hello, upside-down house!" I call.

I've called it this nickname since the day we moved in.

The house is a 1960s tri-level. The main floor houses all of the bedrooms, which my mother hated the moment she stepped foot into the house.

"Everyone will walk into chaos," she said.

A set of open stairs—another design element that horrified a mother with young children—leads up to the living room, kitchen and dining room, yet another feature my mom despised.

"You have to go upstairs to eat and watch TV?" I remember her asking the real estate agent.

But as we slowly walked through the house, other features began to overwhelm the oddities for each of us.

Upstairs, my mother was stunned by the sweeping views of the woods and—in the distance—the river and town of Frankenmuth.

"It's like living in a tree house," she said.

My brother, Finn, loved the ten acres of woods filled with grape vines to swing over spring-swollen creeks, I loved that I would have my own bedroom and my mother adored the midcentury design of the home—from its clean, geometric lines, to the linear fireplace with original brick, the large windows that brought the outside in and the kitchen's vintage avocado appliances and wood details.

But the decision, ultimately, came down to my father, and he wasn't wowed until he made it downstairs. A huge walkout basement with a living space much like the upstairs—small kitchen, open living room and bath—was waiting.

"My office," my father announced, walking around as if in a dream. "My business can flourish here."

My father was also wowed by the price. It was not a typical Michigan house. No one appreciated the midcentury vibe or the layout, and my dad got it for a steal. He was working nonstop, the business was not making much money and the days my grandparents weren't feeding us, we subsisted on a lot of bologna sandwiches and frozen dinners.

My dad ended up buying the home on the spot, and he credits it for inspiring him to take the leap to buy the acreage I discovered for him and expand Wegner's. Today, he could buy any house in town, but he refuses to move.

"You can bury me here," he says.

I realize I am still standing in the foyer.

Isn't it funny how when you return home the place talks to you? The quiet is loud. The silence screams. The walls talk. The floors creak.

In the distance, the glockenspiel chimes.

I haul my bags to my bedroom, which my mother turned into her reading room when I left for college. It's also the place she watches Hallmark Christmas movies to escape the reality of the holidays.

I click on the light.

A pull-out Joybird sofa—in a beautiful harvest-gold fabric—sits against the wall where my bed used to be. An Eames reading chair is tucked under the window, an arc lamp stretched over it. A beautiful Scandinavian-inspired shelving unit—sleek walnut—occupies the biggest wall and is filled with books.

The room smells like my mom.

My mother is an eclectic reader. Copies of thrillers and mysteries mingle with historical fiction, autobiography, memoir, self-help and even a section of old Jane Fonda workout tapes.

I pull out a copy of Jane Fonda's *Lean Routine* exercise tape. The famed actress is wearing leg warmers and a mass of permed curls, her legs in an impossible V over her head.

I can picture my mom and I doing these workouts together on the shag carpet in my grandparents' basement, or doing Denise Austin while listening to "YMCA" or "Let's Get Physical." After we'd work out, my grandma would inevitably bring us down a tray filled with Capri Sun, Cheez Balls and pizza rolls.

So much for the workout, Grandma.

I slide the tape back into its home, and my eyes scan the base of the immaculate, clean, midcentury wall unit. A photo of me graduating from the University of Michigan is framed next to one of me graduating from high school. They've been in this same spot forever.

Things never change.

Suddenly, a thought clicks.

Do they?

I open the rattan doors at the bottom of the cabinet.

"Yes!" I scream in the quiet.

An old safe sits in the cabinet, as outdated as an Edsel.

I'd forgotten!

I give the big handle a tug.

Locked.

If things have truly not changed, then I already know the code to the safe and what's inside.

I take a seat on the floor, and use my index finger to punch in the numbers.

"One, two, two, five, pound," I say.

Just like the gate code. Just like Wegner's address. Christmas Day.

It's always Christmas.

I inhale sharply and pull the door.

It pops open.

My father's tax returns—as they always have been—are stacked in folders. No matter how much time has passed, no matter how much the business has grown, my father still does his own taxes. My father still puts the paper files in here. He only trusts himself to do his taxes. He only trusts his family.

I feel sick to my stomach, but I think of Benjie's text and I forge on.

I grab a stack from the top and begin to open the folders.

I finger through the papers, eyeing how much Wegner's has made annually, how much they have paid in taxes, how much they have written off, the value of its assets, the building and land, how much my parents pay themselves and Finn.

Wegner's has made a lot of money.

Wegner's has also lost a lot of money.

I tear through the taxes, trying to make sense of it all on the fly.

I can see the business took a big hit the last few years during Covid. But they also seem to have made a big comeback of late, despite the fact they have too much overhead.

I grab my cell and begin to snap photos, going back ten years.

I immediately begin to see ways to cut costs to make the profit bigger and more appealing to Vance as well as how a sale could be structured to benefit both my parents and Vance.

I text the photos to Benjie and Bea with my thoughts.

A few seconds later, Benjie texts a big thumbs-up with the words GREAT INTEL! HART HENRI DOES IT AGAIN! IT'S GOING TO BE A VERY MERRY CHRISTMAS! in all caps.

I exhale.

I can actually pull this off. Just a little parental convincing now.

I begin to place the tax folders, exactly as I found them, back into the safe. That's when I notice—on the side—a large stack of something rubber banded together.

I pull the stack from the safe and remove the rubber band.

Christmas cards?

I begin to open them, one after another.

My parents have saved every Christmas card I've sent the last decade.

I look at the cabinet, the TV, the cards.

A Hallmark stand-in for the real thing.

Each pretty, glittery holiday card is filled with a hollow, handwritten excuse as to why I wouldn't be returning home yet again for the holidays.

Promotion.

Work.

Travel.

Takeover.

At the end of every card, I wrote, "I love you, Mom and Dad. See you next year."

A decade of excuses.

And the moment I finally return home, it's to pull a fast one on the people who love me more than anything in the world at the time of year they love more than any other.

I put the cards back and lock the safe.

As if on cue, I receive a text from Bea.

It's a sad-faced emoji crying a single tear.

10

They say that Santa knows when you've been naughty or nice, but my father seems to know instantly when I'm up to something, too.

"I just can't believe that you're actually home for Christmas," my dad says, shaking his head.

"I have about a hundred days of vacation stockpiled," I ad-lib. "My boss said I better take some of it, or I was going to lose it. New company policy. They're not going to pay for accrued vacation any longer. Trying to cut corners."

My dad looks at me the same way a store Santa might a child who swears she's been a good girl after he just saw her tug her sister's hair while waiting in line.

"Speaking of cutting," Finn says, as if reading my mind. "Remember when you and Sofie butchered Hannah's hair at that sleepover in middle school? You gave her those blunt bangs, and she cried for a week."

He laughs and grabs another slice of pizza.

"She wanted a new look," I insist.

"Well, you gave her one," Finn continues, shoving a slice of supreme into his mouth. "She wore a wig to school like Jan Brady."

"It was an accident," I say.

"Right," Finn says. "Like when you and Sofie 'accidentally' replaced Hannah's baton during homecoming, and it wouldn't light during her fire baton routine. The entire stadium went dark, and she just stood in the middle of the field doing a routine no one could see while 'Burning Down the House' by the Talking Heads blasted."

"She still won homecoming queen," I say, a bit too defensively. "Don't forget that she ripped down all of my and Sofie's posters."

"That royal court was worse than *Game of Thrones*," Finn says with a laugh, taking a swig of his beer.

My brother has never changed. His whole life has been a never-ending episode of *Happy Days*, surrounded by childhood friends, falling in love with his childhood sweetheart, working with Mom and Dad at the local business.

From my spot in the living room, I can see down the stairs, through the hallway and into Finn's bedroom. We used to tease my parents that they bought this house just so they could always keep an eye on us.

His room remains as it always has. His band and baseball trophies sit on a shelf. Even his light—a red-white-and-blue basketball, an ode to the Harlem Globetrotters—looks ready to swish through the net over his bed.

I know the framed photo of Finn that sits next to his trophies was taken at the Sears Portrait Studio at the mall in Saginaw when he was a boy. He is holding a baseball glove and not just smiling, but beaming.

Finn has always been okay with just *being*.

He's always been okay living in a small town. He's always been okay knowing what every day will bring. He's always been okay spending his life with the first girl he ever loved. He's always been okay traversing in my father's shadow, okay with being not the king of Christmas, but an essential elf.

Why can't I just be okay?

"I missed you like a toothache," I say to him, joking to end the focus on me.

"You were the one who got braces and refused to wear your retainer," Finn says with a wink. His voice softens. "I missed you too, sis. How long are you staying?"

I shrug.

"Hmm, that seems ominous for such a planner," he says. "Either you got married, won the lottery or are here to destroy the family business."

The room spins, as if I entered a fun house at the circus.

"I'm just joking," Finn says before I can say a word. "You look like you just saw Shep."

What is it about little brothers?

"How's Clare?" I ask, changing the subject. "And Ethan?"

"Great," he says. "Busy. Tonight was his high school Christmas formal. Clare and the other moms had a pre-party, took photos and now they're drinking wine and watching *Pretty in Pink*. It's as much about the moms these days as it is the kids."

I laugh.

"Ethan went with a sweet girl named Aimee. Not *A-m-y* but *A-i-m-e-e*. He took a girl named Cyndee to homecoming. Not *C-i-n-d-y* but *C-y-n-d-e-e*. I don't even try to spell kids' names anymore. If it were Hangman, I'd get hung every time."

I laugh again. "And I thought I had it rough growing up with a boy's name."

My cell trills.

An endless stream of texts from Benjie.

Haven't I done enough in one night?

"How's business?" Finn asks, nodding at my cell.

"Insane," I say, tucking my phone into my pocket. "How about Wegner's?"

My mom, dad and brother look at each other.

"Insane," they say as one, before laughing.

It hits me that, in my sustained holiday absence, the three of them have formed an even closer bond, as if they have gone through a war together. They are their own band, and I am the former lead singer who left before it took off, then returned after they became famous, seeking my share of the pie.

I am longer an integral part of the Wegner Band.

"We have a long road until Christmas," my dad says, now checking his phone. "I hope Santa is patient this year."

I stare at my dad, a real-life Santa.

We do bad things and then try to convince Santa—and ourselves—that only a fine line separates naughty and nice. But most of us—whether we're a child giving a frenemy a disastrous 'do or an adult returning home on a holiday ruse to steal her parents' business—know the difference between right and wrong.

And when we intentionally do the wrong thing, we can feel our hearts crack. Because we can see it in the eyes of Santa.

My father's eyes meet mine.

"Well, this is just such a wonderful surprise, Henri," my dad says, finishing his text while sipping a glass of a hearty Cab. "You're usually so busy this time of year with work. I'm just so glad to see you. I'm glad you could finally come home and relax."

I smile.

My father cocks his head at me and takes another sip of wine. His eyes narrow just a touch. "So," he continues. "Everything okay?"

It's a simple question with so much hidden meaning.

My brother kicks my foot.

"Yeah, what's going on?"

"You've always had freakishly long legs," I say, avoiding my father's question.

"And you've always looked like the von Trapp sister no one liked," Finn says.

He kicks me again.

My dad is still watching me.

"Everything's okay, Dad," I say, as my cell continues to vibrate in my pocket. "I promise."

"It's just so nice to have everyone home again," my mom says. "I never expected this." My mom looks around at all of us. "I'm *so* happy."

Her voice warbles just a little at the end, and I can feel tears from a river deep within try to surface.

In the dim lights from the trees and the flickering of the logs in the fireplace, everything is shadowed, including my family's faces.

My mother—the quintessentially all-American girl, Debbie Reynolds come to life—no longer looks like an ingenue. Her blond hair is white, her blue eyes are faded hydrangeas, her porcelain skin a bit more lined.

My brother's smile persists, but his boyish face has morphed into that of my father's a few decades earlier. He looks like the dad in need of car insurance in a State Farm commercial.

But my father has changed most of all, as if Old Man Winter has overtaken his appearance. Eyebrows like big, gray clouds dangle over his eyes. His lips—despite the warmth of the fire and the red of the wine—look ice-bitten blue, shadows are formed in the crevices of his Bavarian Alps of a face, and snowy hair sits atop the mountain peak.

I've been removed from them for such extended periods of time that it's like I'm seeing them anew.

The echo of the glockenspiel's chime envelops the house.

Time is passing so quickly.

How much have I missed?

And why don't I realize I could miss everything—every moment, every Christmas, every laugh—if I intentionally sever my relationship with them?

I rub my eyes.

"You look so tired," my mom says. "Finn, will you help me clean up?" My mother begins to collect our plates. "Your sister's been on the road all day."

"It's not that long of a drive from Detroit!" he complains, sounding just like he did as a kid. "And I'm the one who's been working at the store all day long." He pauses. "It's not like she knows what we all go through every day. It's not like she's ever here."

The silence is so deafening that I can hear the sizzle and hiss from the logs in the fireplace, the low hum of the vintage holiday bulbs on the tree, the snow pelting the window, the flicker from the twinkling lights on the porch.

My mother stands and grabs Finn by the shirt collar, and she drags him toward the kitchen just like a mother cat might a belligerent kitten.

When the room is cleared, my father chuckles.

"Good to be home, huh?" he says. "No wonder you stay away at the holidays."

"It is," I say. "And all I ever want is to be here with you at Christmas."

He leans over and refreshes our wine. I lift my glass.

"Cheers," he says. "To Christmas!"

We take long sips, and when I set my glass down, my father is staring at me.

"You never answered my question," my dad finally says. "What brings you home unannounced? And with no..."

"Expiration date?" I add.

He smiles. "Don't get me wrong," he says. "I love seeing you. Nothing and no one—not even the store—defines Christmas for me more than you being here."

My heart simultaneously swells and shatters.

"But this is so unlike you," he says. "You seem to work as much as we do at the holidays."

"I just wanted to see you," I say lamely.

My dad lifts his glass toward me and winks.

"Okay," he says. "We'll leave it at that for now."

My brother stomps into the living room and picks up the pizza box. He makes a face at me as he leaves and then smiles.

That's when I see—now that the pizza has been cleared—the *Wegner's Wish Book* sitting in the middle of the coffee table, the image of my father's little girl sitting on the floor in her grandparents' basement.

That was so long ago. That was a time when I believed in my father, his dream, Santa, the magic of Christmas.

I look up. My father is staring at me, nodding, smiling.

"I know my little girl," he says. "Better than anyone."

My heart lurches.

"Who wants iced Christmas cookies?" my mother calls in a singsong voice.

"When did you have time to do this," I ask, happy for the distraction, "in between everything else?"

"You always have to make time to bake at Christmas," she says, setting a plate of iced cookies in different holiday shapes—bells, wreaths, trees, angels, reindeer—on the table and then taking a seat. "Your grandma always made time, and so do I. Christmas is about giving, not receiving."

I think of Bea and unintended irony.

I pick up a Santa-shaped cookie—his beard thick with white icing—and bite off his head.

11

December 16

The smell of freshly brewed coffee wakes me from a dream. Actually, a nightmare.

I had returned home for Christmas, but not as Henri Wegner.

No, I was the Grinch.

Yet again.

I was breaking into everybody's home in Frankenmuth that I knew—sliding down Finn's chimney, under Sofie's door, shimmying through a decorated window into Wegner's—and I was stealing everything I could get my hands on and shoving it into a big Birkin bag: ornaments, trees, cookies, wreaths, turkey dinners. The money I found—in envelopes on Christmas tree branches, hidden in holiday cookie jars—wouldn't fit into the Birkin, so I had to stuff dollars into my pockets but also into my mouth.

I was literally consuming cash.

As I was sneaking out of Wegner's, the elfin *Weihnachten* woman I met yesterday made me sit in the throne for a picture. When she handed me the Polaroid, the image was not of me but a green, yellow-eyed monster with a devious smirk plastered across its face.

Moreover, the photo of my body was an X-ray, and my heart—just like the Grinch's—was three sizes too small.

I jolted awake.

I hold out my hands again.

They look normal.

I lift my phone, reverse the camera and look at my face in the screen.

Exhausted, a touch green around the gills, but definitely me.

I sniff the air again, smelling the coffee, and glance at the clock: 5:02 a.m.

Like father, like daughter.

For as long as I can remember, my father has been up before dawn even considers waking in order to brew the coffee and get his day started.

Like most Americans—although unlike many men his age—Dad has evolved on the caffeine front, from making Folgers to making espresso or a pot of Starbucks blend that would put hair on the chest of a yeti.

I accidentally hit Photos on my cell, and my sleepy eyes suddenly see the surreptitious tax pictures I took yesterday. My hands tremble slightly. I put the phone down, my eyes wandering from the clock on the shelf to the wall unit hiding the safe.

Safe.

Am I?

Are any of us?

My eyes scan the base of the immaculate, clean midcentury wall unit.

A thought enters my mind, and I hate myself for even thinking it: *Did I miss any other pertinent information my parents might have hidden in there?*

I stand, slide my feet into a pair of slippers and pull on a University of Michigan sweatshirt over my pajamas. I walk over to the cabinet and open the rattan doors.

The cabinet next to the safe hides a tangle of slithering, snaking wires and cables jutting from a very new TV, a very old VHS player and set of speakers.

More irony.

My father may have been the one with the dream to start Wegner's, but it has been my mother's guiding hand that has built the brand and kept the connection between past and future while hiding all the messy wires from public view.

"You never want a cord to show," I can remember my mother telling me as a girl as we decorated for Christmas. "Otherwise, it ruins the illusion."

She spent as much time tucking wires behind branches, hiding cords beneath tree skirts and disguising ugly adapters and surge protectors with a forest of bottle-brush trees and faux snow. My mom has done the same thing with Wegner's. I've yet to see a cord in any photo that's been taken, and I've yet to witness any public discord.

I kneel and begin to search the cabinet.

What else can I find in here?

"Busted!"

I scream and fall onto my rear.

I turn my head, and my mom is standing there in a fluffy buffalo plaid holiday robe.

Think fast, Henri.

"No, you're busted!" I laugh. "You still do these workout tapes? I was just remembering when we did them together."

"I do," she says. "Sometimes, I'll pop in a Jane Fonda. Sometimes I'll run a yoga class from my cell to the TV."

"Fancy," I say.

"And sometimes," she says, "sometimes, I come in here and tell your father I'm going to work out, shut the door and watch a Hallmark Christmas movie."

I chuckle.

She continues. "It's a requirement at the holidays," Mom says. "And sometimes I feel like I need to escape from the reality of our own Christmas world. Don't you?"

I nod.

My mom stops, leans back out of the doorway and swivels her head left and right in the hallway.

"We're going through a lot right now," she confides quietly.

I'm too surprised to speak for a second. This isn't what I expected to hear from my mom, especially after nearly getting caught snooping.

But this could be the leverage I need to convince them to sell.

"Meaning what, Mom?"

"Meaning..."

There is rustling in the hallway, an echo of footsteps.

"What are my two favorite girls whispering about at dawn?"

My dad appears in the doorway, already fully dressed, smelling like Irish Spring and Old Spice.

I inhale.

Some things do never change.

"Conspiring to overthrow you," my mom says with a big wink.

Her joke is like a jab to my ribs.

"And we can't do that without coffee," I say.

"This way," my father says.

We follow each other like partridges upstairs to the kitchen, walking in the light of the still nearly full moon, which makes night seem like midday. I emerge in the midcentury tree house, the moon dangling above the woods, a black-and-white winter portrait, long shadows from the trees moving like fingers across the snow. In the distance, the creek of my youth glistens, partly frozen, partly alive.

My father hands me a cup of coffee.

As I lift it to my mouth, I realize he has intentionally picked out the mug just for me.

My Favorite Dad Gave Me This Mug!

I take a sip and notice my dad's mug.

Nobody's Walking Out on This Family Christmas! We're All in It Together!

I retreat to the dinette set as my dad and mom begin to work in tandem and in silence, pulling ingredients from cupboards and cabinets.

"Pancakes?" I ask. "I thought you were oatmeal people these days."

My mother turns to look at me, whisk in the air. "Are you insinuating we're old?"

"Not old, healthy."

"Well played," my mom laughs. "But our little girl always gets pancakes shaped like reindeer on her first morning home for Christmas. It's just…" she hesitates "…been a while."

"Some things should never change," my father adds quickly, heating a skillet, "save for turkey bacon because of my cholesterol."

I smile and sip my coffee.

"You did see the latest medical study?" my dad asks.

"What was that?"

"One bowl of oatmeal offsets a week of pizza and wine," he says.

"Oh, the Dr. Wegner diet," I say.

"Yes," my mom adds. "The one that says twelve iced cookies are as good for you as a kale salad."

"Now you're just getting confused," my dad says. "That's the Santa diet, and it's a good one, too."

I laugh, watching the easy camaraderie between my parents, that balance of love and friendship, light and laughter.

That's when I see first light peek in the kitchen window. The counter glows. Sitting by the window is what looks like a dead branch emerging from a beautiful McCoy vase featuring a pretty pink blossom on its base.

There is a Bavarian Christmas tradition that my parents still follow in which they cut a winter's branch from a cherry tree and place it in a vase of water. In the warmth of the holiday home, the branch—with love—should blossom by Christmas. My grandparents always placed a cherry branch in a vase in December, too.

I stare at the dead branch.

This is called "forcing" a branch to bloom. In essence, you confuse it with the warmth to believe that it's spring.

You lie to the cherry branch.

My gaze moves from the branch to my parents.

You make it believe that it's time even though it's not.

My stomach groans.

"Someone's trying to talk," my father says with a chuckle. "Here you go!"

A plate appears before me that is as magical as a Wegner's display: reindeer pancakes!

Two pancakes—a smaller one sitting on the edge of a bigger one—form the head and body. The eyes consist of two dollops of whipped cream with blueberries in the center, another big squirt of whipped cream and a maraschino cherry for Rudolph's nose, and turkey bacon juts from the top pancake to create antlers.

My parents sit, and I take a photo of my breakfast with my cell—a sweet photo to offset the spy mission—before drizzling my reindeer with pure Michigan maple syrup.

"What are your plans today?" my mother asks. "You're up so early. I take it you have to work?"

"I do have to work," I say. "With you. I thought I'd spend the day—actually the next few days—working with you at the store."

My father drops his fork.

"Is that okay?" I continue.

"Of course it is," my mother says. "We'd be delighted to have you." She takes a bite of her pancakes. "And the extra help."

My dad picks up a piece of bacon and waves it at me.

"You've never wanted much to do with the store at Christmas before," my dad says, eyeing me warily. "What gives? What about your job?"

"Jakob," my mother says. "Henri doesn't need the third degree at dawn."

"I told you already," I say. "I have so much time to take, and I don't want to lose it. I can easily go back to bed if you don't want to see me or need the help."

My father laughs.

"I would love nothing more than to be around you every second of the day."

Another crack in my heart.

"Me, too," I say.

"Well, wonderful then," my dad says. "A true Christmas miracle. We all need one."

He finishes wolfing down his breakfast and stands.

I hear a tinkling.

"Mabel?" I ask. "How did you get up here?"

"For this," my dad says.

He grabs a piece of turkey bacon and holds it in the air.

Mabel barks, and he hands it to her. She scarfs it down.

"She eats with the same grace as her best friend," my mom observes.

"Ha-ha," my dad says.

"You're the true Christmas miracle, aren't you?" I ask Mabel.

She trots over to me and collapses on my feet.

Dad retrieves the pot of coffee, brings it to the table and refills our cups as well as his travel tumbler.

"I'm going to brush my teeth," he says. "Can you be ready in a few minutes, Henri? I like to be in before seven."

"Sure," I lie, knowing it takes me an hour to get ready before I even feel comfortable going through a Starbucks drive-through.

"And can you bring Mabel with you to the store today?" my dad asks my mom.

She nods, and he patters down the stairs.

Once he's out of earshot, I say to my mom, "What were you going to tell me earlier? What is it you're going through?"

My mother holds a finger to her lips, as if she's a librarian shushing me for talking too loudly. She waits until she can hear the water running downstairs and then whispers, "Your dad is too proud to admit that it's been a rough few years."

"Really?" I say.

"Covid. Inventory issues. Inflation. Staffing problems. Outdated systems."

I look at her, incredulous.

"You'll understand what I mean when you get in there," she whispers. "Your dad wants to do it all. The way it always was."

"What about Finn?" I ask.

"Finn is loyal. He's okay with things as they are."

She cocks her head, making sure the water is still running.

"Your brother thinks everything your father does is perfect. Doesn't rock the boat. And your father tunes me out. Says I'm a worrier."

My mom places her hand over mine.

"I think it was fortuitous you came home. Your timing is impeccable."

A glimmer of light in my darkness?

The water stops running, and my mother gets up to clear the table.

As I watch my mother, I think of mentoring countless business owners and corporate executives about the danger of keeping secrets—from your board to accounting—and not listening to your most trusted advisers.

My mom turns on the faucet.

She walks back over to me and says, "This is just between us."

I nod. "Of course."

My mom is like her cabinet: she is hiding all the cords and wires.

She turns off the water.

"Better go get ready," my mom says happily with a big smile.

Part three

12

As my father drives, the tires groan over the newly fallen snow.

Although the sun has started to rise, the road before us is still dark, and the lights from my father's oversize truck bounce up and down, left and right, along with my arm.

"You're doing that on purpose, aren't you?" I ask.

I am trying to put on makeup. The passenger mirror in my father's car is not as large or well lit as the driver's mirror in my SUV. Moreover, with each and every pothole we hit, my mascara wand skitters across my upper lid and forehead, my lipstick flies across my cheek and the foundation ends up in my hairline.

My dad glances over.

"You look a bit like Tammy Faye Bakker," he says, voice deadpan. "That should be a boon for business."

One of Michigan Governor Gretchen Whitmer's most famous campaign promises years ago was to "fix the damn roads," and she has kept her promise. But Michigan winters are like aging—relentless and unending—and it takes constant patching to cover all the potholes.

I glance at the road before me, then to the side, before looking at myself in the dim light surrounding the mirror.

My fair skin—especially when I'm exhausted and wearing little makeup—is beginning to resemble the sad, gray slush.

"You're a natural beauty," my father says. "You don't need a stitch of makeup."

Don't most fathers look at their daughters the way they did when we were just girls? Bright eyed, rosy cheeked, taut, dewy skin.

And don't most daughters look at their fathers as unable to do any wrong?

"Thank you, Dad," I say.

I put my makeup down and look at myself. My appearance is somewhere on the scale between clown and killer clown.

Please don't let anyone I know see me today, God.

My father—as he has done since the first day he has opened the shop—parks in a spot flanking the road far, far away, adjacent to the Silent Night Memorial Chapel.

"Our customers should have the best spots," he says, as if I need reminding.

I watch him gather his things—cell phone, briefcase, coffee tumbler—the truck filled with the spicy zing of his soap and aftershave. In a world where we've been taught by too many of our political and corporate leaders that greed is good, mean is normal, nasty is okay, my dad is still a good man.

I glance around at the lights gleaming up and down Christmas Lane.

I think of my mother's whispered confessions.

But doing things the same way is not always good business.

"Why are the lights on?" I ask.

"They remain on twenty-four hours a day," he says.

"Why?" I ask again.

"So people driving by day or night can see them. It's good for business."

I turn in my seat to look at him.

"No, Dad, it's bad for business."

"It's marketing, Henri. Branding."

"Dad," I say, keeping the tone of my voice steady. "Just think of the cost savings you could incur if you shut the lights off, say, when the store closed."

My father's face turns beet red. I take a breath to let him decompress and then continue.

"Hear me out. Not that many people are on the road around here late at night. If they are, they can't stop to shop. And those who live here and shop here already know about Wegner's and what to expect." I take another breath. "And it's so dark here in December, I bet the lights are on all the time because the sensor can't tell whether it's day or night. We only get a few hours of sunshine a month in winter, if we're lucky. Why not invest a little bit of money to put all of this on a timer? I think you could save a lot of money."

My dad scans Christmas Lane, thinking.

"How much would the timer cost?" my dad finally asks.

"Way less than it does to light the world for no one to see." I smile gently at him.

"Let me run some numbers today, okay?" I continue. "Let me help…for once."

"Okay." He nods, getting out of the truck.

I follow suit. It is bracingly, head-numbingly frigid.

"I now remember why I never wanted you here," my dad jokes. "Too many ideas."

"That stings worse than the cold," I say.

"C'mon," he says, taking off in a jog across the snow.

"Don't break a hip, old man," I yell.

"Don't scare any children today, Tammy Faye!"

We race down 25 Christmas Lane, and I am taken back in time to doing this exact same thing when I was still a girl. It was not the holiday lights extravaganza it is today. In fact, my father pulled all the lights we had in the basement of our home, then begged my grandparents for some of theirs, and we draped them over bushes and wrapped a couple of trees. It snowed that first night, and we ran up and down the lane in front of the original store with as much excitement as if we were reindeer trying to get Santa's sleigh off the ground.

As I run this morning with my dad, I can still remember him yelling, "We did it, Henri! We did it! Our own Christmas store!"

My dad skids to a stop in front of the store, slides a key into the lock and immediately begins to turn on interior lights as he goes. I follow, shutting them off.

"Aren't dads the ones who are supposed to run around after their kids shutting off the lights?" he says.

"Store doesn't open for three more hours," I say. "Employees don't arrive for another two. Why waste the electricity?"

I follow my dad through the store to the café, and then into their offices.

"Is it okay to turn on this light?" he mocks.

The lights go on, illuminating my father's face. His mouth is turned down.

"I'm sorry," I say. "I'm just trying to help. Remember, this is what I do for a living. I cut costs. I streamline."

"You sell family businesses to the highest bidder."

Now, my face drops. I can see my father wants to take it back.

"I'm sorry," he says. "I didn't mean it."

I take off my coat and hang it up. My father makes coffee. It is quiet—save for the hum of the lights—for a few minutes.

"You know, Dad, I also help a lot of small businesses make a lot of money. Some aren't equipped to take the next step, some have built a company their whole lives and are simply exhausted, others have no one to run it after they are gone and some are simply bad business owners with a great idea that needs to be taken to the next level."

I walk over to the coffeepot and sniff dramatically.

"And sometimes, people just get burned out," I say. "But

sometimes, Dad, business *is* business. People get laid off. Companies get too fat. Costs need to be streamlined."

"I understand, Henri. I'm not some rube. I may not have gone to the University of Michigan and worked for a huge corporation, but somehow I've managed to grow a small business into a big one without a guidebook."

"Dad," I say, my voice soft. "I didn't mean to put you on the defensive. There's no one in this world I respect more than you. But I know you want this to be your legacy. I know the last few years have been tough for many small businesses, and it's a different world today. Companies have to adapt and change, or they become dinosaurs."

My father looks as if he wants to tell me the things my mother whispered this morning.

"I agree," he says. "It's just hard for a dinosaur to change."

I smile. "I know, Dad."

"And it's hard when you remember every single person who has ever worked here—teenager to grandmother—and you want them to feel like they're a part of the family. Small business in a small community *is* family. Our employees work hard. They deserve to be taken care of. *That* is our legacy."

"Then let me help you retain that legacy," I say. "I'll give input. You can ignore it unless you think it makes sense. And then, just like Santa, I'll be gone after Christmas. How's that sound?"

He pours a cup of coffee.

"I don't want to think about you leaving yet," he says.

I smile.

"Let me help, Dad," I continue. "I want to help."

He hands me a Wegner's coffee mug.

"Okay," he says, turning on the radio to the Muth. "All of our expenses and accounting files are on the laptop, marked by fiscal year," my father says. "I'd love to see what you think we might be able to save on electricity." He looks at me. "And any other ideas you might have, too."

I smile and take a seat at my mother's desk.

I can tell he wants to say more, but his phone rings.

"Sorry, John," he says. "I'll be right there."

He hangs up.

"I completely forgot about a chamber meeting I have this morning," he says. "Can you manage the store until everyone arrives?"

My heart suddenly races.

Can I really be this lucky? An entire morning to snoop uninterrupted? I could have all the intel I need today.

"Of course," I say, trying not to sound too excited.

My dad grabs his coat.

"See you later."

He stops at the door. "Thank you, Henri. It's good to have you home."

My father exits.

As if on cue, "You're a Mean One, Mr. Grinch" begins to play on the radio.

13

I am a modern-day Mata Hari.

I am downloading and copying files as quickly as I can.

I take pictures.

I run numbers.

I pull together a summary report of expenses, what I feel could be cut and enhanced, what I believe Vance could cut and improve, and I send file after file, photo after photo, report after report, to Benjie and Bea.

I am sweating like a madwoman an hour later, glancing so often at the clock that my neck is stiff, and none of this has to do with menopause or even guilt at the moment.

It has everything to do with DOS.

Wegner's is still on DOS!

My father needs my help more than he knows. *Wegner's* needs more help than it knows.

Perhaps my plan is not so evil after all. This place needs new eyes.

I hear footsteps.

My mother walks in and sees me in her chair, bent over her laptop, my spine a Slinky.

"DOS?" I yell when I see her. "You still use *DOS*?"

My mother lifts her finger to her mouth and looks around for my dad.

"He's not here," I say. "And I don't care. This is insanity. I haven't used DOS since I worked at Glamour Shots in the mall in the '80s. I didn't even know it still existed. I feel like I'm trying to decode a nuclear bomb."

My mother hangs her coat.

"I told you, honey, he doesn't like change."

"Change?" I say, my voice rising yet again. "This is like being stuck, literally, in the Ice Age. It's dinosaur refusing to see the world as it is. I feel like after work we should all go to the mall and eat at Sbarro's and then go see *Risky Business*."

My mother laughs.

"I know, it's not funny," she says. "But you look a bit '80s today. What's with your mascara?"

"I did it in the truck at dawn while hitting potholes!"

She laughs again.

"You won't think this is funny. Come. Sit down."

My mom pulls up a chair next to me.

"Do you know what your electrical bill averages out to per day?"

"A lot?" my mom asks.

"Twelve hundred and fifty dollars! Per *day*!" I let the number sink in. "That's nearly a half-million-dollar electrical bill each year."

"No," my mom says, clearly shocked.

"Yes," I say.

I think of running down Christmas Lane, the lights becoming a blur, money becoming snow, just blowing away in the winter wind.

This would be one of the first things Vance Enterprises would eliminate. An easy quarter-mil savings by simply flicking a switch at night.

It would be the first thing I would cut, too.

"I guess I only have ever looked at it month by month," my mom says, sounding uncomfortable. "I feel so dumb."

"No, Mom, don't. It's just one of those things you get used to seeing and paying. You don't look at the overall cost. It happens all the time."

Finn walks in. His big smile fades immediately.

"What have we here?" he asks.

"DOS," I say. "We have DOS here. Welcome to the '80s."

"It's worked all these years," Finn says.

"That is not a plausible excuse or business model," I say. "We also used to throw razor-sharp, pointed lawn darts at each other in the yard. We didn't wear seat belts. We didn't have air-conditioning. Sometimes, things need to change for the better."

Finn pulls his shoulders back, just like he did as a boy, physically daring me to cross the line.

"I'm calling my assistant, Bea," I say. "Tolliver is going through a huge laptop and software conversion right now. I think I might be able to secretly siphon enough to change everything over here. She can help us do that remotely."

"Oh honey, can you really do that?" my mom says hopefully.

"I can," I say definitively, although my mind is asking, *Which team are you on, Henri? Tolliver or Wegner?*

"I'm telling Dad!" Finn says.

"What are you, eight years old?" I scoff.

He starts to walk out of the office. I bound up from my mom's desk, sending the wheeled chair flying behind me. I grab Finn's arm.

He turns on a dime, eyes blazing, and shakes me off.

"No, you're not telling Dad," I say.

"Why are you here?" Finn asks. "Why are you home? This is so not Hart Henri."

How does he know my old nickname?

He smiles smugly.

"Yes, your little brother has read all of the articles about his big sister's—" Finn stops, pretending to search for the right word "—success."

He uses his fingers to make air quotes around the last word.

"Finn Jakob Wegner!" my mother says, standing. She only uses his full name when she's upset. "Apologize to your sister."

He folds his arms.

"Now!"

"I'm sorry."

His words are empty.

"She's just trying to help us," my mother says.

Am I?

I know that my parents' antiquated business practices might raise red flags for Vance Enterprises. They might look warily at a company so behind the times, or try to offer only a fire-sale discount price for the business.

"And we need the help," my mother continues, knocking me from my thoughts. "You know we do."

"Let this be my Christmas gift to Wegner's, after not being around enough," I say, keeping my voice neutral.

I reach out and touch Finn's arm, gently this time.

"Please."

He nods. "Okay. But promise you will loop me in with Mom on how to do everything." I can tell from his eyes and voice that he's hurt. I feel as if I've always hurt him unintentionally simply by being older. I've always felt as if I abandoned him and the entire family, burning down the bridge so he never had the option of leaving.

"I promise," I say. "And just so you know, Dad and I talked this morning, I ran the numbers and we're considering putting the Christmas Lane lights on a timer so we have more control and can shut them off when the store closes. We'll save a ton of money with one easy switch."

"So punny," Finn says. He looks at Mom. "Did you know about this?"

"I think it's imperative we look at every way we can improve and save money," she says. "It's been a tough few years, Finnie. You know that. You've seen the numbers. Business is good, but we're down. You and your father refuse to acknowledge that. We can't bury our heads in the snow anymore."

Finn shakes his head at us. "I feel like I'm watching an episode of *Succession*," he says. "Are you Kendall, Shiv or Roman?"

"It's such a great show, isn't it?" I ask, refusing to play his game.

"Very informative," Finn says.

"You two," my mother says, her voice strong, a warning shot across the bow to behave.

Finn opens his mouth to say something, but my father rushes in the office.

"I shouldn't have gone to that stupid chamber meeting. We had a lot of people call in sick today, or unable to make the commute," my father says. "I need the two of you to fill in on the floor."

I look at Finn.

"Now!" my dad barks. "We're overwhelmed."

14

If this were *Succession*, then Finn just pulled a fast one on me.

"If you need me, I'll be in Villages and Hummels," he says. "Gert will take good care of you, won't you, Gert?"

Finn waves at me as he leaves.

I blow him a kiss. He catches it and holds it to his heart.

I have been banished not to the land of misfit toys but to the world of personalized ornaments. There is no worse Christmas curse for me.

I am the least talented artist you've ever witnessed.

Remember the stick figures you drew in art class as a child?

That's full-on Picasso for me.

Remember the friend in high school art class who painted her face and nails instead of the canvas?

Me.

The one in college art class who couldn't get perspective right in a painting, whose birds looked like frowns, whose suns had happy faces and whose trees looked like they were floating above the earth?

That person was a better artist than me.

"Sit down, sweetheart," Gert says.

Gertrude Heinrich—Gert for short, Grandma Gert to many

in Frankenmuth—is every bit of her ninety years. She taught high school art at Frankenmuth forever, and when she retired, my father hired her to run the store's brand-new personalized ornaments business.

That was over a quarter century ago.

Today, nearly half of the glass ornaments sold at Wegner's are our own designs, handcrafted by global artisans exclusively for us. "Merry Christmas" ornaments in more than forty languages are among the eight thousand styles of ornaments available.

But the biggest seller of all?

Wegner's staff personalizes nearly half a million ornaments annually.

And Grandma Gert taught them all how to perfectly print your grandson's name in gold on a red ornament surrounded by silver snowflakes, write Baby's First Christmas in script or frame a newly married couple's wedding date in the little white window atop their stocking caps.

These personalized ornaments are as beloved a tradition here at Wegner's as the artists themselves. Gert still employs the same vintage lettering techniques used by my father and other early sign painters. It requires precision brushes and oil-based lettering enamel for a glossy appearance.

"Hi, Gert!" I say. "It's Henri. Henri Wegner. Remember?"

Her eyes glint. I can't tell if it's recognition or the result of cataract surgery. And then she says, "Oh, it is you."

Grandma Gert is wearing a Santa cap and an ugly Christmas sweater that reads All I Want for Christmas Is Wine. Gert can wear whatever she wants around here.

Everyone mistakes Grandma Gert for the quintessentially kind grandmother who drinks tea, bakes cookies and loves every living creature.

She is anything but.

Gert, like me, never married. She was married to her work. And she is a true artist. Her landscapes are in the Michigan governor's mansion, and she takes her work at Wegner's *very* seriously. I remember her once telling her team when she was first hired, "When we personalize an ornament for someone, it is like creating a painting. It will hang forever in someone's home and remind them of a precious memory. It must be perfectly done."

"Yes, it's me," I say.

"It's going to be a long day!" Gert calls down the table at the other employees. "Maybe it's best you just handle cleanup," she says to me.

"I want to help," I say.

"'I want to help,' and 'I *can* help' are two very different things," Gert says.

I forgot how, um, candid she is.

"Who did your makeup this morning?" Gert continues. "If the answer is you, we're in big trouble."

I smile meekly. "I did."

Gert exhales as if she's trying to sail a ship with her own lung power. "I guess we could use the help. But you're just doing the simple names like Joe." She gives me another once-over, and her eyes narrow. "Oh, *now* I remember you from high school. Did I fail you?"

"I passed art," I say. "Barely."

"I was feeling generous that year," she says. "Maybe just stick to the two-letter names, like Ma or Pa."

I take a seat next to her at the long table in the middle of the personalized-ornaments room—picture a big, old cafeteria table filled with every possible art supply, from glitter to glue in the middle. I look down the table. A line of skilled, capable artists is happily painting and chatting with customers.

The room is jammed with shoppers. A long line snakes into another section.

I take a deep breath.

A woman in a bright red scarf approaches me holding a blue ornament.

"Hi!" she says, her voice animated. "This is for my son and brand new daughter-in-law who got married in October. This is their very first holiday together, and blue is their favorite color. Can you write on the ornament, Our First Christmas As Mr. and Mrs. Vernon Van Der Raamalt Beenhouwer?"

She beams and hands me the ornament.

I look at it.

Now, I'm not a scientist, but I do know that it is scientifically impossible to write—much less spell—what this woman just uttered onto an ornament this size. I know one is supposed to see the universe in a grain of sand, but you cannot write the novel this woman wants on a tiny blue globe.

I hand her a piece of paper.

"Could you just write that down for me so I don't misspell anything?"

"Of course!" she says. "It's Dutch."

I glance at Gert.

"This is going to be good." She rolls her eyes.

A little boy walks up and asks Gert to write Ben on an ornament twice this size.

Ben!

"Universe is an ironic place, isn't it?" Gert asks me with a laugh.

The Dutch woman hands me the piece of paper and nods, waiting for me to get started.

"Is there a color you'd prefer?" I ask.

"Let's do silver," she says. "Pretty on the blue, don't you think?"

I grab a brush, dip it into some silver paint and start to draw.

I complete the word *Our* and the first three letters of *First* and realize I am not only out of room but that the paint is dripping.

The woman is hunched over me, watching my every move.

I haven't been inspected this closely since I went on vacation to Greece, and every single man and woman on the beach—ethereal beauties who looked as if they had just sprung from either mythology or an episode of *The White Lotus*—turned to inspect me when I removed my beach cover.

Gert glances over.

"Looks like it's going well."

"I don't need sarcasm right now, Gert, I need help." I look up. "This is impossible." I lower my voice and jam my paintbrush at the piece of paper beside me. "She wants *Ulysses* painted on a golf ball."

Gert shakes her head.

She takes a rag and wipes the ornament clean. Then she places it in a little cardboard holder shaped like an egg cup and covers that in white tissue.

"First," she says, picking up a brush and dipping it in silver paint, "don't you remember a thing your father taught you?"

My heart hiccups.

"What do you mean?"

"Didn't you used to sit and watch him make those early signs?"

I nod.

"This is the same technique, just in a different form. Watch."

Gert begins to effortlessly paint beautiful letters just like the ones my father used to carve. She rotates the carton with every stroke to keep the ornament and lettering even.

"You letter using downstrokes to prevent the paint from flaring," she says. "And each letter should have a flourish, and it should look as if it's curved and carved from centuries ago."

Within moments, every word the woman wanted has been painted perfectly on the ornament.

With room to spare.

Gert even paints two ornate snowflakes on both sides of the lettering.

"This will need an hour or so to dry, and then we will wrap it, box it and have it ready for you," Gert says.

The woman leans over the table.

"Thank you sooooo much," she says to Gert. Then she turns to me. "This must be your first day. You'll get the hang of it."

I barely have room to catch my breath when the next woman approaches.

"Just make it to Nancy," she says, handing me a red ornament. "Spelled the usual way. And, in gold, please."

"You got this," Gert says.

I take fifteen minutes—going painfully slowly as Gert guides me—but I'm impressed with my effort when I finish.

"Look at this!" I say to Nancy. "Isn't it beautiful?"

Nancy's face falls.

"I told you Nancy is spelled the usual way," the woman says, her voice rising.

I look at the ornament.

"I don't understand."

"N-a-n-c-e-e," she says. "Nancee."

Gert chuckles.

I think of Finn and what he said over pizza last night about the spelling of the names of Ethan's girlfriends.

"Listen, Nancee, just for your information, that is not the *usual* way your name is spelled," I say sweetly with a big, dumb smile plastered across my face.

"That's not true," she says.

I grab my cell. "Let's just google, oh, let's see, Nancy Sinatra or Nancy Reagan." I hold up my cell. "It's *y* not *e-e*. Fancy is not spelled *f-a-n-c-e-e*. Neither is your name."

I smile again.

"Did you try one of those online tutorials to do your makeup today?" the woman asks.

"Ouch," Gert whispers.

"Your ornament will be ready in about an hour," I reply. "With a *y*."

She storms off.

"I would high-five you for that, but—" Gert stops talking and nods.

I look up. My father is standing before the table.

"That is not the Wegner way, Henri. You know that," he says. "*You* may treat customers and employees like this in the way you conduct *your* business—as if they do not matter—but it's not the way we do things here. Got it?"

My cheeks are on fire. I haven't been spoken to like this by my dad since I was a kid.

I blink. I want to cry.

"Yes, sir," I say.

"Good."

He walks away.

I look around. The table of painters is staring at me. When I glance at them, they nervously begin to paint again.

I am so flustered. The tinkling sound grows louder and louder until I have to shut my eyes. When I open them, Mabel is beside me.

"You know," I say, hugging her. "You always know when I need you, don't you, girl."

Gert leans down and pulls a poufy pillow from underneath the table.

"Your dad has one of these in every section for her," she says. "Mabel likes to visit everyone. She's been here as long as I have, it seems." Gert reaches over and touches my hand. "And she does know when we need her."

I bend down and give Mabel another big hug.

"I'd like this ornament to say, For Quinn, A Michigan Girl Forever."

I know that voice. I would know it anywhere. Even after so long.

I look up from Mabel and crack my head on the edge of the table.

"That must've hurt," Gert says.

I know those eyes, that smile, those lips.

I would know them no matter how much time has passed.

"Shep?"

"Henri?"

"What are you doing here?" I ask.

"What are *you* doing here?"

I don't know what to say. Whatever comes out will be a lie.

"She's a fill-in," Gert says to Shep. "But my gut says this will be her last day."

15

"You'll be lucky that Gert did your ornament," I say. "She's the best."

"I remember your high school art days," Shep laughs. "Took a lot of therapy to forget."

He is wearing a beautiful wool sweater that I know he made in his shop, a heathery blue gray that matches his eyes perfectly.

Shep has only gotten better looking with age.

When Sofie and I saw Rob Lowe in *The Outsiders* and then in *St. Elmo's Fire*, we lined our bedrooms with posters of the young star. As Shep got older, he began to look more and more like the actor, and every girl in a hundred-mile vicinity of Frankenmuth wanted to date him.

"You look great, by the way," Shep says.

Vintage Shep. He can disarm you with a compliment out of the blue, a wink of his perfectly colored eye, a rub of his perfect jaw and five-o'clock shadow, raking his hand through his still full hair that falls just so.

Does he think I look great? Is he just being nice?

And how can a woman who has been so successful in her life—who has stared down billionaires and led meetings of a thousand people—be reduced to silence, transported to her teen years—*No, returned to the days of DOS!*—simply when an ex compliments her?

I struggle for the right words to say, my brain mired in quicksand.

And then I catch a million reflections of my image on a wall of shiny silver ornaments hanging behind Shep.

"You're a great liar," I finally say. "It looks like a caravan of circus monkeys did a makeup tutorial on me. I got up at dawn to help out here."

"You've always had that quick, self-deprecating humor," he says. "I think that's proof of someone who knows themselves really well."

Or, someone who doesn't want to know themselves at all.

"Speaking of proof—in this case, a hundred proof—have you seen anyone from high school lately?" I ask. "Like Sofie?"

He laughs.

Ah, humor. It is the great unifier and divider. It can bring someone closer, or it can deflect attention. I've always believed a thin line separates humor from heartbreak.

"See?" he says. "Always funny." Shep stops. "It's a small town. You see everyone. Whether you want to or not."

I think of Hannah. I think of living here. Anonymity. Another reason I ran.

"I was sorry to hear about you and Hannah. I wanted to reach out, but it didn't feel right."

He nods.

"How are you doing?" I ask.

"Better," he says. "It took a while. Actually, it took a long while. It's been five years. Therapy has helped. I felt like such a failure. To my family, to my town, to myself. But I finally feel as if I understood why I married Hannah and why my marriage failed. I've changed so much, Henri. I'm a different person now. I've stopped blaming everyone, including myself. This is the first Christmas in a long time where I actually feel as if I'm an active participant in my own life again, not just some ghost of Christmas Past. I actually feel…happy."

What is with all the Scrooge references?

"That's a lot of information to share so quickly, I know," Shep continues. "But I've wanted to tell you that—and a lot of other things—for a long time."

He's been thinking of me?

I want to ask him so many questions right now, but I simply nod and say, "I'm so glad, Shep. How are the kids?"

"Better, too. I think they've actually learned to stop blaming themselves for all of my and Hannah's issues. They are incredible kids."

"So Quinn is following in my footsteps at the University of Michigan?" I joke.

"She is," he says. "And I'm so proud. I encouraged her to go there." Shep hesitates. "Because of you. She's a brilliant kid. She wants to make her own mark on the world, just like someone else I know."

I can feel my face flush. I know that it shows. With my German complexion, I am a human traffic light.

"And you do look great," Shep insists. "A bit heavy on the mascara, but great."

I laugh. "I paint my face as well as my personalized ornaments."

"You've never been great at accepting compliments," he continues. "Why is that?"

I've never truly believed compliments when they've been given to me, I think. I guess I've always wondered what the person complimenting actually wanted.

I shrug instead.

Shep shakes his head. "You know, sometimes it's easier just to say thank you."

"Thank you," I say.

"See how easy that was? I can't believe Miss Mabel is still

going," Shep says, squatting down to pet our old mutt, who has followed us into the corner of the personalized ornaments and lain down directly atop my feet. "She's still so attached to you. It's like she waited for you to come again for Christmas after all these years."

His words seem laced with deeper meaning. Or am I reading too much into the situation?

"It's been too long," I say.

"Time goes so quickly," Shep says. "I feel as if we were just dancing in May Day."

I laugh.

"Remember?" he asks.

May 1977

I ran to my window and threw open the curtains.

The sun was shining.

In the distance, the woods were filled with trillium, and yellow daffodils still dotted the hills. A blur of green was beginning to develop on the shrubs and canopy.

I didn't believe my eyes, so I tugged open the window.

A warm breeze rushed through the screen and tossed my long, blond hair around my face. The sweet scent of lily of the valley filled my nose.

"May Day!" I yelled, racing from my bedroom, down the hall and upstairs to the kitchen.

In Michigan, you never knew if May Day might bring a surprise snow, a spring thunderstorm, a cold rain or—sometimes—a day like today that took your breath away.

"Big day," my dad said, pouring me a bowl of Quisp cereal.

"Can I have Pop-Tarts instead?" I asked. "I need my energy to dance."

"Of course," he said with a laugh. "What flavor, m'lady?"

"Strawberry!"

My dad popped them into the toaster, poured me a glass each of orange juice and milk, and then leaned across the counter.

"Are you ready?"

I nodded. "I am! I know every move."

Besides Christmas, there was no bigger holiday in Frankenmuth than May Day. The town put up a massive Maypole downtown, the downtown lampposts were wrapped in ribbon and the high school's May Day and crowning of the May Queen drew the entire town.

Our grade school's celebration was small in comparison to the high school—where the girls dressed in beautiful white gowns and danced intricate numbers—but for every little boy and girl, it was the entire world. Nearly every single day of school during the spring semester, from art class to music, centered on May Day.

And I, Henri Wegner, was chosen by my school as the girl to kick off the dancing, the girl whose ribbon would be the first to weave around the Maypole.

I knew that nearly every little girl who had been chosen to lead May Day in grade school went on to become the May Queen and become part of Frankenmuth history.

My Pop-Tarts sprang from the toaster, and my dad grabbed them quickly, yelling "Hot! Ouch!" and placing them on a plate and setting them before me.

"You know—" my dad started.

"I know, I know," I said. "Mom was May Queen."

"Yes," he said. "But do you know why May Day was started?"

I sighed and looked at him.

"I live in this town, don't I? I live in this house, don't I? I just wrote a paper about it."

He laughed.

"Humor me."

"May Day is a European festival that marks the beginning of summer. Traditions include gathering wildflowers and green branches, weaving garlands, crowning a May Queen, setting up a Maypole."

"A little encyclopedic, but very good, Henri," my dad said with a laugh. "And in Germany, especially in the rural regions and the Rhineland, young men deliver Maypoles—trees covered in streamers—to the house of a girl they like. It's a symbol of their love. It's a symbol of spring." My dad smiles. "I did that for your mother in high school. She said it was the most romantic thing in her life."

"It was."

My mother entered the kitchen and kissed my father.

"Gross," I said.

"Tanz in den Mai," my mother said to my father in German. "Dance into May."

He began to hum, and the two danced in the kitchen, my father turning my mother, who pirouetted round and round, before returning to his arms.

"*So* gross," I repeated. "Can't I just eat my breakfast in peace?"

I removed the crispy edges from all four sides of my Pop-Tart, dunking the pieces in my milk before eating them. Then, carefully, I separated the frosted top side from the bottom jam side, eating the strawberry bottom of the tart first before savoring the frosted side last.

"Do you know what's gross?" my father asked.

I looked at him.

"The way you eat a Pop-Tart."

I laughed. My dad was funny, like a big kid.

"Hurry up and eat," he continued. "Big day, and you don't want to be late."

Our May Field sat in a cleared-out notch in the woods just down a hill from our gymnasium. It was ringed by trees and a beautiful circle of spring flowers that the garden club planted annually.

"Are we ready, fourth-graders?"

My teacher, Mrs. Kline, wrung her hands nervously. This was her first year teaching in Frankenmuth, and the rumor was if you couldn't pull off a perfect May Day—much less one that trumped the previous year's celebration—your contract would not be extended.

We all nodded.

Mrs. Kline caught my eye.

I smiled and nodded my head with confidence.

The girls wore matching white spring dresses with a pretty eyelet pattern, the boys in white polos and shorts. The girls had crowns of fresh freesia with daisies of purple, yellow and white.

My special crown was made of pretty peonies. I smelled like a floral shop.

We marched into the May Field by grade, with the lower school band playing recorders to the tune of "Frère Jacques." I had listened to my brother play this stupid song on his recorder for months. When we were all gathered, the chorus joined in, singing along with recorders:

I see daisies, I see daisies,
Bloom in May, bloom in May.
May's the month for flowers,
No more April showers.
May is here, May is here!

I looked around. My parents and grandparents were seated on a blanket at the edge of the May Field. My heart began to pound. Mrs. Kline stepped into the center of the field.

"Welcome to the annual May Day Festival at Frankenmuth Elementary!"

The crowd applauded.

"The folk tradition of May Day can be traced to a festival held long ago in honor of Flora, the Goddess of Flowers and the Bride of the West Wind. Today, we continue to celebrate its history as a way to honor the start of spring and summer in our town."

The crowd clapped again.

"As you all know, your children have been working on this all semester long, making ribbons in art class, practicing songs in band and choir, writing papers and continuing a beloved tradition. Many today say that May Day is too old-fashioned, but I believe that today's celebration is an appreciation for our history as well as the beauty that surrounds us. It allows us to gather, to celebrate, to be one community. It allows us to dance."

Mrs. Kline pointed to the music teacher, and the choir began to sing "Here We Go Round the Maypole High."

Each grade danced and spun on the May Field. I was sandwiched between Sofie and Shep. I had been sandwiched between them since the day in gym in first grade when we wrapped ourselves in ribbon. Sofie grabbed my hand and squeezed it hard.

And then we were off, skipping onto the field to the music, me leading the charge.

We picked up a piece of ribbon off the ground—pink, purple, yellow, white, blue, mine bright red—and began to circle left, then back again. The fourth-graders stopped. The boys began to skip around us, exchanging places, the ribbon intertwining, making an intricate mess. And then the girls skipped around the boys, and the ribbons were even, parallel again.

In the distance, I heard the glockenspiel chime over the music.

For some reason, my mind wandered. I thought of the children being led out of town. I saw my grandmother and remembered what she told me about the history of the fable. I saw my mom. My teacher's words rang in my head.

History.

What if I mess up history?

Suddenly, I turned left instead of right, and I ran directly into Shep. We connected so hard, in fact, that his momentum knocked me to the ground and knocked my crown of flowers off my head.

The crowd gasped.

The music stopped.

Tears rose.

Shep looked at me—right in the eyes, daring me to be strong—and winked. He put his hand over his mouth and pretended to laugh, pointing at himself as if it were his mistake. Then he picked up my crown, flicked it high into the air and caught it behind his back. The crowd gasped and applauded.

Shep placed my crown back atop my head, extended his hand, lifted me off the ground, twirled me round and round—my red ribbon encircling my waist like a beautiful sash—and then he spun me the other way until we were back to normal.

The music began again, and we wrapped the Maypole perfectly.

When it was over, everyone came running up to me.

"What happened?"

Sofie, Mrs. Kline and my family all asked the same question at the same time.

My heart was in my throat.

"We've been planning that all year," Shep said. "We wanted to surprise everyone, make this year's May Day the one everyone remembered. Right, Henri?"

I could only look at him, wide-eyed, nodding my head.

"Sorry we didn't say anything, Mrs. Kline," Shep said.

"It was amazing," she said. "The way you caught her crown and then turned the ribbon into a sash, just breathtaking."

"Well done," my grandpa said to us. He turned to Mrs. Kline and said with a wink and a nudge, "Looks like we'll see you next year at Frankenmuth."

After all the pictures had been taken, and the field had cleared, I walked up to Shep.

"Thank you."

"Nobody can dance alone," Shep said.

My heart melted.

What fourth-grade boy said stuff like this?

The next morning was a Saturday, and my parents woke me up and handed me a small wrapped package.

"What is this?" I asked. "Thank you."

"It's not from us," my dad said. "We found it on the front porch."

Inside was a key chain in the shape of a boy and girl in Bavarian costume dancing on May Day. Next to it was something, well, gross.

I handed my dad a wet napkin, my face contorted in disgust.

"What is it?" I asked.

"It looks like a sapling," he said. "Read the note."

Every day should be as magical as May Day. You can't dance alone. Plant this cherry tree so it will stand forever as a symbol of spring… & Christmas!
Shep

"It's not a tree covered in streamers," my mom said, "but I think this might be the sweetest, most romantic gesture I've ever seen in my life."

When my parents left, I stood on my bed and jumped up and down.

And then I got dressed, hopped on my bike and raced all the way to my best friend's house to show her the note and key chain.

"Henri!"

I jump out of my skin and return to the present.

Gert is waving wildly at me from across the room, trying to get my attention.

"We're backed up over here!" Gert yells. "The boy break is over!"

"I'm sorry," I say. "I have to go. It was great to see you again, Shep."

"You, too, Henri. It's been way too long."

We stand there awkwardly for a second, my hands stiff by my sides. Shep leans in and gives me a hug.

"How long are you here?" he asks.

I shrug. "Through the holidays for sure."

"Wow," he says. "That's a record for you, isn't it?"

I nod.

"Maybe I'll see you around town," I say.

I sound like an idiot.

"I hope so," Shep says. "Maybe you can stop by the shop sometime. I'd love to show you how we've grown and expanded over the years. I think even the mighty Henri Wegner would be impressed."

"Mighty?" I say.

"Just say thank you."

"Thank you," I say. "And I promise to stop by. I'd love to see what you've done."

"It's a date," Shep says.

My heart flip-flops.

Date?

Date!

My face flushes.

"And I'm not dating anyone, by the way," he says. "I've been taking time to focus on myself, my kids and my business. But the timing is feeling right to date again."

What?

What!

He could read my face.

"G-good to know," I stammer.

Shep accompanies me back to the painters' table. Gert shows him his ornament.

"Perfect!" Shep says. "Thank you! She's going to love it!"

Gert touches it to make sure it's dry and then packs it up for him.

Have we been talking that long? I think, checking my cell. *We have. Time does indeed fly.*

"Thank you, Gert," Shep says. "Henri, see you soon. Bye."

"Bye!"

As soon as Shep walks away, I grab my cell and call Sofie. My words come out in a rush.

"I just ran into Shep at the store. Of course, I looked like I had been attacked by raccoons who did my makeup. My head is still spinning. It felt weird and yet like old times. Am I crazy?"

"What? Really?" she says. "You've always been crazy. Wait… What are you doing at the store?"

"Helping my family. Did you know Wegner's is still using *DOS*? I feel like time has stopped, like we're still working at Glamour Shots."

"Ha!"

"That's led to fighting. Which led me to be being banished to personalized ornaments by Finn."

"You?" Sofie laughs. "The girl who can't even draw stick figures? The girl who made gingerbread houses that looked like haunted houses?"

"I get it," I say.

"Is Gert still there?"

I reach out my phone. "Say hi, Gert."

"Hi, Gert," she says.

"She hasn't changed, has she?" Sofie laughs. "She won't take any guff."

"Tell me about it," I mumble into the phone. "Listen, Shep told me the timing was right for him to date again. What does that mean?"

Suddenly, I hear Sofie yell, "Can I get your attention, please! My BFF has boy troubles, and I need to leave early tonight."

Sofie continues, "Can you meet me at nine thirty at Prost tonight?"

"That's leaving early?" I ask.

"In the restaurant biz, yes," she says. "In this town, yes."

"I'll be there."

"Be there. Or be square," Sofie says, saying the same thing we used to say when we were kids. "Never forgotten, forever alive, we're the Class of '85!"

I hang up.

In the distance, I see Shep wander by. He turns and lifts a hand. I wave.

Gert clears her throat. She does it in a not-so-subtle way that makes it sound as if a cement mixer is churning chain saws.

"We have a Ben and an Ann waiting here," Gert says. "Do you think you can handle that? Or do you want to talk to boys all day long?"

"No, ma'am," I say, nervous. "I mean, yes, ma'am, I think I can handle those names."

I set an ornament onto an egg cup and grab a brush. I dip it in silver paint.

Gert leans over to me and whispers, "By the way, I should've painted Shep in the nude when I had the chance."

I drop my brush. It rolls off the table and onto my lap, making it look as if I just wrestled a disco ball to the floor.

"You had the chance to paint Shep in the nude?" I say in a stage whisper, grabbing a rag to wipe my pants.

"Goodness no," Gert says. "I just wanted to get a reaction out of you." She looks at me. "I remember you two from high school. So in love."

I suddenly feel as if my grandma is beside me offering me wisdom and unfiltered honesty.

I concentrate on the ornament before me and paint a perfect *B* on the ornament.

Gert leans over.

"You do know what Henrietta means in German, don't you?"

"I should," I say, "but I don't."

"It means 'ruler of the house.'"

I turn to look at Gert.

"I'm not fooling you," she says. "And do you know what Gert means?"

I shake my head.

"'Strong as spear,'" she continues. "We're both very much alike, Henri, both very connected to the meanings of our names, our careers, our heritage. But sometimes that can be a bad thing."

"Why is that?" I ask, painting a perfect *E* and *N*.

"Because you don't get too many chances to paint a life with a perfect partner," she says. "I never got one. I've had a great life, don't get me wrong, but I still wonder sometimes."

Gert picks up her brush and gets back to work.

"You wonder what?" I ask, finishing the *A* and two *N*s on the next ornament.

She stops painting and looks at me.

"What a fully finished canvas might actually look like," she says. "What it would have felt like to have my spear hit the right target."

16

"Prost!"

"Prost!"

A group of semi-drunken holiday revelers seated behind us—all wearing Christmas sweaters—joins me and Sofie in our cheers to one another.

"Prost!" they yell.

The little restaurant at the end of downtown is packed. Many visitors who have spent the day shopping at Wegner's and filling their bellies with chicken and noodles at Z's or Clausen's Chicken Haus end up here for a nightcap.

Prost is a wine bar and charcuterie restaurant offering up some very fine pours and delicious dishes—dips, salads, regional charcuterie platters—most sourced locally. It's a hidden gem for many locals, who want a city-feeling dinner and nice glass of wine as well as a hideaway from tourists after catering to their whims all day long.

Sofie and I are situated in the back corner of the restaurant, near the bar, against the large windows that face the outdoor patio that is jammed in warmer weather. The young waiter approaches. He's all hipster bangs and '50s glasses, dressed all in black.

"We'll have the German Heritage Charcuterie Board," Sofie says.

I laugh out loud. "I thought you'd do *anything* but German."

"When in Rome..." She shrugs.

"But we're not in Rome," the waiter says.

Sofie and I look at each other, trying to keep a straight face. She sighs.

"What is it with young people and irony?" I ask, thinking of Bea.

"I bet you don't even like *Seinfeld*," Sofie says to the waiter. "Do you?"

He shakes his head.

"It's mean funny."

"Life *is* mean funny," Sofie says.

"Right?" I agree. "Just look at me. I'm a fifty-plus-year-old single woman who's returned home for Christmas with her family. I woke up at dawn, put my makeup on in the dark in my father's pickup on a road filled with potholes, and saw my ex before I even had a chance to sneak off and fix my face and then spent the day personalizing holiday ornaments while getting 'read' by a feisty ninety-year-old woman."

"See? You can't make this stuff up," Sofie says to the waiter.

"So," he asks, "you're not the feisty old woman in this story?"

I nearly do a spit take with my Michigan dry Riesling.

Sofie stands and high-fives him. "You just mastered sarcastic irony! You are officially a child of the '80s! Congratulations! A-plus!"

He bends at the waist as if he's bowing to the king. "Thank you," he says. "But I was being mean."

"No, you were being honest," Sofie says with a laugh.

"No," I say, staring down my BFF, "you were being *ironic.*

I believe if you can't laugh at yourself, it's going to be a long, hard life."

"When in Rome," the waiter says. "I'll put your order in."

"And another glass of Riesling, please," Sofie says. "We're going to need it to wash down all our irony."

"Yes, ma'am."

"And don't call us ma'am," Sofie adds as he walks away. "That's mean-funny."

The waiter laughs and gives us a big thumbs-up.

"Speaking of mean-funny," Sofie continues, "I have something I want to show you before you tell me all about your meet-cute with Shep."

"It was more like a meet-not-cute."

"Even better," she says. "This is more of a *not*-cute, too."

Sofie grabs her tote bag and pulls out a photo album.

I stare at her.

"DOS and now a photo album," I say. "Ah, it's good to be home."

Sofie throws open the cover with a flourish, and I immediately bust out laughing.

"I totally forgot you had this!" I continue.

"Remember now? We absconded these photos from our days at Glamour Shots," Sofie says. "We'd sneak out the best of the worst photos people didn't buy. Isn't it a time capsule?"

More like a time machine. Sofie and I once worked side by side at Glamour Shots. We both needed one summer away from our family businesses, a touch of independence, and we found it at the mall. We spent our days setting up tackily surreal backgrounds for the photographer, styling customers—and I use the term *styling* very loosely—and wrangling pets that customers brought into the store to be photographed alongside.

"No!" I yelp in horror.

The first photo is of a young woman whose hair is teased and sprayed so big it extends outside of the picture frame. She is wearing a teal dress, a thick gold headband and a matching gold glove that holds up her chin just so.

Then there is the family of four wearing matching Hulk Hogan T-shirts and faux Hogan horseshoe moustaches.

"Oh, there's more!" Sofie says.

The next page is a photo of a young couple holding a cat. The husband is dressed as Luke Skywalker, the wife as Princess Leia and the kitty as Chewbacca. In the background, the photographer has placed images of the family of three floating in outer space, looking as if they are about to enter a battle with Darth Vader.

Opposite them is a boy in a Karate Kid outfit doing battle with a replicated image of himself, and a young woman in a cowboy hat blowing smoke off what looks like the end of a real rifle.

And it keeps going and going and going.

"I can't," I gasp. "I'm dying."

I can feel tears run down my face as I am greeted by a woman with mammoth octagonal glasses wearing an Elizabethan collar to match the cone her pug is sporting, and then a photo of four teenage boys dressed as the members of KISS.

"Wanna know what's worse than all of this?" Sofie asks. "The prom pictures."

I am laughing so hard, I'm crying and can barely catch my breath.

"You think that's funny?" Sofie asks.

She turns the page.

I roar.

There is a picture of the two of us, thinking we looked totally rad. Our hair is permed and teased, our blue eye shadow extends to our temples, and we are attempting to pose like supermodels. The background behind us is split in two. Behind Sofie is downtown Frankenmuth. Behind me are skyscrapers.

I stop laughing.

"Your German Heritage Charcuterie Board," the waiter says, "and your Riesling."

Sofie scooches the photo album to the edge of the table.

"Featured on your board is Black Forest Schinken, Kern's Pistachio Jagdwurst, Summer Sausage, Willi's Liver Pâté, Butterkäse cheese, House-made Caraway Seed & Beer Mustard, Sauerkraut, and Bread & Butter Pickles."

The waiter glances at the open album.

"Is that you?" he asks, his voice rising.

"In the flesh," Sofie says.

"Wow, you do need to be able to laugh at yourself in life."

Sofie turns to the page of the boy dressed as the Karate Kid.

"Yes, sensei," she says. "Now you understand sarcasm. Wax on, wax off."

The waiter looks at her.

"Google it," she says with a wink.

"Enjoy," he says.

"You've grown awfully quiet," Sofie says, taking a bite of cheese and sip of wine. "What's up?"

I want to tell my best friend everything. I never keep anything from her. It's literally killing me. I need her advice, support, brutal honesty.

And yet I don't want to tell her anything. Because what if it's too much? What if she hates me for what I'm doing?

Instead, I decide to take a baby step. I reach for the photo album and return it to the picture of us. I tap my finger on our picture.

"Did I always want to leave Frankenmuth?"

"Ah, the prodigal daughter returns home filled with guilt."

"I'm serious."

"So am I."

Sofie looks at the photo of us and then at me.

"Complete honesty?" she asks.

"Is there another option with you?"

"True that," she says. "I think you always felt torn. I think you loved Frankenmuth—I think you still do—but so much of your childhood was defined by your father's dream. I remember the days when your family was struggling. I think that left an impact. And then, over the years, your dad came to personify this town, and I think you secretly wondered if people liked you for you or because of your dad. I felt the same. I think that's why we became friends."

Sofie takes a sip of her wine and continues.

"I also think you saw yourself in me and Shep and freaked out when you'd return home after being away at college. You saw there was a bigger world out there, and I don't think you could see yourself forever wearing a dirndl like me or wearing an elf costume when you're fifty. You didn't do anything wrong by living your own life, Henri. But maybe it's not the life you want anymore."

I stare at her, shocked at her insightfulness.

"I can read between the lines," she continues. "I know you've not been happy lately. And that's okay to admit, too. Doesn't make you a failure. Just means you're a different person now."

"The last few years have been hard." I search for the right words. "I feel like I'm at a crossroads in my life and career. And there's a train barreling toward me. And I might be tied to the tracks."

Sofie raises an eyebrow.

"Sounds like an old movie," Sofie says. "Who's the villain with the creepy moustache?"

It's me! I want to scream.

Sofie laughs and continues.

"Let me share my old movie with you. I took over my family's business, and as soon as I did, everyone in town began to say that Z's was headed for failure." Sofie rolls her eyes. "I changed a lot of things—I added new events, new menu items, healthier options, I updated our marketing, I brought in tour buses. Any time you try to change a beloved tradition, people question you or hate you for doing it. But they're not running the business, seeing the numbers, understanding things must evolve to keep that tradition alive. Sometimes, it takes fresh eyes and a new perspective to see that. You know the old adage about the three-generation rule for family businesses? Shirtsleeves to shirtsleeves in three generations?"

"I know it," I reply. "The belief that the third generation can't manage the business and wealth they inherit, so the family company ultimately fails, and the family's fortune and legacy fades with its failure."

"But you're the second generation, Henri. You have the knowledge, drive and passion to keep your family's business going for generations," Sofie says. "I'm sure Wegner's is facing challenges, just like every other business today. I mean, we barely survived Covid. I'm thankful the town rallied behind us and ordered takeout for months on end."

"Wegner's online business could certainly be strengthened," I say, thinking of what I've recently discovered. "Not to mention ditching DOS. And so many other things." I sigh. "Not to mention my dad still does all of the hiring. Or that I just found out our annual electrical bill is nearly half a mil."

"You're not in competition with your dad," Sofie says. "Only with yourself."

"And Amazon," I add.

"Always," she says with a shake of her head.

"I can't help but feel like I am in competition, though," I say. "With my dad and my brother. I mean, they both got furious at me today."

"Change is hard. Take a breath. Tread gingerly. I didn't turn my chicken ship on a dime my first year in the water or I would have hit an iceberg and had a *Titanic* on my hands. Steer slowly."

"That's quite an analogy," I say.

"I didn't want to use another chicken metaphor," Sofie says. "Leg up. Wingman. Tough skin. See what I mean?"

I smile. "Thank you," I say. "For everything."

I squeeze her hand.

"This is a strange little town to grow up in," she says, shaking her head. "Especially for us. It was a hard decision for you to leave. It was a hard decision for me to stay. Home is filled with lots of memories, good, bad, raw, beautiful. Some folks leave home for the right reasons, some for the wrong ones. Some stay where they were born because they love it, others because they're too scared of what the unknown holds. Time can either enlighten and embolden us, or hold us prisoner. We're both at an important stage in our lives. Our parents are aging. My kids are having families of their own. We have to make big decisions about our careers, retirement, family businesses, who takes over. Will a family member take over, or do we sell?"

Sofie's word hit too close to home.

I can't keep lying to my friend. I open my mouth to tell her everything, but a group in the restaurant suddenly whoops out loud, and the moment is gone.

"I just don't know what to do," I say.

"I don't either most of the time. I do know I plan to work for a long time because I still love what I do—it's a part of my soul—but I have to make plans, too. I want to travel some. I want a day off. What do you want?"

I consider my job, my reasons for coming here, the urge to do what is right for me versus what is right for my family.

Sofie taps the photo album with her finger.

"Time passes so quickly," she continues. "This seems like it was just yesterday, doesn't it? I want a photo of us together as old women with blue hair and cataract glasses drinking wine on a beach to go next to this one of us as kids."

I laugh. "Thank you being my number one, my ride or die, the chicken to my noodles."

"Always."

As Sofie hugs me, I have a revelation.

It's humbling and bit terrifying to realize, when you really stop to think about it, that when you reach the age of fifty there are only, perhaps, five people in the universe who truly "get" you. And the sad part? They all now probably live in a different city than you.

Did I leave Frankenmuth for the right reasons or the wrong ones?

Have I returned home for the right reasons or the wrong ones?

So many questions unanswered.

"Can I ask you a question?" she asks.

I nod at Sofie.

"Why are you really here?" she pushes. "It's so anti-Henri. I mean, I wasn't even wearing control top pantyhose the last time you were home."

It's time for the truth.

I take a sip of wine to gird myself, open my mouth and begin to reveal the secret reason I've returned home when I hear, "Wow, twice in one day."

I look up. Shep is standing at our table.

"My lucky day," he says.

Sofie kicks me under the table.

"We were just talking about you," Sofie says with a wink.

"We were not!" I insist.

"Just kidding. We were just reminiscing," Sofie says. She opens the scrapbook and turns it toward Shep.

He laughs. "I fell in love with that?"

My eyes widen. Sofie's jump out of her head. My look to her says, *I told you.*

"We all make mistakes," Sofie says to cover. "What are you doing out on a school night, Shep?"

"Having a holiday drink with Mouse. He said he already saw you, Henri."

I look over and wave at Mouse at the bar, blowing him a kiss. "Yes, when I got to town yesterday."

"How are you doing, Sofie?" Shep asks.

"Not a spring chicken anymore," she says. "See? Did it again. Another poultry pun."

Shep chuckles.

"Speaking of chicken," Sofie continues, "how's Hannah? I saw her the other day, and she seemed so fragile. I hope she's okay."

Shep nods. "The holidays can dredge up a lot of memories," he says. "I know they do for Hannah. It's been a hard few years, but I think we've all changed." Shep stops before adding, "For the better." He glances at the scrapbook. "But she's doing much better. Thank you for asking and for reaching out to her. She needs that."

"Maybe we can all get together this Christmas. Celebrate old times."

"I'd like that," Shep says. "We all used to be so close."

Mouse waves at Shep and points at a small table that's come free.

"I better go," he says. "Stop by and see me at the shop anytime, Henri. I told you, I'd love to show you how we've expanded."

"I will," I say. "I promise. See you soon."

Shep begins to turn, but he stops on a dime. His eyes focus on the table. I follow his gaze.

My key chain is sitting on the table.

"You kept it," he says. "All these years."

I run my fingers over the faded images.

"Yeah, you know, just a bit of nostalgia for my parents' house keys," I say awkwardly, trying to dismiss his comment.

The tiniest of smiles filters across his face, and it brightens, as if sunlight has emerged from the clouds.

He turns and heads back to his table.

"What in the hell was that!" Sofie says as soon as he's across the restaurant.

"I told you."

"This was totally meant to be!" she says. "You can't tell me all of this is pure happenstance. You were *meant* to come home. You were *meant* to cross that wooden bridge again."

"Stop it," I say. "Too much water under that bridge."

"Puh-lease," Sofie says. "He's hot as ever. Still looks like Rob Lowe. My husband turned into Dumbledore."

I laugh.

"Hank's a good man," I say.

"Yes, he is," Sofie says. "And so is Shep."

I glance down at the scrapbook, looking at us as girls, remembering what Finn said about the silly fights we used to have with Hannah.

Over what?

I don't even remember.

I do remember whenever we'd see her at school, Sofie and I would start blurting out as many palindromes as we could—*radar, mom, noon, civic, taco cat*, even *Yo, banana boy!*—just to annoy the Pukey Palindrome.

But I didn't even really know Hannah that well. Just an image of her.

Perhaps she finally saw herself clearly.

Have I?

Maybe I've seen everything backward my whole life.

Sofie motions for two more wines.

"What are you doing?" I ask. "I'm going to be blitzed."

"My night out. My rules. We're going to get a little drunk and sing '80s songs."

She clears her throat.

"Come on, Eileen," Sofie sings.

And that's all it takes to get an entire bar singing and for me to forget about my troubles for another night.

17

"Hello, old friend."

I am standing in the parking lot of the Bavarian Inn staring up at the glockenspiel.

The town is silent, save for the soft whisper of the snow as it gently falls.

Even at night, even quiet, there is a majesty to the old Bavarian clock tower.

After our third glass of wine, Sofie and I decided it was best not to drive home. She texted her husband, Hank, to pick her up, and I texted my father to pick me up after realizing there were no Ubers available in Frankenmuth in the winter late at night.

"It's good to see you, Henri," Hank said when he arrived. "Didn't take you two long to pick up where you left off."

I laughed. "She's the chicken to my noodles," I said, using our favorite analogy.

"Hey, I want to be the noodles for once," Sofie said, her head out the window.

"We can drive you home," Hank said.

"No, it's late, and you live on the other side of town. My dad is still at work. He's on his way."

"That man is like Santa," Hank said. "A true saint. And he never sleeps during Christmas."

"For some reason, I still feel like I'm twelve years old," I said.

"In dog years," Sofie laughed. "Hey, Hank! Guess who we saw tonight? Shep!"

Sofie said his name—*Shep!*—like schoolgirls do when a crush passes by in the hallway.

"Ah, the old flame. Bound to happen. It's a small town," Hank said. "Guess who I saw tonight? The Domino's guy."

I laughed.

"You're a good guy, Hank," I said.

"I'm a lucky gal," Sofie said, leaning over to kiss Hank full on the lips. "He's the headmaster of my Hogwarts."

"I'm guessing this has to do with my beard," Hank said. "I grew it during Covid. Either this or an air fryer. Now I can't get rid of it. I think it makes me look Michigan manly."

"It makes you look like a wizard," Sofie said. "But I love you anyway."

The two took off, and I stood in the snow, waving goodbye.

Sofie stuck her head out the window as the car drove away, and yelled, "Wham! How could we forgot to sing Wham!"

And then as if pulled by a magnet, I began to wander downtown, past Shep's Woolen Mill—where I stood staring into the windows at bins of wool comforters and pillows like a crazy woman—and directly to the glockenspiel.

"You are an old beauty," I whisper. "A history in this town as old as mine."

I know every fact—like I know every bell—by heart.

The glockenspiel was imported in 1967, and the construction of its bell tower was like completing a work of art. The carillon uses a special double keyboard, which gives the sound of seventy bells.

Just above the stunning large clock face with gold-covered numerals and hands of copper with leaf-gold covering is a stage.

Every few hours, the glockenspiel plays several selections, followed by the chiming of the hour.

And then, two doors—depicting the curtain of the stage—open, and moveable, colorful lifelike figurines—fifteen total, four and a half feet tall—come to life to depict the legend of the Pied Piper of Hamelin based on the famous narrative poem by Robert Browning.

I stare up at the stage, remembering the first time my entire family—parents, grandparents and me—came to see it. I was just a little girl, and my family thought I would be mesmerized by the fable and figurines. Instead, I cried, scared by what I'd witnessed.

"Was that true?" I remember asking my grandmother.

"It's just a fable," she said. "A part of our history. It's not meant to frighten you. It's meant as a folk tale, a reminder of important lessons."

December 2013

"I knew I'd find you here. I'm so sorry, Henri."

Without a word, I collapsed into Shep's arms and wept.

"I know how much she meant to you," he whispered. "She meant a lot to me, too."

I'd seen Shep at my grandmother's funeral, seated at the back of the church and then standing beyond the tent at the graveside service.

"I can't imagine life without her," I said. "I can't imagine Christmas without her."

"I know," he said softly.

"Seems fitting she would pass right before Christmas," I said. "It's as if she wanted to go before the holiday so we'd all have a chance to be together in order to heal. I can't believe I couldn't make it home in time to say goodbye."

I began to cry anew, and Shep held me until my tears subsided.

"This is where you two always came to talk, wasn't it?" he asked.

I nodded.

"Ever since I could remember," I said. "She loved a story with a lesson."

I lifted my head and looked at Shep.

"Tell me a good story," I asked.

"Okay," he started. "There was once a fair maiden of Frankenmuth who was known as the Christmas princess."

"Stop," I said, with a small smile.

"All true," he said.

"Thank you for coming to the service," I said. "I know it's a little bit awkward with how things ended between us, my past with Hannah..."

"Hannah and I are separated," he said. "We need some space. I don't know what's going to happen, but—" Shep looked into the winter sky "—I'm tired of being sad."

I hugged him as the glockenspiel chimed.

"Our timing has always been off, hasn't it?" he asked. "We fell in love so young. I was too quick at the draw. I wanted a family, I wanted to stay here forever... I never considered what you wanted or needed."

I held him at arm's length.

"You didn't do anything wrong," I said. "You didn't do anything wrong by asking me to marry you."

"And you didn't do anything wrong by saying no."

The cold wind whipped across our faces.

Why did it still sting so much then?

"Your grandmother was an amazing woman," he said. "Believed in your parents, believed in you and your brother, believed in the goodness of the world. You know, I felt like I lost part of my family, too, when we broke up. I grew up with your family. You grew up with mine. Sometimes, I drive by your parents' house and your grandparents' house and just remember what it was like when everything was okay."

His words strike a chord in my heart.

"Growing up sucks, doesn't it?" I asked.

"I think I stopped growing at some point," Shep said. "I admire you, Henri. You've seen so much."

"I have," I said. "And I've missed so much, too."

The bell chimes.

"Time," Shep said. "There's never enough."

He hugged me again.

"You take care of yourself, and if you ever need to talk, I'm just a phone call away," he said. "Bye, Henri."

I watched Shep trudge through the snow, just as he did so long ago on the bridge.

And then he was gone.

Again.

The glockenspiel chimes.

I jump.

I glance at my cell.

It's midnight.

The five-bell Westminster chimes to sound the hour.

I stare at the glockenspiel.

The stage comes to life, the figurines moving as the snow dances around my face.

The doors open, and a man's voice echoes through downtown, the figurines appearing to tell the story of the Pied Piper, who came to the beautiful German town of Hamelin to drive out the plague of rats by playing a magical melody with a silver flute. But when he succeeded and the town refused to pay him, he returned for payback: he led all the children out of town with his flute, and they vanished through a rock into the mountain. Only two children could not keep up the pace and were left behind. They related the tale to the parents who made a long search to no avail. Their children had disappeared from the city, forever, never to be seen again.

The doors shut, and the stage goes quiet.

My heart is beating so quickly that it sounds like the echoes of the chimes.

I can hear my grandmother's voice as clearly as I could hear the story just now.

"Oh, Henri, this tale is not meant to be scary. It's simply a fairy tale, a story that's been passed along over time."

"Why?"

"Well, a Pied Piper is a person who attracts a following through charisma or false promises," she told me. "He entices people to follow him, on the premise of good fortune but actually leads them to their doom. When you 'pay the piper,' it means you must face the consequences of your decisions, especially when you lie to good people."

"But that's scary," I said.

"I know it seems that way, but it's not. This is really a lesson for grown-ups, sweetheart. It's meant to remind us to be honest and good, and to do the right thing," she said. "We shouldn't lie, especially to those we love. Keeping a promise is a very big thing. Children learn from their elders. We are the role models. I hope this silly little fable instills in you not to be scared but that our town—any town, big or small—can instill in you wonderful values and beautiful memories that will last forever, so even if you're not here, they will live within you and remind you to always do the right thing."

I remember my grandma taking me into her arms.

"It all seems like such an easy thing, doesn't it?" she continued. "But it gets harder the older we get."

Tears well in my eyes.

My phone trills.

I think it's my dad running late, but it's not. It's a text from Benjie.

Been working all day on this, but great news: Vance is a GO! Your intel and reports allowed them to peek behind the curtain. They are one hundred percent convinced this is the right moment and right deal. They want this on a fast track, completed by Christmas so they can announce and take advantage of the good PR. I've attached their offer. Your parents will be taken well care of. Get your dad to sign. If not, I'll turn up like an unwanted uncle on Christmas Eve. Merry Christmas!

Pay the piper.

A car honks.

I turn.

My father is waving.

I move toward the car but stop at the last minute and look back at the glockenspiel. I stare at the stage.

I am the rat who's returned to town.

18

"I'm sorry I got mad earlier today," my father says.

His voice is hoarse. He reaches for a bottle of water. It's empty.

My father reaches for a tiny candy cane, opens it and pops it in his mouth.

His pickup, like every coat pocket, is filled with candy canes. The glove box, the drink holders, the floorboards, blazers, winter coats are littered with the red, curly Christmas candy.

When I was a kid and Wegner's was taking off, I remember my dad stalking the store one holiday season. He would go department to department, hiding behind trees, and watch the mothers and grandmothers shop, plucking ornaments from trees, studying them, talking about which would be perfect on their trees or as gifts for family members or friends. Most would shop for hours.

The husbands would trudge behind, complaining, bored out of their minds. After a while, kids would begin to get distracted after the thrill of the lights began to fade. Older ones would gripe; little tykes would cry.

The next week, my father had a big TV delivered to Wegner's main entrance—in a spot across the room from Santa's throne—and turned the channel to a sports station. That never changed: football in the fall, basketball and hockey in the winter, baseball in the spring and summer. It immediately became known as the Christmas Cave and became so popular among the "shopping single" husbands that my father had to add an entire section of couches and recliners. Husbands actually *wanted* to accompany their wives to Wegner's, and business doubled.

Moreover, my father—stealing a holiday decorating idea right from my grandmother—began to cover the trees with tiny candy canes to appease the children. As shoppers pushed carts from tree to tree, kids could pull a candy cane right off a branch and be entertained with something sweet for half an hour.

I think of my grandmother, Shep, my father, Benjie, parents and children, rats and doing the right thing. Somewhere in between all of those things lies the story of growing up, the story of me…the story of all of us.

I begin to cry.

"Hey," my dad says, slowing the car. "Are you okay?"

I wipe my face with the arm of my coat.

"I was thinking of Grandma while I was waiting," I say. A lie that isn't a lie. "Just a little emotional." I look at my father. "And a little drunk."

"I know there's a lot of emotions this time of year," he says. "You've been through a lot at Christmastime."

"Thanks, Dad," I say. "So have you. And it's okay about this morning. I know I'm a lot sometimes."

"You're not," he says. "You're just trying to help."

I can feel the tears come again, and I squeeze my eyes shut to stop them.

I watch my father's profile as he drives in the dark. His face is gray in the dim light.

How many hours has he worked? How many nights has he worried? How many people has he employed? How many dreams has he made come true?

My head grows dizzy, not from the buzz of the wine but from a revelation.

I learned everything about business from my father.

Perhaps I was born and raised to be an entrepreneur, a visionary, but was lured by the Pied Piper of…

Money?

Independence?

Broken hearts?

All of the above?

"I have something to show you."

I realize we are in the parking lot of Wegner's. 25 Christmas Lane twinkles in the dark.

"What are we doing here, Dad? Did you forget something?"

He turns off the car and picks up his key fob. He holds it toward the lights and clicks.

Wegner's goes dark.

"It's called a 'treemote,'" my dad says with a husky chuckle. "Wish I would have thought of that. It's a remote for all the lights."

"How did you do this? When did you do this?"

"Today," he says. "Had J.J.—my longtime electrician—come out. He did it in a day. Cost us a chunk of change, but will save us a mountain of money."

I stare at him.

"I listened to you, Henri," he says. "I yelled at you because I didn't want to yell at myself."

My dad doesn't just look at me; he implores me with his eyes.

"I need your help, Henri."

His face is illuminated from the soft light coming from a lamppost.

And that's when I see it.

A lone tear trailing down my father's cheeks.

Oh, to see your father cry!

To witness fragility from the man who has embodied strength

your entire life, the man who has kept you protected and safe, the man who has risked everything for you to have a better life, who has allowed you to make your own decisions without an ounce of judgment.

I know that this single, solitary tear represents a flood of emotion to this man, a thunderstorm that has likely been building his whole life, and to witness it firsthand is like having my heart cleaved in half.

In an instant, I see a Rolodex of memories in his eyes, the age on his face, the fact that the lights are slowly dimming.

"I want to help you, Dad," I say. "I'm here to help you."

There is one more tear—this from the other eye.

He clears his throat and tightens his jaw.

I am shattered.

Once again, I dissolve into a heaping wreck of tears. My father opens his arms and holds me, rocks me, until I stop.

"You okay?" he asks.

I wipe my face and nod.

"It's been a tough few years," he admits after a moment of silence. "Costs have increased. Inflation is crushing small businesses like ours. We can't hire enough employees. We can't retain the ones we have. No one wants to work retail. Amazon undercuts us at every turn. We're still making great money, but we're losing more than ever. How can we continue to grow our business and invest in our people without hemorrhaging cash and changing the philosophy that made us who we are?"

My father says this in one big breath of air.

"I have a lot of ideas, Dad."

"Mind starting again with me tomorrow? I promise I won't yell at you again," he says.

I smile.

"Especially with the hangover you're going to have."

"Ha-ha, Dad."

"Do you remember how tall that Santa Claus is?" my father asks, nodding at the signature Santa that stands as sentinel outside Wegner's.

"Seventeen feet," I say.

"You remember everything, Henri. Amazing."

Do I?

"I'll never forget when John Wayne called the store two weeks before Christmas to order a Santa suit," my father says.

This is one of his favorite stories.

"I picked up the phone, and he said, 'This is John Wayne,'" my dad says, imitating the actor's drawl. "I thought I was being pranked by schoolkids. So I said…"

"'And this is Santa Claus,'" I finish.

My father laughs.

"See, you do remember everything about our history," he says. "And the Duke says, 'That's actually why I'm calling. I need to buy a Santa suit.' And we got one to him before Christmas. He sent a thank-you note a few weeks later that read, 'Thank you, Pilgrim, for saving Christmas. The Duke.'"

My dad continues, "One of my favorite quotes of his is 'Life is getting up one more time than you've been knocked down.' I refuse to stay down, Henri. I want Wegner's to continue forever. It's my legacy to my family, this town, the spirit of Christmas." He stops. "But mostly to myself."

Do not cry again, Henri.

I take a deep breath.

"I promise to do what I can, Dad."

"Courage is being scared to death and saddling up anyway."

"Your quote?" I ask. "Or John Wayne?"

"His," my dad says. "And ours."

He starts the car.

I am in a battle. I feel like I'm in the Wild West. I have ridden into town, but I still don't know if I'm here to save it or burn it down.

"Here," my dad says, as if reading my mind. "This will make you feel better."

I look over.

My father is holding out a candy cane.

19

December 17

"There's something magical about having a job where you decorate Christmas trees for a living, don't you think?"

Barb Weinhardt has been working at Wegner's since I was a girl. Her kids were a few years older than me and Finn. She rose from customer service through the ranks to become manager of the ornaments department.

"Three hundred and fifty-three trees to be exact," Barb continues with a laugh.

After I downed four glasses of water, three aspirin and two cups of coffee—as much to deal from my hangover from Benjie's text as well as my real hangover—my dad suggested I start my day with Barb, who oversees about a quarter of the nearly thousand seasonal and full-time employees. Though there are a hundred other things I should be doing instead—coming clean, having my dad sign Vance's offer, running for the hills—I find myself standing in the middle of the Friends, Family & Home ornaments department.

Perhaps I can use this as a way to gather more information.

Although whether it's for my father or for Benjie is yet to be determined.

"Is it okay if I ask you a few questions about operations?" I ask, treading gingerly. I know—from my vast experience—how employees feel when a "big-city stranger" descends into their world asking questions and offering suggestions. That leads to changes. Downsizing. Cuts. Reorganization.

That leads to a place either they no longer know, or a place that will no longer exist.

But Barb could be a great guide to what's good and not so good.

Barb offers a loud, husky laugh. People love Barb for her booming bravado.

"I know you're here to spy," she says. I wince inside. "The prodigal daughter returns home. Ask away. I'm always honest."

I ask Barb about staffing issues—how difficult is it to hire and retain new employees—as well as sales volume throughout the year, what she feels could be improved, what she feels should stay the same.

She acknowledges many of the same issues my mother and father have outlined.

"Many younger adults simply don't want to take a job like this," Barb says. "They either feel it's beneath them, or that it doesn't pay enough. And if they start here, they complain, or simply don't go the extra mile. Now, it's not universal, but it's certainly a pattern.

"Some simply don't want to put in the time like we both did," she continues. "They want instant gratification—a promotion or job increase immediately. They refuse to pay their dues and then say I'm not being a fair manager. That's a huge issue, because we're constantly in training mode. I feel like I'm a hamster running on the wheel. Rather than being able to move people up the ranks and promote them into jobs where they have a full grasp and focus on sales, I'm forever rehiring, retraining, over and over."

Barb twists hangers on ornaments that have turned backward so that their pretty sides are facing out on the tree's branches to entice customers.

"I certainly think we need to bury DOS along with perms," Barb says, a quick laugh booming from her body. "The time it takes to train people on an antiquated system they've never used and will never understand is a total waste of time. And it's costing the company money. I've begged your father to update that system for years."

"I used it at Glamour Shots," I say. "Am I dating myself?"

Barb laughs.

"Between us," I say, "I'm doing an overhaul of the entire computer system. New laptops, new software, everything. It should be implemented after the first of the year."

"Wow," Barb says. "That's amazing. I'm thrilled you could push your father to change. I've been trying for years."

I nod.

"Speaking of dating…?" Barb asks with a wink. "Are you?"

I do a double take at Barb. "Just myself."

"You're quick," Barb laughs. "I like that. My son is divorced. I could give him a call."

"Last thing I need to do right now is date a divorced man," I say quickly.

"Shep?" she asks. "You two were like Bogie and Bacall. Now am I dating myself?"

I chuckle.

"Long story," I say. "Looong story."

"I understand," she says with a wink. "Small town."

"People keep saying that," I say. "At least this feels like another world in here." I look around at the bustling holiday shoppers.

"It is," Barb says. "It's like the North Pole every day. We now have over two million visitors a year, including fifty thousand the weekend after Thanksgiving, and over twenty thousand children visit Santa here from Thanksgiving weekend through Christmas Eve."

I note this info on my cell, knowing it will impress Benjie and Vance, while keeping a carrot dangled in front of them in order to give me a little more time.

Barb continues. "Your father has built a magical world here that people want to be a part of. That's a rare thing in this day and age."

My heart drops as I finish sending the text.

Barb turns to a cart and opens a box. She holds out a glass blown ornament in the shape of an old-fashioned station wagon. The wagon is bright red, a green Christmas tree on top, a mother, father, young boy and a happy dog—tongue out—smiling, rosy cheeked, heads sticking out the window.

"Do you remember what it was like to feel like this?" she asks, rotating the ornament in her hands.

I have a flashback of going with my grandparents to cut down a Christmas tree at Fir the Love of Christmas Tree Farms. I'd race around with my grandparents, searching for just the right tree.

"The back has to be as pretty as the front!" my grandma would call.

Then we'd chop it down, and the tree farm would wrap it up and put it on top of the car while we sipped hot chocolate.

After we moved to the upside-down house, my brother would head out to our woods the first day of December. He would cut down a pine, drag it inside, set it in the tree stand and drench it in tinsel even before the lights and ornaments were on it.

"Now it's ready to decorate!" he'd yell at the top of his lungs when he was finished.

One year, Finn cut down a tree that was much too tall, the top bending at the ceiling.

"You can't cut the top!" my brother pleaded to my father. "It's perfect for the tree topper."

My dad managed to cut a good two feet from the trunk and prop it up so that no one would notice the stem was missing.

My father has always propped us up.

He's always made me feel as safe and secure as that tree.

"I do," I finally say. I touch the ornament and then Barb's arm. "Thank you for reminding me."

"That's all we want, Henri. People just want to feel safe, especially in these times. Marriages collapse, people get sick, we lose the ones we love, we fight over politics. All people want is to be able to feel happy and hopeful. We just want a bit of escape at Christmas. And if that's buying a Christmas ornament or snow-kissed Victorian village at Wegner's, or it's tucking into a good holiday movie or book, then what's the harm? If Santa can return every year and if the glockenspiel can chime on the hour, why shouldn't your father's legacy last forever, too?"

I need another aspirin.

"Do you mind if I ask you a question?" Barb continues.

"Go ahead."

"Do you think your father feels safe?" Barb asks. "How do you imagine he feels most days?"

"That's a good question, Barb. I guess I haven't thought about the business that way."

Barb grabs a silver hook from a tangle of ornament hangers and places the station wagon on the branch. A heat vent kicks on in the store, and the car looks as if it's actually moving, headed home to set up the family tree.

"Your father is like this ornament hook," Barb continues. "He's the conduit, the lifeline for all the fragile beauty around here. He keeps families fed and gainfully employed. He provides healthcare and retirement for countless people in this town. He keeps small businesses afloat, not only his own but hundreds of suppliers around the US and world."

My gut churns. I know it's not the hangover.

Barb cups the ornament with her hand. "Nearly half of the glass ornaments sold here are Wegner's own designs. They are handcrafted by global artisans just for us. Your father doesn't just talk the talk, he actually supports the dreams of others. What he started so many years ago in your grandparents' tiny basement continues to this day. Christmas isn't just a day to him, it's a way of life."

"I think I've gotten more used to seeing things from a large corporate point of view," I confess.

"You know what sticks in my craw?" Barb continues, on a roll. "We all complain about the cost of everything, and yet we refuse to buy a twenty-dollar electric mixer that's made in America over a ten-dollar one that's manufactured overseas and then we have the gall to complain about the fall of the American worker. Your father has never forgotten. Some of our items may cost a bit more because they are handmade here in the US, but that keeps countless dreams alive."

My stomach rolls over again. I think of what Vance will do with these ornaments once they take over. I know they will manufacture them overseas, as cheaply as possible, and every single one will be a cookie-cutter replica. Not works of art, but plastic trash.

Barb takes a breath.

"Do you really know what needs to change?" she asks me. "Your dad needs a little help. He's in his seventies. Your mom is, too. Finn is a hard worker, but he's not a visionary. Wegner's is no different than my great-grandmother's silver flatware that I pull from the china cabinet every Christmas to decorate my table. It's perfect the way it is. No one ever wants it to change. Just needs a bit of elbow grease to shine it up so you remember how special it really is."

I spot my father across the store, Mabel at his feet. My father points at me. Mabel comes trotting, as best she can, one arthritic hobble at a time, until she runs right into my legs. She jingles excitedly like the ornaments on the tree.

I kneel down and hug my beautiful, aging mutt.

"Who's my special girl?" I ask, kissing her head. "Who's my baby? You glad I'm home?"

My father is waving at me in the distance.

I realize I whisper the same things to Mabel that my father used to whisper to me when he would come home late from work and tuck me into bed.

"Sorry if I said too much," Barb says. "You know me. Always speak my mind. But I will never lie to you."

I will never lie to you.

My father walks away.

I feel guilty tears gallop toward my eyes. I take a sharp breath to keep them at bay.

"Your honesty is a breath of fresh air," I say. "Thank you. For all you do for Wegner's, for all you've done, for everything."

"That's so sweet, Henri. Thank you."

Mabel barks.

"She's the honest one," Barb says, her laugh booming through the store. "Telling me to keep my mouth shut, aren't you, Mabel?"

Barb bends down and scratches Mabel's head.

"Why can't we just learn from old dogs?" Barb asks, straightening. "Despite all the aches and pains, they are joyous simply being surrounded by those they love. Humans? We're always staring at our phones, thinking about tomorrow, consumed with guilt and worry. Mabel? She just lives in the moment."

My cell trills.

Great work, Henri! Get daddy to sign now!

I take a seat on the floor and bury my face in Mabel's fur, not only to be in this moment for once in my life but also to mask the guilt I can no longer keep hidden.

20

December 19

If you think Santa's elves are busy this time of year, you should see Wegner's fulfillment center.

Phones are buzzing, envelopes are being stuffed, catalogs labeled, and ornaments are secured in Bubble Wrap and placed in boxes that are sealed with shipping tape.

"Wow!" I say to Finn and my father.

It is the Christmas epicenter—Santa's hotline—for the store's catalog, shipping and website fulfillment.

"We mail nearly three million wish catalogs every year," my father says over the noise. He picks one up and taps the cover. "You're our cover girl."

My face flushes.

"Yeah," Finn says, "for some reason we featured the woman who wanted us to end the wish catalogs." He gives me a pointed look.

"It's a big expense," I say, defensively.

"Nearly three-quarters of our online orders are a result of the catalog," my father points out.

"I was obviously wrong," I say. "I'm not always perfect. Sorry."

"We ship over a quarter million packages around the world each year," my dad says, "and they are all handled in-house. I'm very proud of that. Would it be cheaper to have a site like Amazon handle all of our fulfillment? Yes. But we are not Amazon. We never want to be Amazon. I want our customers to know that we personally oversee each and every order."

"I understand completely," I say, "but..."

"Butt out," Finn says.

"Finn!" my father warns.

"I know she's got some idea up her sleeve that will end up costing people their jobs," he says.

I pick up a wish catalog along with a small box.

"Have you ever considered implementing mail processing automation?" I ask.

"What do you mean?" my dad asks, skeptically.

"It automates the process of sending letters and packages," I explain. "It reads and sorts incoming mail. It would significantly reduce inefficient, labor-intensive mail flow, like the wish catalogs."

"Here she goes." Finn rolls his eyes.

"Yes, here I go, Finn! I'm sorry, but there are a lot of antiquated systems still in place here that are costing us a lot of money."

"Us?" Finn asks. "Is there a mouse in your pocket?"

No, a rat.

"Stop it!" my dad says. "Henri has some good ideas. Business has been her life, Finn."

"And Wegner's has been *my* life, Dad! I think it's time you remember that!"

Finn storms off.

"I'm sorry, Dad." I sigh. "I didn't intend for this to happen. You asked for my thoughts. After speaking with Barb the other day, I just wanted to be as honest as I can."

Liar.

"Finn will be fine. He's just a little sensitive that you're home and full of ideas. You two have always had a bit of a quiet rivalry. Go on. I want to hear more."

"You'd save time and money, Dad," I say. "It would be an investment up front to automate and retrain, but many of these workers who are spending their days sorting and mailing could be placed on the floor or in the call center to make money for the store, and we could put the extra dollars into public relations, marketing and social media. People are obsessed with Christmas. I mean, with all the summer visitors flocking to Michigan, we could have a Christmas in July that might create a new holiday season here in the midst of a slow season."

"Would you mind putting together a proposal for me to review?" my dad asks. "I mean, if you have time. I know this is supposed to be a vacation for you, I know you must still be swamped with your own job and I know you probably need a break, but I'd love to have you finish overhauling our computer system and then look closely at automating."

"Thank you, Dad," I say. Then I laugh. "I mean, Mr. Wegner."

"We make a great team," he says. "It's so nice having you home for a bit. I feel—" he searches for the right word "—safe."

"I'll get right on it," I say, thinking about Barb and Mabel.

My phone buzzes with a text.

Another day, another dollar, Henri. Has your father signed the papers? We only have a few days to get this deal done...or else! Please update NOW!!!!!

"Speaking of work," I say.

"I'll leave you to it. See you back in the store."

I glance around and begin to type.

Nearly done. Working on last-minute proposal for my father to update outdated computer systems and automate fulfillment. I want it to be a win-win for both. Give me 48 hours!

Bubbles appear.

48 hours.
Done before the 25th.
Or your Christmas goose is cooked.

The holiday irony continues.

"What's going on?"

Finn is standing behind me. Between the secretive texts and all the noise in the fulfillment center, I didn't even hear him come back.

I jump at his voice and drop my phone. It bounces on the floor, once, twice…

Please land facedown, I think. *This isn't a peanut-butter-and-jelly sandwich. It's my life.*

It lands facedown.

I sigh and grab my phone, sliding it into my pocket.

"Nothing," I answer.

"Henri," he says, his voice dropping. "Why are you suddenly so interested in a business you had zero interest in for so many years? I mean, you typically spend less time in our house at Christmas than an iced cookie."

"What do you mean?" I feign innocence. "I'm home for a visit and thought I'd help out at the store."

"Show me your phone, Henri."

"It was my boss, if you must know. I'm actually still working even on my vacation. I know you're a little jealous I'm having so much input. I don't mean to overstep any boundaries. I really don't."

"And I know you're up to something. I know my big sister." Finn crosses his arms.

"I only want to help," I repeat.

"Right, Henri," Finn scoffs. "You're the polar opposite of Dad—you're the antithesis of the Wegner way."

"And you're stuck in time, Finn, being a yes man to someone you don't want to upset or disappoint," I say. "You may not want to hear it, but the way Wegner's is headed, there's a good chance there won't be a business left to run into the ground when you take over."

"How dare you!"

"How dare *you*?"

I look up. Employees are staring. My face flushes. I'm embarrassed for myself and for my father.

I give them a wave.

"We can't decide what to order for lunch?" I say with a laugh.

The employees nod and smile and go back to their work.

For a moment, we stand in silence facing one another.

"Do you know how hard it has been for me to live in your shadow, Henri?" Finn whispers angrily.

"What?"

"Firstborn child," Finn says, mimicking my father's voice. "Henri is so smart, so strong, so independent. *My Christmas Prinzessin*."

"Oh, come *on*, Finn—"

"I couldn't leave here," he says. "I couldn't leave home. How could I be the one to leave Mom and Dad all alone?"

"That's not fair, Finn. That was your decision."

"Really, Henri? I had the choice to leave them all alone? Who was going to help them as they got older? Who was going to take over the family business? Who was going to give them grandchildren? I certainly couldn't be the one to disappoint them. You had a choice, Henri. I didn't. You literally burned down my bridge out of town."

My anger suddenly turns to sympathy. His true feelings—ones I have long suspected but buried—have finally been unearthed.

Suddenly, I want to reach out and grab my brother, hug him until all the hurt goes away.

"Hurting and helping are not interrelated, Henri," Finn continues. "I've seen what you do to the companies you take over. You hurt them, but you lie to yourself that you're helping people. Wegner's is not a widget, Henri. It's not another line item on your spreadsheet. It's flesh and blood, it's dreams, it's decades of hard work."

I clench my jaw.

"I *know* that," I say.

"And it's *Christmas*, Henri," Finn says. "Maybe before you set off changing things, step back and remember why this company was founded and why it means so much to Dad and so many people. I know you can't spell *Christmas* without the letters *m* and *a*, but that doesn't mean we have to be another of your mergers and acquisitions. Christmas is not run by shareholders. It's run by the heart."

With that, Finn turns and walks away.

I watch him go, blinking in shock.

My kid brother never had the chance to cross his own bridge.

Part Four

21

December 19

"There's nothing like cheese and chocolate to make a girl feel better," I say to Sofie.

"There's nothing like cheese and chocolate to block a girl up," she says. "You're closer to sixty than sixteen, honey." Sofie pats my tummy. "One look at that bloated belly right now would make any gastroenterologist reconsider careers." She watches as I stuff another handful of candy into my mouth.

The woman at the counter watches me carefully.

"You know you still have to pay for all that," Sofie continues. "They might have to put you on a truck scale to weigh you, and no one wants that."

I nearly choke on a piece of saltwater taffy.

"Maybe you should slow down." Sofie sounds concerned now. "Both your mind and your eating."

I had to escape the drama of my brother, my family business and my life for a moment, and begged Sofie—after bringing her up to date—to meet me for a "wandering lunch" like we used to do during school. As seniors, we got an hour for lunch off campus, and Sofie and I used to come downtown and eat like tourists, hoovering cheese from Mouse's family's store before wandering over to the old candy store for "dessert."

I met Sofie at the Cheese Haus, where Mouse stuffed me with endless free samples of Swiss, goat, Havarti, Pinconning, Frankenmuth, cheddar and cheese curds, and regaled me with stories from school to make me feel better.

"Remember when you won the state debate tournament against that big Detroit high school by not saying a word?" Mouse asked.

"That's right!" Sofie said. "The final round was pro and con on whether women's rights were making strides internationally."

"And when it was your turn," Mouse said, continuing where Sofie left off, "you gestured dramatically as though you were speaking but never uttered a sound."

"The moderators thought your mic was broken at first," Sofie said, "but then at the very end, during the last few seconds of time you had left, you simply said..."

"Women's voices are being silenced across the globe, and until every woman in every nation has equal rights, no woman has rights," I finished.

Where did that passionate girl who wanted to change the world go? I wondered as my friends laughed. *When did she become another cog in the system working to silence entrepreneurs and quash dreams?*

Then Sofie and I wandered down the street to Rau's Country Store, which is not only like stepping back to my childhood but also like stepping back in time. It truly resembles an old general store with wide-plank hardwood floors and narrow aisles whose shelves are lined with wood crates and glass canisters crammed with old-fashioned candy.

After Sofie's warning, I head to the counter with my bag of candy—Nik-L-Nip wax bottles, jawbreakers, candy sticks, gummies, suckers, lollipops, jelly bellies, candy bars and Claey's Candy—along with my all-time favorite, saltwater taffy.

The cashier looks inside, then at me, raising a suspicious eyebrow.

"I'm paying for the empty wrappers, too," I say, my mouth filled with taffy.

"You should debate on the pros and cons of taffy," Sofie says, sidling up next to me. "You'd probably win *and* lose."

I pay for my candy, and we head outside and stand under the covered porch beneath an old wooden sign reading Michigan's Most Unusual Country Store.

"Ever notice," I say, sliding a candy stick into my mouth, "that everything in Michigan is the 'most' something? Your restaurant is 'world famous,' Wegner's is 'the world's biggest,' Mouse's store is 'the legendary'? Why is that?"

Sofie looks at me and then up and down Main Street. Bundled-up tourists crunch up and down the snow-covered sidewalks. Tour buses ease by, faces pressed to the steamed-up windows, eyes big, taking in the town.

The skies have cleared—a winter blessing of living on the eastern side of the state, where blue skies appear a touch more often than on the west coast, where Lake Michigan's presence can keep it cloud covered for months.

"We're a big state filled with people who have big hearts," Sofie says, still staring out at Main Street. "Michigan is surrounded by water, and every town up and down the coast has some fascinating, quirky history, just like our little Bavarian wonderland."

She grabs a cotton candy stick from my bag—her favorite—and waves it at me.

"It's about history, Henri. We're all shaped by it. Most run from it. But it's still in there." Sofie stops and points the candy stick at my heart. "How you come to terms with it is what matters."

Sofie opens the wrapper and pops the candy stick in her mouth. She continues.

"My great-grandmother once told me that the Great Lakes were formed by the blood, sweat and tears of our ancestors," Sofie says. "That still gives me goosies to this day."

Sofie points her candy stick down the street.

"You know my family risked everything to start our restaurant, selling their farm and borrowing money to make their dream come true," she says. "We opened on Mother's Day in 1929—just before the start of the Depression—and served guests for a dollar each. One day during the Depression, our receipts totaled seven cents—a man named Fred Goetzinger purchased a single Speckled Sport cigar."

Sofie shakes her head and continues.

"Your father did the same. Wegner's is now known around the world, and that didn't come easy for him. I'm sure there were many days his receipts totaled seven cents, too." Sofie puts her hand on my shoulder. "History is not a straight line, Henri, and I think history is actually what brought you home for Christmas this year."

And, with that, my eyes well up.

"Oh, honey," Sofie says.

She opens her arms, and when I lean in, her candy stick pokes me hard right in the face.

I laugh through my tears.

"You wanna tell mama what's going on?" Sofie asks. "Or are you going to keep eating taffy until you turn into Violet from *Willie Wonka*?"

"I can't."

"That bad, huh?"

I sigh. "Promise me you won't hate me."

"Go on."

"I'm about to be fired from my job," I start. "I mean, my boss was going to let me go before the start of the year. But I had this idea about Vance Enterprises…"

"The huge Vance Enterprises?" Sofie asks.

I nod. "My idea was that I could save their reputation and reinvigorate their business by convincing my parents to sell Wegner's to them."

Sofie's eyes bulge from her head. *"What?"*

"You promised me you wouldn't hate me," I say.

"No, I didn't," she says. "Keep going."

"I came back to convince my parents to sell," I say. "It's just that... Well, I didn't tell them that. I've been spying, taking photos of tax returns and downloading accounting files, sending them to my boss. Vance is ready to jump. My boss wants this wrapped up by Christmas. He wants my father to sign the papers today. I not only can't even bring myself to broach the topic with him, but I hate myself more every day. I feel like the worst daughter in the world."

"Oh, Henri. What a mess. I don't know whether to slap you or hug you." Sofie shakes her head as she eats her candy stick. "Okay, okay, let's remove all the emotion here and think about this in a logical way. Do your parents want to sell?"

"I've tried to rationalize my Scrooginess with the fact that they're getting older, the company needs to be modernized, they could retire without a care in the world and Finn and his family could be set for life, too."

"Does Finn want that?"

My eyes tear up again. "No. Finn knows something is up. He doesn't trust me. And, honestly, I've only seen him as my little brother. He's never gotten a shot to be his own person, and that is absolutely breaking my heart." I wipe my nose. "Either I get fired and lose my job, or I keep my job and lose my family." I scrunch up my face. "Now do you hate me?"

"No more than usual." She stares at me, shaking her head. "I'm really disappointed in you, Henri."

"I know."

"No, I don't think you do. You're playing Russian roulette

with your entire life. The Henri I knew never would have even considered duping her father or family."

"I *know*," I repeat. "I've lost my entire perspective for the sake of my career."

"I get that," she says. "I really do. Because there have been so many times I've put my business before my family, and I have so much guilt about that. I know it's taken a toll on them, too."

"What do I do, Sofie?"

"Well, you should have told me a long time ago," she says. "Friends don't keep secrets from one another. I'm pissed at you for lying to me. And I can only imagine how your father—the sweetest man on earth—is going to react."

"You're not helping."

"Total honesty?" she asks.

I nod.

"You came at this from a completely selfish, narcissistic point of view," my best friend starts. "And I do kinda hate you for that. You're a better person than that."

"Am I?"

"You know the answer to that, Henri," Sofie says. "But I can also see this from a rational perspective, too. Listen, I've been approached to sell many times, and I have to admit some of the offers have been very tempting."

"Really?"

"Really. I don't think my children have any intention or interest in taking over the restaurant. They see how many hours I work. I told you, they've seen the toll it takes on family. I don't think they can imagine dealing with the responsibility and hours. And I hate to say this, but I don't even know if they're capable of doing it. I have some big decisions to make in the coming years, but I'd love to keep it in the family, and will do my darnedest to try and make that happen." Sofie takes a deep breath. "Do you think your parents would even consider it?"

"I don't know," I say. "I can't imagine my father would want to sell to a big corporation. You know him. That goes against everything he believes."

"You know, it's not a bad thing if they truly want to slow down and enjoy the rest of their lives without all the stress and worry. I think of that every day." Sofie touches my arm. "But you have to come clean, Henri. You're not a liar. You've never been a liar. I'm not going to beat you up because you already know what you're doing is wrong. But don't hide the truth from them any longer. Don't lie to their faces every day. You haven't been home at Christmas for years. Please don't ruin that forever for them."

"You're right," I say. "I feel sick."

"You should with all the candy you just ate."

I hit her shoulder.

Sofie twirls her candy stick in her mouth and then puts a hand under my chin. She lifts my face until I'm looking her square in the eye.

"I actually think you came home to test yourself."

"What do you mean?"

"Santa always has a naughty and nice list," Sofie says. "I think you know which list you want to be on, but you just haven't been honest with Santa yet."

I shake my head at my friend.

"Thank you," I say. "I love you."

"I love you, too," she says. "But do the right thing, Henri."

Sofie sticks her hand deep into my bag, grabs a heaping handful of candy and stuffs it into the pockets of her dirndl dress.

"You owe me."

22

Bea texts me as I stand outside Shepherd Woolen Mill.

Benjie wants to know when he can expect the signed papers. He even follows me to the bathroom whenever I leave my desk.

I reply, I'm so sorry. I'll let you know more ASAP. This will all be over soon I promise.

Speaking of which: As soon as the deal is done, I'll be submitting my resignation. I don't want to leave you in the lurch before the holidays, but I also don't think this is the right place for me. I'm just not cut out for cutthroat. And I believed in my heart you might see things differently once you got home. I hope you understand.

My heart rises into my throat.

I call Bea.

Voice mail.

"B-Bea," I stammer, "just give me a bit more time. Please. I'm begging you. There's a lot going on behind the scenes that you don't know. Call me so I can explain."

I wait for my cell to ring, but it remains silent.

I think of what Sofie just said about history as I stare at the hand-painted Bavarian murals depicting the history of the state's oldest woolen mill. The beautiful murals that grace the store and sides of the historic mill illustrate how raw wool is turned into beautiful bedding in six steps.

I study the once-brightly-colored images—now slightly faded by time and harsh weather—of sheep roaming in bucolic fields, images of yore.

When I look back in ten years, what do I want the history of my life to look like?

What will I say to my parents? Benjie? Bea?

First, what am I going to say to Shep?

I open the door to the woolen mill and, again, feel as if I am falling back in time.

The store is pure Americana, with a wood floor and vintage lightshades that look as if you wandered into your great-grandmother's house.

The store is lined with shelves filled with beautiful wool comforters, wool pillows and wool mattress toppers. I roam the store, mesmerized by the beauty and craftsmanship of the products. I stop at a display of items that I've never heard of before.

"Those are wool dryer balls."

I turn, and a very pretty young woman—long hair twisted casually over her shoulder and down the front of her tan wool turtleneck—is smiling. I glance at her name tag.

"Ada," I say. "What a pretty name."

Another palindrome. What is going on, Frankenmuth?

"Thank you," she says. "I hated my mother my entire childhood for naming me after my grandma, and then all these old-fashioned names came back in style." Ada halts for a moment and smiles anew. "It also turns out my grandma was the coolest woman in the world. It's an honor to carry on her name."

I can feel my heart swell with emotion.

Ada grabs a dryer ball.

"What are those?" I ask. "I've never heard of wool dryer balls."

"Those are our newest addition, and all the rage right now," she says.

"You just pop three in your dryer, and they reduce static and cut back on drying time," Ada says. "They're made from wool roving without chemicals, which is wool fiber that has been processed but not yet spun into yarn."

"Wow," I say.

"They replace chemical dryer sheets, plus they last for a thousand washes," Ada says. "All the cool kids are using them."

I laugh. "I've always wanted to be cool," I say. "Sold!"

I hand her a box.

"I'll take this to the counter," Ada says, "while you continue to shop."

"Actually," I say, following her toward the counter, "I was wondering if Shep was here today."

Ada nods. "He is."

She points at a row of windows in the back of the store that lets customers look into the basement where the wool is processed.

I walk over to them. Shep is hunched over an old bathtub washing wool.

I watch him work, washing the wool in a row of old tubs filled with hot water to strip the soil and impurities from the fibers.

"After the raw wool is picked, which is a process of opening up the wool fiber, the wool is put through a picker, which opens the locks and blows the fluffy wool into a room where it is raked up and bagged," Ada says, coming up behind me. "The wool is then cleaned with a biodegradable soap and washed and rinsed with water fresh from the Great Lakes, namely our neighbor to the north, Lake Huron. The wool is combed into the soft filling that is sewn into bedding. It's then bagged and prepared for shipment."

"You know your stuff," I say. "You have to around these parts, don't you? Care to hear my spiel about Wegner's?"

"Oh, my gosh!" Ada says, pantomiming hitting herself in the head. "Duh! You're Henri…Henri Wegner. *The* Henri Wegner."

"In the flesh."

"Shep talks about you all the time," she says. "He was so excited you were back in town. He was actually singing while he worked. Some weird childhood song."

"'Frère Jacques'?" I ask, humming it for her.

"Yes!" she says. "That's it."

My heart swells.

"And some other song about May Day," Ada continues. "I actually grew up in Chicago, so all these Frankenmuth traditions are still fairly new to me."

Ada raps on the window.

Shep turns and looks up. In slow motion, his face morphs from confusion to…*elation*?

A bright smile covers his face, and his blue eyes brighten, his lips curling, his cheeks flushing hot pink.

"Ugh," Ada says. "He's so hard to look at, isn't he? My boyfriend says I only watch Rob Lowe TV shows so I can daydream about my boss. I told him that was creepy, but it's kinda true."

I laugh.

"He does talk a lot about you," she says, her voice now serious.

"He does?"

Ada moves off to attend to another customer as Shep motions for me to come down.

I head down into the basement.

"I'm so glad you stopped by," he says, beaming. "I mean it."

"Of course," I say. "And when you stop washing the wool, I think I'm the one who needs a bath to rinse off all the bad juju."

"Bad day?" Shep asks.

"You have no idea," I say.

I didn't mean to say that out loud. I pivot.

"Nothing like family," I say, showing him my big bag of candy.

"You and Sofie did the cheese-and-candy wandering lunch, didn't you? Just like you did in school."

I nod. "And my stomach is not happy."

"I bet," he says. "Want to help me wash some wool to get your mind off of everything? For old times' sake?"

"Why not?" I take off my coat, and tuck my mittens and scarf into its pockets. I place it on a small bench in the back alongside my bag of candy.

I walk back, roll up my sleeves and say, "To old times."

Summer 1985

Shep took handfuls of dirty wool from a laundry basket and placed them in the soapy water. Then he gently moved the wool around the tub with a pitchfork, pushing it through the water and suds, before lifting it to ensure each bundle was soaked.

Shep was shirtless, a Shepherd Woolen Mill apron draped over his torso, and I watched his muscles flex and torque as he worked in the basement. It was cooler down here in July, but still close, and sweat dripped down his chest, off his arms.

"Your turn," he said.

I followed suit.

"There's something comforting about this process," Shep said as I stirred the wool. "It never changes. It can never change." He put his hands on mine, his body pressed against me, and whispered, "We will never change."

His words made my body tense.

We were off to different colleges next month, and Shep's long-term plan was simple: nothing would ever change. Everything would always remain the same.

Forever.

I loved him so much, but did I want a life I already knew to be my future, already written?

I pushed the wool through the water.

"Life is constant change," Shep whispered into my ear. "But I know what I want."

His breath was hot, his voice thick. He kissed my neck.

"Shep," I said. "Everyone can see."

I motioned with my head. Shep looked up. Tourists were gawking into the basement.

"Let them watch," he said. "They're just jealous."

He ran his hands down my back. Goose bumps covered my body.

I wanted Shep, I needed Shep, I loved Shep but I also knew that if we didn't have some sort of separation, we'd be unable to walk on our own.

"Are you excited about school?" I asked.

"I'm excited to see you when you come home on break."

He kissed my neck again.

"What do you want to see most in the world?" I asked.

"You," he said. "When you're home on break."

"I'm serious, Shep," I said, annoyed.

He lifted his hands as if he were caught shoplifting and stepped back.

We finished going through the tubs of wool, and then took a seat and popped open a soda. We had to wait before we could put the wet wool in the extractor to remove the excess water.

He leaned back and stared at me.

"I am being serious, by the way," Shep said. "I love you, Henri."

"I love you, too, Shep." My voice was not as sharp.

"Isn't that enough?" he asked. "Why do I have to see the world when I have the entire world?"

It was the sweetest sentiment in the world, and yet, it felt simplistic. Shouldn't we experience the world before we settled down forever? Shouldn't we do everything we dreamed of doing before we became replicas of our parents forever?

"Where do you want to go one day?" I asked.

"Lake Huron," he said. "With you and our kids."

Kids?

Suddenly, I saw myself in the future, here, doing laundry and washing wool, racing between work and sports practices, nothing ever having changed.

"Where do you want to go?" Shep asked.

I looked at him but didn't answer.

I didn't know for sure, but I also didn't know if the answer was here.

"Good work, Henri," Shep said, knocking me from my thoughts. "It's like you never forgot a thing."

I tried, but I didn't.

"We have about an hour to wait before we can put the wet wool in the extractor to remove the excess water," I say.

Shep laughs. "See? Not a thing." He smiles at me. "Do you want to sit and talk for a bit? I mean, if you have a few minutes."

"I do," I say. "I'd like that."

He nods to the bench, I slide my coat over to the side and we take a seat beside one another.

"So, tell me about all you've done with the business," I start.

"I've taken a huge piece of the business online," Shep says proudly. "Online sales now account for over half of our entire business. I hired a full-time publicist, and with the world being fascinated with 'old being new' again—cooking, knitting, bread-making that started during Covid—we've struck a chord with a younger market. Did you see our dryer balls?"

"Ada showed me," I say. "I'm buying some." I look at him, shaking my head. "You always believed technology was the future. You always saw the future."

I stop short of saying "personally and professionally."

"Thank you, Henri. That means a lot coming from you."

"And you've headed in the direction my father needs to go. Wegner's needs to be modernized in so many ways."

"Well, you're the perfect person to do that," he says. "No one smarter or more talented."

"Shep," I start.

"Remember? Just say thank you."

"Thank you," I say. "Not easy coming home. I've fought with my dad over changes. I just had a major blowup with my brother over it, too."

"Finn's a complicated guy," Shep says. "Youngest kid, little brother, never rocked the boat."

"How do you know so much about him?"

"I grew up with him, Henri. I see him every week. We play on the same summer baseball team. He's a good guy."

"I forget how small small towns really are," I say. "And he is a good guy."

"Finn just wants a little respect," Shep says. "Remember how Lucy used to pull the football away from Charlie Brown?"

"Yeah?"

"I think your brother feels a bit like Charlie Brown," Shep says. "He wants a chance to kick that ball, but it keeps getting yanked away, over and over. He never really knows what he can do. So he doubts himself, and he just keeps trying and trying, missing and missing, falling and falling, over and over again. You and your father are a dynamic duo, Henri. Maybe give Finn a chance to kick for once."

"Thanks, Shep."

"I love your family," he says. "I know it's been a long time, but I miss your grandma. I miss seeing your parents. Hanging out with Finn still makes me feel close to them. You know, he's the one who told me you were in town."

"He did?" I ask.

"Yeah," Shep says, ducking his head. "I think he was playing matchmaker a little bit. He's the reason I stopped by to get that ornament for Quinn. I wanted to see you."

The emotions of the day overwhelm me, and I'm a mess again.

Shep pulls me close, and I lean my head onto his shoulder.

"Why'd you come home, Henri?" he says softly. "It's been so long. And you don't seem yourself at all. You can tell me."

And so I do.

Everything.

He's silent at first, and my mind begins to race with how he must hate me, how he must be judging me, how grateful he must be to have never gotten tangled with such a monster.

"That's a lot of pressure to contend with, Henri," he says. "I can't imagine."

"Why am I such a monster?"

"You're not a monster. You're human."

I stare at the tubs of wool.

His voice is as comforting and reassuring as the routine of washing wool.

"You're not mad?"

"I'm certainly not happy with what you're doing," he says. "And I don't like how you've lied to your family and friends, but I certainly understand the predicament you're facing."

"You do?"

He nods at the tubs.

"We all have a lot of dirt that needs to be washed away."

I sit up.

"I wasn't a good husband, Henri," Shep says. "I thought I loved Hannah, and I thought she loved me, but it was just pretend."

"You don't have to tell me all this," I say. "It's none of my business."

"I've spent a lot of time working on my emotions," Shep says. "I sound so Zen, don't I? But sweeping things away as if they never happened—you turning down my proposal, my issues with Hannah—doesn't solve anything. When you say them out loud, they become real, and so you face them."

I nod.

He continues, "I've changed since my divorce. I don't bury my emotions any longer." Shep turns to me. "Hannah and I thought we could fix each other. Her childhood was not the easiest, Henri. Her dad treated her like crap, her family never thought she was capable of taking over the business, and that's a big reason she acted the way she did in high school. I thought I could heal all her pain, and she thought she could erase all my heartache over losing you."

"Shep," I start.

"No, it's okay, Henri," he says. "But love can't do all of that heavy lifting. Love is just a Band-Aid. And, eventually, if that love is not completely real and authentic, it ages, gets a bit worn and falls off, and you realize the original wound never healed. The scar tissue remains forever. The only way Hannah and I could heal was to heal ourselves, and we realized we had to do that separately. We could only do that by not hurting each other—or beating ourselves up—anymore. It's a sea of change, day after day. It took a long time, but I'm proud of the person I am."

Shep puts his hand on my leg.

"I want to be proud of the person I am," I say.

The buzzer rings.

"Then you need to wash away all that dirt."

I nod.

"Do you know why sheep flock together?" Shep asks out of the blue.

I cock my head at his question, not understanding.

"They run from what frightens them and band together in large groups for protection," he says. "Family and friends flocking together is the only protection they have from predators."

Shep looks me deeply in the eyes.

"I think you came home for protection from predators."

"Maybe you're right," I say. "Thanks for listening, Shep, but I better go." I grab my coat, and Shep walks me toward the basement door.

"It was so good to see you, Henri," he says. "I hope this isn't too presumptuous, but I'd love to see you again. Even if it's just a pizza down here, like the old days, or a walk on the bridge."

"I'd like that, too," I say. "And I can't thank you enough for the good advice and for not hating me."

"I could never hate you, Henri."

He opens his arms, and we hug, tentatively at first, and then tighter.

My heart races.

You know that exact moment when you hug someone you're attracted to, and you don't want to hold on too long but you also don't want to be the first to let go?

This is that moment.

Finally, when we part, our faces are just inches from one another.

Shep's face, of course, is more weathered and more lined than it was when we were young, but—to me—it's even more handsome because it tells a story, just like that beloved vintage Christmas ornament you pull free from its box. It may have a few cracks and hairline fractures, but it's still beautiful because it has...

A history.

Shep's eyes are soft, the color of Lake Huron in early summer, when the weather is warm and the water is still cold.

His lips are so perfect that it's ridiculous.

23

On my way back to Wegner's, it begins to snow.

A commercial sponsored by my father begins to play on the radio, followed by another Christmas song in the endless stream of Christmas songs.

I start to change the channel, knowing I will be surrounded by Christmas music the rest of the day and month, when I hear "Jingle Bell Rock."

I can feel my soul smile.

Finn played trombone in band, marching band and jazz band in junior high and high school, moving from the recorder to a short-lived career as a drummer and, finally, to the loudest and most obnoxious instrument this side of the tuba.

The walls of our upside-down house reverberated for years whenever Finn practiced. Birds relocated to Canada to escape e cacophony.

Naturally, since Frankenmuth was Christmas City USA, marching band was invited to countless holiday parades all oss Michigan.

Jingle Bell Rock" was the song the band played every sin- ear.

Shep's breath is on my face, on my lips, in my mouth.

I feel as if I'm in a trance. I lean forward.

Suddenly, the timer goes off again, snapping us back into reality.

"Time to get the wool into the extractor," Shep says. "It needs to dry."

I start to turn and leave, but Shep reaches out and grabs my arm.

"I've missed you."

"Me, too."

"More than you can ever imagine, Henri."

"Me, too. I'll see you soon, Shep. Thank you for everything."

I head back upstairs to the store. But before I leave, I feel as if I'm being pulled by a string back to the windows.

I look down at Shep working.

His eyes drift up—as if he knows instinctually I am there, that I have always been there—and catches me staring.

And then he gives me a wave and returns to his routine, and I suddenly feel very calm.

It became engrained in my soul, resounding as loudly there as the glockenspiel's chimes.

Finn's involvement in band was a major dilemma for my parents, whose work schedule—often eighteen hours a day at Wegner's during the holidays, literally starting the day after Halloween and continuing through New Year's—was overwhelming. Finn's baseball schedule came during a more forgiving time of year, but finding time during the holidays to drive Finn to band practices, football games, weekend bus pickups and neighboring towns was not an easy task.

I remember my parents used to play rock, paper, scissors to determine who would drive Finn. They could not wait until I was able to drive so I could take on some of their parental duties.

I remember how annoyed I used to be having to spend my very precious Fridays or Saturdays driving my little brother to his stupid band parades. Once I drove him to Saginaw, in a blinding snowstorm that came out of nowhere, to march in the town's holiday parade. I was so scared driving him in the snow and so mad at my parents for making me do it that—when we arrived—I took my frustration out on him.

"Aren't you getting out of the car to watch me?" he asked.

"No!" I screamed. "I hate you!"

I can still see Finn standing there, snow piling atop his two-foot-tall marching band busby shakos hat—red imitation fur with a mile-high feather plume—jacket with gold buttons that matched his trombone, polyester bibbers, white gloves and black boots.

One tear found its way free. Then he turned and marched off in the snow.

That's when it hit me: I was simply furious at Finn for being a kid.

He was just a boy still, and the only thing he wanted was someone to watch him play and march.

He just wanted someone to be proud of him.

I shut my eyes, ashamed that I'd been such a crappy sister.

Later, when Finn saw me standing along the parade route, waving like mad, his face lit up more brightly than the float in front of him. He marched higher, moving his trombone left and right, up and down, to "Jingle Bell Rock."

The band stopped in front of us and began to play.

The bass of his trombone reverberated in my soul.

The road before me blurs as tears fill my eyes.

Finn has always just wanted to be seen.

I suddenly make a U-turn and head toward home.

I rush into my parents' house and race to the big tree in the living room.

"There you are!" I say, grabbing an ornament off the tree.

I race back to my car and instead of heading back to Wegner's I drive my car farther into the woods. I smile when I come upon Fir the Love of Christmas Tree Farms. I drive under a wooden arch with a beautiful wreath and down the long, snowy drive.

I park and head out into the snowy forest. I walk between the rows of trees, going farther and farther, following the advice of my grandfather.

"No one ever goes all the way to the back, Henri. That's where all the beauties are!"

I glance up in the snow, and I see it: a dandy Douglas fir, its needles a bluish, dark green, radiating from the branches in all directions, is standing happy and tall, dusted with snow, thrilled to see me.

Just like Finn.

I call to a passing employee, waving my hands.

"Over here! This one, please! It's perfect!"

I head to Wegner's, the tree on top of the car. I park under the porte cochere, jump out and untie the tree. I motion for some employees inside to help. Barb sees me and gathers a small army.

"I'm not even going to ask," she says with a laugh.

The image of us dragging the tree through the entire store is not, I'm sure, such a magical holiday scene. We pull the tree through the ornaments section, and I smile when I see the ornament of the red station wagon with the tree on top.

"This way!" I say to the troops.

We don't stop until we reach the privacy of the office.

"What in the world are you doing?" my father asks. "And where have you been?"

"Getting into the Christmas spirit," I say.

"I thought you'd gotten drunk," he jokes. "Again."

"Ha-ha. I'm just high on cheese and chocolate." I glance at the tree. "And life."

"Need this?"

Barb returns with a tree stand and tree skirt.

"You think of everything," I say.

She winks and exits.

"Don't just stand there," I say to my father and mother. "Help me."

My father is looking at me as if I've temporarily gone insane and is too nervous to say anything.

They help me place the fir in the stand and then watch as I wrap its base with the tree skirt. Barb picked a winner: the skirt is a green velvet adorned with colorful Santa and sleigh appliqués accented with shimmering stitching, sparkling sequins and white pom-poms.

"Perfect!" I exclaim.

"Where are you going?" my father asks.

I don't answer. I beeline to the customer service department, and I scooch next to Betty Lou Preston, who's been the "voice" of Wegner's forever.

I punch a button on her phone, lean in and say, "Attention, Finn Wegner! Attention, Finn Wegner! Please report to the office immediately! There's an emergency! Thank you!"

Betty Lou looks at me and raises one thin black eyebrow,

which she's penciled on for decades since the day she plucked out her last brow hair.

"I'm not even going to ask," she says, before hitting a button. "Good afternoon! Wegner's Winter Wonderland! How may I direct your call?"

I rush back to the office—nabbing a box of silver icicle tinsel garland on the way, now followed by a curious Gert—and a few moments later a bewildered Finn races in.

"What's going on?" he asks, looking around. "What's the emergency?"

He stares at me and then the silver tinsel in my hands.

"Here!" I say, handing him the tinsel.

"Have you lost your mind?"

"No," I say. "I think I've found it."

I nod at the tree.

"Remember when you used to go out and get our Christmas tree every year? I just wanted to return the favor for once. Please accept my apology for earlier today. I hope you know how much I love and respect you."

I watch the years melt from his face. He is no longer a grown man, mad at his older sister and overwhelmed at work; he is a boy.

His cheeks relax, and a smile—that infectious, natural smile of his—brightens his face.

"I haven't been listening to you," I continue. "I don't know if I ever have."

He meets my gaze.

"Thank you, sis."

"I think I missed something after I left," my dad says.

I nod. "A lot actually," I say. "I had lunch with Sofie and saw Shep…"

Everyone's eyebrows raise at once, as if a curtain is being lifted.

"And as I was driving back here, 'Jingle Bell Rock' came on the Muth."

Finn laughs, remembering.

"Memories."

"You know the funny thing about the trombone I finally realized, something that you've always known?" I ask. "It's rarely the lead instrument. It's always the background. But you can't have a song without its backbeat. It would be flat and lifeless."

"Henri," he says, his voice embarrassed but pleased.

"Do your thing," I say, nodding at the box of icicles.

He begins to dangle silver tinsel on the beautiful branches. Finn holds the box toward me. I grab a few and toss them on.

"You have to carefully place them, Henri," he says. "That's the secret to hanging icicles."

He sounds just as he did as a kid. My heart swells with emotion.

When we are done, he stands back and admires his work.

"Oh, I forgot one thing," I say.

I reach into my pocket.

"First ornament for the tree."

Finn shakes his head at me again, not understanding.

"My Charlie Brown ornament?" he asks.

"A good friend told me today that Charlie Brown just needs a chance to kick the football," I say. "Tell me everything you want me to know about Wegner's. Tell me what you think needs to be changed." I stop. "Or left exactly the same."

Finn hangs the ornament on a bluish branch, steps back and crosses his arms.

"Get out on the sales floor to get a real feel for the business, our employees and our customers," he says. "Feel the magic."

Finn turns toward me.

"If there's one thing I think you've missed your entire career, it's the connection to people. You're always behind the scenes, making deals, looking at systems, cost cutting, the bottom line, but you rarely see a business from an emotional point of view. Why do people shop here? Why do they choose to spend their hard-earned money? Why do they return, year after year, with their grandparents, children, best friends? Because it resonates in their souls. It makes them feel safe."

I think of sheep flocking.

I can hear the tinkle of the ornaments and Mabel approaching.

In the distance, the bells chime.

"Deal," I say, extending my hand.

"Deal," he says.

I see in my peripheral vision my father put his arm around my mother's waist. He kisses her on the cheek, huge smiles on their faces.

Gert is beside them, watching this unfold.

"A real tree is a nice touch in here," Gert says in a stage whisper to my parents. "Henri has some good ideas."

Gert takes a beat and then adds, even more loudly, "But I do have to ask if she drinks on the job. Between her makeup the other day and dragging a tree into the store, I'm a bit worried about her."

Another beat.

"Not to mention how bloated she looks today."

"I'm standing right here, Gert!" I say, turning. "I can hear you! And, by the way, it's the cheese and chocolate that has me so bloated." I look at her. "Although, after the day I've had, I could use a drink."

"See?" Gert says. Then she winks at me. "I keep a flask in my purse, too."

My father places his hands over his ears, and my mother ushers him away from the Christmas chaos.

24

December 20

My texts and calls to Bea have gone unanswered, but Benjie persists like the flu.

Call me, Henri! Time is running out. Bea is hiding from me. Victoria Vance is about to have my head. You promised me. I promised her. If not, I'll have your head. Do we have a deal? Tick-tock.

"Here's Brady!"

A grandmother shoves her very sturdy grandson—who must be all of three—into my arms. He grabs my cell, and I consider letting him text a babbling reply to Benjie.

It would likely be more coherent than the thoughts in my jumbled brain as I try to think of what to say to my father and Benjie while trying to save my head, and keep my family, friends and Bea.

Brady puts the phone in his mouth.

"Mine," he says.

You can have it, kiddo.

Per Finn's request, I am working on the floor at Wegner's,

and he has strategically started my day in Villages, Collectibles & Nativity Scenes because he knows these are the most particular of any of the Wegner's customers.

Ironically, retail experience, especially at the holidays, is a skill I often look for when hiring at Tolliver.

In today's world, more and more young people have held summer jobs or internships that center around technology or social media, but—call me old-school—I prefer, as my grandfather used to say, real boots-on-the-ground experience.

For the last ten minutes, I've watched Brady's grandma swat his hands away from intricate, highly breakable Dickens and North Pole villages with all the skill of a trained martial arts assassin, yelling, "No! No, Brady, no!"

Brady reaches out and yanks my hair.

Hard.

"Hair!" he says.

"He has a thing for hair," his grandmother says. "Loves to rip the heads off of his sister's dolls. I'm sportin' a few bald spots myself."

Holding Brady is akin to holding a cannonball with octopus arms that's been rolled in syrup.

"No! No, Brady, no!" I yell.

His grandmother laughs.

"You're gettin' the hang of it now," she says. "Do you mind if I take this one out of the box?"

"Not at all." I smile and nod.

She unboxes yet another North Pole village shop, this one called Nina's Knit Mittens, a little porcelain shop that looks like a bright red knit mitten with a green front door and a snow-covered ball of yarn in front of it.

"Hmm," she says, placing a hand under her chin. "I don't know."

She gestures at the different collectible shops before her: a gingerbread bakery, a North Pole pizza parlor, a Christmas quilts store and the Knit Mittens.

"What do you think, Brady?"

"I like!"

The grandmother steps back to study the different options.

"You know," she says, "for the last thirty years, I've come to Wegner's to buy my Christmas decorations. I sold all of my mom's holiday decorations after she died because it was too painful for me to remember." She shakes her head. "Dumbest mistake of my life. So I started coming here to buy tree skirts and nativity scenes to replace the ones I gave away. When I had my daughters, I came here every Christmas with them, and we started buying these North Pole villages, one piece at a time. Now, I have a grandson, and I have North Pole villages that run throughout my entire house, from the kitchen, to the living room, and under the tree. A train track runs from room to room, and Brady has a toy train he operates that visits all the little villages. You love them as much as I do, don't you, Brady?"

He gives his grandma a mighty thumbs-up.

She continues, "I can feel my mother again—I can feel the spirit of Christmas again—every time I pull the villages free from their bins each year and start to create the magical towns."

The woman looks at me, her eyes misty.

This is why you work retail.

This is why Finn wanted me on the floor again. *To remember.*

"I think you should go with the Knit Mitten store," I say. "It's adorable. They just started making it this year, and it's a limited edition. What do you think, Brady?"

"I want pizza!" he says.

I laugh. "Well, Brady loves pizza, so I'd add that one, too. I think you need to start adding village memories for your grandson, too."

"Sold!"

After Brady and his grandmother depart, Finn sidles up to me and says, "You're good."

"What are you doing out of the office?"

"Watching how my older sister does things."

"Bring it on. What's next?"

He laughs. "You know I'm not intentionally trying to torment you."

"Yes, you are," I say. "And I probably deserve it."

"The elf at the entrance just called in sick," Finn says with a grin more mischievous than any of Santa's little helpers, "and so we need a Wegner's *Weihnachten* woman." He stops. "Actually, we need the original Wegner's *Weihnachten* woman."

"No."

"Yes."

"Then we're good?" I ask.

He waits a moment, drawing out the tension, and finally nods.

"Better go get dressed," Finn says with a laugh. "There's an extra costume in the office. Yours!"

I burst into my parents' office, which—despite the recent expansion—is anything but fancy.

"What are you doing?" my parents ask at the same time.

They are hunched over the new laptops that Bea recently sent to me when we were still communicating. The laptops are a few years old in the real world, but light-years ahead of what my parents were using, especially since Bea installed all new software on them. Once I have my parents fully trained, we plan to get newer laptops for the entire staff and train them after the holidays.

If any of us are still around, that is.

"Finn is still torturing me," I say. "Where is the extra elf costume?"

My father can't stifle a laugh.

"I'm glad to see you two working things out," he says. "You

actually make a good team. Remember how you used to beat everyone—us, your grandparents, friends, the entire neighborhood—when we'd play board games and you'd team up?"

"No one could beat the two of you," my mom adds.

My father points. "Extra costumes are hanging back there," he says. "Including your original costume."

"Thank goodness we let it out for that Christmas party years ago," I say.

"And," my dad continues, "the extra caps and shoes are in a large box marked Wegner's Elf."

I head behind a makeshift partition from the '70s that used to be in the restaurant. This area is kept hidden behind the large partition, and it's more like a catch-all closet meets department store dressing room.

I begin to change into the costume, knowing my brother is going to get a big laugh out of this.

My cell buzzes, and I grab it quickly, hoping it's Bea.

I'm going to cancel Christmas if I don't hear from you by five p.m.

"I can't deal with this," I mumble.

"What?" my father calls. "Did you say something about a deal?"

My heart sinks.

I should just walk out right now and tell him everything.

"Nothing," I yell. "I can't deal with this costume. Where's that box with the caps and shoes, Dad?"

"Box marked Wegner's Elf, probably under a bunch of other boxes," he calls. "We haven't had time to organize lately."

"Lately?" my mom asks. "There are boxes back there from the '70s, from when you were just a girl. If you stayed around, we'd have this place in better shape than Suzanne Somers's thighs."

I laugh as I riffle through boxes. I pull one off another,

looking for the elf accessories. I finally see the right box at the bottom of a stack. On top of it is another box simply marked Henri on the side in faded Magic Marker. I open the lid and am stopped cold.

Sitting on top is a flag.

My flag.

I reach down and unfold it.

The flag is red, the following words as green as the pine tree stitched onto it.

Holiday Land: Where Every Day Is Like Christmas

1977

In lower school, my teacher had the wonderfully creative idea that the class form its own new states and governments. This was in the year following the bicentennial, when America was still feeling decidedly united. The goal was to familiarize students with government and the duties of citizens within their government. Our class was divided in half and tasked with electing officers, and creating branches of government, rules of law and a constitution. I was elected president of my state, which I named Holiday Land.

My rule of law was quite simple: kindness.

"When creating laws," I remembered essentially saying, "we must always ask ourselves, 'Is this good for all? Are we making the world a better place?'"

Our country's name, like my governing philosophy, was naively hopeful. I ran into problems when I had to send our rules back to the citizens to be ratified.

"What about me?" was always the number-one question. "What do I get out of it?"

I had my grandma, the seamstress, make a beautiful flag, with a Christmas tree as our symbol.

The local newspaper came out and took pictures of the president, senators and state reps. When the article appeared in the paper, my mother cut it out and hung it on the refrigerator, like most mothers did at that time. Over dinner, my father asked how the new state I was helping to create would be different.

I reiterated my philosophy.

"I'm so proud of you, Henri," he said. "You will be an amazing leader. Smart, kind, always thinking of everyone other than yourself."

He then said, "Just know that the world won't often appreciate that philosophy. We become jaded. We become selfish. We forget what matters most in the world—each other. But, more than anything, we forget the magic of Christmas, its meaning and purpose—that there is something bigger than us. There is hope."

When I went to school the next day, my country's flag had been stolen. My teacher found it stuffed in the corner of the coat rack behind our little jackets.

It had been torn in half.

I look at the flag.

My grandma sewed it back together.

"No one can rip apart a dream someone has built," she said. "We must always remain stronger than the bullies."

I place the flag back in the box, pull on my shoes and cap and ready myself to come clean to my parents about the big bully in my life, and how I'm the one trying to rip their holiday dream in two.

My father applauds when I walk out.

"Just as I remember."

My mother simply shakes her head.

"You're supposed to be on vacation, Henri, remember?" my mother asks. "I thought you came home to rest and relax, not get into a bickering match with your little brother and work at Wegner's 24/7. You need a break."

"I know," I say, just wanting to unleash weeks of torment, "but it's not much fun sitting home by myself when the people I want to visit are here all day. This way I get to see you guys."

Mabel looks up from where she's been napping and begins to bark.

"It's okay, baby," I say. "It's me. It's Henri." I kneel and hold out my hand for her to sniff. She barks happily and then does an arthritic jig. I stand.

I catch my parents' eyes. They are staring at me and Mabel, smiling in a wistful way, as if they want to capture this moment in their minds forever.

"You know, I can still remember sewing that costume with Mom as if it were yesterday." My mother shakes her head, and I can see her disappear for a moment. "Your father was working day and night, and he had all of these ideas constantly, as if lightning were striking him or God was speaking to him. We were watching *How the Grinch Stole Christmas* with you in Mom and Dad's basement, and you were still a baby, but when you saw all the characters, your eyes lit up. You were mesmerized."

My mother looks at me.

"Remember, Jakob?" she asks.

"As if it were yesterday," he says.

"Your father was watching you watching the cartoon, just as closely as Mabel is watching you right now."

I glance down at Mabel, her eyes alert. I move, my shoe jangles and Mabel places a big, old paw atop the bell to stop it. She removes her paw, I jingle the bell, she barks and does it all over again.

"Then years later, when you were in junior high, we were watching that same special, and you were still mesmerized by it. Your dad yelled, 'That's it! We need someone to welcome every guest to Wegner's so their eyes will look just like Henri's when they enter our store. So they feel the magic!' Your grandmother started sketching a costume that moment. You remember what a great seamstress she was?"

"I do," I say, remembering the flag.

"We stayed up nearly all night—and then a few more days and nights—making that first costume," my mom says. "And you became Wegner's first elf. Customers loved how cute you were. It's like..."

My mother stops, smiles and begins to tap on her keyboard again.

"Go on," I say.

My mom shakes her head.

"Go on," I urge.

"It's like we tailored this entire company just for you," my mom says. "I'm sorry."

"Mom," I start. "It's okay. Don't be sorry."

"You don't need to hear any sob stories from me, and I don't mean to lay any guilt trips on you, Henri. I just got a bit nostalgic. What you need to hear is how proud your father and I are of you for carving your own niche and for being so successful." She nods her head and forges on. "But, as I keep telling your father, we must begin to make some big decisions."

"Meaning?" I ask.

This is my moment. Play it cool.

"Meaning we're not spring chickens. We're firmly in our seventies. How much longer can we keep going at this pace? How much longer do we *want* to keep going at this pace? What does our life look like without this place?"

"What about Finn?"

"We love Finnie, and we think he is the hardest worker and most loyal soul in the world..." my mom says.

"But?" I prompt.

"But," my dad cuts in, "—and I'm speaking here as a business owner and not a father—Finn has always excelled when he's part of an ensemble, just like in baseball or band. He needs a coach. He responds to a drum major. That's what I've been to him. That's what you've always been to him as a big sister, Henri. When you two are in sync, you can rule the world."

I open my mouth. It's time.

"I need to talk to you about something important," I say. "I don't know how to say this, but..."

Finn appears at the office door.

"Customers are waiting," he says, snapping his fingers. "Time we put that elf on a shelf."

He grabs me by the arm and pulls me out of the office, the sentence that could change all our lives replaced by the jingling of my shoes and cap.

25

By 5:00 p.m., I have—in this exact order—been:

*Barfed on three times by children who have either gotten overly excited by the magic of Wegner's, frightened by my appearance or—like I have been guilty of—overindulged on chocolate and cheese;

*Hit on by two men, one in his nineties with a walker who said I looked like liked Betty Grable (he pinched my rear end), and one on college break who asked me to be "his sugar-mama elf";

*Hypothermic, from being assaulted by the north wind rushing through the front doors every thirty seconds;

*In pain, since I have had to hold my head at an odd angle from keeping my cap from sliding off;

*Unable to hear a word anyone says, since there is a bell jingling mere inches from my ear every time I breathe or move;

*Unable to check my phone due to the never-ending line of customers.

"Smile!"

I hold up the camera and peer at a family perched on the Wegner's throne.

A grandmother and grandfather are seated beside one another on the king-size chair of red velvet. Each holds a boy and girl on their lap, while the parents are perched upon the ornate gold arms on opposite sides.

The entire family is dressed in red turtlenecks featuring bright green trees on the front. Underneath, it reads in a pretty scroll:

The Gardner Family Tree
Christmas 2023

The Polaroid shakes in my hand.

Everyone should feel like family, I can hear my father say.

The words jangle in my head, just like the bell.

I lower the camera and think of what my mother just said.

It seems like only a few photos ago—a flash of a camera bulb—that my grandparents were alive and well, and my father was starting this store. I was a girl who waited all year long for Christmas. I was a girl who dreamed of making wishes. I was a girl who dreamed of home.

"Is everything okay?"

"Yes," I chirp happily. "The camera was just acting up for a second. Smile!"

I wait for the photo to emerge.

"Perfect," I say. "Take a look."

They all rush to see the Polaroid.

"You know," the grandmother says, "I just cannot thank you enough for continuing this tradition. We all take photos on our cell phones then forget about them or delete them. But every year I take the Wegner's Polaroid and put it in our family photo album. I will give that album to my daughter, and I hope one day she will give that to her children. So even when I'm no longer here, they will be able to remember these moments. Christmas is a special time. Our family reunites too infrequently due to distance, work, travel, but Wegner's makes us come together, at least once a year. Thank you."

I open my arms, and the woman hugs me.

I watch them enter the store, and take a moment to recover.

"Hello?" I hear a man call. "Are you going to take our picture?"

Over the jingling of my cap's bell and the tinkling of the ornaments in the store, over the heat vents, hum of the customers and the Christmas music, I swear I recognize the voice calling to me.

I turn and say, "*Frohe Weihnachte!* Welcome to Wegner's!"

"Are you kidding me?"

If I were a character in a Christmas cartoon, my eyes would pop out of my head and roll around on the floor right now.

"Henri?"

Benjie and Maya are seated on the throne. He is holding her—in a *very* non-Christian way—in his lap.

"What are you doing here?" I gasp.

"I told you," Benjie says, a look of supreme annoyance on his face, "that you had until 5:00 p.m. to get the deal done. I truly hope the way you're dressed is all part of your big takeover plan because I'm beginning to feel as if you're being totally...elfish," he sneers.

I jerk my head around to see if anyone in my family is nearby.

I want to come clean with him. I want to come clean with everyone.

I just need a bit more time to get my sleigh ready for takeoff.

"It actually is," I say, leaning into them. "I've been working every part of the store—sales, marketing, inventory, distribution, accounting—to get an insider's peek at where things stand and what Vance could cut or duplicate. It's part of the final report I'm preparing for Vance. Take what I'm wearing, for instance. This getup is sort of like the greeters at Walmart."

A shopper enters the store and takes a photo of me.

"See?" I whisper. "Can you imagine how popular this could be? Happy elves are exactly the sort of publicity Vance needs to erase all the negative press of late."

"Okay, Henri," Benjie says, temporarily appeased. "I'm not totally buying it, but I'll cut you a little slack."

I sigh.

"For now."

"Thank you," I whisper.

"Why are you whispering?" Maya asks. "And once Vance takes over this store, I'm suggesting that we make this costume way sexier, right, hon?" Maya runs her fingers through Benjie's hair, and I have to stop myself from audibly gagging. She turns her eyes on me. "Sheer leggings, red leather skirt, and the jacket should be low cut, with fur trim around the bust. And there should be bells *everywhere*!"

I don't really know any elves who strip, I think. This is a family business in Frankenmuth not a club in Vegas.

"We can work out all these details once the papers are signed," Benjie says.

"Now take our picture with that weird camera," Maya adds.

I step back and aim the camera.

In that instant, I see what my dad sees when he walks in the store every day.

The Christmas display my father made by hand decades ago for a department store no longer in business—the chair of velvet, the candy canes, the Wegner's Winter Wonderland sign—has never changed despite how much the world has the last fifty years.

And sitting on it are two people—dressed in form-fitting designer suits—who know nothing of this history, who simply wish to change it all for the sake of the almighty dollar.

Context, out of context.

And behind them are the wooden signs that started it all, carved by my father in my grandparents' basement, when all either of us had were wishes and dreams.

"Take the picture already!" Maya yells.

I take the picture.

When it appears, I hand it to them.

"Do I look fat?" Maya asks, squinting at the image.

"Never," Benjie purrs.

Cue gag reflex again.

"My turn!"

Maya lifts her cell and snaps a photo of me.

"This is so going on Insta," she says with a laugh. "Our Tolliver elf!"

"Everything okay, Henri?"

I jump at the sound of my father's voice.

"D-Dad!" I stammer.

"The man of the hour!" Benjie says, standing up and extending his hand, nearly ejecting Maya off his lap.

"Dad, this is Benjie Tolliver," I say. "My boss."

"Well, well, well," my father says, extending his hand. "It's nice to finally meet you. I've heard so much about you."

"And, Dad," I add quickly, so no one can get in a word, "this is Maya Jenkins. I work with Maya as well."

"Oh, my goodness," my father says. "You used to be Henri's assistant, right?"

Maya's face turns bright red. "I did," she says.

"We met a very long time ago," Dad says. "It's so good to see you again."

Maya nods and begins to scroll through her phone.

My father turns to Benjie.

"I met your father many years ago when we visited Henri in Detroit. I was so sorry to hear about his passing. Henri adored him. We had a lot in common, your father and I. Started our own businesses with nothing more than a dream. Worked with family. You should feel proud of all you've done to continue and grow that legacy."

Benjie's expression softens, and a sweet smile emerges.

Speaking of heart, is exhaustion making me imagine this, or did my father's kindness actually make Benjie's heart grow three sizes this day?

"Thank you," he says, sounding genuine.

"So what brings you to Wegner's?" my dad asks. "Vacation? Checking in on Henri? I have to say we are thrilled that you gave her extra time off this year to spend with family."

No!

Benjie raises an eyebrow and shakes his head at me. His expression says everything. *Busted, you little elfin liar.* The Grinch has returned.

"Oh, Mr. Wegner," Benjie starts. "We need to talk..."

Benjie's mouth is still open—ready to utter the words *in private!*—when I hear someone say, "Are you Maya Jenkins? Miss Michigan?"

Maya beams that she's been recognized by a customer.

"I am."

"You so should have won Miss America," the woman says. "You got robbed."

"I did!" Maya says. "I mean, no one gave a better answer than me. And that evening gown I wore? Right?"

And then, Betty Lou's voice comes over the intercom, "Jakob Wegner to the office immediately, please. Jakob Wegner to the office."

"You'll have to excuse me," my father says to Benjie. "But Henri is the perfect tour guide to Frankenmuth. Enjoy your time in town and at Wegner's. Merry Christmas!"

He hurries off.

"Oh, Henri," Benjie says. "What have you done? Or, rather, not done? This is going to be an interesting dinner."

"Dinner?" I ask.

"We have reservations," Benjie says. "It was meant to be a surprise celebration, but now I think it's going to be more along the lines of the Red Wedding episode of *Game of Thrones*."

I wince. *I never should have watched that show.*

"Just give me a few moments so I can change," I say.

I turn, but Maya grabs my arm.

"Oh, no!" she says. "You look way too cute to change. You have to go out like this. I insist. A local elf in her Christmas hometown. It's perfect, right, Benjie?"

I have an impulse to push Maya into the set of candy canes, but children are watching, and the image of an impaled former Miss Michigan might leave a lasting mark on their Christmas memories.

"Right," Benjie concurs.

"Then let me just grab my purse," I say with a smile.

As I head to the office, I finally power on my cell. An endless stream of texts and messages appear.

Call me!

Call me NOW!

Where are you?

Benjie & Maya are on their way to Frankenmuth!

I'm sorry I've been MIA. I'm just so upset and disappointed, but I don't want you to be caught unaware.

When I come to Bea's last text, I don't know whether to laugh or cry.

Run!

Although it's much too late to flee, and I might not make it out of dinner alive, I'm relieved that Bea is finally responding.

At least I might have someone left to plan my funeral.

26

Benjie insisted on driving, so I am stuck in the back of his Land Rover feeling like a sullen teenager who's had a huge fight with her parents right before a family dinner.

My mind whirs as I mentally try to play out how I will navigate this nightmare.

Benjie is eerily silent, but he keeps glancing at me in the mirror, his eyes flashing with anger.

"That little shopping area looks like you're visiting the Swiss Alps, doesn't it?" I ask, hoping my perkiness will outweigh my panic.

"What's that?" Maya asks.

"The glockenspiel," I say, tapping on the window.

The two look out at the beautiful clock tower illuminated in the snow.

"It puts on a live show with moving figurines that tell the tale of the Pied Piper," I add.

Benjie slows the car, and for a second, I think they are enchanted by Frankenmuth's Bavarian beauty.

"Isn't that about a bunch of rats?" Benjie asks.

I gulp.

"It's so *provincial*," Maya says.

Something inside me flames.

Growing up here, I feel as if it's okay for me to say Frankenmuth can feel a bit too small-town, but it's not okay for an outsider to say it.

"It's not provincial, Maya," I say, my voice tight and testy. "If I'm not mistaken, didn't you grow up in Jackson, Michigan?"

Maya's head spins like an alarmed owl, her eyes big, flashing anger.

"And I got out," she said. "Just like you."

As if on cue, the bells chime.

My soul, for the first time, seems to be in sync with them, rather than discordant.

As the bells ring, I feel a rush of emotions: guilt, sadness, clarity.

But mostly I feel truth ring inside me.

I open my mouth to respond when Benjie says, "I made reservations for dinner at the famous chicken restaurant. Should make for a fun night."

His voice drips with sarcasm.

I sigh.

At least I will have Sofie as my literal wing woman to protect me.

Benjie parks downtown, and when we all get out, I head across the street to Z's.

"Where are you going?" Benjie asks, pointing. "I made reservations here."

My stomach drops.

"You made reservations at Clausen's Chicken Haus?" I ask.

"Yeah? Why?"

"You said the famous chicken restaurant."

"Aren't they both famous?" he asks. "They both say they are."

"C'mon!" Maya calls, rushing for the door. "I'm freezing."

I text Sofie as I baby step across the street.

Save me! I'm having dinner with my boss at Clausen's. He knows I haven't told my father. It's going to be a nightmare.

P.S. I'm dressed as the Wegner's elf.

Dots undulate.

Don't lose your cool.

I make it to the door when my cell lights up again.

P.S. The costume still fits you?

I take a deep breath and open the door.

"Reservations for three," I hear Benjie telling the hostess when we enter. "Tolliver."

"Right this way, sir."

Now is the one time in my life I would like to be invisible. I would like no one to see me, notice me, be aware of my existence.

And yet that is impossible because—as I pass by a large mirror in the entryway and see my face morph into horror—I am dressed like an elf.

The movie *Legally Blonde* springs suddenly to mind, specifically the scene when Reese Witherspoon's character gets duped into believing she has been invited to a costume party, and she shows up in a bunny costume.

That's exactly the way I feel right now.

Except *way* older and *way* less hot than Elle Woods did in her costume.

As we're led to our table, every head in the restaurant turns to watch me.

I jingle.

People snap photos. Children point. Waiters nearly trip.

When we're seated, Maya grins. "Told you it would be fun to wear that out tonight."

I want to crawl under the tablecloth, bash her in the kneecaps and burrow my way out of here.

"Would anyone care to start with a cocktail?" the waitress asks when she arrives.

"Oh, yes," I say. "I'm going to need many, many cocktails."

Benjie and Maya order glasses of a popular German Riesling. The waitress looks at me.

"Ma'am?"

"Double vodka on the rocks."

Benjie smiles. "The lady is going to need a strong drink."

Maya is still eyeing me warily after our car confrontation, and I know I must keep her happy to make Benjie happy.

I also know I must dance for as long as I can to avoid the inevitable confrontation with Benjie.

"How is the TaterTot Toys closure proceeding?" I ask Maya. "I've seen it everywhere in the trades."

I'm guessing here. I haven't looked at the *Wall Street Journal*, *Bloomberg* or *Crain's Business* in days.

She smiles.

"Thank you for asking, Henri. It's going very smoothly. We should be wrapped up by year's end, and I expect we'll exceed my closing profit projection by about seven percent."

It feels like there is a lump stuck in my throat, and I swallow, then take a big drink of water.

"That's just, um, amazing, Maya."

"It is, isn't it?" Benjie asks. "At least someone is doing their job. Maya killed it this year."

Killed it.

I can clearly picture the closing of the original TaterTot Toys office, manufacturing plant and department store in Gatlinburg, Tennessee, all of those people out of work on Christmas Day.

I can see the toys being made at a massive manufacturing plant overseas.

I can see the little department store downtown being turned into a mattress showroom or Starbuck's.

I can see the faces of those who are out of work and didn't even see it coming at all because of corporate greed, all because someone could make a bigger profit on a toy when the actual windfall is simply seeing the joy on the face of the child who receives it on Christmas morning and the happiness of the parents who worked so hard to put it under the tree.

And over this movie in mind, there is a soundtrack. One of my grandmother's favorite Christmas songs by Dolly Parton is playing. *Lord, it's like a hard-candy Christmas.*

Our drinks arrive, and I polish off half my cocktail in one gulp to calm my nerves.

"Are you ready to order?" the waitress asks.

"We gotta do the All-You-Can-Eat World Famous Chicken Dinner, right?" Benjie asks. "When in Rome."

Benjie reads from the menu. "'Heaping platters of golden chicken, bountiful bowls of mashed potatoes, dressing, egg noodles.' I mean, I feel like I'm getting off a horse and buggy for Christmas dinner at Grandma's in the 1850s. Strap on the feedbag!"

The waitress finishes jotting on her pad.

"I'll be right back with all of the appetizers that are part of the family platters," she says. "Creamy cabbage salad, homemade cranberry relish, cheese spread with garlic toast, homemade chicken pâté, freshly baked breads and whole fruit preserves."

"I'll be full before dinner," Maya says, running her hand over her taut tummy. "We might have to run in the snow in the morning, babe."

I tap my glass at the waitress.

"I'm gonna need one more."

She gives me an *Are you sure?* look. I nod.

"She's gonna need it," Benjie says.

"I'll be right back."

Benjie looks around the restaurant.

"Wouldn't this actually be a great idea?" he asks. "Buy these dueling chicken restaurants and franchise them across America, sort of like a chicken-themed, northern version of Cracker Barrel?"

I think of Sofie and our quaint little downtown filled with only small, independent, family-run stores—woolen mills, cheese and old-fashioned candy shops, Christmas stores and chicken restaurants—being turned into yet another big-box store, cookie-cutter town filled with the same things and zero personality.

I strum my fingers on the glass, buying time but also remembering. I lift my head.

"Did you ever have a TaterTot Toy?" I ask.

"No," Maya says with a laugh. "How old do you think I am?"

"When I was a little girl—before there were cell phones and Amazon—there were these big Christmas catalogs that would come every year from Sears, JCPenney and Montgomery Ward called wish catalogs. They were as big as a Buick and contained every toy, game and article of clothing any boy or girl could ever dream of wanting for Christmas." I smile at Maya and Benjie. "My grandmother would give me a red marker, and my brother a green marker and tell us to circle every item in that catalog that we wished to receive from Santa for Christmas. 'Point arrows at them, too, so he'll make sure to see,' she told us."

I take a big sip of my drink.

"Then, a few weeks before Christmas, we'd return those catalogs to my grandma, and my parents and grandparents would take us to see Santa at Tingleman's department store." I turn and point out the window to where it used to be. "It's closed now. My father built the holiday throne you had your picture taken on for Tingleman's. We kept it in order to continue their legacy in our store. My dad wanted everyone who entered to feel like family, just like we did when we walked in Tingleman's."

"What's your point, Henri?" Benjie asks.

"Anyway," I say, "I would whisper every gift I wanted from those wish books into Santa's ear, and then my family would eat a big chicken dinner just like we're having tonight. One of the gifts I wanted as a little girl was a TaterTot Toy. I don't know if you even know this, but they were cloth dolls with plastic heads, and they were the size of a real baby with the most adorable faces and big dimples. They looked like potato babies, and their bodies were all chubby and sewn with little stitches that looked like potato eyes. The amazing thing about these dolls, though, was that each one came with its own history and name, like Spud, Yam, Murphy or Tater. You got papers with each doll as if you were adopting it. That made it all even more special, because each little girl felt like each TaterTot was actually hers. You wanted to care for it as if it were your own, real baby."

"Did you get one for Christmas?" Maya asks.

"I did. Her name was Small Fry because she was tinier than the other dolls. Her papers said she was a fighter because she was smaller than most and had to work hard to survive. She had blond hair just like me and wore the most adorable overalls with a gingham shirt. I remember she came in a box wrapped in red foil paper with a big gold bow. I cried when I opened the box and saw her. I carried that doll everywhere for years, to dinner, to bed, to school. She was my best friend until Sofie came along."

I realize that Maya and Benjie are just staring at me now.

"Maybe you should tell the new company to make adult TaterTot dolls called *Vodka*," Benjie says, nodding at my glass. "Get it? Potatoes."

Maya laughs. "I will. What a great idea, babe."

"I know it seems like I've gone down memory lane here, but the reason I'm telling you this is because all of these places—Wegner's, this restaurant, TaterTot Toys, Tingleman's—have a history. It seems a shame that it's all simply being erased."

Benjie shakes his head at me.

"Okay, enough BS and stalling here, Henri. I appreciate the tour down memory lane, but the point is you're trying to prevent that," he says. "You're here to protect your family history. By convincing your father to sell to Vance, you're protecting your past *and* securing your future." Benjie cocks his head at me and pierces me with those unflinching eyes. "But you haven't even brought that up with your father yet, have you, Henri? Do you care to explain?"

"I just need a little more time," I say. "I don't know if my parents are ready."

"I don't give a damn if they're ready! I'm ready!"

Benjie slams the table with his hand. I sit up, eyes wide. People turn to stare.

"Time is up, Henri," Benjie says, leaning across the table. "You've gone soft on me, Hart Henri, and you know I don't like soft."

Just quit, Henri. Right now. You know the right thing to do.

I think of what my parents just said, though.

Is this the right time for them to sell?

"You all ready to move into Henri's corner office, Maya?"

Maya beams. "It's time for a remodel," she says. Maya shoots me an *I win!* glance, which infuriates me to the core.

"Just a little more time," I beg. "Please."

Benjie smiles.

"Either I have a signed deal by Christmas Eve, or you're fired. Got it, Henri?"

"Henri Wegner?"

Hannah Clausen is standing over Benjie's shoulder.

She is staring at me, even more intensely than Benjie was.

How much did she overhear?

"Hannah!" I exclaim. "Hi. It's good to see you. Um, this is my boss, Benjie Tolliver, and my colleague Maya Jenkins."

"It's nice to meet you," Benjie says. "Great restaurant. Atmosphere is so…vintage."

Maya notices Hannah's dirndl.

"Does everyone in this town dress in costume?" she asks.

"We're proud of our history and heritage around here," Hannah says. She turns to me. "It's been a long time, Henri. It's nice to have you home at Christmas."

"It's nice to be home," I say. "How are the kids?"

"Big," she answers, smiling. "Happy."

"That's good," I say. "How have you been?"

She scans her restaurant, as if considering my question.

"The holidays are busy around here and filled with a lot of mixed emotions," she says. "As you well know."

I nod.

"How have *you* been?" she asks.

She emphasizes *you* as if she can see into my soul.

"Busy," I echo. "A lot of mixed emotions."

Hannah eyes Benjie and then me. I cannot tell what she's thinking. I cannot tell what she's heard. My heart is thumping in my eyeballs.

"Well, you haven't changed," she says, reaching out to touch my elf cap and jingle the bell. "At all."

I smile and nod at her dirndl.

"Frankenmuth forever!"

She laughs and then leans over to me and whispers, "We need to talk."

She hands her cell to me.

"Put your number in, and I'll get in touch."

I nod and do as requested.

A group of dirndl-wearing servers appears with platters of food.

"Oh," Hannah says in a chipper voice. "Your meal has arrived! Enjoy Clausen's famous chicken dinner, and—on behalf of my staff—I wish you a Merry Christmas."

Hannah moves off to another table to greet a group of diners.

She heard everything.

She is going to blackmail me. She still holds a grudge. My goose is cooked.

Or, rather, my chicken is fried.

I feel like I'm in shock.

Complete and utter shock.

Benjie puts a forkful of cabbage salad in his mouth, and then grabs a slice of bread from the basket—still hot and steaming—and layers a spoonful of blackberry preserves atop it.

"This is so good," he says. Benjie stuffs the piece of bread in his mouth and looks at me. "A real down-home meal. I can feel the Christmas spirit. Can't you, Henri?"

He makes the simplest sentiments feel like a threat.

Hannah seemed to do the same.

Our waitress appears.

"Your cocktail, ma'am."

"Thank you," I manage to say. "You have impeccable timing."

27

Wegner's Silent Night Memorial Chapel is—fittingly—completely, utterly silent.

The snow has stopped, and the skies have cleared. Through the round window over the chancel, stars twinkle, and the moon makes it feel as bright as day.

Somehow, I made it through dinner, feeling as if my soul had died and only the shell of my body remained, washed up on the shore like an empty mollusk.

Benjie and Maya dropped me off at Wegner's after dinner, Benjie stuffed on chicken and the knowledge that he had me dangled over a fryer.

I could not go home to face my father, so I texted him saying I was staying at Sofie's for a girl's night and then texted Sofie saying that everything went surprisingly well with Benjie.

Lies, lies and more lies.

Somehow, I found myself walking down 25 Christmas Lane before noticing the lamppost-lined walkway displaying "Silent Night" in over three hundred languages.

When I looked up, I was standing outside the chapel.

I pulled out my key, let myself in and took a seat in one of the pews.

All alone.

A large Advent wreath, star and crown hang from the ceiling. A Swiss crucifix—presented as a gift to my father and carved in 1818, the same year "Silent Night" was first sung with a guitar—sits on a mantel behind the altar.

Gert carved an angel as well as an inscription on the altar in German: *Friede den Menschen auf Erden die einer guten Willen sind.* "Glory to God in the highest and peace to His people on earth."

My mother and father went on a European buying trip when I was a girl and discovered the St. Nicholas chapel in Oberndorf, Austria. The chapel is famous for being the place where "Silent Night" was written, and played for the first time in 1818, accompanied by a guitar.

People in town thought my father had lost his marbles when he set out to re-create an octagonal replica of the church on a piece of land next to Wegner's. My dad believed this fifty-six-foot-tall landmark nestled on nearly thirty acres of landscaped grounds would not only remind visitors of the real meaning of Christmas but also welcome them to Michigan's "Little Bavaria" as they entered Frankenmuth.

Of course, "Stille Nacht," or "Silent Night," became one of the most beloved Christmas hymns in the world and has been translated into more languages than any other religious holiday song.

The year after "Silent Night" was performed in St. Nicholas Church, an organ builder brought the song to his home in another province of Austria, and the Strasser and Rainer folk singers included the song in their concerts, helping the carol spread throughout Europe.

In 1839, the Rainers brought "Silent Night" to the US when they sang it in front of Wall Street's Trinity Church in New York City.

Today, the song is ever present at Christmas, and people from around the world come to this little chapel to visit, meditate and pray. My father has never charged a penny for admission.

Every year on Christmas Eve, at exactly 3:00 p.m., my father breaks from working at Wegner's to lead an annual sing-along of "Silent Night." Hundreds attend the ceremony.

Each and every moment of my father's life has been defined by a dream, faith, family, hard work and believing in the good in the world and mankind.

I zip up my coat and stare at the pots of poinsettias that line the little chapel.

What traditions do I have in my own life, separate from my family?

I mean, Bea had to force me to put up a tree and decorations.

What traditions will I continue when my immediate family is gone?

I take for granted that my family won't be here forever. But who will be the conduit—in life, holidays, traditions, business—that will keep that legacy going?

Finn has his own family. At dinner the other night with Clare and Ethan, I felt a bit like a stranger to the teenager. He knows his aunt Henri, but I'm really just someone who sends birthday cards and passes through his life on occasion. When Ethan has children, will Aunt Henri even be a part of that, or a distant star?

Who will lead the sing-along?

Will Wegner's weather the changing of the guard?

Will I?

Bea's words return to me in the quiet:

You need your parents…

Bea is right: one day, they will be gone. What will be the legacy of my father's company in the hands of Vance? And what will my legacy be without my family?

Soon, Bea might be gone, too.

I could be totally, utterly, deservedly alone in the universe.

I stare through the window and into the silent night.

When this chapel was being built, my father used to come

here and pray. One December day, I sneaked inside and watched him kneel on snow in front of two-by-fours, his head bent before rafters.

There was still no roof on the chapel, and snow was falling inside.

"What are you praying for, Daddy?" I asked.

There was a large construction blanket nearby, and my father shook it off and put it beside him. He patted the blanket, and I knelt beside him.

"I just pray I have done the right thing," my father said. "I am praying that I am not a selfish man. I am praying for my family."

"Why?" I asked.

My father looked around the chapel.

"I am a simple man, Henri. A husband. A father. An accountant. But I have always had this dream—this vision—to bring Christmas to life for people. To show them the true beauty and magic of Christmas, the reason for Christmas." My father stopped, and his voice broke. "I fear that pride has gotten the best of me. I fear that I am no longer humble. I fear that I have let my family down. I fear that this father has let his Father down."

I put my arm around my father's back and patted it like he did mine when I was scared or upset.

"Doesn't the Bible say that God speaks to us in visions and dreams?"

My father turned his head to look at me. His face, sad, changed to surprise. "That's right." He nodded.

"I think we should listen to our dreams," I said. "Otherwise, we just wander through this life. Right?"

My father shook his head at me.

"My brilliant Henri," he said. "What would I do without you?"

I lay down on the cold, hard wood and faced reality.

"Help me, God," I say. "I am a simple woman. I fear that

pride has gotten the best of me. I fear that I am no longer humble. I fear that I have let my family down. I fear that I have let my father—and You—down."

I clamp my eyes shut and weep.

In the silence, I hear a voice.

It is mine.

Returning home, after all these years.

I think we should listen to our dreams. We should listen to God. Otherwise, we just wander through this life.

And then I fall asleep on the pew.

I dream that I am standing before the glockenspiel, and I am living inside it as one of the figurines. The bells chime. I come out as the Pied Piper of Hamelin. At first, I lead all of the rats out of town, all of whom have faces just like mine.

The gathered crowd cheers.

When I return to collect my money, the mayor balks. I grow angry and lead all the children from Frankenmuth. All of the children are my Frankenmuth friends and family: Sofie, Shep, Mouse, Finn, Clare, Ethan, Mom and Dad, Hannah.

I lead them out of town, into Wegner's, where they steal every Christmas ornament.

The town boos.

One little girl is left behind.

Her voice rings out through the town.

"If we could only remember the real meaning of Christmas," she says. "I was left behind to remind you."

The doors open, and the little girl appears.

It is me.

The town cheers.

I jump awake.

I open my eyes just in time to see a shooting star flash across the sky.

28

December 21

I am in the middle of another dream: a strange woman is standing over me, staring, watching me drool.

"Gah!" I yelp, sitting up much too quickly.

I wipe my mouth.

This is not a dream.

"Are you okay?" the woman asks.

"What time is it?" I ask.

The woman looks at her watch.

"Nine a.m."

"No!"

I sit up and look around, my back aching, my neck sounding like a movie popcorn machine.

The pain is real.

The Silent Night Memorial Chapel is filling with tourists, all gathered around, staring at the crazy woman who's passed out inside.

People lift their cell phones and snap pictures of me.

I realize I am still dressed as an elf.

"I'm the fourth wise man," I say, trying to make a joke.

"Shecky. I was sent from the North Pole, got lost on the way to the manger and ended up here."

A woman in the back laughs. "Bet it wasn't a silent night, though, was it, Shecky?" she asks with a wink, her voice much too loud and echoing off the walls. "And bet that manger turned out to be a bar."

"You get me, ma'am," I say.

A man walks up to me, kneels, lifts his cell and takes a photo. "Elf on a shelf!" he crows. "Live and in person!"

I stand.

Well, *stand* is a generous verb.

I crouch. And groan. Then try to move.

"Ow!"

A woman in her fifties cannot sleep on a pew.

I grab my purse and take three steps forward but end up moving like a mummy.

The sun blinds me when I walk outside.

It is a crystal clear, freezing December day in Michigan. The sky is so blue, the snow so white, that I can barely see.

I zip up my coat and reach for my mittens.

I can feel my phone vibrate when I do.

There is an endless stream of text messages.

From Dad:

Are you okay?

From Mom:

Where are you?

And Finn:

Hello?

Bea:

On pins and needles here. What happened? How did it go? I'm so sorry. About everything. I tried to warn you!

I race to my car, turn on the engine and crank the heat.

I answer all the texts, relieved my father didn't get too suspicious.

The date on my cell glows before my eyes.

December 21.

I only have a few days to decide my and my family's fate.

Otherwise, I will forever be the town rat.

29

I race home to shower, letting the hot water soak my lower back. I stand there forever.

I turn off the hot water only when I'm able to move without wincing.

I grab the blow dryer and turn it on high, pointing it directly at the mirror to dissipate the fog. The fan in my childhood bathroom has never worked well, and—even after all these years—my father has yet to change it.

Slowly, my image comes into focus.

I look around the bathroom. The blue ceramic dolphin I bought when we went on vacation to Florida still sits on the shelf underneath the window next to the pink conch shell I found on the beach. Some of my girlish perfumes still rest on a pretty tray in the corner of the vanity: Love's Baby Soft, Opium, Obsession and a slew of Designer Imposters.

My mother may have turned my bedroom into her "library," but the bathroom not been touched since I left. I wonder…

Is it still here?

I open a vanity drawer, moving a pile of towels aside.

I laugh.

There, in the back, is my Lady Schick Speed Styler with

comb attachment, the one Farrah Fawcett used and was spokeswoman for, the one that gave her those famous "flippy curls."

I pull the dryer free from the back of the cabinet. I unplug my hair dryer and plug hers into the wall.

Nothing.

I take two steps toward the trash can and hover the hair dryer over it, but I cannot part with it. Instead, I return it to the cabinet and cover it with a pile of towels.

As I dry my hair, I stare at my reflection.

I am no longer a little girl.

But many days—like when the snow is newly fallen, the spring wind warm, the pools are packed on a July day and I smell Coppertone and hear pop music…

I cock my head as the glockenspiel echoes in the woods.

When the bells chime, I am still a girl, no different than I was decades ago.

I begin to put on my makeup.

I grew up without makeup tutorials on TikTok or a nearby Ulta. I grew up with Sofie, studying photos of Cyndi Lauper and Madonna while holding a tray of blue eye shadow saying, "Trust me."

Memories are like that dolphin, that shell, that perfume, that Farrah hair dryer.

Some you just cannot let go even if the girl is no longer a girl.

You hold on to them for a reason.

I can remember picking up that shell on the beach as if it were yesterday.

Something behind it catches my eye.

I walk over. There is a red ribbon wrapped around the dolphin and other trinkets from my childhood. It is a bit dusty. I pick it up and smile. It's a sash that reads Christmas Court 1985 in a pretty scroll.

I was nominated for Christmas Queen, along with Sofie and Hannah. We all wanted to win, but I sort of knew I would win May Queen, and Sofie would win Christmas Ball Queen. Whereas Homecoming was based on beauty and May Queen on history, Christmas Queen was based on personality, and Sofie was friends with everyone. She won.

After the ceremony, my father hugged me and whispered, "You will always be my Christmas Prinzessin."

I place the sash back on the shelf and return to the mirror. I stare as if seeing myself for the first time.

As I turn to leave the bathroom, my cell vibrates.

Meet me under the Holz Brücke at 3 p.m. We need to talk.

It's Hannah's number.

It's all over.

I start to head out of the bathroom again, but the red sash catches my eye again, and another memory—long forgotten—comes flooding back into my mind. My heart cracks.

For some reason, I turn back around and douse myself in Love's Baby Soft, the perfume of my teen years, hoping the familiar scent might help bridge the looming battle I have coming with Hannah.

30

"Under the bridge?" Sofie asks. "What is she, Bavarian mafia?"

Sofie's eyes grow large. She is in the kitchen making her family's egg noodles alongside the chef and other staff, and flour dances in the air around her.

"What should I do?" I ask.

"Don't worry. I'll drag the river for your body."

"Seriously, Sofie, she overheard Benjie. She knows *everything.* I'm worried she's going to tell my father to get revenge on me. Or use it against me in some way. She's always held a grudge against me."

"Okay, okay," Sofie says. She finishes the batch, wipes her hands on her apron and says to the kitchen staff, "I have to deal with an emergency. My best friend is about to be murdered. I'll be back in five."

Hilariously, not a single person in Sofie's kitchen bats an eye, flinches a muscle or gives her proclamation a second thought.

I follow Sofie into the vestibule that separates the bar from the restaurant.

"What should I do?" I ask again.

We take a seat on a floral bench that sits before the restaurant's wide front windows. I can't help but glance across the street to see if Hannah is watching.

"She's as busy as we are with the lunchtime rush," Sofie says. "She's not coming for you. Yet."

"You're not helping."

"Just listen to what she has to say, Henri," Sofie says, her voice instantly calm. "She's different, I swear. When she let me hug her a couple of weeks ago, it was like she needed a friend." Sofie stops. "No, it was like she needed a parent to hold her. She seemed like a scared kid. I think the divorce changed her and Shep deeply."

A cat suddenly races by on the sidewalk.

"Did you see that?"

I nod.

"We have these feral cats that show up every Christmas when it starts to get really cold outside and busy inside," she says. "They come to the back of our restaurant after lunch and dinner for food. They know the routine—we feed them the chicken scraps and give them water, but whenever we try to pet them or take them inside, they run. They want love. They just don't know how to show it or accept it. They're too scared they'll just get hurt again. Even though they have a pack around them, their instinct is to survive on their own." Sofie stops and looks at me. "Hannah reminds me of these feral cats."

"You're making me not hate her."

"I don't think she hates you, Henri. I think she's wounded and trying to heal. Just hear her out, okay?"

Sofie takes my hand in hers.

"Okay," I say.

She stands and claps her hands together.

"I gotta get back to work," she says. "I know you're just here for the free chicken and advice anyway. I'm a way better deal than Lucy's nickel psychiatric counseling in *Peanuts*, aren't I?"

"You're the second person who's given me very sound therapy advice based on *Peanuts*," I say.

"Cartoons and Christmas," she says. "Welcome to Frankenmuth!"

She puts her arm around my back.

"Now come eat some fried chicken and buttered egg noodles," Sofie says. "Mama's cookin' will make it all better."

31

This is where it ends, I think. *How fitting. Under a bridge, just like Benjie hinted.* Game of Thrones *style.*

Hannah is seated on a knoll below the bridge. In the spring and summer, it's green and grassy, and kids sit with their feet dangling over the edge—the bridge a few feet above and the river a few feet below—and toss rocks into the water.

The area is protected from the bridge in the winter, and the heat from the passing cars keeps the knoll snow free.

I slow as I approach.

Hannah is still so pretty. While I'm, well, to continue the analogy, *Game of Thrones* icy, Hannah is all-American adorable.

I take a seat beside her, wincing slightly, my back still aching, and dangle my legs over the edge.

It will just make it easier for her to push me in the river and get it all over with.

"Hey, Hannah."

She looks up.

"Do you know why I asked you to meet me here?"

No nonsense.

"I have my ideas," I say.

She laughs softly.

"This is where I used to come and hide," she says, her voice pensive. "While everyone else was up there, I was down here. My dad couldn't find me."

The memory I had earlier comes flashing into my head.

After Sofie was crowned Christmas Ball Queen, there was a photo on the front page of the *Frankenmuth News*. I am standing beside Sofie, my mouth open, cheering for my friend. Hannah is on the other side of Sofie, her eyes looking the other way, as if searching the crowd.

There, at the edge of the photo, was her father, face gnarled in anger, his disappointment and humiliation at her loss etched—completely unedited—for the world to see.

I knew her dad was a disciplinarian. My father said he was a tough businessman, and I know my father tended to avoid him, but I don't think I ever realized how bad it was until I saw that sash again, until this very moment. Even though she won Homecoming Queen, nothing was ever good enough.

"Did you ever wonder why I was so mean to you in school?" she continues. "Because that's how I was treated at home. Looking back now, I was jealous of what you had, Henri."

"Me? What?"

Hannah shakes her head.

"You had an idyllic life, Henri. You had a good father, you had a best friend, you had an amazing boyfriend." Hannah plucks a rock off the ground and tosses it into the Cass River. "I lashed out because I wanted to hurt you, even a little, just to make you feel what it was like to be me even if for just a second."

"Hannah," I start.

"No, let me finish," she says, looking at me. "There's a point to all of this, I promise."

I swallow and take a deep breath.

She continues. "I think that's why I went after Shep after you two broke up. I wanted to hurt you again. But I also thought he and I could fix each other. I thought he could heal all my pain, and I thought I could erase his heartache over you. But no one person can save another. That's too much pressure. That's too much expectation. And expectations are just preconceived resentments." She looks at me and winks. "My therapist taught me that."

"I never realized all you were going through," I say. "I'm sorry. I never meant to ruin your fire baton routine…"

"Yes, you did," she laughs. "And I probably deserved it." She waits until I look at her. "I overheard what your boss said to you at the restaurant."

Hannah puts her hand on my back.

Time to go in the drink.

"Bullies bully," she continues, rubbing my back sweetly. "I'm truly sorry for being one and hurting you. But bullies turn innocent people into replicas of themselves, and the bullying won't stop until you stand up for yourself."

I do a double take at Hannah.

"Your boss is like my father. You get so used to the abuse that you think you become immune to it, but you don't. You simply become a shell of a human, shutting out the world and all your emotions, and then one day you realize you're a bad person, too. You forget the person you were, the person you want to be. You put a Band-Aid on your heart, but it's not enough to heal a lifetime of hurt."

I think of what Shep said, and another memory dances into my mind.

This time, I'm in first grade. I am crying because I fell over one of my father's stupid stacks of wood he left in my grandparents' basement, hit my head and had to wear a big bandage on my forehead the day of our elementary school Christmas concert. Mrs. Hartley, our teacher, tried to console me, to no avail.

That's when Hannah came over and stood beside me. She

was sporting a Band-Aid on her forehead, too, with little Santas all over it.

"Everyone will think we both got boo-boos," she said.

Hannah and I *were* once friends. Hannah and I both still have big boo-boos.

"You're so right," I say.

"Your boss...what's his name?"

"Benjie," I say.

"Well, Benjie's a Christmas ham," Hannah says. "Actually, no. He's a Christmas ass. Why do we women still put up with that misogynistic crap? I'm sure he treats you differently than he does his male counterparts."

I nod, thinking of me, Maya and Bea.

"I'm sure he says, 'But I'm giving you a chance... Do it the way a man does... Follow my rules.' No, we get to make the rules for once. Remember when you were president of Holiday Land?"

I smile and nod. "I do."

"That's what we need today," Hannah says. "We need to lead with heart, kindness and empathy. My father believed that was weakness, but it's our true strength. Can I ask you a question?"

"Yes."

"What power does he have over you?"

"My job," I say. "My career. My success. My financial stability."

"You already have all of that," Hannah says. "C'mon, Henri, the only thing he has over you is that you're still seeking his acceptance, and you have to ask yourself why. That's all on you. All you're missing is a little bit of self-worth, and Henri Wegner has owned that her whole life. What happened?"

"I lost myself to my career."

"No, you lost you, Henri," Hannah says. "So did I. Your father gave you all the self-worth in the world, and you just—" she plucks another rock and tosses it into the middle of the river, where the water is still flowing between the ice, little waves rippling outward "—threw it away."

Hannah continues, "My dad never believed I could do anything as well as he did," she says. "He was always disappointed in me. He used to say, 'Jakob Wegner had a girl, but he named her after a boy, and she sure acts as tough as one.' He had to die before I could finally see myself. Isn't that sad? And by then, I'd ruined a marriage. I didn't want to ruin my kids, too. I had to start believing in myself, and I finally did. My restaurant is all women owned and operated. And it's never been more successful. I just don't want to waste another Christmas being mad and sad."

"I'm so proud of you, Hannah."

She grabs my hand.

"I wanted to prove my dad wrong, Henri," she says, her voice now as strong as the river. "Your dad just wants you to prove him right. There's no greater difference in the world."

I lean in to hug her, and we hold each other in the shadow of the Holz Brücke.

Part Five

32

Christmas Eve

I click on the kitchen lights and tiptoe to the fridge.

I pull out a carton of eggs and then retrieve corn syrup, granulated sugar and vanilla from the cupboard.

Simple ingredients for a simple candy.

I pull a bowl from the stand mixer, crack an egg and carefully strain the white from the yolk.

When I finish, I leave the egg whites alone. It's vital they sit for about a half hour in order to come to room temperature.

I pull three baking sheets from the drawer underneath the oven. This midcentury drawer always sticks for some reason, and I have to give it a big tug to make it pop open. I grab the sheets and stand too quickly, my back still in pain from my night sleeping on a pew in an elf costume.

I rub my lower back—trying to stretch left, right—and silently groan. I retrieve wax paper from my parents' catchall drawer and line the baking sheets then bend—very slowly this time—to retrieve a heavy saucepan from beneath the stovetop.

I combine the sugar, water and corn syrup and begin to bring it to a boil. While the pot heats, I pull a bottle of aspirin from my parents' vitamin bin housed in my grandmother's old bread box and down two tablets with a big glass of water.

I return to the stove, stirring the mixture constantly with an old wooden spoon to dissolve the sugar.

The methodical rhythm calms me immediately, like it did washing wool with Shep.

My eye catches the bending branch in the McCoy vase.

Over the last few days, buds have formed.

I hear a jingling, and I look over to see Mabel—with every ounce of strength and willpower she has—make it up the stairs into the kitchen and trot over to me, yawning, tail wagging.

"You'd follow me anywhere, wouldn't you, girl?" I ask.

I lean down and kiss her head.

There is a large pouf over by the table. She totters over and—instead of lying down—falls in a heap. Within moments, she's asleep.

I shut my eyes and listen to her snore.

What is it about a dog's snore that makes you feel safe?

"I want you to live forever," I say to her.

She opens her eyes, looks at me and sighs.

I wave at her, and she falls asleep again.

I turn and stare at the bread box as I continue to stir.

My grandmother used to make divinity every Christmas.

In the middle of the night as Christmas Eve turned to Christmas morning.

I caught her one night when I was staying at her house. My father was working all night long in their basement, and our family came and stayed with my grandparents. I woke to try to catch Santa coming down their chimney. I sneaked downstairs in my footed pajamas and hid in the old telephone nook in the hallway.

The nook was a little cubby about half the size of a powder room. There was a chintz curtain that my grandma would snap shut like a magician when she was on the phone with her friend Erma. I did the same when I talked to Sofie.

A black rotary phone sat atop a little white floating desk that was built into the wall. A tiny wood chair with a spindle back and rattan seat that was as comfortable as bricks was pushed under the desk. The desk held a framed family photo, an old-fashioned telephone index that flipped open, a notepad and a pen. A vintage schoolhouse light was mounted above the desk to illuminate the tiny area, as was a framed needlepoint my grandmother made of the front of her home surrounded by snow-flocked pines that read:

No matter how distant
The highways we roam
Our thoughts use the highway
That leads back to Home

Instead of catching Santa, I caught my grandma making divinity in the middle of the night, humming holiday songs.

Actually, she caught me.

Christmas 1976

"What are you doing wide awake, young lady?"

My grandma threw open the curtain to find me seated on the chair, legs curled beneath me.

"Waiting for Santa," I said.

"You missed him," my grandma said. "He's already been."

I raced out of the cubby, through the kitchen and into the living room.

"Did he eat the cookies we left him? Drink the milk?"

The plate we had left out reading Santa's Cookies only had crumbs left, and the glass of milk was empty.

"What about the carrots for the reindeer?"

My grandma pointed.

Only the green tops remained on the plate with Rudolph's glowing nose.

I turned.

The tree was engulfed in beautifully wrapped gifts.

"What did he say?" I yelled. "Did he look like Santa?"

"Shhh," my grandma said. "You'll wake up the whole house."

"Did he?"

My grandma laughed. "Yes, he looked just like Santa. C'mon. Might as well help me if you're up."

I followed her into the kitchen.

"Want some hot chocolate?" she asked. "Or do I even have to ask?"

"Yeah!"

"Shhh," she admonished again.

My grandma poured some milk into a pot to heat, and she stirred it with one hand as she stirred another pot with her other.

"What are you making?"

"Divinity."

"Yum!"

"Line those baking sheets with wax paper," she said, nodding at everything lined up on her narrow, aqua-blue Formica countertops.

I watched her boil the sugar and then pour it over the egg whites, beating them until they made candy. Then I helped her drop heaping teaspoons of the mix onto the baking sheets.

I grabbed a tray and headed toward the oven.

"No," my grandma said. "We don't bake these, remember? They just sit. We just let them set like this."

As she made my hot chocolate, I whispered, "*Lots* of marshmallows," and my grandma made it rain atop my mug. She patted a chair at the dinette set in the corner of the kitchen, and we took a seat.

"You know you should be asleep," my grandma said.

"So should you," I said.

She nodded and chuckled, grabbed a napkin and wiped my mouth.

"I think," she said, "you're going to turn into a big marshmallow when you grow up."

I giggled.

"Why *are* you awake?" I asked.

She looked at me and then at the drying divinity.

"Lots of memories at Christmas," she said. "Did you know my mom and dad—your great-grandparents who you never met—were dirt-poor?" she asked.

I shook my head.

"We never got much for Christmas," my grandma continued. "Some fruit in our stocking..."

"Fruit?" I wrinkled my face in disgust.

"Yes, fruit," she said. "And usually one special gift that my grandma sewed for us. A pretty sweater, or maybe a coin purse my dad made, on which he'd tool a beautiful flower. But the thing we looked most forward to was her Christmas cookies and candy. Oh, she was the best baker in the world. Her snickerdoodles and frosted sugar cookies were the hit of the annual church Christmas bake sale."

My grandma just sat there, shaking her head.

"But I knew times were really tough when she made divinity."

"How come?"

"It only requires a few simple ingredients," my grandma explained. "Eggs, sugar, water, corn syrup, things she always had in her pantry. I woke up just like you did one Christmas Eve looking for Santa, and I caught my mom making divinity. She said, 'We may not have much, but my family will always have candy on Christmas.' Then she knelt down and looked me right in the eye. 'My family will always have joy on Christmas.'"

One tear popped out of my grandma's eye, and she wiped it away with the napkin.

"Joy only requires a few simple ingredients, too," my grandma continued. "Each other."

She stood and placed some divinity on a plate, then set it on the table between us.

"Made a batch earlier," she said, handing me a piece. "Taste. It's perfect with your hot chocolate."

I put the divinity in my mouth, and it melted. It was like a candy cloud, a mix of marshmallow and nougat.

"It's sooo good," I said.

"Do you know why it's called divinity?" my grandma asked.

I shook my head as she placed a piece of candy in her mouth. She shut her eyes and sighed.

"Because it's *divine*," she said.

I laughed.

"But I think it's more than that," my grandma mused. "Do you know what *divinity* means?"

I shook my head again as I ate.

"How can I put it?" she asked herself. "It's like God or an angel."

"Jesus?" I asked.

"Yes," she said. "He is both perfectly divine and perfectly human. He is all of us. Two distinct natures in one."

"Which is better?" I asked.

My grandma laughed. "Ah, the question old as time. We all want to be good, but that stupid human part gets in the way."

She picked up another piece of candy.

"Do you want to know why I'm really awake?" she asked.

"Uh-huh."

"Worry. Time. The human part." My grandma smiled. "Your father is working himself to the bone to make Wegner's a success. Your mother is right there next to him, all while raising you kids. My parents sacrificed everything for us to have better lives, and your grandpa and I did the same. Now, your parents are continuing that legacy. But, oh, how I worry, dear Henri."

All of a sudden, my grandma pushed her fingers together and crushed the piece of divinity into dust.

"Time, Henri," she continued. "It's such a fragile gift. We wish for everything but time. I sorta miss the days when I was your age. I didn't have much, but I had infinite time. Now..."

Her voice trailed off.

"But," I said, "you still have all the ingredients for joy."

My grandmother shook her head as the tears flowed. She patted her lap, I took a seat and finished my hot chocolate with another piece of divinity, which was, truly, divine.

"Need some help?"

I jump at the sound of my dad's voice.

"That's the trouble with an upside-down house," he says. "You hear everything."

He walks over and pats me on the back, eyeing what I have on the stove and countertops.

"Making Mabel's divinity, huh?" he continues. "Something must be going on."

I answer his question with a question.

"Wanna drizzle the sugar while I beat the egg whites?"

He begins to pour as I whir the mixer, beating and beating, until the divinity sets.

My dad grabs two tablespoons, and we drop the candy onto the waxed paper, working in silence.

"Want some peppermint tea while we wait for it to dry?" he asks when we are finished.

"Thanks."

He fills the kettle, turns the heat on high and, within a couple of minutes, has filled two Wegner's Christmas mugs with peppermint tea. We take a seat at the dinette table by a snoozing Mabel. I look at her then my dad.

"Why are you awake?" I ask.

"Why are *you* awake?"

"Couldn't sleep," I say.

"Obviously, but why?"

"Worry," I say. "Time."

"Me, too."

I nod at the bread box.

"Was just thinking about Grandma," I say. "I miss her."

"Me, too," my dad repeats. "You know, she never wrote down a recipe."

"I never realized that. I guess she kept it all in her head."

"No," my dad says, placing his hand over his heart. "She kept it all right here."

I smile.

"And that's what I've done all these years," he continues. "Probably not the best road map for making candy *or* a business."

My father sips his tea.

"Thank you for your help at the store these last couple of weeks," he adds.

"I haven't done a thing," I say, sipping my tea to assuage my guilt.

"You've helped. A lot. Our overhead has been too high for too long. Our systems have been outdated." He stops. "Just being here. With us. With me. That alone means the world."

He speaks in halting sentences, and I have to duck my head.

"Do you think your mother and I should sell Wegner's?"

I suddenly jerk upright. *Where did that come from this late at night?*

"What? Why?"

"I'm being completely honest and vulnerable right now, and I need you to be the same. Your mom and I are getting older, Henri. And, as we mentioned the other day, there will come a time in the very near future when this will all be too much for us to manage."

"But you have Finn," I say.

"Finn loves the store, but I'm not sure he can do it all by himself. It takes a team. It's too much for one person. It really is. He knows that. Moreover, Clare and Ethan aren't interested in the business at this point in their lives. Who knows if Ethan will ever be, or if he will want to go his own way, like you. This business requires a lot of help. And one day…one day, we won't be able to help."

"Have you asked Finn—"

"Let me just think out loud here for a second," my dad interrupts me. "If Finn takes over and has to hire a lot of outside people to help him run Wegner's, why wouldn't I just sell the business now, knowing it will eventually fall out of the family? At least this way, I would have a guiding hand in its future."

My heart pounds in my head.

I can actually have it all: I can convince my father to sell to Vance *and* keep my job. I can wake up Christmas morning without my father ever knowing the real reason I returned home. I can walk out of this entire nightmare as if it were just a bad dream. I can have every wish fulfilled, like a kid on Christmas Day.

"Your mother and I will be set, Finn, his family and you will have a foundation to do whatever you wish for the rest of your lives, and none of you will have to worry about us, or be burdened with making the decision on what to do about the future of Wegner's."

"Dad," I start.

"Just be honest, Henri. We're all running out of time."

Fate has chosen the ideal moment for me to convince my father to sell right now. No more perfect Christmas gift could have been wrapped and placed before me.

All I have to do is tell him that now is the perfect time to sell. I just tell him I know the perfect buyer, Vance—another family business. I tell him I will take care of everything, and he will get more money than he ever dreamed.

I can put a ribbon on the entire package.

I stare at my father sitting with me in the middle of the night.

I glance at the cherry branch.

It was never forced to do anything. It simply needed to be brought inside at Christmas, nurtured, loved and enveloped with warmth.

Then it realized it was safe to bloom.

Bea was right.

I came home because I finally realized how quickly time passes and because I knew—deep in my soul, in that child-like, divine part of me—the answer has forever been written in my heart.

"Don't sell, Dad," I say.

I can feel my soul exhale as soon as I say the words.

"Why?"

I think of talking with my grandma and then with Hannah.

Your dad just wants you to prove him right.

"Because we still have all the ingredients for joy."

And then I come clean. I tell him everything. Why I really came home, why I now plan to quit my job, why I want to stay and one day take over Wegner's with Finn.

When I am done, I am a mess.

My father sits in silence, just staring at me as if we are strangers who just met and having nothing to say to each other.

He does not try to console me.

We just sit there.

"Dad, please," I finally beg. "Say something."

Instead, he gets up and walks over to the counter. He takes a napkin, places a piece of divinity in it and walks out of the kitchen.

"Dad!" I call.

The clock on the microwave glows: 2:17 a.m.

It finally dawns on me that it's officially Christmas Eve.

As my dad heads toward the staircase, I see his hand clench around the napkin, and the divinity crumbles.

33

Talk about a silent night.

I haven't slept a wink.

The upside-down house is upside down.

And very, very quiet.

My mom and dad have already left for work.

I couldn't sleep but I couldn't face my father in the light of a new day.

What did he tell my mom?

Finn?

I wonder if any of them will ever talk to me again.

He didn't even make coffee.

I open the cabinets, grab a filter and some grounds and, as I make a pot, I manically check my cell.

Nothing.

My cell is as silent as the house, and that quiet is deafening.

I'd rather be yelled at by someone, anyone, than face this complete and total avoidance because I know it's like that dead quiet before a tornado hits.

In the middle of the night, after I confessed everything to my father, I texted Benjie to tell him the deal was off and that I was quitting my job, effective immediately.

I texted Bea to alert her and beg for her forgiveness.

This morning, I even sent a pathetic, inane Hey, how's it going? Busy? text to Finn as a way to see where things stood.

Nothing.

I put my head in my hands and rub my temples trying to erase the guilt and exhaustion.

Part of me wants to pack up right this moment and head for Detroit. But a bigger part of me needs closure, even if that closure means closing the wish book on all I've ever known.

As I wait for the coffee to brew, I look out the kitchen window. It snowed overnight, a beautiful, fresh blanket of white. A sense of calm ripples over my weary mind.

There is nothing like a sunrise over freshly fallen snow.

I look over the countryside.

It is still dark out, but the skies have cleared, the stars glimmer and night is putting its finishing touches on its painting of dawn with glorious streaks of blue.

I crack the kitchen window.

I love the silence of a snowfall.

And then I hear a squirrel romp, an owl hoot, a horse whinnying in the distance.

I hear the night wind whisper to the dawn, *Good morning.*

The pines are flocked, and the trunks facing the north are sporting a shrug of white. The rest of the world—all of its imperfections—has been erased.

Winter white as far as the eye can see.

I wish all of our imperfections could be hidden by a fresh blanket of snow.

But, over time, most of us get a little worn, a little tired, a little dirty.

What did I wish for as a girl? An Easy-Bake Oven, a TaterTot doll, a velvet dress, a Shaun Cassidy sing-along machine with a built-in microphone.

But, mostly, I wished for my family to be safe.

I wished for my daddy's dream to come true.

I wished—long before I wanted to run far away—for Christmas morning, opening gifts, holiday songs, eggnog, divinity candy and frosted cookies…

To spend all day at home with my family.

Somehow, we must continue to seek that source of goodness and light. We must look into our hearts and ask if we've truly been a good person, and—if not—what we can do to be better.

Not only for ourselves but for the sake of others.

Why did I wait for Christmas to come home and express my love?

Every day has a chance to bring the possibility of joy, hope, miracles.

The cherry branch in the vase flutters in the breeze.

I smile.

In just a few hours, its woody stem has exploded in buds.

Timing.

My eyes shift to the cherry tree in the backyard, the one that grew from the sapling Shep gave me on May Day so long ago. The branch budding in the kitchen came from that tree.

I pour a cup of coffee and can hear my dad's voice explaining why he and Mom bring a cherry branch into the house every December.

St. Barbara's Day is an old Bavarian tradition that honors every Christmas the memory of a king's daughter whose mother died when she was very young. Her beauty was so legendary that her father locked her in a tower to hide her from the world. Through her window, she could still see all of God's creations, and she dedicated herself to her faith. Her father tried to force her into an arranged marriage, and when she refused, she was tortured and killed. Lightning struck and killed her father the moment she died. After she died, a cherry branch was found in her tower, which she had sneaked in and kept alive by sharing her drinking water with it. Her faith was restored when it blossomed.

I stare at the tree and then the branch. I shut my eyes, hearing my father's voice.

This tradition is still celebrated today by cutting a cherry branch on December 4 and placing it in a vase of water, hoping that it will bloom three weeks later—exactly on Christmas Day—as a sign there is beauty even in the darkest of days and as a symbol of our faith. It's still believed that should pink blossoms emerge in the warmth of the home on Christmas Day, love will bloom for someone, and they will be married the next year.

Perhaps this cherry branch is a symbol of my own rebirth: it just takes love, warmth and faith—even in the winter of one's life—to bring yourself to life again.

"I hope so, Dad," I say.

I open my eyes.

34

Talk about a Silent Day.

I am standing in Wegner's watching my father greet customers.

It was a madhouse when I entered, and—though my father saw me walk in—he has yet to greet me.

I've yet to see Finn or my mom.

I'm too sick to my stomach to enter the store or seek them out, so I just stand here, busying myself with a mop—ever present during the winter—to wipe down the melting snow people track inside. Then I will pause, lean against the mop, and watch the happy scene that surrounds me, every hug, every smile a reminder of my betrayal.

My father—in a suit, a green tie festooned with tiny round, red ornaments and Santa cap—greets last-minute shoppers coming into Wegner's. Mabel sits by his side, wearing reindeer antlers atop her head and a Christmas sweater that reads Santa's Little Helper. She sits patiently, knowing she will get a cookie for this, and wags at every person who enters the store and pets her.

"Frohe Weihnachte!" my father bellows. "Welcome to Wegner's!"

If he knows a customer, he will pull them in for a long hug.

"Another Christmas together, Jakob," Mrs. Patterson whispers into his ear as she steadies herself on her walker.

"Lots more Christmases together, Verna," my father says.

Each time the front doors swing open, a gust of arctic wind whips in, bringing little tornadoes of snow. You can almost see the face of Old Man Winter standing outside, lips pursed, nose blue, conjuring up the cold.

The store teems with people. They have come to shop. They have come for the sing-along at three o'clock.

No, they have come for my father.

"Already got the game on for you, Bill," my dad says to a couple entering, their hair as white as the snow on top of it. "And, Margie, I held back those two new, limited-edition Snowbaby collectibles you wanted."

"Oh, Jakob! Thank you!" she says, giving him a hug as her husband heads for the TV. "My first great-granddaughter. I wanted to start a new tradition with her. So she can remember when I'm no longer around for Christmas." She places a mittened hand on my dad's cheek. "You are such a kind man, Jakob. It wouldn't be Christmas without you. Next year I'll bring little Adele."

"Promise?" my father asks.

"I promise."

Their words touch me so deeply that I have to close my eyes, take a deep breath and steady myself against the mop.

"Are you okay?"

I jump at Finn's voice.

"Why are you mopping, Mary Poppins?" he continues.

My mother comes up behind him, carrying a cup of coffee.

"You look like you've seen a ghost," she says.

"Just like Scrooge," Finn adds.

I look at my father. "You didn't tell them, did you?" I ask.

My dad shakes his head.

"Tell us what?" Finn asks.

I place the mop in the corner and turn to my brother and mother.

"You were right, Finn," I say. "I've lied to you. I've lied to all of you."

And then I tell them—everything—in a rush like the wind that blows through the front doors.

Finn's expression turns stony. My mother's eyes mist.

"I'm so sorry," I say pathetically. "I selfishly wanted to save my job, but I also wanted to save this place, too."

"But you mostly wanted to save yourself," Finn says.

"I did," I admit. "I didn't realize what I had until I came back here for Christmas." I shake my head. "And then I realized I was receiving the greatest gift, one I never expected to receive, like Ralphie getting the Red Ryder BB gun."

No one laughs. I clear my throat.

"But I know it's too late for all that. I just hope the changes I suggested help you in the future. I never meant to hurt you, but I know I did. I broke your hearts, and I know you can never forgive me. It's the three of you. It's always been the three of you. I've been the one to turn my back on you your whole lives. This is your business. And, Finn, you need your shot."

I look at my family.

"I'll leave after the sing-along," I say. "The least I can do is pretend to show the community that you have a good daughter."

I turn to head out of the store.

I lean down and pet Mabel.

"Promise me you'll stick around," I whisper. "They need you."

"Henri," my dad says.

I straighten up and walk back to my father.

"I love you, Dad," I whisper. "Goodbye."

35

As I walk down 25 Christmas Lane, my cell finally trills. I read it, heart filled with hope, thinking it might be from my father or Finn. It's not. It's from Benjie.

You can't ruin my Christmas without me ruining yours. That's only fair, don't you think? Merry Christmas, Henri. See you soon. Love, Santa

I power off my cell.

I deserve this. I deserve all of this.

Snow falls.

Irony of ironies, it's going to be a white Christmas.

My father's dream is coming true. The ideal backdrop for his beloved sing-along.

I pass a lit display of Rudolph and the reindeer pulling Santa's sleigh.

Rudolph's red nose blinks in the snow, and I shake my head at the accuracy of the children's tale.

We all need guidance. We all need light in the dark.

My father knows that we need the white of the snow and the

light of Christmas, faith, family, friends, each other to brighten our days as we walk through winter.

And Christmas Lane is certainly bright.

The old-fashioned streetlights are wrapped in Christmas greenery tied with bright red bows. The colorful displays of snowmen, reindeer and Santa rock in the north wind. The pines are flocked in snow.

I walk under an arched entrance along the lane designed to look like a bar of sheet music lined with musical notes. Silent Night Memorial Chapel—in a white script that looks very nostalgic—looms above those first notes to "Silent Night."

White wooden signs in the shape of Christmas trees line the sidewalk, telling the story of how "Silent Night" came to be.

I tromp through the snow. A nativity scene—white marble, as white as the snow—sits in front of a holly bush heavy with berries.

Two massive pines flank the chapel.

Despite the snow, there are already a few hundred people braving the weather: store owners, community leaders, family friends.

I scan the crowd. Sofie blows me a kiss. Mouse winks. Shep waves. Hannah smiles.

My heart thumps wildly, booming in my ears, as if Donner and Blitzen have landed on the roof and are prancing around on their hooves.

I wave.

None of them know I am waving goodbye.

Suddenly, the crowd begins to applaud.

I turn.

My father is approaching, smiling, waving, my mom and Finn right behind him.

They glance at me, and I step back into the assembled crowd.

My parents ascend the dozen small steps of the chapel until

they're standing at its entrance. Behind them, the doors are open, and the chapel glows in candlelight.

"Thank you all from the bottom of my heart for coming out on this very Michigan winter's day to celebrate our annual sing-along," Dad says. "And it's going to be a white Christmas!"

The crowd cheers, their collective exhalations creating a fog in the snow.

Dad continues, "Today actually marks the thirty-fifth anniversary of the Silent Night Memorial Chapel and sing-along, and it's all because of you. Because of your faith in us over the years, we have created a magical chorus."

My heart sinks as the audience applauds anew.

"Jakob and I are no longer spring chickens," my mother says, "or—more appropriately—young reindeer, so it's getting harder for us to keep Christmas going year-round. Only Santa can do that."

My parents look into one another's eyes and smile. Then my mother nods.

"Which is why Debbie and I have decided to sell Wegner's," my father says.

The snow seems to freeze in midair along with my father's words.

I see people's mouths opening, forming the word *No!*

My entire world, my entire being, my heart, soul, brain are frozen solid.

Finn glances back at me.

I shake my head and lift my hands into the air, indicating I had no idea this was happening.

Finn turns away.

What is going on?

My ears are buzzing so loudly I cannot hear, much less think. In fact, the sound is so deafening that I must place my hands over my ears. Suddenly, the world goes white. I think I am fainting.

But then I see my brother point into the sky. The crowd is looking heavenward.

God is coming to smite me, I think.

I look into the sky.

A helicopter, blades whirring, making the world a blender of white, descends on an empty plot of land behind the chapel.

People lift their cells into the air to record the commotion.

The side of the helicopter reads Tolliver.

The helicopter lands, and, finally, there is deafening silence.

I stare in disbelief, then look back at my parents, who seem just as bewildered as I am by the chaos.

Are my parents selling to Benjie?

Or is he just here to make my last Christmas at home even more miserable?

No matter what, it's all over.

I've lost everything: my job, my family, my legacy.

I begin to sneak away, unable to face the madness, when I see Bea racing toward me, out of breath, hair wild from the ride and the wind.

"Henri!" she yells.

"Bea, what's going on?"

"Benjie tricked me into coming," Bea says in a rush. "I'd already quit and today was my last day, but Benjie told me he was going to surprise you and needed my help. That he was so inspired by your kindness and loyalty to family that he wanted to personally invest in Wegner's. He said this had all changed the way he looks at business. I actually believed him. Until we were in the air. That's when he told me his plan to ruin your Christmas and turn your parents against you forever."

All of a sudden, the helicopter takes off again, and the world is a swirl of white.

"What happened?"

"He planned on having his helicopter hover over the chapel and create chaos until everyone left. And then tell your parents how you've wanted to ruin their business forever. But then I just lost my mind, Henri. I started yelling at him that his father would be so ashamed of him. I said, what kind of person acts like this at Christmas and asked him what kind of person he wanted to be. I asked him what he wanted his legacy to look like. He looked down at the chapel and sort of melted into his seat. And then he just let me off the helicopter."

"Bea," I say, pulling her into a hug. "I'm so sorry. You were right…about everything. Thank you."

"So…how's it going?" she asks.

"It's too late for me," I say. "But not for my family."

"You still did the right thing, Henri."

Everyone watches the helicopter vanish—along with Benjie and my previous life—and eventually the crowd quiets, and my father begins to speak again.

"Well, that was quite the entrance," he says, to laughter, looking toward Bea and then at me.

Bea gives an embarrassed wave.

"I've caused enough commotion," I whisper to Bea. "I'm going to get out of here while I can."

Bea grabs my arm.

"Don't run away and hurt your family again. Just face it all head-on for once."

I stop. She's right.

"Trust me?" she asks.

"Ok."

"As I was saying," my father says, "Debbie and I have decided to sell Wegner's…to our son, Finn…"

The crowd cheers.

My parents motion for Finn, who joins them on the steps. He waves.

"Finn?" my dad asks. "Would you like to say a word or two?"

Finn takes the microphone.

"I'm so grateful to my parents for entrusting their faith in me," he says, "and I'm so excited about the future of Wegner's and Frankenmuth. Moreover, that future will be even brighter because I'm going to be partnering with my sister, Henri, who will be moving back to Frankenmuth full-time to help me run Wegner's."

What?

My head jerks upright, and I do a goofy double take trying to comprehend what is happening.

"Now, you need to understand that our mom and dad are not done yet," he continues. "Not by a long shot. They will continue to guide and lead Wegner's for the foreseeable future, and Henri and I will take over the reins only when they're good and ready. And I hope that's many years from now."

The crowd cheers again.

"Together," Finn adds, "nothing can stop this family."

Tears blur my vision.

"Henri, would you join us?" my father calls.

Bea yelps and shoves me toward the chapel.

I turn to her.

"I think I'm going to need you here," I say. "As more than an assistant. As a guiding hand and friend."

"I would love to be part of the family," she says. "Now go!"

I climb the chapel stairs and wave when I'm between my brother and my parents.

The crowd cheers again.

My father puts his arm around my back.

"I don't understand," I say under my breath, smiling broadly for the audience.

"I knew you would do the right thing," my dad says, waving to the crowd. "I knew you were that same little girl who wished only for the right things in this world."

"But..."

My sentence is not completed as Barb emerges from the chapel and hands my father a guitar.

He begins to sing, his voice penetrating the hush of the winter snow.

As I join in, I cannot help but finally appreciate the song's lyrics.

Silent night, holy night,
All is calm, all is bright.

When we finish singing, the crowd mobs my family.

In the distance, the glockenspiel chimes.

36

The living room of the upside-down house is a sea of wrapping paper.

Mabel is asleep in the midst of it, a soft cushion for her old body.

She is exhausted from the Christmas chaos.

Finn, Clare and Ethan tore through their gifts in a matter of moments, slugged down some cinnamon rolls and hot chocolate and then tore off to Clare's family to do it all over again.

Last night, over pizza and wine, we were able to discuss our Christmas past, present and future. Somehow—understanding the impossible pressure I was under and being removed from the family Christmas for so long—my parents and Finn were able to forgive me, a true Christmas miracle.

"I'm sorry I broke your trust," I told them. "Mom, you were just waiting for me to come home and celebrate Christmas with you again like Grandma did. Finn, you were just waiting for me to act not like your big sister and just be your friend. And Dad, you were just waiting for me to prove you right for once in my life. I'm sorry it took so long. I won't let you down again. I promise."

"Save that bow!" my mother yells. "Oh, and that ribbon!"

I smile.

Like Scrooge, I feel as if I can live the rest of my life with the joy of Christmas and family in my heart.

God bless us, every one!

I shove wrapping paper into a garbage bag.

"Not that tissue!" my mother says, retrieving it from the trash. "It has those cute candy canes all over it. It's so pretty. I can fold it, iron it and use it again next year."

She heads out with an armful of brightly colored tissue and bows stacked on top.

I smile.

Next year.

"Christmas is only three hundred sixty-four days away," my father says with a laugh. "We don't have much time. You sure you're up for all this?"

I nod with great conviction.

"I am."

My father opens his arms and hugs me tightly.

"By the way, I may still have had DOS, but I also have cameras in the office that I check every night," he says into my ear. "I saw you snooping, Henri."

My eyes grow wide. I feel sick again.

"Why didn't you say something, Dad?" I ask. I can feel a lump in my throat. "Why didn't you throw me out of the house? How could you forgive me, Dad? I don't feel like I deserve it."

"I knew in my heart my little girl could never break it," he says. "And sometimes we all do the wrong thing. I mean, I've been ignoring your mother's advice for years. I've been overlooking Finn."

My father takes my hand and leads me to the couch. He grabs the *Wegner's Wish Book* off the coffee table.

"You are still the same little girl inside you've always been." My dad looks me right in the eyes. "The same little girl who always believed in the magic of Christmas."

"Aren't you still angry?"

"I was, but it was more disappointment than anger. I needed time to think. But you came clean to me, then quit your job and told Debbie and Finn, not knowing how they'd react. A small person does the wrong thing, but it takes a big person to do the right thing." My dad looks me in the eyes. "Fathers will always believe in their daughters. We have to."

"Oh, Dad."

My father grabs my hand.

"A parent can't force his child to follow in his footsteps. Usually, she'll do the opposite, or it will end in disaster. But if we raise our children right—with kindness, love and independence—then a solid foundation will always remain."

"Ethics are doing the right thing even when no one is watching," I say.

"You did do the right thing, Henri."

"Look at this!" my mother says, reentering the living room. "I know you saw it earlier, but I just had to put it out here for us to admire today. It's the perfect Christmas miracle!"

She is carrying the McCoy vase with the cherry branch.

"Our faith has been restored!" my father announces, looking at the branch and then at me.

My mom places the vase in the center of the table, right next to the wish catalog.

"I wonder if love will bloom for someone, and they will be married the next year," my mom says with a wink.

"Me?" my dad says.

"Ha-ha," Mom laughs. "You're stuck with me, Jakob Wegner."

She gives him a kiss on the head and then reaches down, grabs a stick-on bow and slaps it on top of his noggin.

"My Christmas gift," she says. "Too late to return it now, I guess."

My father stands, and the two of them gather another armful of ribbons, bows and tissue paper, leaving me alone on the couch.

My cell vibrates, and I pull it from my pocket.

Still on for noon?

I smile.

After our family dinner last night, I took Shep some pizza, and I shared the drama of the last few days. We ate in the mill, and I felt like a girl again.

He asked me to meet him on Christmas Day to talk.

"I think I'm going to head out to get a little fresh air," I yell to my parents, not wanting to give them too much information. "Work off all the sugar from the cinnamon rolls and hot chocolate. I'm taking Mabel, too!"

I pat my legs and call for Mabel.

She hobbles over to me, wagging her tail excitedly.

I grab her leash, open the door, but turn at the very last second.

"And I'm taking you, too," I say, pulling the cherry branch from the vase.

37

The Holz Brücke is outlined in white lights. The sky is cinder-block gray, snow continues to fall lightly—white flakes twirling about in the air like *Nutcracker* ballerinas—and the lights from the bridge twinkle in the Cass River.

No one is about. Everyone is home with their family, many still in pajamas, eating cinnamon rolls thick with icing and drinking coffee from holiday mugs staring at the tree in front of the fire.

I watch the river flow, scanning Frankenmuth in the distance. The Bavarian buildings are coated with snow and the north wind makes the Christmas lights dance on the tree branches. The only thing missing is the Alps.

Mabel looks up at me, her furry mug as white as snow, her nose thick with a layer of it after sticking her head deep into the powder to sniff.

All of a sudden, and with a strength I didn't know she still possessed, Mabel jumps onto the bridge and scans the river and the town, her golden eyes slowly taking in every detail. The north wind pulses over her long fur, and she lifts her face into the air, closes her eyes, inhales and sighs. Mabel turns her head toward me and barks.

Mabel—like Bea, currently baking cookies with my mom, who immediately tried to fill the holiday void left by Bea's mother—knew in her heart exactly why I came home.

To spend the time I have left with those I love.

I knock the snow off a small bench that sits flush against the bridge, set down the branch, pick up Mabel and hug her to me. I close my eyes and inhale her scent as if trying to lock it into my memory forever. I open my eyes and stare directly into hers. She kisses me, over and over and over, making me laugh like a girl.

When Mabel was a puppy, I used to bring her here and she would bark at the ducks. Oftentimes, Sofie and I would park our cars at opposite ends of the bridge to block traffic, and we would race back and forth through the covered bridge with Mabel, our yells and her barks echoing all around us.

"This is your bridge, isn't it, girl?" I ask, petting her head. "This is your town. What a life you've led. To be so loved. We sure are lucky, aren't we?"

Mabel lifts her head into the sky and barks.

"Hey, Mabel!"

Shep is walking toward us.

Shep kneels, I let the leash go and Mabel goes bounding into his arms.

"You remember me, don't you?" he coos, ruffling her fur and kissing her old head. "Merry Christmas, Mabel."

He grabs her leash.

"Thanks for meeting me," he says. "So, what did Mabel get for Christmas?"

"A Christmas cookie in her stocking, a Christmas sweater—as you can see—that says I'm So Doggone Cute and a new squeaky toy, which she destroyed in under a minute," I say.

"Aw, the perfect Christmas, right, girl?" Shep asks.

Mabel barks happily.

"How was your Christmas?" I ask.

"It was nice," he says. "Hannah and I spent the morning with the kids, and it felt…good."

"I'm so happy to hear that," I say.

"What did you get for Christmas?" he asks.

"A second chance," I say. "At everything."

Shep smiles that smile.

I hold up the branch. "It's taken me a long time to blossom."

"My first gift to you," he says.

Shep reaches into his pocket and produces a small, wrapped box.

My face betrays my shock.

"Don't worry," he laughs. "It's not a ring."

He hands me the gift. "Just a little something," he says.

I set the branch on a railing and open the package.

I laugh when I see what he has given me: a new May Day key chain of a little boy and girl dancing.

"Thought maybe you could use it," he says. "New life, new keys…"

"It's perfect," I say. "I love it. Thank you."

"And I love you, Henri," he says out of the blue. "Always have, always will. Maybe we can try again…with no timeline. And maybe the timing is in our favor this time."

"Shep…" I start.

"You don't have to say it, but I want you to know exactly how I feel. No games. I just want to be completely transparent with you moving forward. How's that sound?"

"Perfect," I say, "because I love you, too. Always have, always will."

He takes me into his arms and kisses me. I don't want to let go, so I don't, and we kiss until Mabel barks.

"See where we are?"

Shep points at the beam.

"Did you plan this?" I ask.

A heart, with our initials inside, is still carved onto the railing.

"You've always completed my heart," he says.

I kiss him again.

I look into Shep's eyes. They are filled with light.

The beauty of a covered bridge is that light glows inside in unexpected ways.

Honeycombs of light from the lattice dance even in the dark.

Ripples of light from the waves shimmer inside.

And light splays from both ends of the bridge, a window of hope, calling you, beckoning you. You may either walk toward it, or away from it. The decision is entirely up to you.

He takes my hand, and we walk into the snow, Mabel leading the way, pink blossoms from the cherry branch mixing in the wind with the falling snow.

"This bridge," I say to Shep, "has finally led me home."

epilogue

Christmas Eve
One year later

"You couldn't have picked a better day to get married? Like, any other day?"

"Nope." I shake my head at Finn, my veil sweeping in the breeze. "It had to be today."

"At least we can kill two birds with one stone," my father says.

"Jakob!" my mother scolds, hitting him on the shoulder before knocking a skiff of snow from his tuxedo jacket.

"How sentimental, Dad."

I scan the Holz Brücke.

Guests are seated underneath the wooden bridge, and votive candles line the wooden railing. The candlelight flickers off the lattice, casting the bridge in an ethereal glow. Pine boughs drenched in white lights and pine cones encase the bridge's rafters. On both ends of the bridge, just outside the entrance, Fraser firs twinkle with lights and the limbs are heavy with hand-decorated ornaments from Wegner's.

Thanks to Gert's talents, not mine.

Heat lamps are poised along each row.

"I should have sold the store to pay for all of this," my father jokes again.

"It's so beautiful," I say, looking across the bridge, snow falling lightly. "Like a dream."

"This is *your* Christmas wish finally come true," my mother says.

"I think we're ready," the minister says. "Whenever you are."

I nod at the driver, and we step aboard the horse-drawn carriage. It begins to move toward the covered bridge. I can see Shep's carriage start forward at the same time at the opposite end of the bridge.

We veer around the firs and when we arrive at the entrance, the carriage stops, and my father and brother escort me off.

I am wearing a winter white dress made in Germany with a snow-white cape. The dress is simple and elegant: fitted at the bodice, flowing at the bottom, an embellishment of ghostly blossoms on the overlay.

I stand at the entrance of the bridge as Shep and his groomsmen take their places. Mouse gives me a wave as he takes his place.

"You all look so beautiful," I say to my bridesmaids, Bea, Sofie and Hannah, who are wearing dresses of dusty pink for a very important cherry blossom reason.

How all of us got this far is a testament to our struggles and strengths, but here we are, united as women.

When "The Bridal Chorus" by Wagner begins, and I enter the bridge, the crowd murmurs.

My father escorts me down the aisle. He leans into me and whispers, "You will always be my little girl."

I hold my tears at bay as my father pulls back my veil, kisses my cheek and presents me to Shep.

I cannot hold back my tears when Shep finally sees me, and a tear trails down his cheek.

He is still heartbreakingly, heart-flutteringly handsome.

Shep shakes his head.

"How did I get so lucky?" he whispers.

"I'm the lucky one," I whisper back.

My bouquet shakes in my hands from excitement, and Sofie steps forward to take it from me.

It is not your typical bridal bouquet. I opted for branches from Shep's cherry tree, which we forced in the farmhouse Shep and I now share, and which are filled with pink blossoms.

Shep asked me to marry him on May Day.

He left a gift on my parents' porch just as he did when he was a boy.

When I opened the door, a May Day bouquet—filled with simple flowers—was hanging from the doorknob. Inside the basket was an envelope. It contained a card that read: "Meet me by the cherry tree!"

I found Shep by the tree he'd given me so long ago holding a velvet box.

"Would you do me the great honor of marrying me, Henri, and making me the happiest man on earth?" he asked, kneeling. "Finally."

"Yes!" I yelled.

I heard a resounding *"Whoop!"*

My parents were standing in the window of the upside-down house hooting, hollering and applauding.

Perhaps, I think, as Shep says his vows, *the old tales are true: between May Day and St. Barbara's Day, I was always meant to marry Shep.*

I just had to cross the bridge again.

Shep and I exchange vows, and when it's time for the ring and it doesn't appear, the crowd goes silent, nervously looking around.

A soft tingling echoes throughout the covered bridge. The rows of guests turn as one.

Mabel comes running, as best she still can, and she doesn't stop until she reaches me. A ribbon hangs from her neck.

"Thank you," I say, untying the ribbon and taking the ring from it. I kiss Mabel on the head.

My dad calls for her, but she doesn't budge.

The guests giggle.

She's right where she's supposed to be.

And so am I.

When Shep places the ring on my finger, I cannot stop my tears.

It's the ring he's kept since we were seniors in college.

Inside are replicas of the initials—along with the heart—that we carved right here on the bridge.

"You are a part of my heart," Shep says. "We are one. We will always be one heart."

Everything is a blur until I hear the minister say, "You may kiss the bride."

Even though it's a cold Christmas Eve in Michigan, I melt into Shep's kiss.

The wedding guests stand and applaud.

"If you'll remain standing," I say, "there's one more tradition before the reception. Dad?"

My father comes to the front of the bridge. He is carrying a guitar.

The crowd grows quiet.

Dad begins to play and sing. "Silent night, holy night..."

When he finishes, as if on cue, the glockenspiel chimes in the distance.

My soul sings and then, finally, after all these years and after all of these Christmases, it stills.

★ ★ ★ ★ ★

acknowledgments

Santa doesn't do it alone, and neither do I. He has an entire North Pole filled with elves—along with Mrs. Claus—working year-round to make dreams come true, and so do I. HUGE holiday hugs and love to:

My agent, Wendy Sherman, who has guided my sleigh for nearly twenty years;

My editor, Susan Swinwood, who makes each book a special present;

My publicity and marketing team, the elves who do everything behind the scenes and get little credit for all their talent and hard work: Kathleen Carter; Heather Connor; Leah Morse; Diane Lavoie; Lindsey Reeder; Danielle Noe and so many others;

The indie booksellers across the US, a gift to us and this world;

The countless authors whose talents I not only admire but whose friendships are a true gift: Nancy Thayer, Brenda Novak, Susan Mallery, Kristin Harmel, Kristy Woodson Harvey, Mary Kay Andrews, Patti Callahan Henry, Robyn Carr, Sherryl Woods, Brenda Janowitz, Jane Green, Zibby Owens, Sarah McCoy, Joy Callaway and countless others;

My mutts, the late, great Mabel, who will live forever in my soul *and* this novel, the divine Doris, all sunshine, light and love, and the great Gerti, our new rescue, found on the streets and now at home in our hearts.

And, of course, to Gary, my greatest gift in the world, no matter the day of the year.

Mostly, to YOU, for making every day feel like Christmas morning!

dear readers,

There is a line in *The Wishing Bridge* where the mother asks her daughter, "Why do we always wait until Christmas to return home and show how much we love one another?"

That is the foundational question in my latest holiday novel.

Growing up in the Ozarks, my grandmother's house was the epicenter—the North Pole—of Christmas to me. She decorated every room, lined her yard with Christmas blow molds and lit anything that didn't move. But it was more than the decorations: it was the feeling I was safe and loved more than anything else in the world.

The holidays can be difficult for many of us, especially as we begin to lose those we love. They are no longer present at the dinner table, or at church service. They will no longer make the iced cookies we love, buy us a special ornament or have a stocking over the fireplace. Some of us avoid the holidays because a family member has hurt us, or because it's hard to recreate the childhood joy we once had.

I know firsthand. I lost my brother when I was young—the one we called "The King of Christmas"—and then my grandparents, and, finally, my mother. There were times I didn't want to return home at the holidays because the memories crowded the house even though it was, by then, largely empty. Even after so many years, the pain was still raw. And yet I understood that I was missing out on the little time I had left with the family who remained and that I hurt so much because I was so deeply loved. And I learned that sometimes you must stop avoiding painful memories and celebrate your past while also starting new traditions.

In *The Wishing Bridge*, Henri avoids going home because of a painful memory, using work as an annual excuse. When she returns for Christmas, under a ruse, she realizes—as I did—that her time with family, as marked by the chiming of the town's old clock tower, will not last forever.

I write winter and holiday novels that are "ropes of hope" for those who need it most, a reminder that—as my Grandma Shipman used to tell me—"Life is short as one blink of God's eye, and in that blink, we too often forget what matters most." Family. Friends. The holidays. Forgiveness, of ourselves and others.

This novel looks at the difficult decisions we must make as adults and how they alter our lives, be it a breakup, moving away from home, or becoming the person you want to be even if that hurts or disappoints those who raise and love us. I took the path less traveled in becoming an author, and that path was a curvy, hilly one filled with potholes and blind turns, and yet it was the best decision I've ever made in my life.

The Wishing Bridge takes place in the very real village of Frankenmuth, Michigan, a beautiful Bavarian Christmas wonderland located on the eastern side of the state along the Cass River just south of Lake Huron. Frankenmuth is known as Michigan's Little Bavaria due to its German heritage and architecture. But it really comes alive at Christmas. I absolutely fell in love with Frankenmuth the first time I visited—and also nearly spent my entire IRA at Bronner's CHRISTmas Wonderland, the world's largest Christmas store, which inspired Wegner's Winter Wonderland in the novel. The town's unique beauty, people and history also inspired me as did its independent stores. You will recognize many of them in the novel—fictionalized, of course—and I hope I honored them and will make you want to visit. Most of all, I hope I did Bronner's justice. It is a magical place, and Wally Bronner's unwavering faith, love of family and friends, and belief in the American dream reminded me of my grandparents and touched my soul, making me want to write this novel the first time I set foot in Bronner's.

Speaking of the American dream, I wanted to honor that idea in this novel. My grandparents worked and sacrificed to have better lives, and that planted a seed in my soul to pursue my own American dream, which I have done as an author.

The Wishing Bridge is about the choices we make in life—some good, some bad—but realizing that if we have a strong foundation, it is never too late to cross that bridge in our lives to become the people we dreamed we could become.

This is a love story—to family, to friends, to finding love later in life and to Christmas. I was swept away writing this novel, and I hope it touches you as much as it touched—and changed—me.

Happy holidays, and I'm so excited to bring you my new summer novel in a few months!

XOXO,
Viola

THE WISHING BRIDGE

VIOLA SHIPMAN

Reader's Guide

1. A major theme of *The Wishing Bridge* is how our memories of the holidays shape us, especially as we age. What are your favorite Christmas memories? What do you miss most about the holidays when you were a child? What traditions have you and your family kept going, and what new traditions have you introduced?

2. Memories are a tricky thing, and *The Wishing Bridge* is filled with them. Do you think our memories are inevitably skewed based on our emotions and personal points of view? Have they altered any relationships, especially with someone you love or loved? How?

3. Another theme in the novel centers on the need to step out of our parents' shadows in order to make our marks on the world. How did your parents influence you? Did you feel a need to do something totally on your own, be it career, moving away from home, not doing something you were always expected to do? How did that change you? What lessons did you learn? How did your parents react to those decisions?

4. *The Wishing Bridge* looks at the difficulty in returning home—especially at the holidays—to face family or your past when you've been hurt in some way. Is this something you've experienced in your life? How? Discuss.

5. I discuss the idea of "the American dream" in this novel: what it means to start with nothing more than a dream and build that into a successful business from scratch. What do you think it takes to realize a dream? How do you think the American dream has changed over the last century? What is your dream and how are you working to make it come true?

6. At the start of the book, Henri is hitting middle age in a male-dominated corporate world. Do you think her feelings around youth and gender in the workplace are valid, or are things changing for women?

7. I have always loved Christmas. I have red and green bins filled with beloved decorations and ornaments, new and old. This novel celebrates many of those beloved decorations. What are your favorite Christmas decorations and ornaments, and why?

8. Setting is always as big a character in my novels as my characters themselves. *The Wishing Bridge* is set in Frankenmuth, Michigan, one of my favorite resort towns because of its history and uniqueness. There is no place like it, especially at Christmas. Do you have a favorite holiday destination? Why?

9. As I write in my letter to readers, the store in this novel is inspired by Bronner's CHRISTmas Wonderland, the world's largest Christmas store. Do you have a beloved place to shop at Christmas (rather than online), be it a tree farm, gift shop or Christmas store? Why is that so special to you?

10. I divide my time between two resort towns on opposite sides of the country, each filled with unique, independent businesses. The spirit of these shops and restaurants make these places special. *The Wishing Bridge* is an homage to independent businesses. What are some of your favorite non-chain places to shop and eat where you live? What makes them so special?

11. Henri's heart was broken by Shep when they were young. The two remember the breakup very differently, and it changed the course of their lives profoundly. Did you have a romance when you were young that broke your heart and changed you (for better or worse)? Discuss. Have you ever reconnected with that person?

Christmas Angels

1

The Tree Topper

"A little more to the left! A little higher! OK, stop!"

Kate Roseberry took a giant step back and suddenly jumped, startled. She turned to see what had stopped her progress, her dark ponytail slapping her cheek as she spun. Her back was pressed against an Auntie Anne's pretzel kiosk.

She laughed at her overreaction and then said to the girl in the smock and paper hat, "Can I get a cinnamon sugar?" before turning back around.

"Perfect!" she yelled to three members of her team, who were each on hydraulic lifts decorating a twenty-four-foot artificial Christmas tree that resembled a majestic mountain pine.

The tree stood in the center of St. Louis Tower, a brand-new glimmering high-rise downtown, near the base of the Mississippi River. A new shopping mall—a cavernous space with a three-story atrium—comprised the bottom portion of the Tower, while offices filled the top floors.

Kate had gone big in her holiday design for the mall, knowing that anything too small would feel out of scale in the wide-open space.

Like putting a bow tie on King Kong, Kate remembered thinking when designing her sketches.

As a result, the massive tree's limbs held silver, gold and red ornaments as big as small pumpkins, an analogy that was all too fitting—and all too soon—for many shoppers.

"It's not even Thanksgiving yet," a woman hissed as she strolled by, still wearing shorts since they were having an unusually warm fall. "Or Halloween!"

Kate smiled as sweetly as she could. "I know," she started, "but..."

Kate stopped herself and blew her bangs out of her eyes. She could explain to the woman—like she had to everyone for years—that she had hundreds of places to decorate in the city, that she couldn't wait to start until after Halloween ended, and that it took months to plan and execute such intricate designs—especially in places like malls, airports and office towers—but no one cared about that. They just wanted the holidays to look perfect. And Kate was the queen of holiday perfection.

"Kate! Kate! Hello?"

Kate followed the rumbling voice of Marvin Stopher, her lead installer, up the tree, his big body dwarfed by the massive trunk. He was like a real-life Disney animator. He transformed gigantic, fake trees—pulling them out of boxes that had been stuffed into a warehouse—and built them piece by piece with Kate alongside him, fluffing each branch until the tree came to life.

People don't know the hard work behind the magic, Kate thought.

"Kate?" Marvin yelled again. "Are you waiting for a pretzel?"

"What? No!" Kate called to him over the Muzak, the Starbucks baristas and frothers, and the muffled footsteps and chatter of shoppers. "I would never do that while you're working so hard!"

She turned her head to the Auntie Anne's worker and whispered, "Hold that pretzel, OK?" before lifting her head and shouting, "Everyone ready?"

Marvin and two seasonal workers nodded. They were tiered on individual lifts at different heights and angles to the giant tree, one left, one right, and one center. Marvin was holding a huge ball of gold ribbon.

That ribbon is long enough to make a cummerbund for Godzilla, should he decide to head to the Met Gala, Kate thought, looking up. She silently chuckled at her monster analogies and reminded herself not to watch any more Halloween horror movies.

Marvin held the ribbon, readying himself to toss it expertly to the next person, who would then catch it and toss it to the next, before they draped it through the branches.

"Okay!" Kate yelled. "Let's do this!"

Like a carefully choreographed Harlem Globetrotters routine, the three tossed and caught the ribbon, before tucking it just so.

"Now it's your turn!" Marvin called to Kate as he lowered his lift to the ground and stepped off.

Kate grabbed a box and stepped onto the lift, toggling the lever and moving up, up, up until she was floating at the tip-top of the tree, above the mall, seemingly ready to ascend through the huge skylight and toward heaven.

She reached into the box and carefully unpeeled layers of Bubble Wrap. Kate smiled. There, smiling back, was an angel, the topper for the tree. Kate stood with the giant angel, positioned herself on her tiptoes, and stretched, placing the angel on top of the tree until it was secure and straight as an arrow. She found the plug on the angel's back and inserted it into the green cord clipped to the branch. Suddenly, the angel came to life, glowing, the LED lights on its wings strobing as if it were flying. A few people in the mall applauded.

For a brief moment, Kate stood nearly face-to-face with the angel, floating above the world.

Tree toppers—be it cupids shooting faux lit arrows on Valentine's Day trees or hopping bunnies juggling colorful eggs atop Easter trees—were Kate's signature. And Kate always topped the tree herself.

To Kate, this final act was akin to an author writing *The End* when a book was finished, an actor taking center stage to bow during a curtain call or a chef bringing out a special dessert. Kate believed every tree deserved an exclamation point of beauty. And she believed that people, especially on the holidays, needed something to look up to, something to raise their heads, something to inspire them.

I certainly do this year, Kate thought as the angel's lights blinked in front of her eyes.

"I don't think I can be as bright as you this holiday season," Kate whispered to the angel. "Just not feeling in the holiday spirit anymore."

Kate reached up to touch the angel's face and look into its shining eyes, her mind whirring back a year.

"No, you do the honors."

Kate sipped a glass of champagne in front of the fireplace of her 1920s St. Louis bungalow, whose walls and stained glass windows were twinkling in the light from the Christmas tree. The spirit of the holidays filled the tiny house, along with the smells of Christmas: a live Fraser fir tree, wood crackling in the fireplace, sugar cookies baking in the oven.

"Are you sure? It's kinda your thing."

Kate laughed at her boyfriend, Tyler. He was standing holding the topper for the tree—an heirloom angel her mother and grandmother had given her years ago for good luck when she started her business—a nervous look etched on his face, like a kid who had to recite a speech in front of the whole school.

"I'm sure," she said. "I've earned a break."

"OK then," Tyler said. "Hope it meets your expectations."

Kate watched her boyfriend—*My boyfriend!* she thought, her

heart skipping a beat—turn and place the heirloom tree topper atop the freshly cut fir.

He looks so handsome in the light, Kate thought, his emerald eyes twinkling, his cheeks rosy, his blond hair aglow. Almost as if he were lit from within, like the antique ornaments on the tree.

"What do you think?" he asked.

"Perfect," Kate said, sipping her champagne. "Never had a doubt."

"And what do you think about this?" he asked again. Kate looked at him, cocking her head in confusion. Tyler was now standing before her, holding a tiny box wrapped in gold foil paper and topped with a red velvet bow. "I thought this would be a fitting gift."

Kate's mouth dropped.

A ring? We've only been dating less than a year, Kate thought, her mind racing. *It seems so soon. But I do love him. I do! Oh, my gosh, I said, "I do!"*

"No, it's not *that*...yet," Tyler said, reading her mind. "It's something I thought would be meaningful to you."

Kate felt a simultaneous rush of relief and disappointment. *Yet*, she thought, smiling to herself. *He said "yet."*

Kate opened the box and, again, her mouth fell open.

"Kate, are you OK?" Tyler asked. "Don't you like it? Is something wrong?"

"Kate, are you OK? Don't you like it? Is something wrong?"

Kate blinked, once, twice, and realized she was still on the hydraulic lift, facing the angel, blinking in motion with it.

She looked down and realized it was Marvin yelling at her.

"Are you OK?" he asked again. "Is there something wrong with the tree topper?"

"No!" Kate yelled, still staring at the angel.

No, she thought. *Except they're not all they're cracked up to be.*

Just like the holidays. It's all just pretend. There are no guardian angels in this world. There is no perfect holiday.

"Are you ready to come down?" Marvin yelled.

I am, Kate thought, lowering the lift. *Just like a fallen angel descending toward earth.*

Marvin was packing up stray boxes when she returned. "Beautiful," he said. "As usual. I'm headed off to decorate Union Station. Meet you there?"

Kate nodded. "Running back to the office," she said. "See you in an hour."

Kate watched Marvin pack up a flatbed dolly and haul it away. As soon as he was out of earshot, she turned to the Auntie Anne's worker and said, "Got that pretzel?"

She had just taken her first bite—her lips ringed in cinnamon and sugar—when she heard a man's voice ask, "Hungry?"

Kate turned. A handsome man, holding an orange-and-black bag, stood before her. Kate's eyes widened. She smiled apprehensively, and the sugar fell from her lips.

"I'm just teasing," the man said. "I'm Chad Cooper. I'm a partner in Cooper, Anderson, Schiff & Hines, the law firm at the top of the Tower."

Kate stared at the man.

"I hired you to decorate our offices for the holidays," he said, smiling. "And you're pulling out all the stops for our firm's holiday party. Remember?"

"Oh my gosh," Kate said, her cheeks flushing. "I'm so sorry, Mr. Cooper."

"Chad," he said. "Please."

"Chad," Kate said, nervously wiping her mouth and rubbing her hand on the T-shirt she had thrown on to decorate. She extended her hand. Chad shook it, then lifted his hand in front of his eyes to inspect it.

"Cinnamon sugar?" he asked.

Kate's entire body blushed before Chad said, "Sorry, couldn't help myself."

Kate laughed and self-consciously smoothed her ponytail with her free hand. "A girl gets hungry," she said. "Again, I'm so sorry."

She looked up at the giant Christmas tree filling the atrium. "I often feel like I'm time-traveling. Living in a world months ahead of everyone else." Kate nodded at Chad's bag. "I mean, it's not even Halloween yet, and I'm already decking the halls with boughs of holly instead of pumpkins."

Chad chuckled. "It's sort of the same in my work," he said. "People only see a five-second interview with me on TV and not the endless hours of work that started months, if not years, ago."

Kate nodded, now remembering how many times she had seen the well-known St. Louis attorney's boyishly handsome face on TV and in the newspaper.

And I didn't remember one of my biggest clients, Kate thought, silently admonishing herself.

Chad seemed to pick up on her anxiety and said, "It's OK. You're busy and distracted. The holidays are hard."

Kate smiled.

"And speaking of the holidays," Chad continued, giving his bag a shake, "I'm still working on Halloween."

Kate suddenly remembered Chad had a son. She had decorated his private school's Lessons and Carols holiday concert and reception a couple years back. Chad had remembered her work, and that's why he had hired her to do his firm's offices and parties this year.

He stopped and looked up at the tree in the center of the mall. "It's so ironic," he said, pulling a costume from the bag. "It's an angel. Like your tree topper."

Kate looked at the picture of the costume on the front of the bag and smiled. The angel's gown was white satin with a gold belt, and it had white wings with gold tips. A halo of white fluff hovered over the little boy's head.

"It's adorable," Kate said. "How old is your son now?"

"Coop is seven," Chad said. "I'm a little worried the other kids will make fun of his costume, but he refused to go as anything else this year."

All of a sudden, Chad stopped. Kate thought she saw his strong jaw tremble. The fierce trial lawyer St. Louisans saw on TV and in the newspaper—the one who never seemed at a loss for words—suddenly looked like a little boy himself. Chad ran a hand through his sandy silver-flecked hair, and then nervously straightened his tie.

"I just can't find any Trick-or-Treat bags that work with this costume," he said as if in a trance. "I've looked everywhere. All the Halloween stores have are pumpkin buckets or spooky bags. And I can't give him a pillowcase. That would make me the worst dad of the year."

Chad shook his head and put the costume back in the shopping bag.

"I don't know what to do," he muttered.

He seems so out of sorts for such an in-control guy, Kate thought.

"I have an idea," Kate said gently. "Why don't I make him a Trick-or-Treat bag that looks like a little cloud? I'll just get a container and glue some cotton balls around it. It'll be perfect. Oh, and I think I have a little harp that I use for Christmas that might be cute for him to carry around, too."

Chad smiled and reached out to touch Kate on the arm. "I can never thank you enough," he said. "Truly."

Kate's heart skipped a beat at the emotion in Chad's voice.

"You're welcome," she said. "Just consider it payback for not remembering you at first, and a thank-you for your belief in me and my company."

"OK," Chad said.

"I'll drop it by your office," she said. "I've got some finishing touches to do here later anyway."

"It was nice to see you again, Kate," Chad said. "And, again, thank you."

Chad turned and stopped, his eyes looking toward the top of the tree.

"Do you still believe in angels?" he asked, giving his bag a gentle shake.

Kate's eyes grew wide. *What a strange question*, she thought. *And why is he asking me that?* Her heart began to race as she again thought of Tyler.

"Forget it," Chad said, starting to walk away. "Odd question, I know."

"Yes," Kate blurted, stopping Chad in his tracks. "I do. Although it's hard to sometimes."

Do I? she suddenly thought. *Where did that come from?*

Chad smiled weakly. "I like your honesty," he said quietly. He hesitated and then mumbled, seemingly to himself, "I used to believe they were everywhere."

He gave Kate a faint smile. "See you later," he said, walking away and disappearing into the crowd of shoppers.

What was all that about? Kate wondered.

Kate realized she was still holding her pretzel, and she took a big bite of the sweet dough, the conversation replaying in her mind.

"Do you still believe in angels?" she could still hear Chad asking. *Do I?*

Kate looked at the tree again, and what she had with Tyler popped into her mind once more. Without warning, the sadness returned. *Last year was so magical*, Kate thought, tears springing to her eyes. As they started to run down her cheeks, Kate turned quickly and rushed out of the mall before anyone could see her.

She made it to the garage, dropped her pretzel into a garbage can and found her van before collapsing into sobs. The painted logo on the side of her van—*HOLIDAYS BY KATE!*—was blurry through her tears. Kate walked up to the van and felt the magnetized banner underneath her logo—*Make Your Christmas Sparkle!*

I wish I could move you ahead to Easter, Kate thought.

Kate changed out the banners for each season and holiday, magnets that rotated between *Make Your Easter a "Hoppy" One!*, *Celebrate Your Graduate in Style!*, or *Turn Your Halloween Party Into a Howling Success!*

But Christmas was—usually—Kate's season to sparkle.

Ever since she was a girl, Kate loved to make the world pretty and the holidays perfect. Her mother and grandmother had taught her the beauty of family heirlooms and traditions.

"Memories are things you can't buy in a box store," her grandmother had always said.

Her whole life Kate had wanted to be a decorator, and she had found her own niche in holiday decorating, one that made her—and everyone around her—the happiest.

Her career had seemed as dreamy as a flocked tree, but now it just seemed like a façade.

Kate's heart leaped into her throat, and she turned to press her forehead against the cold metal of the van to cool her emotions.

When she lifted her face, she finally noticed that someone had stuck a Post-it Note on her van. She took a step back, and its message became clear. The word *UNHAPPY* had been written in Magic Marker on the Post-it Note, which had been stuck in front of her *HOLIDAYS BY KATE!* banner. Kate turned and scanned the mall's parking garage, but it was quiet, save for a few cars parking and shoppers strolling out with bags.

Unnerved, Kate jumped into the driver's seat and navigated out of the parking garage. She turned on the radio to find one of her favorite radio stations. The station was already playing holiday music twenty-four hours a day.

Kate gunned the engine as she hit the interstate and headed

into downtown St. Louis from the riverfront. As she merged into traffic, Kate looked at the driver's side mirror. The sticky note took off, flying, floating in the current.

It looks just like an… Kate thought, stopping herself, willing herself not to say the word. The Post-it Note continued to flitter, growing smaller in Kate's mirror, before it disappeared just as "Hark! The Herald Angels Sing" came on the radio.

Kate flicked off the radio and headed in the direction of her office. In the near distance, the Gateway Arch glimmered in the sun, a halo effect over the silver landmark, its base like a shimmery skirt.

Kate shook her head at the irony of the image in front of her: the Arch resembled a giant, glowing angel that had landed over St. Louis.

2

The Holiday Pin

Kate padded into her tiny kitchen, her slippers sliding across the black-and-white-checkerboard floor, and reached into the old cupboards she'd refinished and repainted herself. She pulled out a mug, sighing at her ironic selection. On the front of her cup was a trio of Santa's elves drinking coffee and working even faster than usual, their little stockinged legs dangling over a banner that read *Did Someone Say Christmas?*

Kate poured herself a cup of coffee and nodded her head in agreement. *That's exactly how I feel, fellas. But now it feels like work*, Kate thought, *and not a calling.*

She stepped into the dining room and looked out the old, wavy double windows that revealed a row of gingerbread brick bungalows each sitting atop a small hill and yard. It was a dark, blustery early December day, and Kate took another sip as her eyes tried to adjust. All of a sudden, the neighborhood exploded in twinkling lights. The trunks and branches of trees sparkled, candy canes blinked, wreaths glowed, and blow-up Santas on roofs came to life.

What the…? Kate thought.

And then she realized the lack of sunlight had triggered many of the home's holiday lights to pop on, tricking them into believing it was already nightfall.

Kate glanced at her own yard, before turning to survey her living and dining rooms. They were emptier than if the Grinch had swept through last night unannounced.

Kate sat in a chair in front of her fireplace and took another big sip of coffee. She tried not to look, but she couldn't help but stare into the corner of the living room, where a tree usually stood guard this time of year, and then around the room, which had been filled with so much holiday joy last year. Kate shook her head, strode into her bathroom, and turned on the shower, undressing as the steam filled the room. She stood under the hot water until her mind cleared.

After her shower, Kate pulled on a turtleneck and slacks, did her makeup and pulled her hair into a work-ready ponytail, and then gave herself a once-over in the full-length mirror. Since she was always on the move—unpacking, decorating, hauling—she tried to dress comfortably but professionally, especially if she was in client offices. She'd learned early on that wearing a skirt on a lift wasn't a good idea, nor was wearing anything too nice, as she ended up snagging it. Moreover, she was covered in glitter nearly every day.

Still, I need something to jazz myself up today, Kate thought. *I can't look as gloomy as the weather.*

Kate opened the beautiful wooden jewelry box that sat on her dresser. Her parents gave her the box for Christmas when she was a girl, and she smiled at the scroll-y *K* carved on top. When she opened it, music from *The Nutcracker* spilled forth.

This is where her favorite heirloom jewelry lived, be it the mood ring from grade school or the pearl earrings her grandmother had given her when she graduated college.

I need a long necklace, Kate thought, rummaging through the box, *or a pin.*

Her fingers brushed a tiny velvet purse, and she picked it up. She opened the tie at the end and gave the purse a little shake. A pin of an angel came tumbling into her hand.

Kate gasped and dropped it as if it were poisonous.

As if in a trance, Kate walked into the living room, stood by the fireplace, and stared at the empty spot in the corner, recalling Christmas a year ago.

"Are you OK?" Tyler asked. "Don't you like it?"

"Tyler," she said, her eyes filling with tears. "Where did you find this?"

"It's an heirloom," he said. "I found it in an antique store. I know how much you love antique things, from holiday decorations to furniture. I just thought...well...that it seemed perfect for you."

The little cherub pin was gold, its eyes happy and bright, and it was playing a harp, which was studded—like its wings—with small diamonds.

"Tyler, no, it's too much," Kate protested.

"No, it's not," he said, walking over and kneeling in front of her. "I love you. You're my angel."

A car alarm suddenly went off in Kate's neighborhood, and she realized she was once again staring into space, listening to ghosts.

Kate shook her head, turned off the lights in her house and grabbed her keys. But as she strode to the door, she stopped, turned, and walked back to her dresser.

"Just because he wasn't ready doesn't mean you aren't," Kate remembered her mother telling her after the breakup. *"It's brave to fall in love and open your heart that much. Guardian angels surround you. You just don't see them anymore."*

Kate opened her jewelry box again, picked up the angel and pinned it to her sweater.

★★★

Cooper, Anderson, Schiff & Hines was nestled on the top four floors of St. Louis Tower, far above the mall below.

Kate merged onto the elevator with a sea of people and pushed the button for the thirtieth floor. When she stepped into the quiet, moneyed lobby of the law firm—which represented the city's biggest figures and businesses, including the beloved St. Louis Cardinals—she couldn't help but laugh out loud.

"May I help you?" a receptionist with a severe gray bob and imposing eyeglasses asked, giving Kate a dismissive look.

"Oh," Kate said. "Sorry. But the letters of the firm's principals spell out CASH. Get it? C-A-S-H. I never noticed that until now."

"May...I...help...you?" the receptionist asked again, her words matching the frigid weather.

"I'm sorry," Kate said, gathering herself. "Kate Roseberry. I'm decorating your offices for your firm's party this weekend."

"Conference Floor, one level up," the woman said. "And please tell your team to take the freight elevator. They're already here...and have been quite, shall we say, disruptive."

Kate mustered up a smile for the woman, wondering if she had a chance to assert her passive-aggressive authority anywhere else except here. "I'm deeply sorry for any inconvenience," Kate said, heading toward the elevator. "Thank you."

Kate emerged one floor up and was immediately greeted by Marvin and Claire, her young assistant.

"Did you meet the Dragon Lady?" Claire asked, her puppy-like enthusiasm causing her wavy red hair to bounce. That's when Kate noticed she was wearing a Santa hat.

"Claire," Kate said as a warning.

"Kate," Claire mimicked. "I'm sorry, but she's cray-cray."

"She's not the only one, Mrs. Claus," Kate said. "Marvin, radio everyone and tell them to take the freight elevator, or this will be our last holiday job here."

Marvin picked up his radio while Claire grabbed Kate's arm and dragged her down the hall. "'Your little group is being quite disruptive,'" Claire said as they walked, imitating the receptionist. "How was I to know she wouldn't like my ensemble? I think it's quite fetching for the holidays."

Kate tried to stifle a laugh, but she couldn't. A dose of Claire was just what she needed this morning. "So, how's it going?"

They rounded a corner, Claire announcing, "Like this."

Kate gasped. The Conference Floor was truly just that. It was comprised of moving walls that allowed the cavernous space to be divided up as needed. In this case, nearly half of the thirty-first floor was being used for the party—and CASH's five hundred employees.

"I'd forgotten how big this space was…and these views!" Kate said, walking toward the floor-to-ceiling windows that delivered sweeping views of the Arch, the city skyline, the Mississippi River and the bridges leading into Illinois. "Amazing!"

"Umm, what about the design?" Claire asked, walking over and turning Kate around.

"Sorry," Kate said, a big smile slowly crossing her face. "Even more amazing."

Claire jumped up and down, her Santa hat bouncing. "Yay, thank you," she said. "We followed your design down to the last bow. Looks like Christmas threw up in here, doesn't it?"

Kate cocked her head at her assistant. "So eloquent," she said.

"Just quoting the queen," Claire laughed. "That's what you said after a few glasses of champagne last year when the season ended. Remember?"

Kate nodded. And, in a definitely lowbrow way, Claire was right. The once bland, empty space was overflowing with the warmth, beauty and spirit of the holidays. Two cocktail bars—draped in shimmering fabric—flanked the room. Food stations would be set up in old-fashioned sleighs. The entire ceiling had been draped in real pine boughs, twinkling with soft white lights. Gold and silver ornaments hung from the boughs at different heights. A dance floor in the middle of the space had been designed to look like a Currier and Ives frozen pond; a DJ booth in a white gazebo stood nearby. Wreaths danced on the many windows, and four silver trees—all dressed in gold—stood in the four corners.

"Stunning," Kate said, as Marvin entered the room. She turned to the rest of the team, who were still tweaking, adjusting and decorating. "You all outdid yourselves."

"No, you did," Claire said, nodding at her boss, her Santa hat nodding as well.

"As usual," Marvin added. "Even..." He hesitated. "...this year."

Kate smiled wanly and began to mouth, "Thank you" when she heard a man's deep voice behind her say, "You really did outdo yourself."

Kate turned, then blushed. Chad stood in front of her, a smile on his face.

"Chad Cooper, this is Marvin and Claire," Kate said. "They really did all the work."

"It's nice to meet you," Chad said. He shook their hands and again turned to Kate. "I just wanted to stop by and say thanks, not only for what you've done here but also for helping my son at Halloween. Some of the kids didn't understand his costume, but..." All of a sudden, Chad stopped. "Anyway, you really helped me out." He reached out to touch Kate's shoulder. "Thank you."

"You're welcome," she said.

"I'm sorry I have to go so quickly," he said, "I have a meeting, but I wanted to say thanks."

"I guess we'll see you this weekend," Kate said.

"Oh, I won't be here," he said.

"I'm sorry to hear that," Kate said.

"I have to work," Chad said. "But I know everyone will

have a great time. Thanks for waving your magic wand here. Or maybe magic candy cane is more appropriate for this time of year."

Kate smiled. "Thank you."

She reached out to shake Chad's hand, but when he glanced at Kate's sweater, his mouth dropped open.

"Where did you get that pin?" he asked as if she were on trial.

"What?" Kate started. "This?"

She looked down at the pin and fumbled her words.

"Um, it was a gift," she said. "Last year. Long story."

Chad nodded and then turned, the shiny leather on his black dress shoes making a subtle squeak. He began to leave the room before suddenly turning and looking out the windows, his eyes darting back and forth as if he were watching a bird fly. He again glanced at Kate's pin and whispered to her, "Angels. We can't escape them, can we?"

Without another word, Chad turned and left.

The room was silent. After a few seconds, Claire said, "What was that about? It was like watching an old movie. He seemed to like you, and then he got very mysterious."

"He was the same way the last time we met," Kate said. "Very sweet and then, all of a sudden, very distant and nervous."

Marvin moved toward the windows and motioned for Kate and Claire. Marvin produced a folded envelope from his back pocket. "Two of the partners came up here earlier and asked that I give this to you."

Kate opened the envelope and pulled out a sheet of paper and a check.

"Must be the last half of the fee," Kate said. "Law firms are so timely."

She scanned the letter, her eyes growing wider as she read it. She looked up at her colleagues, her mouth open.

"Oh my gosh," she said. "Chad's wife passed away last winter, right before the holidays. She had cancer and was sick for a very long time."

Kate continued to read the letter, then looked at Marvin and Claire. "They want me to decorate Chad's home," she said. "They said he won't do it for himself, and they're worried about him and his son. He already told them he's not going to Chicago to visit his or his late wife's families, and he instructed them he doesn't want visitors.

"I can't do it," Kate continued, her eyes darting from Marvin to Claire, shaking her head, her ponytail bouncing emphatically. "It just seems like such an intrusion on his privacy. Who can tell someone when they're ready to heal again and move on? I mean, I'm still not ready, and I didn't experience anything like what he did."

"But what about his son?" Marvin asked in his quiet way. "What if he needs to heal, or even have some second of happiness, and his dad's too sad to see that or help him?"

Kate bowed her head, her mind whirling, and she shut her eyes to say a little prayer. When she opened them, the diamonds on the wings of the angel pin were shimmering, as if it were flying.

"Angels," Kate heard Chad say. *"We can't escape them, can we?"*

No, Kate thought. *We can't.*

She looked at Marvin and Claire, gave the letter and check a hearty shake, and said, "I'm doing it. But I'll need your help and all of your support."

3

The Snow Angel

St. Louis did not handle the snow well. Two inches of snow sent the city into an all-out panic.

In fact, St. Louisans handled even the most modest of snowfalls as if an apocalypse were imminent, and they immediately had to obtain every loaf of bread, carton of eggs and gallon of milk they could lay their hands on.

Kate drove by Schnucks, the local grocery chain. Its parking lot was jammed, even though the snow had just begun to coat the roads.

They expect to be snowbound after four inches of snow? Kate chuckled. *And to eat French toast for a week?*

A line of snowplows eased onto Manchester Road, headed for the highways, and traffic slowed to a stop. Kate cracked her window and watched the snow. Even with the traffic, a hush was already beginning to fall over the city, the kind only a snowfall can bring.

Sometimes Mother Nature forces us all to slow down and stop, Kate thought.

The snow—heavy, wet—made a soft whooshing noise as it

fell. Suddenly, a snowplow honked. Kate jumped and shut her window.

She clicked on the radio, and "Let It Snow" came on.

Holiday irony, you constantly amuse me, Kate thought, smiling.

Growing up in Chicago, snow had been a season unto itself. "What are the only two seasons in Chicago? Winter and construction," the old joke went. Kate had loved the long winters when she was younger. She loved the way Chicago looked in winter: Lake Michigan iced over, frozen waves suspended in mid-air, the city streets continuously freshened with a coat of white, the shock of the icy wind contrasted with the warmth of the shops and restaurants.

Kate had loved to ski and sled. She loved making snow forts, snowmen and snow ice cream.

"You should have been born a penguin," her mother would joke. "Or married Santa so you could live at the North Pole."

Maybe that's why I do what I do, Kate thought. *Maybe it's always called to me.*

Kate eased down Manchester Road, heading west to Chad Cooper's house. The western suburbs were where most St. Louisans lived. St. Louis was divided between the city and the county, and the divide felt cavernous at times. Citizens flocked to baseball and hockey games, the riverfront's bars and riverboat casinos as well as the Italian restaurants on the Hill, but then they left the city behind and took their tax money with them.

Kate was proud to live in the city. She often felt like a pioneer. When she bought her house, everything in life seemed possible.

Kate passed one of the city's historic Catholic churches, which was illuminated for the holidays. Stained glass windows sparkled; luminaries shimmered.

It looks frosty, magical and hopeful in the snow, she thought.

Her stomach lurched as she thought about Chad and the task at hand.

Christmas is either the happiest of holidays if you're blessed, she thought, *or the biggest nightmare if you're not.*

She turned her van onto Warson Road and headed into Ladue, a tony enclave—and one of the wealthiest suburbs in the US—filled with elite prep schools, sprawling estates and old redbrick mansions sheltered from the street. Traffic again slowed as vans similar to Kate's—for plumbers, contractors, interior designers—plugged the quickly slickening streets.

Kate heard happy screams over the sound of her holiday music. She lowered the volume.

In the sloping front yard of a large home, a group of children wearing snowsuits were playing. To Kate, they resembled little, round Weebles, the old toys whose commercials had the tagline, "Weebles wobble, but they don't fall down." The kids were running around in puffy coats and little boots, stumbling, tumbling, playing in the snow, their breath coming out as puffs of smoke.

Kate watched as three of the children ran halfway up the snow-covered slope and suddenly dropped onto their backs, waving their arms and sliding their legs to and fro. They stood with great care, then each of them grabbed the other's hand, and they leaped forward as far as they could.

Snow angels! Kate thought, smiling at the pretty, smooth silhouettes the children had left in the white.

Kate was instantly transported to her home in suburban Chicago. She could see herself as a little girl, just like the kids who were running around in the snow.

"Are you ready?" her mom had asked, grabbing her daughter's hand.

"No!" Kate yelled. "What if it hurts?"

"The snow will break our fall," her mother said.

"Break?" Kate worried. "Fall?"

Her mother turned to Kate, who had been filled with fear

and worry ever since her grandfather had died earlier in the year. It was the family's first Christmas without their patriarch. "If the snow doesn't break your fall, the angels will."

"How?" Kate asked.

"You're honoring them by making silhouettes of them in the snow," her mother explained. "They won't let you get hurt. Ready?"

Kate again grabbed her mother's hand, shut her eyes and fell backward with a yelp, landing softly in a big bank of snow.

Whoosh!

"Now do this," her mother said, making an angel in the snow.

Kate followed suit, and when she had finished, her mother stood carefully in the cleared area and helped her daughter stand. They held hands and took a mighty leap to clear their newly created silhouettes.

"Pretty," Kate said. "They do look like angels."

Yells came from the neighboring yards as kids made snowmen or tobogganed down hillsides.

"Can I ask you a question, Mom?" Kate asked quietly.

"Anything."

"Do you believe in angels?"

"Yes," her mother said.

"Do you think Grampa is an angel?"

"I do," she said, before taking a big seat in the snow and patting a spot next to her. Kate sat with another *whoosh*.

"I think that angels are all around us," her mother continued. "I think that people like your grampa who we love and miss are around us, even if we can't see them. Sometimes they might take the form of a cardinal or a hummingbird, or sometimes their spirit might live on in the heirloom angel we place on top of a tree."

Kate wiped her nose with her mitten and scrunched her face, her cheeks rosy.

"Angels are messengers, Kate," her mother said. "Sort of intermediaries—or go-betweens—between heaven and earth."

"Like our postman?" Kate asked. "The person who brings us a letter?"

Her mother laughed, nodding. "Yes, sort of," she said. "But you have to be aware that angels are present. Most people go through their lives not seeing what's all around them. It's easy to get lost in this world. It's hard to stay present."

A loud honk knocked Kate from her memory, and she realized there were no longer any cars in front of her. She waved an embarrassed *sorry* to the frustrated driver behind her.

Kate navigated down Warson, listening to the friendly voice on her cell give her final directions. She slowed and turned into a driveway, which was canopied with snow-covered trees, and wound back and back through a wooded lot.

Am I in a nature preserve? Kate thought.

Finally, the trees cleared and a redbrick home—*No, that's a minimansion*, Kate thought—towered in front of her. Massive white pillars supported the huge front porch, and the upstairs bedrooms had private terraces.

Definitely Southern, Kate thought. *Very Rhett and Scarlett.*

St. Louis had a significantly more French and Southern vibe running through its history—a contrast from its rival Chicago—although it considered itself more Eastern than Midwestern.

Kate pulled into the circle drive and looked around.

Where is everyone? she thought.

She picked up her cell, closed her map app and finally noticed all the texts.

Stuck in traffic, Marvin had messaged three times.

Huge accident on 40 because of the snow, Claire had sent. *Who knows when I'll get there. Sorry.*

And finally, from Claire: *Three inches of snow sends St. Louis into panic! I need French toast!*

Kate laughed then sighed, opened her door and trudged through the accumulating snow to the front door. She rang the bell. Her eyes widened when a beautiful young woman answered the door.

"Oh," Kate said. "I'm sorry. I'm, um, Kate Roseberry. I was expecting…"

"Mrs. Doubtfire?" The woman laughed.

Kate furrowed her brow in confusion.

"I'm sorry," the woman said. "I'm Janet Edlinger. I'm Mr. Cooper's nanny."

"Oh." Kate stumbled, staring at the woman who looked like a Swedish supermodel turned celebrity nanny, all blond tendrils and rosy cheeks and dewy skin.

Kate self-consciously rubbed her own cheek, which felt as if it had been dehydrated from the van's scorching heat, the cold air outside and the endless hours of work.

"Oh, you're the decorator," Janet finally said, filling in her own blanks. "Come on in. Coop's out playing with friends."

Kate nodded.

"Let me show you the house," Janet said with a smile.

Kate stopped in her tracks as she stepped in the house.

"Don't worry about your boots," Janet said. "With a seven-year-old boy and snow, I'm wiping down the floors nonstop."

Kate smiled, but that was not why she had stopped. The house certainly had a *Gone with the Wind* feel. A marble foyer encircled a grand staircase; oil paintings that looked as if they had been lifted from an art museum were individually spotlighted and lined the massive walls that led to a stunning coffered ceiling.

"This way," Janet said, leading Kate down a parquet hallway and into a living room that was the size of Kate's entire bungalow.

The living room featured a wall of windows that overlooked woods and a ravine—no other homes were visible. A beautiful creek trickled in the distance, its water steaming, snow-covered logs crisscrossing it.

"It's so beautiful," Kate said, before turning and being greeted by a wall of family portraits. She walked up and studied a photo of the family, all dressed in red Christmas sweaters, big smiles on their faces. "And so is she," Kate continued. "Is this Mrs. Cooper?"

"Yes," Janet said. "Ella was her name. She passed away last winter. It's been a tough year on the boys, to say the least. She was diagnosed with cancer just after they were engaged. Mr. Cooper never wavered. Her only dream was to have a child, and she did. She fought every step of the way."

"I can't imagine," Kate said, tears filling her eyes.

"No one should," Janet said sweetly. "Especially a little boy."

Kate turned to look at Janet and nodded.

"Is this where they had Christmas?" Kate asked.

"Yes. This was their hangout spot," Janet said. "And they celebrated Christmas in here."

"I would, too." Kate smiled. "I'll do my best. I just feel…a little awkward about all this, especially since Mr. Cooper doesn't even know I'm here."

Janet walked over and put her hand on Kate's back. "He needs this," she said softly. "And Coop needs Christmas."

Kate smiled weakly.

"Do you need any help?" Janet asked.

"You're used to wiping down floors and kid's faces," Kate smiled again, "and I'm used to hauling holiday deco. We're both Santa's little helpers."

Janet laughed. "Just yell if you need me," she said. "I'm going to make some hot chocolate for Coop. He should be back from the neighbor's shortly. He'll be cold."

Janet turned and walked away, before stopping. "You're like a Christmas angel," she said. "Spreading happiness."

Kate's heart leaped into her throat. The images of snow angels again filled her head.

Kate headed back to her van and began to haul boxes inside. She'd hoped Marvin and Claire would be here, so she could get started on decorating—and keep her mind preoccupied—but she'd have to do it all herself today.

"Thanks, Mother Nature," she said, looking up into the swirling snow.

Kate began piling boxes into the corner of the room. She stopped and nervously opened one.

The partners at Mr. Cooper's law firm had given her no instructions on how to decorate his home, and she didn't know the family at all. But she had taken the comments he'd made to her—about angels and her angel pin—and run with them.

The boxes were filled with angels, and this one…

What's gotten into me? Kate thought. *I even brought a box of my family's antique angel ornaments since I wasn't decorating my own tree this year.*

She pulled out a beautiful, hand-carved wooden angel—an angel that had been carved from wood with a single cut, no glue, its wings fanned in thin strips—and ran her fingers over its face. She had gotten it when she traveled to Switzerland. A wood-carver had made it for her while she watched him work.

"An angel," he had said, creating it without knowing Kate at all, "for an angel."

Hope you still have some magic in you, Kate thought, placing the ornament back in the box.

She headed back out to the van and braced herself for the heavy lifting: an artificial tree—its base and endless limbs divvied up into many long boxes—sat waiting.

Kate yanked a vertical box toward her, steadied herself and grunted loudly. She balanced the box, took a few big, unsteady steps and then—without warning—her feet slid in the snow, and she threw the box, landing hard on her behind.

The box came open upon landing, stiff, green limbs from the artificial tree springing forth and skidding through the snow.

"Are you OK?"

Kate let out a yelp. Standing beside her, looking down, was a little boy clad in a Sock Monkey stocking cap.

"I...don't...know," Kate said.

"Christopher Ogden O'Malley Cooper at your service," he said. "Coop for short."

He extended his hands, and Kate slowly stood.

"Thank you," she said. "I'm Kate Roseberry. I'm here to decorate your house for Christmas."

Coop crossed his arms—the air in his puffy coat making a hissing release—and eyed Kate warily.

"Does my father know about this?" he asked.

Kate gulped.

"Well, no," she said. "Not technically."

"Hmmm," he said, raising a finger to his lips. "Then why *are* you here?"

Kate explained, the boy carefully weighing every word as if he were a judge on *Law & Order.* Kate stifled a chuckle: he was a knockoff of his father in every way, from his looks to his legalese, but he was also just a little boy standing in the snow in a Sock Monkey stocking cap.

As she talked, his face softened and his eyes grew bright. "Oh! You're the lady who helped me with my angel costume! Thank you!" Coop smiled at her, but then skewed his hazel eyes toward the limbs scattered in the snow.

"But this won't do," he said, changing his tone and becoming as formal as if he were a butler on *Downton Abbey.* "This won't do at all."

Kate watched the little boy fold his arms and survey the artificial tree with great skepticism, shaking his head.

Why does he try to act like he's forty years old? Kate wondered.

"What's wrong?" she asked.

"My mom and dad *always* cut a *real* pine tree down from our woods, and we hauled it back ourselves, and then put it in a stand, and my dad gave it a drink of water, and my mom got out this aprony-thing she loved and put it around the tree and then she'd make Christmas cookies in all these cool shapes and then—"

"OK, OK," Kate said, trying to calm the little boy, whose composure was collapsing, his words coming out with more and more emotion. "We can do that."

Can we? she thought to herself. *Am I getting myself into trouble here?*

Kate went to the back of her van. Her job had turned her into a real-life "Girl Scout meets Paul Bunyan," so her van was always filled with any tool for any emergency. She lifted the rubber lining and then a compartment in the trunk and pulled out a saw.

"Wow," Coop said, eyes as wide as those of the Sock Monkey.

"You lead the way, OK?" Kate said.

"OK!" Coop said, taking off through the snow, waving his hand at her. "Follow me!"

The duo trudged through the snow and into the woods, trekking down a small path that led to the ravine.

"Be careful," Kate called, growing worried.

Finally, she came into a swath of woods filled with pines of varying shapes and sizes. Coop was standing in the middle of the trees, slowly pivoting in a circle, his finger again on his lips, surveying each tree carefully.

"Can't be too big or too small," he explained, still turning. "Has to have a lot of sturdy limbs so that you can hide ornaments way back near the trunk. And..." Coop stopped and inhaled "...it has to smell like Christmas."

Kate smiled. "You'd make a great assistant for me," she said. "You're right about picking a perfect tree. How'd you learn all that?"

For a few seconds, Coop did not move or answer. The only sound was the snow falling, the creek burbling.

"My mom," he said, finally turning to face Kate. "I miss her."

Coop's face was wet—with snow and tears—and Kate walked up to him and put her arm around his back.

"I know," she said. "I'm so sorry."

The little boy burst into tears and, without thinking, Kate set down the saw, kneeled and pulled him close. She held him until his sobs subsided.

"Everybody told me she'd always be with me," he said, looking up at Kate. "But she's not. She's not. I'm all alone."

Kate's heart shattered, and she held him even tighter.

How much pain has he already experienced in his short life? Kate wondered, fighting back her own tears. *It's not fair.*

"She *is* with you, Coop," Kate finally whispered, her voice coming out husky and raw in the cold air. "Every second of the day."

"How do you know?" he asked, wiping his face.

"Trust me?"

Coop pulled away and shook his head no.

"A little?" Kate asked.

He nodded tentatively.

"I want you to hold my hand, and then we're going to fall back in the snow," she said. "It won't hurt, I promise."

"You want to make snow angels?" Coop asked, catching on.

"Yes," she said.

"Why?"

"It'll be fun, and I want to tell you a story," Kate said. "Ready?"

The two dropped, fanned out their arms and legs and—as they did—Kate told Coop, first about losing her grandfather and then, for some reason, about losing the man she loved.

The two then stood, carefully, together, hopping free of their silhouettes.

"Cool," Coop said with a smile. "Can I ask you a question?"

"Sure, anything," Kate said.

"Do you believe in angels?"

"I do," Kate said, remembering her mother's words. "I think that angels are all around us. I think people like your mother, who we love and miss, are around us, even if we can't see them. Sometimes they might take the form of a cardinal or a hummingbird, or sometimes their spirit might live on in the tree we pick out at Christmas."

Kate smiled at the boy.

"Angels are messengers, Coop," Kate said. "Sort of intermediaries—or go-betweens—between heaven and earth. But you have to be aware that angels are present. Most people go through their lives not seeing what's all around them. It's easy to get lost in this world. It's hard to stay present."

Coop was quiet for a moment and then he shouted—so loudly that the cardinals sitting in nearby trees scattered—"That one!"

Kate followed his finger point to a beautiful blue spruce that was round and dense, with a perfect perch for a tree topper.

"Perfect!" Kate said. "Why that one?"

Coop looked up at Kate, his earnest face juxtaposed with the one on his cap. "My mom told me," he said, before whispering "I was listening."

Kate's heart leaped into her throat, and she walked over in front of the tree, knelt in the snow and began to saw, her work hiding her tears.

"Timber!" Coop yelled as the tree fell. "Let's get it inside. I'll help you decorate it."

With angels, Kate thought, as the two dragged the tree toward the house.

When the duo got the tree set in the stand and had given it a big drink of water, Kate began to pull out her angel decorations.

Oh, no, Kate thought. *I didn't bring a tree topper! How could I forget?*

She shut her eyes, remembering Tyler placing her family's heirloom angel atop the tree just last year.

I hid it away in an old container, she finally remembered. *I couldn't bear to look at it this year.*

"Wow," Coop said, breaking her out of her thoughts. Kate looked up, and he was hanging the woodcut angel on the front of a limb. "How did you know?"

"Know what?" Kate asked.

"How much my mom loved angels," he said. Coop walked over and pointed to a family portrait on the wall. "See!"

Kate joined him and studied a photo of the family. She leaned in, following Coop's little finger, which was tapping the glass on the photo.

All of a sudden, Kate's heart leaped into her throat. She leaned in even closer to study the picture. Ella was wearing an angel pin exactly like the one she had.

4

The Holiday Cookie Cutter

Kate leaned forward and plucked an iced Santa Claus cookie from the tin that sat on the coffee table in her tiny TV room.

"Ho, ho, ho," Kate said, before chomping off Santa's head. "Sorry."

Kate brushed crumbs off her flannel pajamas, stretched out farther on her couch, and absentmindedly changed the channel.

A Christmas Story? No.

Miracle on 34th Street? Nope.

It's a Wonderful Life? Absolutely not.

Kate stopped at *House Hunters International* and watched as a couple searched for a home on a tropical island.

"I so should have gone somewhere this Christmas," Kate said out loud, grabbing another iced cookie—this one in the shape of a star—and eating all five points off of it. "Somewhere sunny," she mumbled, crumbs again falling out of her mouth.

She looked out at the cold St. Louis night. Her neighborhood was aglow in holiday lights, while her home was dark. Kate tried to stop her mind from wandering back a year, but she couldn't, and she remembered snuggling on this couch with

Tyler watching holiday movies after spending the day making Christmas cookies.

Making iced holiday sugar cookies with her grandmother's heirloom cookie cutters—metal cutouts of Santa, the North Star, candy canes, Christmas trees, bells, snowflakes and, Kate's favorite shape, angels—was one of Kate's treasured childhood memories.

When Kate would press out each cookie's shape, she could feel her grandmother's and mother's hands reverberate in the worn wooden knobs of green and red that backed each cutter.

She had loved the memory and cookies so much that it had become her company's signature thank-you gift to every client who had hired her during the season. Kate had bought new holiday cookie cutters, but they could never match the history and beauty of the heirloom ones.

Kate reached for another cookie—ones that her mother had made and sent to her today—but stopped herself.

I won't be making cookies this year, she said.

Kate then thought of Coop.

Do I really believe in angels? she wondered. *Or did I just lie to him to make him feel better? And did my mom do the same to me?*

Kate nervously eyed the wrapped package that sat next to the tin of cookies.

To: Kate, the gift tag read. *Love: Mom.*

She had been able to open the tin, which was marked *FRAGILE! COOKIES! PRECIOUS CARGO!* in her mother's looping cursive, but she had not yet been able to open the accompanying card or gift as she didn't know if she could yet handle her mother's chipper optimism and unsolicited but well-intentioned advice.

She nervously grabbed another cookie—this one of a pretty bell—and shoved it into her mouth.

"Here goes nothing," Kate mumbled, grabbing the card and gift. She could feel the sugar coursing through her body as she opened the card, which featured an angel sitting atop a Christmas tree.

For my angel, it read on the outside.

Of course, Kate thought.

She opened the card.

My Dear Kate:

These cookies are just a little reminder of how sweet life is. Remember how much fun we had making them with Grandma? We will miss you for Christmas this year. I know how busy you are during the holidays, but I'm holding on to the rest of your gifts until I can watch you open them in front of me. The first week of January will be our delayed Christmas, OK?

I'm worried about you, sweetheart. I know that you're sad. But you know that work won't bake a Christmas turkey with you, or holiday cookies, or sit under the tree with you and open presents.

You need to have some fun. Get back out there. Life is short. Make cookies for your clients. Go have a drink with a friend. I bet you got invited to a hundred parties.

Remember what your grandmother used to say: "Life is a pain in the patootie, and everyone's pain and sadness is magnified during the holidays. But the joy can also be magnified, too."

Life isn't perfect, Kate, like the world you decorate and the parties you throw, but it can still be as beautiful as every tree you light.

My first gift to you this Christmas is the most personal: I hope it helps you find your happiness again, helps you soar, helps you get the holiday spirit again.

Don't lose your shine. You're the brightest light in the world. You're my brightest light, too. You're my angel.

Love, Mom

P.S. And don't eat all the cookies in one night. Put the cookie down, Kate!

Kate laughed out loud and then ran her fingers over her mother's handwriting. She reached for the gift, which was wrapped in *Peanuts* paper—Charlie Brown, Linus and Snoopy around the fragile Christmas tree with the falling needles Charlie had rescued and Linus had wrapped in his blanket.

Kate opened the box and gasped—her family's heirloom cookie cutters were inside.

She set the package down and tried to calm herself. She picked up the remote and again changed the channel to distract herself, this time stopping at the Food Network, where the show was a holiday cookie bakeoff.

Is the universe trying to tell me something? Kate thought.

Her phone trilled, and she picked it up without looking, thinking it must be her mom.

"I put the cookie down, Mom," she said.

A man's booming laugh echoed over the other end.

"Glad to hear it," he said.

"Who is this?" Kate asked, suddenly panicked.

"Chad Cooper," he said.

Kate sat up, her heart racing.

"Is everything OK?" she asked, even more panicked as she realized she hadn't heard from him since she'd decorated his home with his son.

"More than OK," he said softly. "I…" Chad hesitated. "I'm sorry to call out of the blue, but I just had to give you a ring. Your assistant gave me your home number." He stopped. "I can't thank you enough for what you did here."

"Well, it was all your partners' doing," Kate started.

"No," he said. "I mean, the decorating is beautiful, but it's really what you did for my son. He's…" Again, he hesitated, and his voice softened. "…back. He's back to being a kid."

Kate was silent for a moment. The emotion in Chad's voice was palpable, almost as if he were willing the words to come out, and the meaning behind his words touched Kate's heart.

"I didn't do anything," she said.

Wrong thing to say, Kate thought as soon as she spoke the words.

"I think a jury would rule otherwise," Chad said. "If you get a chance tomorrow, Coop would love it if you could stop by. There's something he wants to show you."

"I'm awfully busy," Kate started.

"I know," Chad said. "I just thought..." He stopped. "I just wanted to thank you. Have a great weekend. And if I don't see you, have a great Christmas."

And, with that, Chad hung up.

What just happened? Kate thought.

Kate's eyes darted to the TV, where amateur chefs were making their best holiday cookies. The show cut to a commercial when one of the bakers realized he had forgotten to add baking powder to their dough. Kate began to change the channel, but a commercial for a holiday angel food cake stopped her cold.

Kate stood, grabbed her gift and walked into the kitchen. She clicked on the lights, turned on the oven, pulled out some granulated and powdered sugar, flour, butter, eggs, vanilla, and then readied her aqua-blue mixer. She lined up an army of food coloring—red, green, blue, gold—as well as her best holiday cookie baking friends: colored sprinkles, holly sprinkles, assorted colors of nonpareils, small and large sugar snowflakes, decorating bags and tips, and toothpicks. She set aside her signature handmade gift tags cut out in the shapes of little trees for the holidays. Kate then placed her family's antique cookie cutters on her counter.

Without thinking, Kate said, "Alexa, please play *Holiday Classics* from Pandora." As Bing began to sing, Kate remembered all the holidays she had made cookies with her mom and grandma, all the holidays when family had been near, all of the clients whose lives she had made a bit happier during the year, and even the love she had felt for Tyler.

As Kate began to mix the ingredients, she stopped and picked up the cookie cutter of an angel, running her fingers over its heavenly outline, feeling the wooden knob that had been lovingly held by generations of her family.

A smile crossed Kate's face, and she began to bake.

5

The Tree Topper

"This is a surprise," Chad Cooper said the following day when he opened the door, looking dapper in a black turtleneck and gray pants.

Kate suddenly wished she had put more effort into the jeans, old sweater, big scarf and ancient bomber jacket she had tossed on.

At least I threw on the angel pin, she reasoned.

"I brought cookies," Kate said, the words tumbling quickly out of her mouth.

Chad smiled, but then his face dropped as he scanned Kate.

Why didn't I wear something cuter? Kate thought, seeing his reaction.

"So, did you finally put the cookie down and bring me the leftovers?" Chad deadpanned, shaking his head.

Kate winced and then laughed. "You have a memory like an elephant," she said.

"I'm a trial attorney," Chad said, his hazel eyes glowing in the sunlight. "Come in. It's freezing out there."

He led Kate into the kitchen, and she handed over the cookies.

"May I?" Chad asked. Kate nodded, and he popped open the Tupperware. "Wow! These are works of art. Just like your holiday decorating."

"Thanks," Kate said, her face flushing.

"And delicious," Chad said, picking a Santa cookie and chomping off his heavily frosted beard. "Do you make these for all your clients?"

"I have in the past," she said. "But not this year."

"Why's that?" Chad asked, stuffing Santa's red frosted hat into his mouth.

Kate looked away nervously.

"Sorry," he said. "I tend to ask way too many questions. It's in my DNA. Would you like anything? I mean, you brought me cookies. A cup of coffee, water, glass of wine…?"

Kate checked her watch with great drama. "Wine? It's only two p.m."

"It's Sunday, I've been to church, and I'm Catholic," Chad said. "So wine at two is also in my DNA." He smiled. "Janet took Coop to a holiday thing at the zoo. They should be back in a bit."

"OK then," Kate said. "I'll have a glass of something red."

"That's the right answer—and color—for the Queen of Holiday Decorating."

Chad pulled a bottle from a wine rack and grabbed an electronic opener.

He poured two glasses, handed one to Kate, and said, "Follow me," leading her into the family room.

She took a seat in a Hemingway-esque leather chair near the roaring fireplace and sipped her wine. "Mmm, this is lovely."

"It's a Côtes du Rhône," he said. "I bought a case on a trip to France." He gestured toward the tree with his glass. "Bet you never get a chance to enjoy your own work," he said.

"I don't," Kate said, his simple statement resonating deeply realized: this was the advice her mother had been trying to impart.

I've just been too stuck and depressed to hear it until now, she finally understood.

"Daaaaaddd!"

Just then, Coop came running into the room and jumped onto his dad's lap. "We had a blast at the zoo," he said. "Everyone there loved my stocking cap, too, since it was a monkey!"

"I'm glad," Chad said. "You remember Miss Roseberry, don't you?"

"The Christmas Angel!" Coop yelled. "Yeah! Oh, hold on! I've got something to show you!"

He leaped off his dad's lap and took off running, his footsteps thumping up the stairs. A moment later he was back, out of breath, and hiding something behind his back.

Kate lifted her hands and looked at Chad with a "What's going on?" expression. Chad shrugged his shoulders.

"I—well, we—made a present for you," Coop said breathlessly, using his free hand to pull off his Sock Monkey stocking cap and throw it aside, the static electricity causing his hair to stand on end as if mimicking his excitement.

"What is it?"

"Ta-da! It's a tree topper!"

From behind his back, Coop pulled out an angel made from white construction paper, its base a circle that had been folded to resemble a flowing gown, its wings gold and featuring intricate cutouts like a snowflake. Coop had colored the angel's face with crayons and decorated the front with little hearts. Over its head, the angel wore a halo made from a silver tinsel pipe cleaner.

"It's beautiful," Kate said, standing and taking the angel from Coop's hand.

"Thank you," Coop said. "Remember how sad you were when you couldn't find one for the top of the tree?"

Kate nodded.

"I wanted to make one for you and for us," he said. "And see what it says on the back? *Ella.* My mom's name."

Kate smiled, and overcome by Coop's love for his mom, her eyes filled with tears. "She would be so proud of you," Kate said.

"My dad helped me make it, but I did most of the hard work," Coop said proudly. "But he's the one who thought you should be here to help us put it on the tree."

"Oh, really?" Kate asked, looking at Chad and remembering he'd said it was his son who wanted her to see it.

Chad shrugged innocently before standing. "Ready?" he asked.

The three gathered around the tree, and Chad pulled an ottoman over and stood on it. Coop gave him the angel, which he began to place on top of the tree. He stopped mid-motion.

"This seems more like your thing," he said, stepping off the ottoman and handing Kate the angel.

How does he know that? Kate thought.

"I can't," she protested. "This is your family tree."

"Yes, you can," Chad said, helping her onto the ottoman. "A new tradition to honor an old one."

Kate smiled and placed the homemade angel on top of the tree, adjusting it until it was perfectly straight. When she stepped off the ottoman, Kate felt like hugging Chad.

Kate, she thought, shaking her head. *You only just met him.*

"Perfect," Chad said. "Hey, how about a cookie, Coop? Miss Roseberry brought some iced sugar cookies in all your favorite shapes. There are even some angels!"

"Cookies!" Coop yelled, taking off toward the kitchen.

Kate laughed.

"Hey, I was just wondering," Chad started in a quiet voice, "if you might be free to help me decorate for New Year's. Or, even, maybe just stop by for a glass of champagne."